WHITE COLANDER CRIME

VICTORIA HAMILTON

BERKLEY PRIME CRIME, NEW YORK

**BERKLEY
PRIME
CRIME**

An imprint of Penguin Random House LLC
375 Hudson Street, New York, New York 10014

WHITE COLANDER CRIME

A Berkley Prime Crime Book / published by arrangement with the author

ISBN: 978-0-425-27140-7

PUBLISHING HISTORY
Berkley Prime Crime mass-market edition / November 2015

PRINTED IN THE UNITED STATES OF AMERICA

10   9   8   7   6   5   4   3   2

Cover illustration by Robert Crawford.
Cover design by Lesley Worrell.
Interior text design by Tiffany Estreicher.

Penguin
Random
House

To all of you who treasure "old stuff," what others write off as junk,
I dedicate this Vintage Kitchen Mystery.
Both Jaymie and I understand the pure joy
of finding usefulness in bygone ways, old utensils and vintage recipes.
Happy reading, my friends!

❄ One ❄

BARE FINGERS NUMB from the cold, Jaymie Leighton snipped one last branch from the holly bushes that lined one edge of her backyard, dropped it into the wicker basket and clambered to her feet. December in Michigan: sleety, snowy, frosty, foggy, damp. In turn, but sometimes all at once. At least there was no snow yet, though she was always torn between the joy of watching the first flakes of snow drifting lazily down in spiral paths, and the horror of driving in whiteout conditions and shoveling her walkway and part of the yard so little Hoppy, her three-legged Yorkie-Poo, would have a spot to do his business.

The gallant little fellow was shivering in the open door on the summer porch off the back of the house, vigilantly watching Denver, her crabby tabby, slip through the wrought-iron fence dividing her backyard from the lane that gave her access to parking in her garage. The cat ambled up the flagstone walk. Jaymie carried the basket into the house, made sure Hoppy and Denver were both in, then securely locked up. She set the basket on the long trestle table that was centered in her very vintage kitchen and grabbed an old white enamel colander rimmed in red. She stuck a square of floral oasis in the center with a dab of hot glue, unplugged the hot glue gun and eyed it thoughtfully.

She was making a festive holiday decoration for the Hoosier cabinet that was the focal point—along with the new gas stove—of the kitchen in Queensville Historic Manor, now open and doing nicely in the weeks before the Christmas holiday. Dickens Days in the village had begun, a time when strolling carolers and folks selling packaged homemade goodies made money for the heritage society. This year was especially exciting, with the opening of the heritage manor that would eventually act as a Queensville museum, of sorts. The plan was for artwork and displays that would show the history of their town and its maritime heritage—the St. Clair River was a part of the major shipping route into the heart of North America, the Great Lakes—as well as its connection to Canada. Queensville was named for Queen Victoria, just as Johnsonville on the other side of the river, in Canada, was named for President Andrew Johnson.

Holding her breath, she plunged the end of the first holly branch into the oasis and worked from there. She was not the craftiest of women; her bailiwick was cooking, especially using vintage utensils and old recipes. But sometimes one needed to be a Jill of all trades. She worked steadily with the fresh holly and ribbons.

"What do you think, Hoppy?" she asked her inquisitive little Yorkie-Poo as she pushed the last beribboned bundle of cinnamon sticks in place. She had adorned the holly branches with tiny cookie cutters in the shape of stars and gingerbread men, embellishing her masterpiece with fragrant cinnamon sticks, then finishing it with a rustic plaid bow.

Her little three-legged dog yipped and danced, and she smiled. She could always count on Hoppy to approve. Denver grumbled, sighed and turned around in his wicker basket by her old gas stove, the warmest spot in the kitchen.

"And now to cook!" she said.

She needed some sweet treats to sell to make money for the Queensville Heritage Society's ongoing projects. Thanks to her ingenuity in finding a treasure and solving a murder last spring, they had received a sizable donation in the form of a historic letter that sold at auction for over a million dollars. With that money the society had bought the manor and were refurbishing it back to its mid-nineteenth-century glory, with a few rooms done to turn-of-the-century and Depression-era standards. Much of the windfall money had been prudently invested. The fiscally responsible in the heritage society wanted to run the manor with money from donations and entry fees, as well as whatever society members could make. Dickens Days was the second moneymaker of the year, with the May "Tea with the Queen" event as the first.

So Jaymie was making treats for Dickens Days attendees, some to give away and more to sell. She had investigated nineteenth-century desserts and was overjoyed to find out that brownies were a thoroughly American treat. They were invented by a chef at the Palmer House hotel in Chicago for Mrs. Bertha Palmer, who wanted a lunchbox treat for ladies who came to the 1893 Chicago World's Fair. "Well, Mrs. Palmer," Jaymie said, as she melted chocolate and beat eggs, "your chef hit it out of the park. What does a lady need other than tea and brownies?"

Hoppy yipped in answer, and Jaymie chuckled. "You, sir, are neither a lady nor are you allowed to have chocolate!"

She had been chuckling a lot in the last weeks, and contentment swirled through her. She should be heartbroken because Daniel Collins, her boyfriend of several months, had unceremoniously dumped her for his old flame, Trish. In fact they were already married. Jaymie had gotten an email from him just a week ago, and had sent him a card of congratulations. Jaymie wished them nothing but happiness. She felt the same about Detective Zack, who had *also* found love after his move from the local police force to a more challenging position with the Detroit police. She seemed to be good luck to the men in her life, as they all found their proper partner after being involved with her.

Her present level of comfort and joy was due to a man she had recently met, Jakob Müller: a lover of antiques, junk store owner, proprietor of a Christmas tree cut-it-yourself lot with his parents and father of an adorable little girl named Jocelyn. She sighed. He was the man she had never thought she'd meet, someone who loved where he lived and enjoyed being surrounded by "junk," as her mom and sister, Becca, named all the stuff from bygone eras with which she surrounded herself. In fact, his huge store, formerly a factory, was called The Junk Stops Here; how perfect was that? He owned a piece of land, too, once part of his parents' farm, and had built a log-cabin-style home.

And here she was, sitting and mooning about Jakob instead of working. She would *not* get ahead of herself, she thought, smiling and shaking her head. She had begun to think she needed to just relax and not worry about romance, but that was before she banged on Jakob Müller's front door in a moment of panic, and practically fell into his arms.

She tuned the radio to a station playing Christmas music nonstop and hummed as she made brownies, a double batch since she was going to Jakob's log cabin for a late dinner with just him and Jocelyn and wanted to take some along. It was something to look forward to. With Daniel there had been doubt, with Zack nervousness, but with Jakob there was peace, like a light switch had been flipped on in her soul.

After lunch she was on her way to Wolverhampton, the closest big town, to pick up pamphlets with full-color photos of Queensville Historic Manor. Those of the heritage committee members with harmonious voices would be carol singing through town starting the very next night. Jaymie didn't sing, but garbed in Victorian cloak she would hand out treats and historic home pamphlets.

Tourists would flock to Queensville this weekend for the Christmas sailboat regatta and other Dickens Days festivities. The pamphlet she gave them would encourage them to also visit the Queensville Historic manor just outside of town. The manor was almost ready, dressed up for a real old-fashioned Christmas. There would be carol singing at the candle-topped spinet, and a fire would be blazing cheerily in the hearth as historical interpreters went about their business. Jaymie, when she could, would be in the manor kitchen baking gingerbread men and sugar cookies.

Since she wrote a food column called Vintage Eats for the *Wolverhampton Weekly Howler* and was on good terms with the owner and his wife, Nan Goodenough, she had struck a bargain with them. They had printed, at cost, the glossy color pamphlets, which she had written, and for which Bill Waterman, local jack-of-all-trades, had provided photos, and Jaymie was picking them up. She drove through town past the Queensville Emporium where Valetta, her best friend and the village's pharmacist, stood on the porch, her hands wrapped around a steaming mug of tea. Jaymie waved, and Valetta waved back. Jaymie was scheduled at the Emporium the next morning so the Klausners could go Christmas shopping and visit one set of great-grandkids in Mount Clemons.

She arrived at the *Howler* in Wolverhampton in fifteen minutes. The paper published from a long, low old factory building, constructed of red brick in the thirties to house an appliance manufacturing firm and converted to a printing company in the sixties. That went out of business in the nineties as the electronic age began to take over. Joe Goodenough, a newspaperman, was crazy enough to buy it and convert it to a small town weekly early in the two thousands as a retirement hobby with his second wife, Nan.

Jaymie parked next to her editor's little blue sports car and circled the building, entering through the glass front door, the buzzer indicating her admission. The receptionist who was usually seated behind the front counter was absent, so Jaymie lifted the pass-through and strolled through the door to the carpeted offices beyond the public area. She turned in the direction of Nan's brash New York voice engaged in a heated conversation.

A young man hollered, "You don't know her, Mom. Give her a freaking break, will you?"

"I know who and what that girl is," Nan yelled back. "As if you don't have enough trouble in your life, you have to pick up on a sleazy little piece of trash like that?"

Jaymie hesitated, one turn away from seeing the two, evidently Nan and her son in an argument.

"Screw you!" he yelled back.

There was the sound of a scuffle, ending with a dull thud, and Nan screamed. Jaymie bolted around the corner in time to see the two separated but glaring at each other. Nan's suit jacket was mussed, the shoulder hitched up as if her son had grabbed her. She leaned against the wall and stared up at him. The fellow was tall and lanky, with light brown hair worn collar length. He was disheveled, but Jaymie immediately recognized him; she had seen him around town more than once, and not in good circumstances. He whirled when he heard Jaymie and stared at her as if he didn't see her.

"Are you okay, Nan?" Jaymie asked, slowly approaching, eyeing the son.

The editor straightened, smoothed her reddish hair, coming out gray at the roots, off her forehead, and settled her jacket on her slim shoulders. "I'm fine. It's nothing, just a disagreement. Jaymie, this is my son Cody Wainwright. Cody, this is one of my writers, Jaymie Leighton."

He turned back toward his mother. "I can't believe after everything I've been through you're not cutting me some slack," he growled, his voice shaking with emotion. "I'm happy for once in my crappy life. But you don't want that, do you?"

"For once in your *crappy* life? Do you know how easy you've had it, how—" She broke off and shook her head, with a side glance at Jaymie. She turned back to her son and in a deliberately calm voice said, "Cody, I want you to be happy. But Shelby Fretter is not good for you. If you *knew* what her family was like, how often that name pops up in my newspaper and on the police blotters—"

"Just like me, don't you get it? She's told me how you've hounded her family. I know *all* about your vendetta against the Fretters. No one ever gave Shelby a break, just like *me!*" He whirled and stormed past Jaymie, but stopped and turned back and pointed at his mother. "You've *never* been there for me, but I didn't think you'd sabotage the only good thing in my life!" He disappeared around the corner and the door buzzer sounded as he left the building.

Jaymie turned to Nan. The older woman's face was blotchy and tears welled in her eyes. She forced a trembling smile and said, "You did come at a good time, didn't you? Sorry about that little display. We're a family of shouters."

Jaymie considered Nan a friend as well as a boss, and reached out, touching her shoulder. "Don't think twice about it. You look like you could use a cup of tea. Can you take a break?"

She shook her head. "Everyone's celebrating one of the printers' birthday in the break room with cake. I said I'd cover the front office. Come on out there and have a coffee with me. I'll have the guys get you your pamphlets and we can settle up." Sighing, she tried again to tame her wiry hair. "That boy will be the death of me some day!"

Several minutes later, sitting in an office chair behind the reception desk, a cup of stale coffee in front of her, Jaymie watched Nan work on the reception computer, scrolling through news stories of the day, making note of important political news as well as world events as she spoke to Jaymie. She clicked on a *Missing* poster on a social media site. "That poor girl still hasn't been found," she said, pointing to the screen, which showed a photo of a beautiful young woman along with the day she disappeared and her personal data.

"We put up Natalie Roth posters at the Emporium a couple of weeks ago. Any news?"

Nan shook her head. "She just disappeared, no leads. I spoke to Detective Vestry about it, and all she'll tell me is that there are no signs of a struggle in her apartment."

Jaymie shook her head. "The family must be frantic by now."

"I can't imagine. You know, speaking of kids, Cody *has* had a rough go of it," she said, scrolling down the page, returning to the subject foremost in her mind. "I downplay it because he never missed anything tangible, not like I did. I grew up dirt poor, but Cody and Mandy, my daughter, went to private schools, had the best of everything. But he's the youngest, my baby. By the time he was a teenager my marriage was beyond rocky. His dad and I fought all the time. I was angry, impetuous, moody. Cody takes after me, believe it or not. He just came to live here in the summer after some trouble out of state, but he can't seem to get it together. I was hoping he had, but this Shelby girl . . ." Nan sighed and shook her head. "Her whole family is trouble."

"Does that necessarily mean *she* is?"

"I guess not, but with so many nice girls out there, why did he have to choose a Fretter?"

Jaymie understood what she meant. The name, locally, was synonymous with lawbreaking and fighting authority, because the children—there were four of them that Jaymie knew of—were always getting into trouble. Parents whispered that anything was better than their kid "going Fretter."

It didn't mean that Shelby was a lost cause, but though Jaymie was playing devil's advocate, she had her own qualms about the relationship. She knew what perhaps his mother didn't, that he was already in deep. Just days before, Jaymie had seen the couple arguing. Cody had lashed out, striking Shelby hard.

❊ Two ❊

JAYMIE CHOSE NOT to tell Nan what she had seen of Cody's behavior. Her editor was already worried enough. Twenty minutes later, with the box of pamphlets on the passenger seat, Jaymie headed back to Queensville, troubled by Nan's worried expression. But the editor was a strong woman, and her son's life was his own, to screw up or fix, whichever worked out. She just hoped for everyone concerned that Shelby Fretter and Cody Wainwright broke up; from the outside it looked like a toxic relationship.

At home she spent the afternoon researching recipes for her last Vintage Eats column before Christmas. She wanted it to be festive, but it had to be vintage, too. Her grandmother's handwritten recipe book, a small three-ring binder with a well-worn black leather cover, was on the trestle table and she carefully leafed through it. It was old, from the late forties, fifties and into the early sixties. Some of it was actually falling apart, but turning the pages was like stepping back into her grandmother's life in this very house, in the Queensville of that time period. Young Lucy Armitage Leighton, newly married, cut out recipes and wrote others down in long hand, earnestly planning meals for her small family. Jaymie's dad, Alan, was grandma's only child, but he had clearly been the light of her life, and still was!

The handwritten recipes were most interesting; she wrote in an elegant sloping cursive, and labeled the recipes, some as "family gems" that Jaymie assumed were passed down to her by someone else, perhaps her mother-in-law, the great-grandmother Jaymie had never met. The old binder contained magazine clippings of dresses, too, and crafts. It was a Leighton treasure, and Jaymie felt fortunate that her grandmother had entrusted it to her.

One recipe clipping in particular interested her. Advertised as "no-bake fruitcake," it combined evaporated milk with candied fruits, marshmallows, crushed vanilla wafers and gingersnaps. What woman getting close to Christmas wouldn't want to be able to whip up a no-bake fruitcake? Jaymie had heard it said that family was like fruitcake; it wasn't the same without a few nuts. She smiled and set the recipe aside with her grocery list to try it out on the weekend. It would become her next column for the *Wolverhampton Weekly Howler*.

Her smile died, though, as she tried to erase Nan's anxious expression from her memory. Jaymie felt like she was a late bloomer. Other women seemed to have it all together, while she was still figuring it out. One of those who had it all together, in her opinion, was Nan Goodenough, a tough New York editor who had started, Jaymie knew, as a newsroom intern straight out of high school in the sixties and went on to move up through the ranks until she was managing editor of *New York Metro Life* magazine before retiring and entering into a second marriage with Joe Goodenough. Until this morning, Jaymie had thought Nan invincible, tough as nails and unshakably confident, but now she had seen the editor's vulnerability. It left her wondering, how much of what she took for granted about those she knew was just veneer? What happened when that surface was scratched?

Her cell phone rang and she picked it up, glancing at the call display. "What's up?"

Heidi Lockland, fiancée of Jaymie's former boyfriend Joel, often called for advice, saying there was no one she could trust more than Jaymie. She babbled for a moment about something Joel had done to anger her, then got down to business. "You know the Dickens Days stuff going on?"

"Of course. I'm on the planning committee."

"I was thinking of wearing the gown I had made for the Tea with the Queen event in the spring," she said. "But it's way too summery. Should I wear it? What can I do?"

Jaymie held the phone away and looked at it, then brought it back up to her ear. "Heidi, what are you talking about?"

"I'm going to be strolling with the singers tomorrow night and I want to wear a costume, but the ones the heritage society has given us are just plain awful. I wouldn't be caught dead in one of those hideous woolen coats, so I was thinking of wearing my dress, but it's December and pretty cold."

Jaymie bit her lip. Just when she needed a lift from fretfulness, there came Heidi! "Stop worrying. Even one of those woolen coats couldn't make you look anything less than ravishing. And the whole idea is that the carol singers look similar, you know? Like something out of a Dickens novel." Silence. This was not going over well. "Heidi, it's December. In Michigan. And you're *always* cold!"

Still silence.

Jaymie stifled a sigh and thought for a moment. "How about this: wear the dress. But go out to the manor. In the attic there's a trunk with some red velvet cloaks trimmed in white fur. Wear one of those with some boots and you'll be warm enough. Instead of singing, we'll get you to hand out samples of the food we're selling at the manor and the band shell." Heidi was charming and pretty, sure to be a hit. She was also a truly lovely person on the inside, and kids seemed to adore her. It was actually a great idea. "That way you'll be on your own, and the star attraction! Everyone loves free food."

"I could carry an adorable basket filled with goodies!" she exclaimed. "Jaymsie, I just *knew* you would have an answer!"

"Glad I could help." Jaymie had no sooner signed off than the phone rang again. It was Valetta.

"You do remember that you're working tomorrow at the Emporium, right?"

"Val, seriously, when have I *ever* forgotten to come to work?" Valetta wasn't as bad as Becca in the nagging department, but on rare occasions she did "mother" Jaymie. Valetta, Becca and another friend, Dee Stubbs, all fifteen years Jaymie's senior, had gone to high school together and hung out as teenagers. Jaymie and Valetta were now true friends, bound by common interests, a shared work space in the Emporium and a love of Queensville, but every once in a while the older-sibling vibe came out in her tone.

"Okay, so you've *never* forgotten to come to work or one of your volunteer duties. But you sure are walking on clouds lately, and I thought you might develop love-amnesia."

Jaymie felt her cheeks burn. That served her right for gushing about Jakob after going out with him on the weekend. Valetta was never going to let her live it down. "I'm not in love," she said severely. "I just like him a whole lot."

"Like, love, whatever. You're in deep, kiddo, I can tell. Can't say I blame you. If I had looked over the whole world, I don't think I could have planned a guy better for you than Jakob Müller."

Jaymie was silent. She had a sudden jolt of fear. Love had never come easy for her, and as Val had noticed, she felt far too much already. Should she pull back? Was she letting her emotions run away with her? Everyone warned her that her fondness for romance novels meant that she was impractical and expected too much from real-life relationships. But she believed she had a levelheaded outlook on real-life romance. She had lost at love and lived to tell the story. And yet . . . if something came between her and Jakob, it would cut much more deeply than her previous disappointments.

Taking a deep breath, she settled herself. "Thanks, Valetta, but so far we're just friends. Please don't get ahead of me."

"I won't push, I promise."

"And don't tell Becca *anything* yet! I've only just met the guy. I don't want anyone running off and planning a wedding for me. I'm taking this as it comes."

Valetta was silent for a moment, then said, "Jaymie, honestly, do you think I'd blab to Becca? I thought you knew me better than that!"

"I'm sorry, Val. I *do* know you better than to think you'd discuss this with her or anyone else, for that matter!" Because Valetta was a bit of a gossip, everyone thought she spilled every bit of news she heard, but the opposite was true. As the town's pharmacist, she kept close to her vest most information and could be trusted not to leak anything important. Her gossip was confined to what was already known, or what had been publicly witnessed, and she heard far more than she spread.

"All right, then. See you tomorrow morning!"

Jaymie wrote out the no-bake fruitcake recipe, cut and packaged the cooled brownies, popped some in a tub to take to Jakob's and raced up the creaky stairs, followed by a wobbly, chipper Hoppy, who yapped excitedly. What was she going to wear over to his house this evening? She wanted to look nice, but not like she was trying too hard. She'd need to be able to get down onto the floor if she ended up playing with Jocelyn. The child was adorable, but eerily mature. Maybe it seemed even more so because a form of dwarfism kept her tiny, more like a three-year-old in height than an eight-year-old. But Jakob did not baby her. Calm self-possession seemed her normal demeanor even in a moment of crisis like the one that had sent Jaymie to Jakob's doorstep on a cold, black November evening just weeks before.

Jaymie tried on leggings and a long burgundy sweater, then changed into a long skirt and blouse, then changed back into the leggings and sweater. She regarded herself in her mirror and sighed. Her bottom was starting to widen again, something she was self-conscious about. She couldn't decide if the leggings and long sweater made it better or worse.

Denver had climbed the stairs and sat in the middle of her crazy quilt glaring at her, his expression as annoyed as always. Though she wasn't completely sold on having the animals sleep with her—Denver sprawled, taking up more than his fair share of the bed, and Hoppy snuffled and snored, lone front paw jerking with excited doggie dreams—Jaymie had finally caved and had Bill Waterman build a set of custom doggie stairs carpeted in pale blue for Hoppy. Now he could wobble up the stairs onto the bed and try to cuddle up to Denver, who grumpily put up with the little dog's affectionate nature.

"You'll have the house to yourself this evening, Denver," she said over her shoulder. Hoppy was coming out to the log cabin with Jaymie, since she wanted to introduce Jocelyn to her little dog.

But right at that moment she still had more work to do. She threw on a pair of jeans and a sweater, trotted downstairs and grabbed her keys and the colander centerpiece she had crafted. She was going to take the box of pamphlets over to where they would be stored, at Bill Waterman's spacious workshop-slash-tool museum behind Jewel Dandridge's repurposed vintage shop on the main street. The sharp bite of frosty air made her rethink her sweater and jacket, but as she locked the back door of the summer porch behind her, she decided if she just hustled, she'd warm up. She hastened down the flagstone path, closed the wrought-iron gate behind her, revved her rattletrap van, turned up the wheezy heater and pulled out of her parking space, down the lane and into the heart of town, just moments away.

Queensville was swiftly earning a reputation as a vintage

and antique mecca. There was Jewel's Junk, which featured funky finds and repurposed stuff. Jewel also created pieces out of "hurt" vintage items, thus there were kitchen utensil wind chimes and teacup bird feeders, among other rebuilt and made-over items. Just down from Jewel was another vintage furniture store, Cynthia Turbridge's Cottage Shoppe, which sold shabby-chic furnishings and décor suited to the cottages that lined the banks of the St. Clair River on both sides of the border, as well as Lake St. Clair and beyond.

There was a rumor going around town that a mystery woman had bought a small cottage opposite those two shops and would fill it with more elegant antiques, including china, crystal, silver and jewelry. Only Jaymie and Valetta knew that the mystery woman was actually her sister, Becca, who was planning a store to hold much of her stock, as well as the gorgeous and stately antique furniture that would grace a more elegant home, like the Queen Anne they jointly owned. She ran a china-matching service out of her home in London, Ontario, a few miles inland from the lakes, but thought retail in Queensville would be a good extension and allow her to buy and sell even more. Her husband-to-be was another antique aficionado and loved old electronics, like Bakelite radios and vintage televisions, so the shop might sell those, too.

Jaymie parked along the curb, set aside a stack of pamphlets to take on to the manor house and give to other vendors, and grabbed the heavy box, toting it awkwardly up the walk, past Jewel's shop and back to Bill Waterman's workshop, the size of a small barn, with a high rusty corrugated tin roof and barn wood walls. He had the big double sliding barn doors open as ventilation, and was bent over a paneled door on a sawhorse, painting pungent liquid stripper over it, the surface bubbling and crackling. He glanced up, saw her, and laid a sheet of plastic wrap over it, then grabbed a rag, wiping his hands swiftly.

"Jaymie, let me get that!" He was a big fellow, tall but

slightly stooped, and with graying whiskers sprouting along his jaw and out of his ears. He usually wore overalls, but in deference to the frigidity of the weather, today wore a one-piece long-sleeved work coverall in dark blue over a thick sweater that peeked out of the top. His eyes were shrouded in wrinkles, but they were a bright winter-sky blue, and twinkled in the right light. He insisted on carrying the box for her and led her to an enclosed room, the warmest, driest part of his shop, where he stored his most valuable tools. Once inside, he set the box of pamphlets on a shelf, where it would stay for the duration of the Dickens Days festivities. He grabbed a spare key from a hook and handed it to her, saying, "I set this aside for you. Keep it safe. And don't lose it! Only me, you and Jewel have a key, besides the spare. That way you can come get more pamphlets whenever you need them. You ordered more than this, I hope?"

As she added the key to her key chain, she followed him back out and waited while he locked the big padlock on the inner door. "Actually, I didn't. I guess if things go as well as we plan, we'll need more. A thousand seemed like a lot at the time."

They moved to the front of the shed again, and then he carefully peeled the plastic off the door and began scraping the old dirty paint from the oak wood underneath. As toxic as the chemicals were, he didn't don gloves. "I'd say we'll need another five thousand. Don't forget, the inn wants some, and every shop on Main Street, the Emporium, as well as ones to hand out. And a few places in Wolverhampton might take 'em, too."

"You're right," she said, making a quick decision. "Better too many than not enough." She pulled her cell phone, a gift Daniel gave her during their romance, out of her pocket and brought up Nan's contact information. "It's pricey, but if we want more we'll have to order them now. Do you think five thousand?"

"That'll do," he said, grunting with the effort of scraping.

"I'll support you if Haskell gets tetchy," he said, referring to Haskell Lockland, the heritage society president.

She concentrated as she texted Nan, asked for confirmation, then clicked the phone off. She looked out at the village from his shop, a great vantage point on a slight rise. It had been transformed in the last week. The cottage shops were decked with cedar garlands and wreaths, wound with red-and-green plaid ribbon. At night twinkle lights winked and blinked from the garland depths and the branches of the small fir trees around the shops. The Queensville Emporium had been swathed in festive trim, too. There were long ever-green garlands strung across the street at the main intersection and to the small village green where the information booth for Dickens Days was going to be set up.

All they needed was snow to make the Dickens Days festivities perfect. She sighed. "I guess I'd better get moving."

"You let me know when you get the rest of the pamphlets. Or do you want me to pick them up in Wolverhampton when they're ready? Seems you do a whole lot of driving with no one paying your mileage."

"I don't mind." She hesitated, but then asked, "Did you know Nan Goodenough had a son who's staying with her right now?"

His head snapped up and he stared at her, his mouth turned down. "I know him. He come around here asking for a job. Told him I got no use for those who don't treat women right."

She sighed. "You saw it, too? The way he treated his girl-friend?"

He nodded, tight-lipped. "Whacked her upside of the head."

"Sounds like the same incident I saw. Don't say anything to anyone, but I think he shoved his mom this morning." She explained what she had heard at the newspaper office.

He shook his head. "Don't like him. Don't like any man treats a woman with less than respect." He finished scraping the last bit of paint and grabbed a dirty rag, wiping some of the chemical off the oak door with a splash of mineral spirits,

the pungent scent wafting on the fresh December breeze. But
his dour look lightened and he winked at her. "There are
some fellows out there who know a good woman when he's
found her. Like the Müller's youngest, Jakob. Heard he's
sweet on a real nice girl."

She felt her color heighten and she buffeted him on the
arm. "You stop! Enough of that. We're just friends."

"Sure you are. You say hello to him for me, and that I'll be
out to The Junk Stops Here tomorrow to pick up that antique
sleigh we talked about. I'm thinking about fixing it up and
giving sleigh rides through the village."

She was enchanted, and clapped, jumping up and down.
"Could we maybe plan that for next year's Dickens Days?
Maybe we could even do rides out to the manor house."

"One step at a time, Jaymie. There isn't always snow this
time of year, like now. You go on. I've got to finish this door
for a very particular customer."

She knew he meant Becca and chuckled. Light-headed
with hope and relief—it was good to share her worries about
Nan and Cody with someone who understood, someone as
steady and trustworthy as Bill—she drove her rickety white
van out to Queensville Historic Manor, where she would
deliver a stack of pamphlets, place her centerpiece creation
on the Hoosier and make sure her kitchen had survived the
ins and outs of the various heritage committee members,
some of whom preferred to enter though the kitchen door
rather than circle all the way to the front.

In the slanting late afternoon light, she drove up the lane
and around behind the garage, where some parking spaces
had been delineated for committee volunteers, grabbed her
white colander centerpiece and stack of pamphlets, locked
the van and circled the house to the front to get the full view.
The former Dumpe Manor, now Queensville Historic Manor,
looked wonderful. A massive Queen Anne–style home, with
copious gingerbread and clapboard siding, bound on two
sides with forest and the other with open fields, the house

had been painted a lovely soft blue and the gingerbread a sparkling white. The broad porch and steps had been repaired by Bill and were now safe to mount. The whole was fronted by a lighted sign announcing the name and hours.

She stood near the road and gazed at it, biting her lip and grimacing at the huge blow-up gingerbread man cookie that waved and waggled in the wind, the generator groaning and puttering. Most of the older committee members had been horrified when some of the younger ones had suggested renting a blow-up decoration to draw attention to the historic manor's Christmas opening, but Jaymie had agreed that however you got feet through the door didn't matter. And folks with kids wanted kid-friendly things to look at. The gingerbread man cookie was the best of a bad lot, she thought, better than the Santa on an airplane or sock monkeys on a scooter that were other possible rental choices. But it sure did look tacky in front of the elegant manse! Oh well, it would come down just after the New Year.

She mounted the steps and entered, pausing as she removed her boots to appreciate the beauty of the old house. It never failed to awe her, the lovely old pendant lights, the elegant wood baseboards and beautiful finishing they had all strived to perfect over the last couple of months. An amazing amount had been done in a short time, mostly due to the organizational skills of Haskell Lockland and the handyman ability of Bill Waterman, as well as the dedication of the volunteers, like her, each with their own specialty.

In the main hall they had placed a long, low Chippendale-style table topped by a big mirror, and on the table were pamphlets and what little literature they had pertaining to the Dumpe family and Queensville's history, postcards to buy and one Lucite pamphlet stand just waiting for the literature she had in hand. She filled it with the pamphlets, stacking the rest on the table behind the stand, and then, carrying her boots, strode through the hall to the back of the house where her precious kitchen seemed like an afterthought, when it was the heart of the whole manor house project, if you asked her.

But the kitchen wasn't empty. A fiftyish woman in jeans and a long-sleeved T-shirt, bleached hair pulled back tight in a frizzy ponytail, was on her hands and knees scouring the oven of Jaymie's precious antique gas stove, which was sans knobs, sans burner drip pans, sans grates, sans . . . everything!

❧ Three ❧

"**W**HAT ARE YOU doing?" cried Jaymie, dropping her boots.

The woman jolted, whacked her head on the top of the oven and scrambled out, leaping to her feet and whirling. "What the . . . ? Who are you?"

"Never mind that, who are *you*? And what are you doing to my stove?" Shaking, Jaymie carefully set the decorative colander down on the porcelain top of the green-and-white vintage Hoosier and stood, staring forlornly at her disassembled stove. The same stove she had just thoroughly cleaned according to instructions from a website on antique and vintage stoves, and which she had *just* got working right with a lot of trial, error and burned cookies.

The woman peeled her rubber gloves off, the smell of harsh modern chemicals wafting out of the oven, from which the door had been removed. "I was hired to clean, so I'm cleaning."

Controlling her breathing and carefully inflecting her tone

to somewhat close to politeness, Jaymie said, "My name is Jaymie Leighton, and this is the kitchen I designed and furnished. You must be Lori Wozny. I was on the committee that looked at everyone's references and we were so pleased to hire you. However, I'm sorry if it wasn't clear, but no one meant for you to clean the vintage appliances." She glanced around, noting the knobs laid out on newspaper with some kind of cleaning solution on them. *Argh!* It was almost physically painful to consider the damage that may have been done to them. "Besides, I've already cleaned the stove."

"Not very well," the woman said, her tone huffy, as she tossed the rubber gloves down onto newspaper that was protecting every surface. "It's still dirty. And under the knobs was all this grease! Took me half an hour just to get it off."

Jaymie closed her eyes and swayed. "The grease is there on purpose, just a small amount to make the action smooth. And the knobs are Bakelite. *Bakelite!*" It had taken her some time to establish that it was indeed Bakelite and not another compound. Becca's fiancé had visited and given her the final verdict with some tests involving hot water and a lot of sniffing. After that she had bought the proper cleaning solution, liquid metal polish, and spent hours properly restoring them. And now . . . She took in a deep breath and released it, slowly. It wasn't helping. The woman didn't know, she said to herself. *Stay calm.* "Bakelite is a special material and you never *ever* want to use harsh chemicals on it. *Ever!*"

When she opened her eyes again and looked at Lori she realized she had offended the woman gravely, but she didn't care at this point. "I'm sorry, but I'll have to ask you to just stop," she said, moving toward the stove and touching the surface lightly. "This is an antique and it's precious to me. I don't want to hurt your feelings, but harsh chemicals should never be used on antique or vintage anything. That goes for almost everything in this house."

Lori skittered around, packing up her stuff, throwing things in a blue plastic pail. "*Fine*, then. I was *trying* to do my job, and all I get is *crap*. Typical. If you all want to live in *filth*, or let the public think that's how old people lived, then *have at it*!"

In Jaymie's experience, anyone who talked in italics was seriously angry. "Lori, please, don't get offended. We value your work." It had been difficult to find someone dependable, and the woman had a wonderful reference from Delaney Meadows, the owner of a local job placement company. Lori was the mother of one of his employees, a hard worker, apparently.

But at this moment she was in a full-on snit. Jaymie considered her options and decided silence for the moment was best, and a word to Haskell about her confrontation with the cleaner. Lori stomped out of the kitchen and Jaymie spent the next hour repairing the damage the woman had done. There were scratches on the chrome from the abrasive steel wool soap pad she had used, and it would take some time to tell if the Bakelite knobs had been damaged.

She folded up the newspapers, stuffed them in a garbage bag and turned in a circle, hoping the room was ready for viewing. Some people had already been through the house, but this weekend she was going to start kitchen demonstrations with recipes she had prepared and a costume she had put together with some vintage clothes Jewel had sourced for her. She would wear a longish dress with a patterned pinafore apron over it, her hair done in a twenties or thirties style—a local hairdresser who had recently joined the heritage society showed her how—and black oxford shoes.

The kitchen was now almost perfect, at least for the time being, painted a mellow green, with the green-and-white gas stove that Bill Waterman had found at Jakob's store. There was also a venerable green-and-cream Hoosier, the paint all original, that she had bought at auction, and next to it an antique ice chest donated by the Redmonds, owners of the Ice House restaurant. Vintage and antique egg beaters, cookie cutters, whisks, mallets, muddles and various other implements—most of which had green or red and cream painted handles—were on display, and she had worked up a routine to demonstrate their uses. Her colander with the greenery in it added a cheery and festive note.

She finished up and washed her hands. As usual after she chastised someone, she now felt awful. Lori had only wanted to make the room the best it could be. It wasn't her fault that she didn't know how to care for vintage appliances, nor did she know it was not part of her job. She was one of those who is almost *too* thorough. Jaymie grabbed her jacket from the kitchen chair, where she had slung it after finding her kitchen in disarray, picked up her boots, strode from the kitchen and passed through the parlor to the dining room. Mabel Bloombury was polishing a silver epergne and centered it on the tiger oak pedestal dining table.

"This looks wonderful!" Jaymie exclaimed. She had expected Christmassy red and green, but the table was set with a blue tablecloth, and adorned with all blue and silver.

Mabel stood back and clasped her hands in front of her generous bosom. "Do you like it? The china is one your sister suggested, Sevron Blue Lace, from the nineteen fifties. And the glassware is Libbey Silver Leaf. I thought we'd do it up *this* weekend for Hanukkah, and then go to the red-and-white transferware patterned china your sister loaned us the next weekend."

"What a great idea!" Jaymie said, eyeing Mabel with respect. She hadn't thought the older woman would show so much innovation with the table décor.

Mabel shot her a side glance. "My husband's people started in this country as Blumbergs," she said. "I wanted to honor the celebration of lights, you know." She touched the elaborate silver candelabra in the center of the table and waggled her fingers at the silver and crystal epergne that gleamed softly in the chandelier's illumination.

"I think it's lovely. Say, Mabel, did you see Lori Wozny in the last little while? Is she still here?"

"I think she's upstairs. She stomped through here mumbling under her breath; she seemed in a dreadful mood."

"That's my fault, I'm afraid," Jaymie said, and relayed what happened.

Mabel touched her arm, her fingers icy. "Don't worry too much about it, dear. That young woman seems to be a touch flighty. It runs in the family."

"Runs in the family?"

"She's a Fretter, you know, despite her married name."

Jaymie started and stared at Mabel. There was that synchronicity thing happening. She'd always noticed that once you heard about something or someone, they just kept popping up everywhere. Of course, if she hadn't just heard about Shelby Fretter, it wouldn't have meant anything to her other than a brief acknowledgment that they were known locally as the family whose name was most often seen in the Police Blotter column of the *Howler*. "Is she, by any chance, Shelby Fretter's mother?"

Mabel nodded. "I always felt sorry for those kids. Lori went from man to man to man. The oldest kids' dad—Shelby and her brother are twins—is long gone, didn't even stick around long enough to give them his last name."

"So that must mean Shelby is the one who works for Delaney Meadows, the one who gave Lori her reference? Or is it another of her kids?"

"No, that's right, that's Shelby. She's great friends with my daughter, Lynnsey; they went through school together. Shelby has worked for Meadows for almost a year at his business, some kind of white-collar placement agency. It's in one of those big houses on the north end of town that has been converted into office space."

And now she was going out with Nan's son. Small world. Jaymie made a quick decision. "In the interests of harmony, if Lori's going to keep working here I ought to apologize. I didn't mean to hurt her feelings."

Mabel shook her head, a doubtful expression on her face. "She's one of those who the more you apologize, the more she'll misunderstand. You probably didn't say anything wrong. Some folks just go through life intent on being wounded and seeing insults where none were intended. I'd let it go if I were you."

"But I was kind of abrupt. I feel like I should try." She heard a vacuum cleaner upstairs, and decided to give an apology a whirl. She went through the parlor to the hallway, left her boots by the front door and climbed the front stairs, which ascended to a landing, then made a right-angle turn. She climbed to the second floor and saw Lori Wozny at the end of the dim hall, just finishing. The cleaner turned the vacuum off, yanked the cord out of the plug, and began to wind it up. "Lori?" Jaymie said, as she pulled on her jacket and zipped it up.

The woman started again and whirled, one hand to her chest. "You do love to scare people, don't you!" she said.

"I'm sorry." Was she always going to be apologizing as long as the woman worked for the society? "I just wanted to say I didn't mean to offend you and hope we can be friends."

"If you *heard* the way you sounded!" she said, jerkily finishing winding the cord and pushing the machine down the hall past Jaymie to the broom closet where it was kept. Over her shoulder, she groused, "You'd think I was breaking something, the way you behaved."

Jaymie held her tongue. She knew that she did no such thing and that Lori was overreacting, but there was no way to backtrack now, or it would become a she said/she said argument. "I suppose I'd better get going now."

Lori turned around and glared, hands on her hips. "You oughta be careful, you know. Some folks aren't as easygoing as me."

"I have to go. I have a column due at the *Wolverhampton Weekly Howler*," Jaymie said, looking for any excuse to break off this conversation as she headed toward the stairs.

"You work for that Nan woman, with the evil son? She spawned an abuser, and do you think she cares? Not one little bit!"

Jaymie halted and turned around slowly. She couldn't pretend not to know what the woman was talking about. "Are you talking about the relationship between your daughter Shelby and Cody Wainwright?"

Lori almost smiled—Jaymie thought she enjoyed getting a reaction—but darkened her expression and grimaced. "You bet. That jerk hit my daughter, and she's dumb enough to let him. He tries it again I'll give it to him good, I promise you," she said, balling her hand into a fist. "You tell that to that Good-enough woman."

Torn between silence and defending her friend and editor, Jaymie asked, "Is your daughter going to end the relationship? That would be best all round."

"As if *you* have a clue about it. I've heard all about you." She retreated into the volunteer's lounge and came back out with a red-plaid wool coat that she shrugged into. "You act like you're some kind of detective or something."

Bewildered by the quick shift into a personal attack, Jaymie mumbled a reply, turned toward the stairs and started down. Jaymie pulled on her boots and they both exited at the same time onto the wide-board porch, the crisp December air a bracing wake-up. A beat-up Ford backed up the lane and Lori headed toward it. Hand on the car door, she turned and hollered, "You tell that Nan woman to make Cody Wainwright behave, you hear me?"

The window was down, and Shelby Fretter, a pretty blonde with a downturned dissatisfied mouth, leaned across the passenger seat as she lowered the window. "Mom, why are you talking about Cody? I told you to keep your nose out of my business."

Lori looked uncertain and stared at her daughter, then looked back to Jaymie. "I wasn't doing anything," she said, grabbing the car door and yanking it open. "But some people need to be told that others aren't angels, you know?" She slid into the passenger seat.

How Lori Wozny got from Jaymie's silence that she thought Cody was an angel, she did not know.

"Cody can jam a turnip up his butt, and his mom, too," Shelby said. She leaned across her mother and glared out the window. "Why do *you* care?" she yelled at Jaymie.

"I don't," Jaymie called out, feeling ridiculous but not wanting to engage by approaching the car. "It was just a misunderstanding!"

"Hey, I know who you are. Saw your picture in the paper last month," Shelby said, staring at her. "You're the one who keeps getting mixed up in murder. You think you're some kind of PI?"

Jaymie just shrugged.

"I could investigate *rings* around you!" She rolled her window up.

Mabel Bloombury had come out on the porch and stood by Jaymie. "What's wrong?"

"I haven't a clue," Jaymie said as Shelby gunned the heavy-sounding motor and sped down the lane, turning abruptly and skidding off down the road toward Queensville. "I have *no* idea. I'd better get going," she said and gave Mabel a brief unplanned hug.

She headed home in a thoughtful frame of mind, wondering if Shelby would do what she ought and break it off with Cody Wainwright. And then she thought of how Cody had shouted at his mother that he was happy for the first time in his life. There was trouble ahead, but she hoped it wasn't for Nan.

❖ Four ❖

SHE PARKED THE van in the usual spot by her garage in the parking lane that ran behind the houses on her street and headed into the house. She always left the garage for guests, since her van was so old and decrepit it would go into shock if garaged.

The next few days were going to be busy. Tomorrow morning she had to be at the Emporium for a half day of work, and then there was the evening volunteering for the historic society. Her job, to hand out pamphlets for the historic manor, meant a lot of walking and a lot of talking to folks, dressed in one of the long cloaks the society had for its strolling singers. They were wool, and warm, but also heavy! It would be exhausting, but she was up for it, and looked forward to talking to folks about the historic house.

So her evening at Jakob's log home outside of town would be a pause before the craziness that was Dickens Days. With a mixture of nerves and hope she looked forward to it, but before that, she still had a few tasks. Once home, she got down to some household jobs. The house was chilly, so she turned up the thermostat and raced around organizing herself for the next few days. She brushed down her Victorian cloak and hung it on the hook on her bedroom door, then put together her bag to take with her the next morning for work. Hoppy raced around the house after her, barking his encouragement, while Denver insisted on going outside to sit under the holly bushes and grumble.

The day's light was fading when she finally looked at the clock; time to change her clothes and drive over to Jakob's. She was nervous and excited and her stomach felt faintly ill. Taking a deep breath she stared at herself in the bathroom mirror. Her plump cheeks were flushed with pink, and her brown hair hung in a silky sheet to her shoulders. She smoothed some moisturizer on her face and dabbed dusty rose lipstick on her lips; that was all the makeup she generally used, and tonight she wanted to be wholly herself. Jakob had seen her at her worst and at her best and seemed to like her just for who she was.

She turned from the mirror. Hoppy sat in the doorway looking up at her. Smiling, she waited one moment, then said the magic phrase, "Want to go for a car ride?"

Hoppy yapped and whirled, skittering in his wobbly manner down the stairs to the front hall, then back and through the kitchen, as Jaymie followed at a more sedate pace. She opened the back door, crossed the summer porch and opened the door. "Denver, come on in, sweetie," she called.

Her crabby tabby turned his back and glared at the fence. She sighed. "I'm not leaving you outside. I may be late and it's getting cold." She slipped on the shoes she kept by the back door, crossed the lawn and picked him up, cradling him in her arms. He glared up at her and started purring. He was getting fatter now that she had had his teeth fixed and fed him soft food. He wasn't a whole lot more friendly, but he had never once growled at her, even when he was in pain. And he purred now! Amazing.

"Jaymie, hellooo!"

She peered through the dusk toward Pam Driscoll's voice. Pam was looking after the bed-and-breakfast next door for her friends, Pam's cousin and cousin-in-law Anna and Clive Jones. "How are you, neighbor?" she said, approaching the fence between the two properties. She had thought Pam was going to be a nuisance when she first moved in to look after the place because she seemed kind of needy, but she had turned out to be a surprisingly efficient manager.

Pam stepped out of the doorway onto the deck, which overlooked the Leighton property. She stood close to the deck rail and wrapped her sweater around herself, shivering. "I'm good. Just got off the phone with Anna. The baby is almost due. She and Clive are anxiously awaiting! She's hoping it'll be a Christmas baby, because she's been telling Tabby that there is a special delivery coming! She said to tell you to call or email!"

Jaymie missed Anna and her little daughter, Tabitha, so much! "I'll email her, or maybe we can Skype! I miss her like crazy."

"Me, too. Tell her to email you pics of Tabby in her new Christmas outfit. And of herself. She's enormous! Looks like she'll pop any minute."

"Are your bookings up? I have some pamphlets of the Dickens Days festivities if you want to share them with your guests."

"I'll take them. I'm still learning what there is to see and do around here. I'm fully booked for the weekend. Two are overflow guests from the inn! I guess they overbooked."

"Awesome!" Jaymie paused. She knew some of Pam's history, enough to know that she had been abused in the past by a boyfriend and had escaped. Weighed down by the problems of Cody Wainwright and Shelby Fretter, and how it impacted Nan Goodenough, Jaymie wished she could talk to someone about it, but there was just no way to frame the question in her heart to Pam in such a casual conversation.

She desperately wanted to know why a woman would stay with a man once she had been abused. Impossible to ask of her relatively new friend. Instead, she waved her one free hand and said, "I'd better get this cat inside and get moving. Talk to you soon, Pam!"

"One thing I miss about my life in Rochester, I used to have friends there! I'd love a visit. If you can help me move some furniture so I can clean, we can chat and have a coffee."

"Sure, give me a call."

Pam wrapped her sweater around her more closely, and retreated with a wave.

Jaymie took Denver inside and gently put him in his basket by the stove. He looked up at her, his green eyes wide, and blinked. She smiled. "I know, Denver kitty; you love me in your own way. That's what's important."

She stuck the tub of brownies in a bag and set it by the back door, then pulled Hoppy's little specially knitted sweater, a gift from Mrs. Frump, over him, snapped it under his belly and clipped his leash to his collar. She turned out all the lights except the one over the sink in the kitchen, said good night to Denver and headed out, locking up securely after her. Hoppy wobbled out to the van and waited for Jaymie to pick him up, then settled himself in the passenger's seat, as usual. He didn't know where they were going, and didn't care. He'd be happy as long as he was with Jaymie. That was the wonderful thing about a rescued dog like Hoppy; he was all heart and grateful to be included.

She drove out of town to the highway, and headed to Jakob's place. It had only been a few weeks since the incident that had sent her to his door, but she thanked heaven every day. She had been in terrible trouble, and Jakob's home was the safest place she could have landed besides a police station. It was a twenty minute drive, with a few turns along the way. She tuned the radio to a Christmas station and sang along with "Jingle Bell Rock," trying to settle her nerves.

What was she so anxious about anyway? She knew Jakob

and liked him. They had met a couple of times for coffee in the last weeks, and once with Jocelyn. Each time Jaymie had been mildly nervous, and everything had gone beautifully. But still, this mattered to her in ways she hadn't anticipated. This was dinner at his home with Jocelyn and it felt important, somehow, like a turning point in their relationship.

"You are going to love Jocelyn, Hoppy. She's like you: smart, lovable and cute."

Hoppy put his head to one side as he watched her, his dark eyes fastened on her mouth.

She glanced over at him, then back to the dark country road. "And I hope you like Jakob. I can't imagine you won't."

She pulled into his lane and shut off the van in front of Jakob's log cabin. It was big enough to have a full second floor. There was a barn beyond it, looming dark in the gloomy fall evening twilight. A floodlit sign near the barn read MÜLLER CHRISTMAS TREE FARM—CUT YOUR OWN CHRISTMAS TREE, OR LET US DO IT FOR YOU! It gave the hours—they were done for the evening, which was why the dinner was a little later than the usual dinner with a family would be—and a phone number. This was just one of Jakob's businesses, worked up over the last fifteen years on a ten acre pocket of land in the corner of his family's farm. Like her, he had several responsibilities, because he also ran the store, The Junk Stops Here, from a former car parts factory on a country side road near town.

As she sat for a moment, collecting her thoughts, she caught a glimpse of Jakob in the window of his kitchen, which overlooked the deep porch that fronted the cabin. He was at the sink, tea towel over his shoulder, talking to Jocelyn. He turned, took something out of the oven and set it on the counter, then grabbed a ladle from a container of tools, ladling something out of the pan.

It was a deeply domestic scene. She couldn't picture Daniel or Zack, her last two love interests, cooking and sharing a home with a child. Daniel *said* he wanted children, but there was never a feeling from him that he would be the kind of dad she would want for a child: engaged, careful, loving and participatory. She had tried to explain to Daniel how children changed a woman's life in ways many men didn't understand, how wholly it became a focus, and how she wasn't sure she was ready for that, now that she was finding her way in life, late bloomer that she was.

But with Jakob, she could see it. Her scalp prickled and she swallowed hard. She was anxious and just a little fearful, but knew she was letting herself get ahead of the relationship. She didn't truly know how Jakob felt about her. She needed to just let it be what it was, and take one lovely day at a time.

He looked up at that moment and caught sight of her van and waved. She got out, setting Hoppy down on the frozen ground and grabbing the bag with the tub of brownies off the dashboard. He had the door open by the time she got to it, and opened his arms. She walked right into them, and was enveloped in a hug so warm and comforting she felt all her nerves and tension ease away into the night.

And then chaos erupted as little Jocie trotted to the door, Hoppy yapped a greeting and Jaymie let go of the leash. The two met in a joyful melee of cheerful pandemonium, and raced about for a half hour nonstop. The whole cabin had the fragrance of rosemary and thyme, with a dash of good strong coffee thrown in, and Jaymie pitched in, washing up dishes left over from cooking. Jakob set the kitchen table for dinner with a homely mismatched set of red earthenware dishes on a plaid tablecloth.

She had brought a baggie of Hoppy's food, but Jocie sneaked him bites of delicious homemade meatloaf under the table. Jakob had also cooked garlic mashed potatoes and roasted vegetables. While they ate, Jakob told her about starting his Christmas tree farm.

"I was home from college one summer and thinking of ways to make some money. Papa was thinking of selling off some of the farm, but I asked if I could work it instead."

"Why would he sell part of the property?" Jaymie asked.

"He was thinking ahead to retirement," he said. "For one thing, this part isn't arable for other crops, though it works just fine for conifers. It's hilly and rocky, with outcroppings of stone left from the glaciers, so it won't take a plough. My family has a lot of land, and at that point none of the other boys seemed to want to take over the farm."

"How many of you are there?" Jaymie asked.

"We are five."

Jaymie's eyes widened. "*Five* sons? How did your mother bear it?"

He shrugged and grinned. "She's German. She had no problem ruling us, let me tell you."

"Oma says that they were all *mühseligste*," Jocie said, with a giggle.

"What does that mean?"

Jakob rolled his eyes at his daughter. "That is when my mama is being polite. It means *most troublesome*."

"How old are you all?"

"There was a first child, a girl, Berthe, who was still-born," he said, quietly. "Then there is Dieter, fifty-three. He moved back in with Mama and Papa because my father was in hospital for a while. Franz is fifty-one; he's married and has four kids. They live near Livonia. Helmut is forty-five, not married but living with a lovely woman he met on the Internet. Sonya has two children. I call her my sister-in-law anyway. Manfred is forty-one. He's the wanderer of the family and has been all over. Right now he's living in Papua, New Guinea. Then there's me!"

Jaymie smiled. She already knew Jakob was thirty-seven. "You were talking about your father selling land?"

"This was in the nineties just after I got out of high school. I said instead, why didn't I take over part of it and see how it went. I told him my idea for a Christmas tree farm. We always planted our own Christmas trees over the years, my brothers and I, and we competed for the honor of having one of our trees chosen to be the season's Christmas tree, so I knew what I was doing." He shrugged and grinned. "Or I thought I did. It was a lot of work, and we knew it wouldn't pay off for years, but I was young and ambitious. I got a couple of my buddies and we planted ten thousand seedlings one April."

He paused. Jocie was getting restless, kicking the leg of the table and shifting. "Let's have our dessert, the wonderful brownies Jaymie brought, in the living room by the fire," he said to his daughter.

Jocie hopped down and helped her father clear the table, as he insisted Jaymie go make herself comfortable by the fire. Then the little girl raced around some with Hoppy, who began finally to lag a bit, sleepy after so much unaccustomed exercise. Jakob sat with Jaymie on his new sofa—he had replaced the two chairs he had in front of the fire with a red plaid sofa, and moved the chairs off to one side—and they watched Jocie lying on the rug by the hearth with Hoppy. They were playing some milder game that only the two of them understood, where she would put her hand on the rug and he would put his paw over it, then she would cover his paw, giggle and let go. They did it over and over, with Jocie laughing every time.

Jaymie sat with her feet curled up under her, completely content in that moment, at ease as Jakob turned the TV on and tuned it to *A Charlie Brown Christmas*.

"We watch this every year," he confided, setting the remote down on the side table. "I hope you don't mind me putting it on?"

"Not in the slightest," she said.

The cabin was comfortable, if a bit drafty. Jakob had explained that when he built it from a kit he didn't know as much as he should have. He was now having to correct the mistakes he had made in his youthful enthusiasm.

"Are you warm enough?" he asked, looking over at her.

She wondered what would happen if she said no. Would he move over and keep her warm? She smiled to herself. A bit too soon to be thinking things like that. "I'm good," she said, watching him.

Jakob was a solidly built man, more substantial than Daniel, who was gaunt and bony, or Zack, who was lithe and fit. Jakob was strong, with broad shoulders and big hands, not too tall, probably five ten or so, with a hint of a paunch. His black curly hair was longish, just touching his red-and-black plaid shirt collar, and he had a bit of beard coming in. All in all he looked very much like a lumberjack.

"Jocie, Charlie Brown is on. Do you want your chair?" he asked.

Jocie turned from her game with Hoppy, smiled over at them, and Jaymie's breath caught in her throat. Jocie was a little person. Her face was round and her hair a halo of blond hanging in natural ringlets. Her eyes were a chocolatey brown, not quite as dark as Jakob's but with the same long lashes, and expressive, full of hope. She nodded, then turned to Jaymie. "Can Hoppy sit with me?"

"He can do whatever he wants," she replied. "If he'd like to stay, he will."

Jakob crossed the room to the toy trunk and picked up a small chair beside it that was actually in the shape of a big teddy bear. He plopped it down, pointed at the TV. Jocie gently picked up Hoppy and sat, carefully settling the little dog in beside her. Hoppy was sleepy and docile after two hours of excitement and play, and snuggled close to her with a little doggie sigh as she watched Charlie and the gang find the perfect Christmas tree, which turned out to be a straggly little thing that was beautiful in spite of its faults.

"I'm not sure the lesson from Charlie Brown is one a Christmas tree farm owner ought to embrace," she joked, as Jakob sat back down just a little closer to her.

"But it's important. I tell folks, don't look for the *perfect* tree, because nature makes room for imperfection, just as we should. Not one of us is perfect."

She put her hand on his arm and gazed steadily at him with a smile. "That is *so* the perfect answer!"

He met her gaze. "It's what I believe. I like to give folks second chances, you know? And let things go that aren't perfect. Even if you once believed in perfection; that goes out the door when you have a kid."

She glanced around at the faintly shabby room, toys piled on a chest by the bookcase, where kids books were jumbled in with old texts, battered paperback fiction and one whole shelf of books on arboriculture, which Jaymie didn't even know was a field of agricultural study until she met Jakob. "Perfection is highly overrated," she said softly. She squeezed his arm and released, feeling just a little self-conscious and knowing she was blushing.

They chatted quietly as Hoppy snoozed, kicking at Jocie with his hind legs as she giggled and made more room for him on her comfy chair. The Peanuts gang put on the nativity play, and Snoopy decorated his doghouse with glowing lights. They ate brownies, which Jakob declared were the best he had ever eaten as he licked his fingers. Jocie nodded in enthusiastic agreement, brownie crumbs on her pink bow lips, before her gaze returned to the TV, as the gang sang together around the now beautiful Christmas tree.

"So did you finally find someone to work the tree farm?" she asked, as the show went to a commercial. Jakob had almost despaired of finding anyone who could work the farm and help folks cut down trees in the daytime while he took care of the junk store. He had one fellow, but needed a second.

"I finally did. As a matter of fact, his mom is the editor at the *Wolverhampton Weekly Howler*, the one who hired you for Vintage Eats."

❧ Five ❧

"DO YOU MEAN Cody Wainwright?" she asked.

"Sure. He came out in response to my help-wanted ad in his mom and stepdad's paper, and I told him I'd give him a shot. He's already worked all week for me. Great worker, very energetic."

She was silent, staring at the fire and biting her lip.

"I thought you'd be pleased," he said, watching her. "I know how you feel about Mrs. Goodenough."

She had to tell him, and explained what she had witnessed just that day and what she had seen before, of his confrontation with Shelby Fretter.

Jakob shoved his fingers through his thick hair and sighed, shaking his head. "*Gott im Himmel*," he muttered, staring into the fireplace. He often sprinkled his speech with phrases in German, which was spoken in his home growing up.

"What are you going to do?" she finally asked.

He took a moment, frowning down at his hands, which

were now folded together, the fingers interlaced. Jocie yawned and he said quietly, "I'll put Jocie to bed, and then perhaps we can talk more. I'm not keeping you, am I? I know you're busy tomorrow."

"I have time," she said.

He picked up a snoozing Jocie. She awoke enough to say good night to Jaymie, then he carried her upstairs. Jaymie retrieved her dog and set him on the rug by the fire, then moved Jocie's chair back in place and decided to do the dishes. It was the least she could do. She stood by the kitchen counter staring out into the dark and waited for the sink to fill with hot soapy water. Oddly enough, she was overcome by a feeling of déjà vu, and yet she had never done this exact thing before, washing dishes alone in Jakob's cabin.

She shook herself and started. By the time he joined her she was done and hanging up the tea towel on the rack by the stove.

"You didn't have to do that," he said.

"I know," she answered, turning and looking up at him. She felt a moment of intent, like he had an impulse to kiss her, but then it was gone and instead he took her hand and pulled her toward the living room. "Jocie said that she forgot to kiss Hoppy good night."

"Tell her tomorrow morning that I kissed him good night for her."

They sat facing each other on the sofa. Jaymie brought her knee up onto the cushion and examined his face. He was troubled, his eyes shadowed with his dark brows.

"I was so pleased about Cody," he started. "I know how much you like his mother."

"I'm sorry," she said reflexively.

"For what?"

She thought a moment and shook her head. He was right; she had nothing to apologize for. It was information he needed to have about an employee.

"I guess I'm disappointed," he said. "He seems like a nice fellow, eager to work. I've hired a lot of kids his age over the years and I can't be fooled by that."

"But those things aren't mutually exclusive," she commented. "An eagerness to work and anger control issues, I mean."

"You're right, of course." He reached for her hand absent-mindedly, and sat looking down at their two hands together. "I had thought better of him. Especially regarding his mother; he seems to truly love her."

"I didn't actually see what went on between him and Nan. I'm just guessing," she said about her comment on the scuffle she overheard. "Nan is intense, and she says Cody takes after her."

He nodded. "I'm going to keep him on for now. It's just seasonal work ending Christmas Eve day. I'd like a chance to talk to him."

"Talk to him? Why? What do you mean?"

He looked up and met her gaze, stroking her palm with his thumb. "Remember I told you about my brother, Manny, the globetrotter?"

She nodded.

"He was troubled when we were young. I don't know why; I've never known. We were all raised in the same house, so why one should have troubles and not the others I can't say. But he got in with a crowd of stoner friends and started smoking weed. That wasn't so bad—he was just kind of mellow and disassociated when he smoked—but then he got into harder drugs. He had a girlfriend, a nice girl. Young. Scared all the time. He hit her; I saw it and was shaken to the core. That's not how we were raised. He was sorry after, but they always are, aren't they, men who hit women? And maybe women who hit men, I don't know."

Jaymie was sad for him, he looked so troubled. She put one hand over their clasped hands, but didn't say anything, not wanting to interrupt his deeply personal story.

"My father tried to talk to him—so did my brothers—but

nothing worked. He was angry, said we were taking everyone else's side and not his. He took off and went away for a
while, a couple of years, actually. My mama was so afraid
for him. Papa thought he'd get himself killed."

"I'm so sorry, Jakob."

"But he didn't end up dead, thank God. And when he
came back he was different. Still troubled, but . . ." He shook
his head. "It was like when he would have one of those
moments of rage, he would pull back into himself and stop,
just . . . stop. I heard him talking to Mama one night. I
remember it so clearly; I was sitting in the living room fum-
ing that he was back, because Mama and Papa were so happy,
and I thought, why?"

"You mean, why were they happy?"

He nodded. "He had caused them so much pain and I
was so angry at him for that. It took me longer than anyone
to get over his behavior; I think maybe because we had once
been so close. The closer you are to someone the more they
can hurt you. But anyway, Mama asked him what had
changed. He told her that a man gave him a job and talked
to him. Not all the time, and he didn't preach. He just . . .
talked. The guy must have been a miracle worker. Manny
thought about things, and got the idea that he wasn't taking
responsibility for his own behavior. Which was exactly what
Papa had told him years before, but I guess he had to hear
it from someone else. From then on he said he felt changed.
He went looking for help and got it. It didn't happen overnight, but it happened."

Jaymie didn't say a word, knowing he wasn't finished. She
should get going, she supposed, but she was in no real hurry.
This felt important, the sharing of difficult stories from their
families. It was what had been missing in her relationship
with Daniel.

"I'm grateful you told me about Cody," Jakob said. "I'm
going to keep him on. Do you mind if I call Nan and talk
to her about her son?"

Jaymie thought for a moment, feeling a thread of trepidation. Nan was a very private woman. But Cody needed help and if Jakob could offer it, then it was important. "What would you say?" she asked, hedging.

He paused. Jaymie had noticed this about Jakob; he never spoke in haste. When she asked a question, he often took time to form an answer.

"I suppose I'll let her know that I did hire him, and ask if he's spoken about it. I'll look for an opening, perhaps say that I've heard he's troubled by his dating life, or something like that. I'll try not to be intrusive, but maybe I can ask if she knows anything that's bothering him."

"I'm not sure she'll talk to you. I hope she does. You're a good man, Jakob Müller."

"I've been blessed in life."

She knew, though, that all had not been sunshine and roses for Jakob. His wife, deeply unhappy, left Jakob and Jocie, fleeing the US for her homeland, Poland. Once there she fell back into old ways and took an overdose of prescription medication, either accidentally or on purpose, no one knew for sure. Tragically, she died. It was a terribly sad thing for Jocelyn to have lost her mother when she was just three.

She felt a yawn rising and sighed deeply instead. "I had better go," she said. "I do have a long day tomorrow. Will you and Jocie be able to come to Dickens Days in the evening? Can you get away from the tree lot?"

"I hope we will. Gus, my buddy and partner, is looking after it tomorrow afternoon and evening, while I work all Saturday."

Jaymie stood, as did Jakob. He hugged her close and she felt cocooned, sighing against his chest. They hadn't kissed yet. She hoped they would, but when they both felt the time was right.

He carried Hoppy out to the van for her and helped her in, then handed her the sleepy dog. "Good night, Jaymie. *Träum was schönes.*"

"What does that mean?" Jaymie asked, pausing in the act of putting her key in the ignition. His face was shadowed and she couldn't see his dark eyes.

"Sweet dreams," he said, his voice husky.

"I will surely have those," she said softly, her breath puffing out in steam in the frigid air.

He closed the van door for her and retreated to the porch, where he was illumined by light from the kitchen window. He waved, and she backed out as Hoppy snuffled and snored on the passenger side.

Home, bedtime routine and bed, no time to even read before turning out the light. She didn't need a romance novel to guarantee sweet dreams, featuring her and Jakob's first kiss. She could only hope it was as lovely in real life.

MORNING CAME TOO quickly, as usual. She raced around the house making breakfast and getting her stuff together. It was Friday of the first official weekend of Dickens Days. The next day would be the grand opening of Queensville Historic Manor, with the mayor of Queensville presiding at the ribbon cutting. But first Jaymie had a morning of work at the Emporium.

She felt like she was floating as she speed walked to work, arriving ahead even of Valetta. Her friend, key out, joined her on the board porch of the old general store, but stared at Jaymie for a moment. "There's something different about you," she said. "You'll have to fill me in. Something tells me you spent the evening with a certain junk man."

"We had dinner, which Jakob cooked, and my own brownies for dessert, and we watched *A Charlie Brown Christmas* while Jocie cuddled with Hoppy. We talked, and I went home."

"He cooked *dinner* for you?" Valetta asked, as she unlocked the Emporium and let Jaymie in ahead of her.

"Meatloaf and mashed potatoes. It was awesome!" Jaymie said, turning on lights and shrugging out of her coat.

"Does he have any unwed brothers?" Valetta asked, before she headed back to her pharmacy counter.

"As a matter of fact he does, one or two."

"If they're all as domesticated as he is, send one on over to me. I never could find a man who was good for anything, but maybe there's hope yet."

They went about their business with a flurry of early shoppers and met up, as usual, at eleven for tea. Elevenses, as Mrs. Bellwood, the town's resident who played Queen Victoria, called the midmorning tea break.

"Come on out to the porch," Jaymie said, as Valetta carried her steaming mug of tea toward the front. "I want to scope out the town and see where I'll stroll this evening."

Valetta grabbed a heavy sweater from the hook behind the cash desk and pulled it on, then followed Jaymie outside. "I'll be here this evening. I caved when Haskell called, and so I'm working here on the porch as kind of an information center for visitors. He doesn't trust the Snoop Sisters."

She was referring to Mrs. Imogene Frump and Mrs. Trelawney Bellwood, the two Queen Victorias, who had mended a longtime rift and were now inseparable. The ladies would be taking care of the booth where warm cider and information about Dickens Days and the Queensville Historic Manor would be dispensed to tourists.

Jaymie and Valetta huddled on chairs on the wide-board porch and sipped their tea, which steamed in the chilly air. Bill Waterman and a couple of young fellows wheeled a heavy wooden structure on a dolly cart down the street from his workshop. Jaymie recognized one as Cody Wainwright. Odd, because Bill had been emphatic about not hiring him, but there weren't many day laborers available for work in Queensville, so maybe that had changed his mind. The teenage boys who would be helping later were in school, and fellows like Johnny Stanko, who used to take odd jobs whenever he could, now had a steady gig bussing tables, washing dishes and tending bar at a place out on the highway.

They wheeled the dolly cart just beyond the Emporium to a spot of public property known locally as "the village green." It was merely a small triangular plot bounded by the intersection of three roads: the main street, the road leading to the river and docks and a residential street that led to Jaymie's home, but it had been serviced with electricity and water so that the town could use it for just such events as this. The cubicle would be centered over that electrical outlet so lights and small appliances could be plugged in.

"Bill did such a good job on the booth," Jaymie said, as she and Valetta watched.

"I love the musical notations above the counter!" Valetta said.

The stand was a square enclosure with a marquee over the counter on which Bill had painted some sheet music with "O Come, O Come, Emmanuel" picked out in notes and with the words in script. Hot cider would be available to strolling tourists who had come for the beginning of Dickens Days. Unofficially, Dickens Days lasted all of December, but officially, it was a two-week period before Christmas when the town was lit up.

The men got down to business screwing the booth together and leveling it. Cody was the harder working of the two young guys Bill had hired, and eagerly took direction from the handyman on what to do and how. Jaymie was glad Bill had help. He was getting older. It hadn't slowed him down, but she often felt the town relied on him far too much. He needed extra hands.

"Have you got all your shopping done?" Valetta asked her, as they watched.

"As much as I'm doing," Jaymie said, glancing over at her friend, for whom she had commissioned a hand-knit sweater made by Mabel Bloombury. It had a colorful depiction of Valetta's pretty cottage home, with little house-shaped wooden buttons down the front. Gifts made by expert crafters, whether knitters, woodworkers or others, were original.

She loved giving them even more than getting them. She already had it, and it was wrapped and ready.

"I was done in September," Valetta smugly replied. "William and Eva are getting educational toys whether they want them or not. I will be *that* aunt!"

"I wish I had a niece and nephew to spoil," Jaymie said, standing and stretching. "I'd better get back to work. My tea is cold, anyway, and so am I. There are some cobwebs in the rafters just begging to be eradicated. I'm going to have to get out the sixteen-foot ladder to handle them."

Valetta's eyes widened. "Oh, Jaymie, please don't! Let the Klausners hire someone to do that!"

"I can do it," Jaymie said. "I've done it at home before." She had done the ceilings of her home, but they were twelve foot, not the twenty-foot-high ceilings of the Emporium. She went inside. Valetta didn't follow right away, so she assumed her friend was finishing her tea.

Getting the ladder out of the back storage room was trickier than she thought it would be. She was trying to maneuver it when she felt it move on its own and yelped, looking up to find Cody Wainwright on the other end.

"Mr. Waterman sent me in to help," he said, his gaze sliding away from hers.

"I should have known Valetta wouldn't let it go," Jaymie grumbled, as Valetta scooted past her into her enclosed pharmacy.

"I don't want to see you dead, so shoot me," Valetta said, then closed the door, going back to work as a customer came up to her counter.

Jaymie explained what she was doing, and she and Cody worked in silence all the way around the Emporium, as Jaymie took a duster on a long handle around the ceiling, sending cobwebs drifting down to the floor. Jaymie was actually glad of the help. Cody was fairly intuitive and didn't need a lot of direction. He was careful and proactive, too, making sure obstructions were out of her way as they moved the ladder around the store. When she was done, she and Cody folded the ladder and carried it back to the storeroom, the task made easier with another pair of hands.

After, as they walked together to the front of the store, he lingered and shuffled his feet, picking up candy bars and putting them back, then tidying a plastic tub of child's hair ornaments. Finally, he looked her in the eyes and said, "Look, I'm sorry about what happened between my mom and me, but it's not what you think. I didn't . . . I mean she . . ." He sighed and shook his head. "I didn't hit her or anything. I would never do that."

Jaymie watched him. He was young, a good ten or more years younger than her, his face just beginning to thin out into the planes of manhood. He was good-looking but unkempt, with a shaggy mane of hair that looked like it hadn't been combed or washed in a few days.

"It's not for me to judge," she finally said. "Your family is your business."

He nodded.

"I know that my friend Jakob Müller has hired you. He's a good guy, and he likes you."

"I love working with the Christmas trees, and I like helping folks cut them down. I'm going out there to work after I finish with Mr. Waterman."

The bells over the door chimed and Shelby Fretter entered and started down the baking aisle. Jaymie felt rather than saw Cody stiffen. She hoped he wouldn't accost the girl, but he followed her down the aisle and grabbed her coat sleeve as she was reaching for a pound of shortening. Jaymie watched, holding her breath, as he said something and Shelby snatched her arm away.

"Leave me alone, Cody Wainwright," she said loudly, her voice echoing in the upper reaches of the Emporium.

He stared at her in puzzlement.

Her gaze slid over to Jaymie, then away, as she turned to face him. "I told you never to talk to me again, and I meant it. You leave me alone or I'll have the cops on you so fast you'll spin like a top."

His eyes wide, he stared at her then muttered, "You can't treat me like this, Shelby! You can't jerk me around and then expect me just to slink away like some dog you've kicked."

Jaymie decided she had better intervene. She was coming round the corner of the aisle when Shelby tumbled to the floor and screeched.

"Get away from me!" she cried, hands raised to shield her face.

"Shelby, what's—"

"I said, get away from me!"

He bent over and grabbed at her as she covered her face with her hands. Jaymie lunged forward and got hold of his arm. "Just leave her alone, Cody. She said she doesn't want to see you!"

He whirled and shook off Jaymie's hand. "Get off me!"

Shelby was skittering away from him on her butt, sliding along the hardwood floor of the store. "Just leave me alone, Cody!" she said.

He stomped from the store as Jaymie helped a distressed Shelby get up. She refused to talk about it and refused further offers of help, just buying what she needed—some shortening, baking powder and bandages—and leaving. Valetta, who had been busy with a customer and so didn't see what happened, came up to the front.

Jaymie quickly told her everything. "I'm worried about her. He doesn't seem willing to accept that she doesn't want anything to do with him. I'd better make sure Cody has really gone."

Valetta followed her out to the porch. Cody was nowhere in sight, and Shelby was stomping off down the street past Jewel's store. A fellow coming toward her accosted her and she stood talking to him. It seemed an impassioned chat; she waved her arms and he took her shoulder at one point, but she shook him loose, calming down and nodding as he talked.

"Who is that?" Jaymie asked, rubbing her arms to try to warm herself up. A breeze was blowing around the corner of the Emporium, riffling her hair and freezing her butt. "I feel like I've seen that guy before, but I can't tell at this distance."

"He's been in the store before when you've been working. That's Delaney Meadows," Valetta said, burying her hands in the sleeves of her sweater, a particularly cheery Christmas confection with bells all over it. The breeze made her jingle like a wind chime. "He owns a white-collar employment agency. Runs it out of the old Belcker Building on Munroe."

"Of course! I know who you're talking about. She works in his office."

"He found an administrative assistant for Brock's real estate office last month," Valetta went on, naming her brother, who was a local real estate agent. "He said Delaney was great about sending them referrals."

Jaymie still watched. Shelby appeared just as abrupt with him as she was with Cody and Jaymie herself. Maybe that was in the Fretter DNA, given how Lori Wozny seemed the same: quick to take offense and get angry. "She still seems pretty upset."

Meadows was putting up both hands, and shaking his head. He reached for her arm, but she jerked it away and stomped off. He turned to watch her walk away and called something after her, but she just turned in one smooth move, flipped him the bird and kept walking.

"What's wrong, Jaymsie?"

She turned at Heidi's lilting, questioning voice. Her friend was bundled up a little warmer than she was wont to do, now that winter was threatening Queensville with icy fog some mornings and flakes of snow that danced downward some nights. But nothing could hide her beauty: long silky blond hair, small features, tiny waist, petite all over. Jaymie had felt gawky and enormous in her presence at first, but even though the girl had "stolen" Joel from her and was now engaged to him, Heidi's sunny personality and sweet nature soon had her at ease. They had become fast friends.

"We were talking about Shelby Fretter," Jaymie said, indicating the tableau down the road of Shelby walking away from Delaney Meadows, who was now walking after her, trotting to catch up. "She seems pretty mad at the world. It must be this stuff with her boyfriend that has her upset," Jaymie said, and explained.

"I don't know about that," Heidi said. "I think Shelby Fretter hates everyone. She sure does hate me!"

✳ Six ✳

"HATE *YOU*? YOU know her?" Jaymie asked in amazement.

"She's going out with this guy who is in the same business as Joel, so we all went out to dinner. She was so *rude* to me!"

"Wait a sec," Jaymie said, before Heidi could complain more. "You and Joel went out with Shelby and Cody? But Cody Wainwright's not in the pharmaceutical business."

"Cody Wainwright? Who's that?" Heidi asked.

Valetta laughed. "While you two talk at cross purposes, I'm going in. I have work to do."

Shelby and Meadows had disappeared around a bend in the road. Jaymie eyed the sky, which was a robin's egg blue with light puffy clouds skidding along like paper sailboats on a stream. She wasn't fooled; the crystalline nature of the day meant snow by nightfall, hopefully not enough to interfere with the evening's festivities. Jaymie grabbed Heidi's sleeve and tugged. "Come in and talk in the store. It's too cold out here."

Heidi trailed after her into the Emporium and slipped off her ski coat while Jaymie served a couple of customers who had followed them in, one wanting buttermilk, which they had, and another wanting pickled quince, which they did not have, and in fact no one in the history of retail had ever carried. Jaymie then turned to Heidi, who was perched on a chair by the part of the counter where Jaymie had her picnic basket rental counter. Good, she had some stuff to do there anyway, to make the display more festive.

"You've got such nice handwriting, Heidi. Would you make me up a sign saying special Christmas themed baskets are available for rental for the Dickens Days festivities?"

As Heidi lettered the sign using red and green felt pens, Jaymie redid her rental basket display and quizzed her friend on what she meant by saying she went out with Shelby Fretter and a boyfriend who worked in the same industry as Joel, pharmaceutical sales.

"Joel knows this guy, Glenn Brennan, and he wanted to find out how the guy was stealing doctors."

"Stealing doctors?"

"I guess Glenn managed to get some doctor who Joel has been wooing for ages to refer his drugs over the ones Joel's company makes. It's a similar drug, something for man private parts or something. I don't ask."

"Can't say I blame you. So you all went out to dinner: you, Joel, Glenn and Shelby?"

She nodded. "Shelby and Glenn had gone out a couple of times, and he was totally into her. She treated him awful, but then she treated me awful, too. She seemed angry to be there and said they were supposed to be out to dinner alone."

Jaymie's mind teemed with questions, but she let Heidi print the advertising card first. The girl was on her fourth attempt; she'd never get one done if Jaymie kept distracting her with conversation. Jaymie focused on her rental basket display instead, set up on a wooden shelf behind the sales counter. She had a fifties-era poinsettia-printed tablecloth draped on the shelf. The display was a little aluminum Christmas tree and a vintage tin red-plaid basket. She propped the lid of the basket open, created a snowy scene inside with a miniature mountaintop of felt "snow" and bottle-brush trees. Tiny Christmas village figurines were set on the slope, skiing, building a snow man and having a snowball fight. She created a stack of snowballs with cotton puffs.

"When was this?" Jaymie finally asked, righting one of the figurines that had fallen over.

"Hmm?" Heidi said, carefully adding a holly drawing on the bottom of the sign.

Jaymie looked over her shoulder, then turned and examined the sign more closely. "Wow, you're good at that, Heidi!"

"Really?"

"Sure!" Jaymie said. "I was asking when this was that you all went out." She expected the answer to be some months past, because she knew Cody and Shelby had been dating for over a month and a half.

"About three weeks ago. And I saw them out together just last week when Joel and I went to Ambrosio," she said, naming a restaurant on the highway out of town.

"Three weeks ago? And you saw them together just last week." Jaymie had the impression that Cody believed he and Shelby were semiserious, or at least exclusive, but that was apparently not the case.

"Why does it matter?" Heidi asked, holding the sign out to Jaymie.

She wouldn't care less except Cody was Nan's son, and now he was also Jakob's employee. But that had nothing to do with Shelby, she thought. "Nothing," Jaymie said with a shrug. "But why would she be rude to you? Everyone loves you, Heidi."

Heidi jumped to her feet and hugged Jaymie. "No, *you* love me. I don't know why, but I'm just grateful. You and Bernie are the best friends I've ever had!" she said, naming their friend Bernice Jenkins. Bernie was an officer on the local police force and aspired to become the first female African American detective on the town's force.

"But seriously, Heidi, from the sound of it the girl just hates everyone. Like mother like daughter." She told Heidi about her run-in with Lori Wozny. "The woman was bound and determined to take everything I said and did as a slight."

Nodding eagerly, Heidi said, "Shelby is like that, too! No matter what I said, even when it was a compliment, she made it seem like I was insulting her! I said she had a nice hairdo, and she said well, no wonder I didn't like it since I could afford hundreds of dollars for a cut and color. I told her I liked her dress, and she made some crack about taking hand-outs when she was a kid and shopping in thrift stores, but oh, I wouldn't know anything about that." Wide-eyed, she shook her head. "And here I thought it was just *me* she didn't like."

"She has a chip on her shoulder and I think it runs in the family. I felt bad about my run-in with Lori, too, until I heard she's always like that."

She sighed. "I feel better now. So she's dating a couple of guys at once?"

"I guess so. Nothing wrong with that if everyone knows about it, but I can't imagine juggling two guys at once."

"Rumor is, you won't have to worry about that anymore," Heidi said, with a sly glance.

Jaymie was silent. The downside to living in a small town was that everyone knew about your business, and felt entitled to comment on it. It was a testament to how far Heidi had come in Queensville that she was now in the loop. Just months before, townsfolk, siding with Jaymie and her broken heart, had frozen Heidi, seen as the interloper, out. But Jaymie's friendship with her had solved that little problem. Coupled with Heidi's naturally warm personality, it meant that the girl was now quite popular. Jaymie remained silent and Heidi didn't push.

"What is this Glenn guy like?" Jaymie asked.

Heidi wrinkled her nose. "I don't like him at all. He's so . . ." She wriggled her shoulders, an expression of distaste, for her. "When Joel was up getting us drinks and Shelby went to the ladies' room, he kept saying things to me, even though he's on a date with Shelby and I'm with Joel. It felt creepy."

"He came on to you?"

"Kind of. Nothing too outrageous or I would have told Joel, just compliments."

"But Glenn seemed into Shelby?"

"He was all over her, you know, touching her shoulder, sitting with his hand around the back of her neck . . . I *hate* that! I don't know why some guys do it. She didn't seem all *that* into *him*. Nonchalant. Is that the word? She acted like she couldn't care less. Maybe that's why he acted all crazy about her when she was there, trying to reel her in." She slid off the stool.

"What did they talk about?"

"With each other? Nothing. Joel and Glenn did all the talking. That guy brings out the worst in Joel. It was like constant one-upmanship. Who had what clients, who had more sales . . . That kind of stuff." She pulled on her coat. "So the sign is okay? I'm so happy to help! I got one of the robes you told me about, and I talked to some of the ladies and they all liked your suggestion about me strolling and handing out goodies."

"I'll see you this evening, then."

The rest of her shift was straightforward. After lunch Mr. Klausner, silent as always, took his post behind the cash register with one of his granddaughters, Gracey, who he was training to work.

At home Hoppy was overjoyed to see her, but gave her a brief tail wag and bounded out into the yard to piddle then bark at Trip Findley, her behind-the-lane neighbor, who was out repairing his back fence. Denver slunk out, too, and Jaymie began the mad dash to get ready for the first real evening of Dickens Days. The next day she would be at the historic house in costume, baking cookies in her hopefully still working and very *very* clean vintage oven. But first, this evening she would stroll the town, give out pamphlets and maybe see Jakob and Jocie.

She consulted her list and took care of several things, including phoning in a food order to the Queensville Inn. The chef there handled the food supplies for her vintage picnic basket service. Three families were picking up deluxe baskets to enjoy near the river while the Queensville Brass Chorus played Christmas tunes in the bandstand near the boardwalk.

Midafternoon the phone rang. It was Becca, so she caught up with her sister while she raced around doing other things. Becca, Kevin and maybe even her Grandma Leighton would be joining her in Queensville a few days before Christmas. Her mom and dad, driving up from Florida, would meet them there, then they would all cross the border to London, Ontario, Canada, where Becca would host them for Christmas with her fiancé and one of his kids. Becca was uptight and worried, but Jaymie got her calmed down and even laughing with a description of her run-in with Lori Wozny.

By the time she signed off, had dinner, got Hoppy and Denver their meals and let them out in the yard again, it was dark and time to get going. She changed into her Victorian cloak, made sure the animals were inside and comfortable, then headed out, walking first to Bill Waterman's shed for a stack of pamphlets.

The large workshop was brightly lit, beckoning and warm even though Bill had the door propped open. He was at his workbench near the locked storeroom in his shirtsleeves and jean overalls, working on some kind of electronics.

"It's one of the speakers from the PA system I've installed in the cider booth," he said, in answer to her query. "It keeps shorting out."

"Do we need that?" Jaymie asked. The storeroom was unlocked. She retrieved a pile of pamphlets and stacked them in her wicker basket, then came back out to stand by Bill, who bent over the back of the speaker box.

"Fletcher wants to use it tonight. He said 'Make it a priority, Billy Boy.'"

Jaymie chuckled at Bill's impersonation of their hail-fellow-well-met mayor, Eddie Fletcher, who tended toward a false hearty friendliness. It was funny how as the success and self-funding nature of the heritage committee became more evident, Fletcher had suddenly become interested in the Dickens Days celebrations, though he had originally opposed the town putting up any money for policing and servicing the two-week event. Regardless, the heritage committee welcomed his participation and he would be there that evening, as well as at the next day's official opening of the Queensville Historic Manor.

"Do you still have your key for the storeroom?" Bill asked, as he stripped a wire.

"Of course," Jaymie said, jingling her keys in the pocket of her hoodie under the cloak. "You can lock up when you leave."

"I'll be around most of the evening to stomp out any fires. Tree and Imogene have been plaguing me nonstop about the booth. They keep blowing fuses and won't listen when I tell them not to plug so much into one extension! Darned slow cookers full of cider."

"Don't let them bully you, Bill!" she said, and left, emerging into the frosty air.

The workshop was on a slight rise above the main street, so she paused for a moment, enchanted by the transformation of her town. The town's deciduous trees had long since lost their leaves, so the only green was a sprinkling of firs and pines. All along the main streets householders and business owners like those of the Queensville Emporium, Jewel's Junk and the Cottage Shoppe had decorated the conifers on their property with dazzling white lights that twinkled and gleamed. Even the oak trees had been gussied, with strings of lights wound around their trunks and lower branches, like ghostly trees shining in the darkness.

As she predicted, snowflakes had begun to flutter down, dancing on the breeze, just enough to make it festive! She smiled as she watched people strolling through her town, looking at the displays folks had set up, and pausing at the booth for a cup of cider before proceeding to the park, the bandstand and the river, where the few boats still in the water this late in the fall would be decked with lights on their masts and along their railings. Taking a deep breath, she descended the hill and walked toward the village green.

"Jaymie! Merry Christmas!"

She turned to see Dee Stubbs, her and Becca's lifelong friend, pushing her mother-in-law along the street in a wheelchair. It was Mrs. Stubbs who had called out to her, waving her cane, her wrinkled face wreathed in a smile. Jaymie approached; Dee looked tired, but smiled. She had recently returned to the workforce after raising her kids, and worked the emergency ward at Wolverhampton General a few shifts a week. But she still made time for her elderly mother-in-law, since her husband worked long hours, and her brother-in-law, who owned the Queensville Inn and provided a home for his mother, was glued to the inn most of the time.

"Hey, Mrs. Stubbs, Dee!" Jaymie leaned over and gave the woman a hug. "I'm surprised to see you two here!"

"Mother Stubbs' mobility chair is acting up, but we didn't want to miss this. We thought we'd take in the sights, since the forecast is calling for real snow setting in over the next couple of days," Dee said. *Real* snow to a Michiganian had to pile up enough to shovel.

"DeeDee is good enough to push me around even though the battery on my chair is dying. I wanted to check up on Tree and Imogene, make sure they don't make a hash of the booth," Mrs. Stubbs said.

The woman had a new lease on life, it seemed, since getting

involved in the heritage society skirmish over the history of the former Dumpe Manor, now Queensville Historic Manor. Maybe it was realizing that as one of the few citizens over ninety, she was the keeper of the town's memories. She was still crotchety and occasionally difficult, but she and Dee had made peace, at long last, once the woman realized her daughter-in-law was a little afraid of her, and cautious.

"I'm just heading there myself to set up a display of some of the heritage society pamphlets for our friends to hand out."

They walked together to the booth, smiling and nodding to the many strangers, most with kids, who strolled the streets, cider cups in hand. The ladies handed cider cups to a young couple, and turned to Jaymie and the others as they approached.

"Jaymie, Dee, Mrs. Stubbs!" they cried out in unison. Mrs. Bellwood, the more spry of the two, filled a cup with cider and shimmied past her friend out of the narrow booth, bringing it to Mrs. Stubbs.

Just at that moment all the women looked past Jaymie, smiles on their faces.

"Isn't she the cutest little thing!" Mrs. Frump cried, clapping her hands joyously as she, too, emerged from the booth.

Jaymie turned and saw Jakob and Jocie, hand in hand, Jocie in a hot-pink snowsuit with white faux-fur trim and white galoshes. Jakob was in a heavy parka and dark jeans, his curly hair uncovered by any hat. Her heart thudded with joy. She clutched the pamphlets to her chest and walked toward them, shyly sharing a hug with Jakob and reaching down to peck Jocie on the cheek. She turned and together they walked back to the booth.

"Jakob, do you know these folks?"

"*I* know him," Dee volunteered. "Hey, Jakob. My hubby is heading out to the junk store Monday. He needs a file cabinet for the shop."

"We have a few, four drawer and two. Tell him to say to Gus that I'm giving Joe a good deal."

Dee smiled. "Have you and Jocie met my mother-in-law, Mrs. Stubbs?"

"I don't believe so," he said, and Dee made the introductions.

He took his daughter by the hand and led her over to the elderly woman, who bent forward, smiling down at the little girl. Mrs. Stubbs put out one gnarled, wrinkled hand and touched Jocie's smooth, plump cheek, pinkened by the cold. Jaymie watched and her eyes misted; the juxtaposition of the wrinkled hand and the child's perfect skin was heartrending and strangely beautiful. She swallowed hard, past a lump. Jakob glanced over at her and took her by the arm, pulling her toward Mrs. Stubbs.

The elderly woman looked up at them, then at their linked arms. She nodded. "Your child is beautiful, Mr. Müller."

"Jakob, please, ma'am. Thank you. Jocie is the joy of my life."

Jocie looked up at Jaymie and her father, then to Mrs. Stubbs. "And Papa is the joy of *my* life," she said, in a clear tone.

The adults laughed. Jaymie introduced Jakob and Jocie to Mrs. Bellwood and Mrs. Frump, then the group broke up. Jaymie and the Müllers strolled briefly and chatted, with a cup of cider each.

"I'm so glad you could get away. Were there a lot of people at the tree lot tonight?"

"It was busy, but Gus is there and Cody, too. He's been helpful. I had a chance to talk to him briefly, but I told him I wanted to talk more tomorrow," Jakob said, with a significant look to her. "He's coming to the junk store for a cup of coffee."

She nodded. He was going to have a chat with the guy as he promised, and that was good. She had a feeling Jakob was the kind of man who always kept his promises. They talked a bit more, then he had to get Jocie home. Jaymie watched them leave with a sigh. It was going to be a busy few weeks for all of them. Who knew how much she would be able to see a man who ran a Christmas tree lot? She got back to her task, which was making sure that every person in Queensville that evening had one of the pamphlets and knew about the historic home's grand opening the next day.

It was cold, but she was warmly cloaked, so she strolled and talked herself hoarse and encouraged families to come visit the Queensville Historic Manor. She met up with Heidi and gave her most of the brownies she had brought to sell, all money going into the donation jar at the cider booth. But Heidi was soon cold and bored; once all the brownies were gone she headed home to sit by a roaring fire.

It *was* tiring. Two hours in and she was starting to feel the numbness in her toes. As she finished one complete route from the village proper to the band shell in the waterfront park and back, Valetta waved at Jaymie from the Emporium porch. Jaymie climbed the steps and sank down in one of the chairs. "I'm exhausted!" she said, wiggling her frozen toes in their booted confinement.

"Take a load off for a few minutes at least. No one wants you to kill yourself, you know." Valetta had a table in front of the chairs with pamphlets from the Queensville Inn, a local winery, the *Wolverhampton Weekly Howler* and the local bed-and-breakfast society.

Jaymie added a stack of the historic manor pamphlets to the collection. "I guess I can take a break."

Valetta hauled out a thermos and poured a steaming cup of tea, handing it to Jaymie. "This is better than the cider, trust me."

"I'm not such a big fan of warm apple drink," Jaymie admitted. She sipped, relishing the peculiar taste of "thermos tea," the flavor a combination of being made hours before and taking on the essence of the thermos. It tasted like camping to her, because most summers since she was twenty she had ventured north to a campground in Canada to meet with friends. One staple they enjoyed was tea out of a thermos as they ventured out on a road trip, sat on the dock fishing or took a long hike in the woods on a chilly Ontario morning.

Valetta asked about the meeting among Jakob, Jocie, Mrs. Stubbs and the others, and Jaymie told her what was said. As they talked, she noticed Lori Wozny strolling along the main street with her daughter. Even from a distance it was clear the two were mother and daughter, with the same blond hair, a little frizzy, and slight frames. There was even something in their stance, the way they stood and walked, that was similar. But Lori had on her red plaid wool coat and Shelby wore a smart but too thin leather jacket.

With them was a young man, taller, but probably a brother, given his resemblance to Shelby. Jaymie reflected on her confrontation with Lori, and later with Shelby and Cody. Heidi's information about Shelby dating another man shed some light on her wish for distance from Cody, but why did she keep dating him if he was so dangerous to her? Cody appeared genuinely confused by Shelby, as if her actions were contrary to what he had been led to believe they would be. Still, he wouldn't be the first guy who refused to take no for an answer when a woman attempted to break off their affair. Jaymie tried to keep from judging other women's choices. No one knew what another went through, or how their life affected them.

"I'd better get going," Jaymie said, standing and brushing down her cloak. "If I sit too long, I'll be here for the night; you'll find me here in this chair in the morning, asleep."

"*I* won't find you. I'm off tomorrow!"

"Oh yeah!" Jaymie said. "I must be tired not to remember that. You found that new fellow from Wolverhampton to fill in every other Saturday. Good for you!"

"I need to do a little shopping," she said. "It's strange having someone to rely on, though. Thad will be working the pharmacy, and Gracey Klausner is at the cash desk . . . A whole new generation at the Queensville Emporium!" Valetta said, patting the clapboard wall behind her.

Taped to the wall were a number of public notices, one about the missing young woman from Wolverhampton. It was a solemn reminder that in their own community was a family dealing with sorrow and uncertainty at a time of year meant for festivity and happiness.

"Once more into the breach for me," Jaymie said, grabbing up what was left of her pamphlets and descending the stairs. She turned at the bottom and looked back up at her friend who had stood and was folding the blanket she had wrapped around herself. "Will you be coming to the manor opening tomorrow?"

"I'm not sure. I'll try to be there, but not in time to watch Mayor Fletcher bluster."

Jaymie descended the slight incline to the main street as Valetta packed it in for the night and headed home to her cottage two streets over. A caroling group from the heritage society strolled toward her and she stopped to listen to them. They sang "It's Beginning to Look a Lot Like Christmas" as tiny flakes still fluttered down from the inky December sky and dotted the dark cloaks of the singers. One of the men had a leather belt of jingle bells and kept time. She glanced around and saw many had stopped to listen; Brock Nibley was there with his two kids, and Ruby and Garnet Redmond were strolling arm in arm.

She also noticed the Fretter family again. Lori was listening to the group, but Shelby and her brother were having a fierce argument in each other's faces. She finally shrugged and turned away from him but he grabbed her shoulder and whirled her around. They continued arguing until Lori said something sharp, then all three listened to the singers for a moment. But the fight was not over, Jaymie could tell by both of the younger people's stiffness and taut expressions.

Jaymie set off toward the river for one last stroll and listened at the band shell to the brass chorale play "God Rest Ye Merry, Gentlemen." She threaded through the crowd, handing out pamphlets and talking about the historic home opening, answering questions about other things going on. Cody Wainwright was there. She had thought he'd still be at the tree lot, but he was likely done for the evening.

Finally Jaymie climbed the grassy bank to the boardwalk and strolled down in the direction of the docks, stopping by a few other people just as the last of the boats were passing, their Christmassy lights blinking off, one by one. She stared out across the river to Heartbreak Island, where twinkling lights were going out, too, as the evening wound down to a close. The Leighton family cottage was one road in, hidden by the pine trees that lined the shore. It had been winterized, but she would go out one more time before Christmas to make sure everything was all right. She could just see the Ice House restaurant down the shore, but as she watched the restaurant lights went out.

Time to take her weary bones home. She ambled back through the village, enjoying the quiet. A few stragglers, mostly young couples, strolled, enjoying the lights.

The lights were out at Jewel's Junk. Jewel, a vivacious redhead in her fifties, had kept the shop open for the evening but by now had closed up and taken her little doggie Junk Jr., Hoppy's best canine buddy, home. Jaymie ascended the rise and strolled past the shop, then picked her way through the gloom across the increasingly slick grass as flakes of snow began to stick, dotting the dark green grass. It occurred to her that she should have just taken the rest of the pamphlets home, because the stack in her basket was much smaller than it had been, but now that she was at the storeroom she may as well put them away.

She opened the door into the shed and headed to the small internal storeroom, fishing in her hoodie pocket under the cloak for the key. The door was open, though, and the light on. Bill must be still working, she thought. She headed toward the light and pushed the door open the rest of the way, setting her basket aside on the workbench and turning. A moan made her whirl in place, and she saw a person on the wide-board floor, just a heap of red plaid.

"Lori!" Jaymie cried and raced to her side, kneeling by her. The woman moved, whimpering, and Jaymie helped her turn on her back, which was when she saw that it was not Lori Wozny but Shelby Fretter wearing her mother's coat, and she had been beaten terribly, her face badly bruised and blood streaming from her forehead.

Without a second's hesitation Jaymie raced to the door and screamed *help* into the crisp night air, hearing it echo back to her in the empty town.

❧ Seven ❧

NO ANSWER. WITH one glance backward, noting the young woman's labored breathing, Jaymie knew she had not a second to lose. The girl needed professional help. Whimpering, Jaymie stripped off her cloak and laid it gently over the girl, muttered a quick prayer and exited, looking around to see if anyone was still about.

Not a soul! Jaymie made up her mind quickly, then stumbled and slid across the grass to the nearest house, that of Cynthia Turbridge, owner of the Cottage Shoppe. She trotted up the wooden steps to the porch, hammered on the door and screamed, "Help!"

A light went on in the cottage, and she could hear the latch of the door drawn; a sleepy and suspicious Cynthia looked out from a crack in the door. "Who's there? What do you want?"

"Cynthia, it's me, Jaymie Leighton. There's a woman hurt at Bill Waterman's workshop. Call 911 and tell them. I've got to get back to her, but call! *Please* hurry!"

Cynthia paused for a second, rubbed her eyes, stared at Jaymie and said, "Right away." She slammed the door.

Jaymie whirled and fled back to the storeroom, muttering angrily at herself all the way as she shivered, skidded and concentrated on not falling. Of all times not to bring her cell phone! But it was in her purse, and there had been no reason to carry that on a stroll around town.

She huffed and puffed up the rise to the workshop, then bolted through the darkness to the bright light of the storeroom, praying Shelby was still alive. She could hear the distant wail of the ambulance or police. She strode into the storeroom and knelt by the girl's side, adjusting the navy wool cloak so it covered her up to her bloody chin. Shelby was alive, but she didn't look good. Around the bruises and cuts her skin was pale and waxy, and blood dripped from her mouth now.

Fear clutched at Jaymie's stomach and tears welled in her eyes, but she sternly pulled herself together. "You're going to be okay," she said, her voice quivering and her breath coming in puffs of steam. "You'll be all right, I pro—" Her voice cracked.

She couldn't promise. The bruises seemed to become a deeper, angrier shade of purple; it was as though Shelby's life was draining away one drop of blood at a time, streaming from open wounds to discolor the cement floor under her and collecting in pools in the awful bruises. Her breathing became erratic and slower, with a sound like a harsh rattle on each gasp. A sob bubbled up in Jaymie's throat; who had done this awful deed?

"Hurry up! *Please!*" Jaymie muttered under her breath, like a prayer to urge the rescue providers to more haste. She looked over her shoulder out the open door into the workshop. "We need you!"

Why was the storage room open? Had Shelby come in on her own, been dragged there, or what? Trying to distract herself and stay calm, Jaymie looked around and noticed blood on the edge of the bench, spatter in a couple of places and a random bit of cloth stuck in a cracked section of the bench where wood had splintered. It was a torn section of silky navy fabric, looking out of place in the rough workshop. Where had she seen fabric like that recently?

She couldn't think, couldn't comprehend what had happened. The poor girl had been beaten here, in this storeroom, while just yards away was the help that would have saved her from so much pain. Sirens wailed, coming closer, and finally they cut, replaced by the thrum of heavy motors and men talking. But she couldn't leave Shelby's side. Jaymie felt as though she was breathing for Shelby: in, out, in, out. Slow. Even, but fading. *Definitely* fading. The rattle had stopped, becoming more of a soft gurgle. The voices were closer. "We're in here!" Jaymie shouted, "Hurry! She's alive!"

Moments later she was crowded out of the way by a paramedic team of a man and woman, uniformed and swift, fast but deft. Jaymie answered what questions she could, which was not much beyond Shelby's name, her mother's name and that she had seen them together just an hour or so before in the Dickens Days crowd. Police pushed in, one she recognized as Officer Ng, his black eyes alert and absorbing every detail. A gurney was trundled in, a backboard gently slid under Shelby and the young woman lifted carefully onto the stark white-sheet-covered mattress, an oxygen mask over her nose and mouth. There was no hastiness, and yet all was done speedily and with tender competence. They pulled the backboard out from under her, discarded Jaymie's woolen cloak, and covered Shelby in a blanket, then secured her to the gurney with straps, arms at her side.

One of the paramedics brushed past Jaymie's basket, where it had been set aside on the workbench, and it toppled, the pamphlets fluttering out in a spill of color, one landing in a puddle of the blood, soaking it in, the paper warping into dark waves. She swayed, but Officer Ng took Jaymie's hand and pulled her to her feet.

"Come out to the workshop," he said. A couple of other police were there already, cordoning off the area. One rushed past them and looked in the storeroom door. He caught Ng's eye and both nodded. He turned and crossed his arms over his chest, barring entry to the awful, bloody scene.

Jaymie shivered as she tried to wrap her mind around it all. Shelby had been beaten, but by whom? Her first thought was Cody Wainwright. But there was at least one other explanation, given the adversarial relationship she seemed to have with the young man Jaymie assumed was her brother. Some people, Jaymie had learned in the last few months, almost seemed like a lightning rod, the complex nature of their lives attracting complicated responses and multiple possible explanations when they were murdered. It was like they were the knot at the heart of it all, and to figure it out required the careful picking apart of threads tangled by emotion and violence.

Shelby was alive, thank heavens, and would be able to identify her attacker. Jaymie slowed her breathing. This would all be okay. The answer would be evident from the beginning, unlike the other more complicated occurrences over the last seven months in Queensville.

"Can I go home now?" she asked Officer Ng. "I'm so cold!"

"Please wait. I can help the cold." He snapped his fingers at a young female officer and barked out, "Blanket!"

Jaymie grimaced at the loud command, and regarded him covertly. He was a good-looking guy, very serious, with straight black hair and black eyes, his expression perpetually stern. She had thought his ancestry Vietnamese, but the name was Chinese, Bernie had told her and Heidi. Their friend had gone out with him for a little while, but Jaymie had never really met him or been involved with him. She didn't like how he treated the female officer, but it may just have been his way with any new recruit.

The young officer brought a folded-up plastic-wrapped

blanket and Ng tore the plastic off, handed that back to the officer and held the blanket out to Jaymie. The female officer sighed, jerked the blanket out of his hands and unfolded it, then helped a shivering Jaymie drape it over her shoulders and wrap it around herself.

"Thank you," Jaymie murmured and smiled shakily at the girl, a petite blonde who looked more like a cheerleader than a cop. To Ng, she said, "Why am I waiting? I didn't see anything or anyone. I was just coming to the shed to bring back the pamphlets I had left at the end of the evening and I found her."

"Just wait, please."

A car pulled up to the curb and Detective Angela Vestry got out. She was an angular woman, with scraped-back hair and cold eyes. Jaymie had briefly met her in the trouble that had happened the month before, and thought her competent, if a little gray and grave in personality. She appeared to scan the scene, the whirling light of the cruisers parked at the curb flashing their blue and white lights across her pale face. She eyed some of the villagers gathered, dressed for the most part in parkas over housecoats and galoshes, standing at the curb in clusters, chatting among themselves. Cynthia was among them, wearing a vintage mink coat over pink silk pajamas.

The detective then looked up the rise to where Ng and Jaymie must have been framed by the lights now on in the workshop. Bill Waterman was talking to an officer down by the curb, who was taking notes as the handyman spoke. The handyman looked up the hill at Jaymie and raised his hand in a greeting. She fluttered her hand back, then regarded the detective who now approached.

"Miss Leighton, we meet again," Detective Vestry said, with absolutely no hint of humor or reproach. "Could you tell me what happened?"

She related her evening, as crisply as it would come to her, up until her decision to call it a night. "I suppose I was the last volunteer working. I was bringing the rest of the pamphlets back to the storeroom; that's the inner room in Bill Waterman's shed."

"Was he leaving it open for you?"

"No, he gave me a key," she said, and pulled the unused key out of her hoodie pocket. "One of . . . four, I think? But the workshop was open, and when I entered I could see that the storeroom was, too, and the light was on."

"Didn't you wonder why?" the detective asked, watching Jaymie's eyes intently.

"Bill was here earlier working on a speaker. I thought maybe he was still there, or back again working on it. That's why I walked right in, and that's when I found Shelby. Actually I thought it was her mom, Lori Wozny, at first, because of the coat."

"The coat?"

She explained about Lori's red plaid coat and that the woman worked at the heritage house as a custodian. "I saw them earlier, and Lori had that coat on. Shelby was wearing just a skinny leather jacket, and I thought how cold she must have been. It was starting to snow, not much, just like it is now. I saw Lori, Shelby and a guy, maybe her brother? He kind of looked like her, that's why I thought . . . Anyway, I thought it was Lori at first, but when I turned her over I found that it was poor Shelby. She was just covered in blood! Is she going to be okay? Maybe she can tell you what happened."

"Did you see anyone leaving, or have any impression of someone here?"

"Why?"

"Just answer the question."

Jaymie's stomach turned. "I didn't see a soul. I think I paused for a moment before going in; it was such a nice night! But it was *quiet*. I'd have heard if anyone was still there."

"So you saw her earlier. Did you speak to her? Or see anything?"

"I didn't speak to her. She was arguing with the fellow that was with her and her mom, the one I think is her brother. Other than that, I didn't see anything else."

"It looked like you remembered something just then. What is it?"

"Nothing, except . . . earlier today she did have a couple of run-ins," Jaymie said, and told the detective about Cody and Shelby in the Emporium, and her apparent argument with her boss, Delaney Meadows. "I think I saw Cody Wainwright here, near the band shell. But I didn't see him anywhere near the village."

"You can go home. I may want to see you tomorrow."

"I'll be out at the Queensville Historic Manor most of the day, but you can find me there," Jaymie said. The manor was where a murder had happened just a few weeks before, so Detective Vestry definitely knew where it was. The police chief had virtually taken over that investigation, and for the first time, Jaymie wondered if that had irritated the detective, undermining her chance to solve the crime. The police chief was a different kind of guy and followed his own rules, while the detective seemed a straitlaced and unimaginative, though competent, investigator.

"I know where it is, if I need you," the detective said.

Jaymie walked down the slope to where Bill was just finishing talking to the officer. The chatter of police radios and thrum of heavy motors filled the night air. Somewhere in the distance a dog barked, startling a flock of Canada geese that took to flight, unusual at that time of night. They honked in irritation, dark blots against the indigo sky.

"Are you okay, honey?" Bill said, grabbing her shoulders and looking into her eyes. "You don't look like yourself."

She was shivering, shaken to the core, and perhaps her shock showed on her face. "She was so badly hurt, Bill," she said, wrapping the blanket more tightly around her shoulders, trying to warm up. "I hope she's going to be okay."

His eyes misted and he put his arm around her shoulders. "I knew her when she was just a little thing; drove the school bus for a while, and she and her brother were always going at it hammer and tongs. But just let one of the other kids taunt one of 'em and they'd stick together."

"Are they Lori's only kids?"

"Nah, she's got a couple of younger ones from Walt Wozny, her ex."

"Did you see them tonight? They were all here: Lori, Shelby and I guess her brother?"

He nodded. "Yup. Lori and I talked for a few minutes. Shelby and Travis were arguing about something, I think it was some boyfriend of hers he didn't like, and some girl he'd been seeing. Anyway, they were going at it. She screamed at him to mind his own business and leave her love life out of it."

Was Shelby defending Cody or Glenn? Or was there another boyfriend? Jaymie prayed that she would recover soon so she could tell the police who had done such an awful thing to her. It would be a long road to recovery, given how bad her injuries had looked to Jaymie, but she had family, and that was the most important relationship of all. "I'm so tired," Jaymie said. "I have to be up early because I have to get everything ready for the manor house grand opening tomorrow." She moved from foot to foot. "But I can't stop thinking about her. The poor girl! She was beaten badly, Bill. Very badly."

"Let me walk you home. You seem kind of woozy."

She was grateful. She had known Bill Waterman for years, but lately, with her work on the historic house, she had the chance to work alongside him. He was dependable, helpful and gracious, a real down-to-earth guy. "I appreciate it."

He took her arm and walked her back to her place in silence. Jaymie realized for the first time how close to home this hit for Bill. It was his workshop, and more especially his storeroom, and he'd known Shelby as a child. "How do *you* feel?" she asked, as they turned down her street, one street-light fluttering and going out as they walked past it.

"I understand now how you felt last spring when that fellow was killed on your back porch. It gets you in your gut, doesn't it?"

"It does," she said feelingly, squeezing his arm to her side. "It feels like . . . oh, how to put it? It feels like it belongs to you somehow, like you need to see it solved."

He nodded and sighed as they approached her front door. "Shelby will come through. She's a strong girl, a real sweetheart at the core of her, though she seems a kinda tough nut."

She gave him a quick hug and said, "We'll keep sending good thoughts her way. And to her mom." She paused. "Bill, one question. When I came up to the workshop tonight the storage room door was unlocked. I remember now that the padlock was hanging from the hasp, so it wasn't jimmied with a bolt cutter or anything. Did you leave the padlock undone?"

"I did *not*! It was locked up right and tight when I left it after fixing the speaker."

"Who all has keys?"

"Me, you, Jewel and I keep an extra hidden."

"Hidden where?"

He grimaced. "On top of the door frame, in case I forget mine or need someone to open up the storage for me."

So, not as secure as Jaymie had thought. Anyone could have known about the extra key, or have even seen him get it down. Including Cody, who had been working with Bill that very day, coming and going from the workshop.

He patted her shoulder and turned to head away. "I'll see you tomorrow, Jaymie, at the manor. You get some sleep now, and everything will look brighter in the morning."

IT WAS EARLY, but the day was going to be a busy one. The phone was ringing and Jaymie hopped back to her bedroom from the bathroom on one foot, her slipper coming off at the heel. She plunked down on her bed as Hoppy barked and wobbled up the steps to get up on her bed on his own. "Hello?"

It was Valetta. "Jaymie, I just heard about last night. It's terrible!"

"It was awful, Val. I can't believe my rotten luck."

"Well, sure, but poor Shelby!"

"Of course you're right," Jaymie said, chastened. She sat down on the bed and petted Hoppy with her free hand. "Actually, I'm grateful I found her, or she would have lain there all night and may have died."

"The church is starting a donation to help Lori out."

"Count me in for whatever you need. I'll check with the others and make sure Lori doesn't have to work at the manor but still gets paid. I don't want her to have to worry about anything but getting Shelby better."

"Hold on a sec!" Valetta said. "I've got another call coming in."

The phone went silent. Jaymie pulled her slippers off and wandered around her room with the phone to her ear, putting away a book, a contemporary Christmas tale she had finished the night before when she couldn't sleep, and getting out another to put by her bedside. A comfort read . . . Mary Balogh, *Christmas Beau*, an old Regency, and a second, *A Christmas Bride*. They would do. She selected the three books from her shelf and stacked them on her nightstand.

She glanced out the window. It had snowed overnight, but only an inch or two; it was blowing around until she couldn't even see her backyard at times. That made her clothing decision for the day easy. She would wear thermal leggings until she changed into her thirties-era housewife costume. This was a day she had been looking forward to for months, the official grand opening of the Queensville Historic Manor, but her enthusiasm was dampened as she thought of poor Shelby and her mom. The phone clicked again, and Valetta came back on the line.

"That was Dee," she said. "Poor Shelby is in a coma."

Jaymie was shocked. "Oh, *no*! Is it medically induced?"

"No, it's a result of a blow to the head, from what I

understand. She was not only beaten, but hit her head on something."

"Maybe the workbench," Jaymie said, remembering the blood on the edge of it. And the shred of fabric caught in a splinter.

"She was conscious when she got to the hospital but lapsed into a coma during the night, Dee says."

Jaymie squeezed her eyes shut and took a deep breath, whispering a prayer. She opened her eyes. "I hope she comes out of it."

"Me, too. I wonder if the police found out who did it yet?"

"I was hoping she'd be able to tell them. Maybe she did before she became comatose."

"I guess we'll know if they arrest someone. I have to get going. I'm picking up William and Eva to take them shopping so Brock can get some work done. Eva wants to buy her dad a Christmas gift. What the heck do I tell a nine-year-old to get for her father?"

"Gloves. There isn't a man alive who has a complete pair of gloves or can keep track of them if he does have them."

"Good thought! I'll inspect Brock when I see him and try to finagle out his glove situation."

"Or maybe a personalized mug!"

"Ooh, I like that better. You know how I feel about mugs."

Jaymie got dressed and walked Hoppy, fed the animals and baked some treats to take to the manor, all the while thinking of Shelby. Just as she was taking a tray of brownies out of the oven, the phone rang. It was Jakob!

"Hey," she said softly, smiling just thinking about him.

"Hey," he said, his tone husky. "I heard what happened last night, that girl being hurt and you finding her. Are you okay?"

"I'm all right. It was awful, but I'm grateful I found her. She was hurt so bad." She told him what she had heard about Shelby lapsing into a coma. "Maybe the coma is her body's way of healing. I know doctors sometimes put someone in a coma so they can get better."

"Poor kid." He paused for a moment, then said, "I've been thinking about you all night."

A warm glow kindled in her heart. "It was so nice to see you and Jocelyn. Are you at the store?"

"I am, and someone is with me and wants to say hello."

There was a pause, and a high voice said, "Hello?"

"Hey, Jocie, how are you?"

"I'm very good, thank you," she said, her manners impeccable. "Miss Jaymie, my oma asked if you would like a *Lebkuchen*."

"Uh . . ." What did one say when one didn't know what you were being offered?

She heard a whisper, Jakob's voice in the background. Jocie protested, then came back on the line. "It's a spice cake, Daddy said to tell you, but I said you'd know what it is because you know how to bake."

Ah, the reliance of a child on an adult's all knowingness! "I think I would love a *Lebkuchen*. My family is coming just before Christmas and I could share it with them." A new tradition perhaps; *Lebkuchen* for Christmas.

"I'm putting Daddy back on. See you later!"

"Hey, me again," Jakob said. "My mom told me to tell you that if you're staying in Michigan, you're welcome at her home for Christmas Eve, or *Heiliger Abend*. That's when we do our big Christmas thing."

She felt a tug at her heartstrings. "I won't be able to," she said, with real regret. "I'll be on my way to Canada Christmas Eve morning. We're headed to London to have Christmas with my grandmother and sister, Becca."

"Oh. Of course. We'll see you before then, though," he said.

"I hope so."

"I have to go. Take care today. I'll keep that girl in my thoughts and hope she recovers."

As he hung up, Jaymie clicked the off button on the phone in a thoughtful frame of mind. As much as she looked forward to her family Christmas, she would have given much to be with Jakob and Jocie on Christmas Eve, and to meet his family, as nervous as that made her. It was frightening how fast that imminent meeting had become so important to her.

She roused herself from her reverie; today was a big day, one she had been working toward for a while, and she had to get moving and focus. Today was the grand opening of the Queensville Historic Manor.

❧ Eight ❧

SHE WALKED, BECAUSE she knew that if everything went as hoped, parking would be at a premium. The heritage committee had paid a local landscaping company to mow the field beside the manor and pound fence posts into the still unfrozen ground, along which they strung several rows of wire to form a parking lot. Volunteers would direct traffic and keep it relatively orderly.

As she approached she could see the blow-up gingerbread man, a menacing look on its manic face as it wavered and gesticulated in the wind that whipped down the country road. "Whatever it takes to get people through the door," she muttered, averting her gaze. She trotted up the steps and entered the warm home, now a hive of activity as heritage society members did last-minute touches.

Jewel, of Jewel's Junk, was up on a tall ladder threading holly through the branches of the chandelier in the parlor, while Cynthia Turbridge, owner of the Cottage Shoppe, stood at the bottom, holding the ladder and making comments.

They had both hired help for their shops in Queensville, committed to the historic home's opening success. Mabel Bloombury was placing a flameless menorah in the center of her lovely table. Everyone had agreed that there would be no historically correct real candles used; too much chance of someone forgetting one, or a child or clumsy adult tipping one over. Haskell Lockland, president of the heritage society, was directing, as usual, while managing to do nothing. Others were bustling about, racing up and down the stairs and tweaking the decorations.

"Jaymie! Thank heaven you're here," Haskell said, striding toward her and taking her by the elbow. "What are we going to do about Lori Wozny? Can we expect her to work today? She was supposed to come out tonight and clean up the mess people will inevitably make. What are we going to do?"

"Mabel!" Jaymie called. "Jewel, Cynthia . . . Can you all come here?"

The women gathered in the hall and Jaymie explained her thoughts. In three minutes they had solved the crisis. Each would be responsible for their own area cleanup, and they would enlist others to help. Collectively they would clean the common areas and volunteer lounge. It would all be done. "And Lori should still be paid," she added, meeting each woman's eyes. All nodded. "I don't want her having to worry while she's at Shelby's bedside."

"I don't think that's at all appropriate," Haskell said. "Bad precedent. We can't have anyone thinking they can work for us and get paid for not working!"

Mabel glared up at him. "Haskell Lockland, have a heart! Her daughter was horribly injured. I know for a fact that family is always one step away from poverty, and I can't imagine, at this time of year or any other, letting her worry for one minute about paying her bills and making a living while her daughter lies in a hospital bed in a coma."

"I agree," Jaymie said. "We can afford it, Haskell."

"But she's barely started working for us!" he protested.

"I don't care if she started yesterday or has worked for us for years, it's all the same," Cynthia said softly. She glanced at each one of them. "A wonderful part of living in this village for me has been the support in difficult times."

Recently, Cynthia had some troubles that had resulted in her lapsing back into an addiction that she was now battling with the support of friends, new and old. Jewel took her arm, hugged it to her and nodded.

"I agree," Jaymie said. "I say we pull from the emergency fund, pitch in ourselves and take it up at the next meeting."

"Here, here," Jewel, Cynthia and Mabel all echoed.

Haskell, with bad grace, said, "Fine. But I want it to be known that I disagree. That's how this country got soft, paying people to not work. Ridiculous. If you gals want to do the work, then go ahead. But the house must not suffer." He turned and strode off somewhere else where his input would be vitally unimportant.

Jaymie rolled her eyes and the other women sighed, almost in unison. "Let's get this show on the road *gals*," she said, with heavy emphasis.

She checked the kitchen, which still looked pristine, then trotted upstairs to the staff lounge, one of the old bedrooms with an attached bath and decent-sized wardrobe where clothes for the docents were kept. The room was bare bones, no décor at all to speak of, just a battered folding-leg table by one of the big windows, several discarded office chairs, a fridge, kettle, a countertop and some file cabinets. Haskell had demanded a proper office, so there was a small reading room for his use just down the hall. It and the staff rooms would be locked during opening times.

Jaymie grabbed her costume from a hanger in the wardrobe, slipped into the washroom, changed and then folded her clothes neatly, stowing them in the wardrobe on a shelf and pinning her house keys inside her costume. She glanced at herself in the mirror, her hair coiled in an old-fashioned hairdo and makeup limited to some lipstick. It would have to do. Her stomach roiled with excitement as she slipped down the back stairs to her lovely vintage kitchen. She stood in the center of it, turning in a complete circle, trying to see it from a stranger's perspective. Would anyone get why they were preserving this? Did anyone care?

The walls were a soft green with glossy off-white trim, and the floor black-and-white checkerboard tile. The cupboards were painted cream; the green-and-white Hoosier, untouched by her so it was still in its original state, and the green-and-white stove continued the color scheme. Jaymie tiptoed over to the window, pulled aside the lovely curtains Mabel had sewn, white with a pattern of cherries and ivy, and fastened them with the matching ties, then watched flakes of snow dance through the air.

Someone, a housewife or housekeeper, had done exactly this, she thought, looking anxiously out the window, wondering if her visitors would enjoy the festive goodies she was about to make. She turned away from the window and set up the oven to preheat, shivering at the cold, dressed in her unaccustomed just-below-the-knee-length housedress and hard oxfords.

They were to open at two and unbelievably there were folks lined up to get in. The mayor was in attendance, as well as a couple of councilors. The other ladies and gents who were volunteers were dressed in appropriate garb, as Jaymie was. Jewel wore an Edwardian tea gown, like a lady from Downton Abbey, while Cynthia wore a long-waisted twenties flapper-style dress and a feathered headpiece. Haskell had donned a tailcoat and top hat. All gathered on the porch, across which had been strung a blue ribbon that the frigid wind flipped and fluttered.

The mayor made a speech and Haskell made a much longer one, all while the volunteers stepped from foot to foot, freezing in the cold. All except Mabel, who had on an ancient fur stole over her shoulders, her hands stuffed in a muff.

Mayor Fletcher finally held up the brass scissors and said to the waiting crowd, "I now declare Queensville Historic Manor officially open!" He clipped the ribbon and there was polite applause from the crowd, which was anxiously waiting, kids chattering and folks craning their necks, trying to see inside the front door. They flooded into the warmth of the manor home.

Jewel was her charming self, the redhead's gregarious nature making her the perfect hostess, while Mabel, deeply knowledgeable about every aspect of fine dining in the nineteenth and early twentieth century, acted as the original homeowner, Mrs. Latimer Dumpe. Imogene Frump, as one of the few living relatives, was gowned in her rarely worn Queen Victoria getup, as was Mrs. Bellwood. Both ladies, still trying to one-up each other even though they had mended their broken friendship from years gone by, had arrived after the opening ceremonies.

Jaymie ruled the kitchen. She set her colander centerpiece on the kitchen table and rolled out sugar cookies on the Hoosier tabletop. Using vintage cookie cutters in star and angel shapes, she cut the cookies, sprinkled them with sugar and baked them in her new old oven. The first batch was burned, but after that she got into a rhythm and began turning them out in a nice pale golden color.

She kept expecting Valetta or Jakob and Jocie to visit, but they didn't. Maybe it was for the best, she decided, as she cleaned up mess after mess, because she didn't have a single moment to talk. Families, hungry for pre-Christmas kid-friendly things to do, streamed through nonstop. She handed out the sugar cookies she was baking and helped kids decorate them with colored icing and sprinkles, trying to keep the dusting of crumbs to a minimum.

After a few hours she was wretchedly tired and overdone with people, but then Haskell blustered, "Jaymie, there's a photographer here from the *Wolverhampton Weekly Howler*. Pose with your stove." He introduced her to a young fellow in a parka, galoshes and glasses, holding a fancy camera by the lens. The guy smirked at her outfit and rolled his eyes at the kids jostling his arm.

Her careful coiffure now askew and dark dress dusted with flour, Jaymie took a deep breath, smiled and greeted the photographer. So Nan had come through after all, she thought, and her smile faltered as she thought of poor Shelby, lying comatose in a hospital bed with her anxious mother hovering over her. Nan would have someone covering the incident in Queensville. She eyed the photographer. He might even have been dispatched to take photos of the crime scene, but she couldn't ask him what he knew or what he'd seen, not with tourists present, anyway.

He took shots of her bending over helping a winsome child decorate a cookie; Jaymie fervently hoped he didn't angle it so her butt looked huge. As the last person drifted out of the kitchen, the photographer asked her to stand by the Hoosier, which was decked again with the white colander holding her own holly. She smiled and held up her floury rolling pin.

"Great," he said, with no enthusiasm. "We're done." He glanced around. Haskell had gotten antsy with the presence of children and had retreated, and the last of the families seemed to have drifted off, so it was just her and the photographer. "You're Jaymie Leighton, right? That girl who keeps finding bodies and who works for the paper?"

"Sure," she said, frowning at him in irritation.

"Nan is *really* mad at you. She told me to tell you she's been trying to call you all afternoon."

"Mad at *me*?" she said, alarmed. "Why?"

His expression was sly, and confirmed her immediate dislike of him. "I heard her with the boss. She was screaming that after all she's done for you why would you backstab her that way and tell the cops you saw her son at the scene of the crime? She says Cody told her that he was working last evening at the Christmas tree farm and wasn't anywhere near Queensville."

Jaymie's breath caught. "But I didn't say that, not exactly. I didn't say I saw him at the scene of the crime."

He shrugged. "All I know is Cody Wainwright has been arrested for assault. I took a photo of him when they had him do a perp walk after picking him up at the Christmas tree place. Nan is out of her mind, mad as blazes, mostly at you."

AFTER SWIFTLY CLEANING up the kitchen and helping with the rest of the house, Jaymie caught a ride back to town with Mabel Bloombury, who cast troubled looks at her all the way. Mabel and the others knew what was wrong—that her editor's son had been arrested for the assault on Shelby Fretter—but as they all cleaned the house they respected her need to process it in silence.

She told Mabel she'd see her the next day, the second of the grand-opening weekend, then stood and waved good-bye at her front door. She turned, fumbling in her purse for the key, and at that moment her lights, on a timer, came on to help her see. She entered and locked the door behind her as Hoppy wuffled and wriggled at her feet. She let out a desperate-to-piddle puppy and a nonchalant Denver as the snow thickened. Normally, on an evening like this, she would be looking forward to curling up by the fire in the parlor with a book and cup of tea. Like many readers she had a few books going at the same time, so besides the romances on her bedside nightstand, there was a biography of C. S. Lewis waiting on a table by the settee. But after such a harrowing twenty-four hours she couldn't even think straight, much less look forward to anything. On the phone was an angry sputtering message from Nan, and another from Detective Vestry to call the police station, but she ignored them both and called Jakob first.

Once they had greeted each other, she asked, "Did they really come out to the Christmas tree farm to arrest Cody?"

"They did," he said. "The police officer was nice enough. I told him I didn't want my little girl to see one of my employees arrested, and he let me get Jocie away with no fuss. I told them that he was working all last evening, but that was before Gus told me what really happened."

"What was that?"

"Cody received a text message. He was supposed to work until ten, to help with some of the cleanup, but he told Gus he had a family emergency and took off early."

"But there was no family emergency," Jaymie said. "Not that I know of. I saw him in the village in the crowd, but he was just watching and listening to the brass band. Nan is blaming me for telling the police that I saw him, but what else could I do?"

"You did the right thing. He shouldn't have lied to the police."

"He lied?"

Jakob sighed deeply. "When he was first confronted he told them he'd been working all evening on the tree lot and hadn't left until ten. I confirmed it, but Gus spoke up and told the truth. He feels bad about it now, but he was right not to let the kid get away with that. I won't be his cover-up. Even if he didn't hit that poor girl he didn't do himself any favors by lying. I haven't forgotten what you told me about Cody, Jaymie. I'm praying he didn't do this."

"Me, too." She wondered if he had told the police he was at the tree lot until after ten because he knew what time she was found. Or did he know what happened to her because he did it himself? She had walked up to the walkway and watched the lights on Heartbreak Island after seeing him at the band shell; he had time to get back to the village and attack Shelby, and she had already figured that he could have known about the spare key to the workshop from working with Bill earlier that day.

"How was your day at the historic house? I'm sorry we didn't get there, but I left Jocie with my mother. Today was crazy, and with Cody being arrested I just couldn't leave Gus to take care of everything, and the junk store, too. This is one of our busiest days of the year."

"I understand, Jakob. Please don't apologize. I'm okay. I tried to put it out of my mind, and the day went well. Will you hire someone else to work at the tree farm?"

"It's kind of late to find anyone now. My oldest brother, Dieter, will pitch in. He's done it before and he's free tomorrow."

"I suppose I'd better go," Jaymie said, reluctant to hang up, knowing this was probably the sweetest moment of the day for her. It was only going to get worse once she returned Nan's and Detective Vestry's calls.

"You know what?" he asked softly.

"What?"

There was a pause, and then he said, "I miss you. I wish I could see you tonight."

She was amazed by a welling of emotion, a tear rising into her eye and trickling down her cheek. The wonder of his admission, when she had been feeling exactly the same way but afraid to say it, made her silent for a moment.

"Did that sound wrong?"

"No," she said, her voice catching. "Far from it, Jakob. I miss you, too. I wish I was there with you right now." His cabin was just twenty minutes from town. But no, she had promised herself not to rush things, even when this felt so right. "But I can't be."

"Call me later if you need to talk."

"I will." The one and only thing she missed about going out with Daniel was having someone to talk to late at night. "If I can't sleep, would it be okay to call fairly late, like eleven or so?"

"I'd like that."

They hung up. Jaymie stared at the phone in her hand, then scanned through her saved contacts and hit Nan's home number, kind of hoping she didn't get her editor. She was out of luck.

"Hello? Jaymie, is that you? I've been trying to get you all day."

"I'm sorry, Nan, but today was the first official day of the historic manor being open and I was there most of the day."

"I know, but this is a mess. Why did you tell the cops you saw my son at the scene of the crime?"

"I didn't say that. I *did* say that I saw Cody at the band shell watching the brass band just before I finished up for the night."

"Why did you tell them that?"

"Because it was the *truth*, Nan," she said, unable to hide the exasperation in her voice. Why did her editor *think* she would say it? She moved to the stove and put on the kettle for tea. "Cody was there, I saw him. He didn't tell the police the truth, probably because he was scared they'd think he hurt Shelby."

She was silent.

"You *know* I wouldn't make something like that up. I just talked to Jakob Müller. Cody lied to the police, saying he was working all evening at the tree farm when in truth he asked to leave early because of a family emergency."

Nan sighed. "Damn. I hoped he was telling me the truth and that everyone else got it wrong. What am I going to do with him?"

Jaymie was silent, not knowing what to say.

"But I do not believe he beat that girl. I just don't!"

Jaymie made a sympathetic noise, but she couldn't offer reassurance. She'd seen him hit Shelby; was it so far-fetched that he'd beat her?

"I should have known you wouldn't lie, Jaymie. But Cody is my son." She was silent for a long minute except for a sigh. "I've hired a lawyer, so I hope he'll be able to post bail after the weekend. It kills me to think of him in jail for days, but there's nothing else I can do."

"I'm so sorry, Nan."

"Not your problem, kiddo. Get to work on your column. The news biz goes on."

Once Nan hung up, Jaymie made herself a cup of tea and some dinner, just a homemade frozen dinner of turkey, mashed potatoes and corn that she had saved from Thanksgiving, heated in the oven. Denver was curled up in his basket by the stove and Hoppy was sitting up on a kitchen chair, where she had placed him on a cushion, watching Jaymie eat.

The phone, which was lying on the table by her plate, rang, and she glanced at the call display. It was Valetta!

"Val, how are you!"

"I'm okay. Jaymie, I just heard some bad news."

"Bad news? Is Brock okay? The kids?"

"It's nothing to do with any of them. Dee just called. Shelby Fretter has died."

❊ Nine ❊

"OH NO! IT can't be true." Her imagination raced. Shelby Fretter would miss so much; no marriage, no career, no love, no children, no . . . anything. "That's *terrible*!" Tears welled and she sniffed. "I thought she would recover. What happened?"

"Dee had some technical explanation," Valetta said, her voice quavering. "It's something she called TBI, traumatic brain injury. They did their best, but . . ."

They were both silent. Jaymie sighed, finally, pushing away her unfinished dinner, the part she had consumed sitting like a leaden lump in her stomach. "It never occurred to me that she would die; it just didn't seem possible. I don't know what else to say. She's so young!"

"I guess Lori is a basket case. Dee wasn't supposed to tell me, and I'm not supposed to say anything to anyone, but I knew you'd want to know."

They talked for just a moment longer, then signed off, but Jaymie didn't put down the phone. Anger fueled her. Whoever did this had to pay, and any help she could give she would offer. She called Detective Vestry, but was told that the detective wanted her to come to the police station the next morning as early as possible.

What followed was a sleepless, weepy night. Even her comfort reads couldn't save her, and she threw one across the room and wept into her pillow. Her relationship with Jakob was far too new to subject him to such an emotional overload. Her instinct was that if she did call him he would be gentle and supportive with her sorrow, but her connection to him was like a new and tender plant; calling and sobbing in his ear would be like stomping on that plant, subjecting it to too much stress while it was so young. It might recover, or it might not. So she toughed it out, her tears finally ended, and with her eyes swollen almost shut, she finally got some sleep.

SHE WAS UP early and followed her routine as much as possible, walking Hoppy, feeding the pets, cleaning up the kitchen, but it was just distraction and make-work. All she wanted was to talk to the detective. Finally it was time. She locked up and headed out to her van, driving on automatic to the police station, her mind racing. She waited in a small room for Detective Vestry.

The detective entered and closed the door after her and told Jaymie that their interview was being videotaped. Jaymie already knew Chief Ledbetter was out of town for the weekend, so there would be no intervention from the sometimes genial chief of police. But she was happy to talk to the detective. Her thoughts on any man who would beat a woman were not something she planned on sugarcoating. She didn't care to whom she spoke, so long as she could help.

"Witness interview, Jaymie Leighton, eight oh three, Sunday, December thirteenth," Detective Vestry intoned for the benefit of the taping. "Why don't you tell me your timeline of the evening, up to the moment you entered the storage shed and found Shelby Fretter."

Detective Vestry's cool composure was beneficial. It allowed Jaymie to disconnect her emotions somehow. She went through the evening, including seeing Shelby, Lori and Travis together. She spoke of Shelby and Travis fighting. She talked about who she met and talked to. "It was busy. I saw a lot of folks I didn't know."

"Did you see anyone who might be known to Shelby or her mother or brother?"

"I don't know them that well, but . . ." She thought back. "I *think* I caught a glimpse of her boss, Delaney Meadows. I'd seen them arguing that morning and I recognized him."

The detective made notes, her pale eyes blank of expression. "Why did you go to the band shell?"

"I had been there twice already before my last time. It was my job to make sure I caught everyone I could, to give them the brochure."

"And you saw Cody Wainwright there?"

"Yes. He was watching the band. I didn't say anything, and I don't think he saw me. From there I walked away up to the boardwalk—what townies call the boardwalk—and watched the last boats that were lit up, and saw the lights go out over at the Ice House restaurant. I didn't check my watch, but maybe they know what time they closed down."

"How long was it from the time you saw Cody to the time you got back to the village proper?"

She thought about it. This was pivotal. "I would say it was about twenty or twenty-five minutes. Maybe a little more, but certainly not less. From the time I saw the lights go off over at the restaurant it was ten minutes or so. If Cody had headed straight to the village after I saw him he would have gotten there a good ten or fifteen minutes before me."

"Are you saying you think he did it? Did you actually see anything that leads you to believe that?"

Jaymie thought for a moment, looking down at her hands.

She rarely thought about how her hands looked; the nails were chipped and a little rough from work. She always seemed to have them in hot water, like *she* often was. She should take better care of them for all they did for her. "No," she said. "I didn't see him near her, and I don't have a real reason to think that. Other than a couple of incidents I saw between them a few days before."

"What incidents?"

She told Detective Vestry about the other morning in the Emporium. "It was weird," she said, staring up at the acoustic-tile ceiling and catching sight of the camera. She looked back down. "It seemed like . . ." She shook her head. "I don't know. I would have sworn he didn't touch her, but she fell down and blamed him for pushing her. He looked surprised." Jaymie met the detective's cold eyes and thought back.

"And then there was the one before that. It was another one of the mornings I was working at the Emporium. I normally go out to the porch for tea midmorning, unless it's too cold. Usually Valetta is with me, but she was . . ." She thought back. "Yes, I remember. She was on the phone with a doctor and couldn't leave the pharmacy. I saw Shelby and Cody over by the fence that separates the village green from the street. I had seen her before, but not him, so I didn't know who he was until the other day, when I saw him at Nan Goodenough's office. I couldn't hear anything, but they were having a heated argument. You could tell by their body language. She said something, and he balled up his fist and clubbed her on the side of her head, knocking her sideways."

Vestry's eyes riveted on hers. She had stopped jotting notes, and the tick of the clock on the wall was the only sound. After a few moments she asked, "What day was that?"

Jaymie thought back and told the detective the date.

"Did you call the police?"

"No. The fight broke up and she stormed off. I didn't know what to do. If she'd been hurt . . . I mean, it *must* have hurt, but she didn't look like she needed my help. I thought if she wanted to, she could call the police herself because she had her phone out."

"So she was not incapacitated?"

"No. Not that that matters, right? I mean, it indicates something about their relationship, a violence at the heart of it."

Detective Vestry watched Jaymie. The woman's gaze was calculating and she appeared to be deciding something. "Have you ever experienced domestic violence, Ms. Leighton?"

"No, I haven't. Why?"

"Just asking. So you did *not* see the victim speaking with Cody Wainwright at any point during the evening of the crime."

"No."

"Did you see her with *anyone*?"

"Yes, of course," Jaymie said, beginning to feel impatience well up in her. "As I've already told you, I saw her with her mother and brother. No one else."

"And she was arguing with her brother, you said."

"Yes, I guess that must have been her brother, Travis. A thin fellow, taller than her, with a bit of a beard and a slouch woolen hat?"

"That description matches."

"Do you think *he* could have done it?"

The detective remained impassive. "Can you think of anything else at all that happened that evening?"

"Like what?"

"Did you see or hear anything unusual? Anyone behaving oddly?"

She thought for a moment and shook her head. "No, but one thing I thought of . . . Bill told me there were only four keys to the padlock, and that one was kept up on the ledge above the door. It was just earlier that day that Cody helped Bill in and about the workshop."

"Yes. Well. You seem eager to prosecute Cody Wainwright."

"No, not at all," Jaymie said, stung. "I'm just telling you everything I know or have thought of."

"I think we're done here, Ms. Leighton. Thank you for coming in." The detective stood. "If you think of anything else, please let us know." She paused, then added, "But I don't want to hear about you snooping or getting anyone upset. This is a police investigation and I would have no problem charging you with interference if you get in our way."

Chilled to the bone, Jaymie said, "I won't interfere." As she slunk from the police department she felt chastened and misunderstood. How much better it was to work with Chief Ledbetter, who had a more creative outlook on policing. Jaymie understood that she needed to not interfere, but there were times when she stumbled on things that may never have come to light if she hadn't been interested. And there were times when she had ended up in danger because of that. She hoped she now knew the difference.

She drove back to town, parking the white van when she saw Bill Waterman on the street outside of Jewel's Junk. He was gazing sadly toward his workshop, which was still taped with crime scene tape. She got out of the van and joined him, threading her arm through his. "It's terrible. I'm so sorry, Bill. I know how you feel."

His weathered face was grim. "I was just thinking about Lori, actually. I feel real bad for her. I have a daughter. I don't know what I'd do if someone killed her."

"I was just at the police station. The detective asked me if I saw Cody and Shelby together that night, but I didn't. I hope he didn't do it. For Nan's sake, I hope he's released soon."

Bill glanced over at her. "I guess you haven't heard everything, then. Cody lied, Jaymie. He was seen with Shelby that evening."

"Who saw them together?" she asked.

"Her brother, Travis. He saw her with Cody, and they were arguing, but she told him to take off, that it was private, so he left them alone."

"What time was that?" Jaymie asked.

"I don't know. Does it matter?"

Yes, it did, Jaymie thought but did not say. It mattered a whole lot.

JAYMIE COULD NOT stop thinking about the tragedy, but she still had responsibilities. As she had promised, she dropped in to help Pam Driscoll move some furniture for cleaning. They climbed the stairs together to one of the empty rooms, a small but pretty robin's egg blue room with floral curtains and shabby-chic furnishing. Pam was upset about the murder.

"I know Lori," she said, tugging at the end of the bed. "She was so nice to me right away when I moved here and she must be suffering so bad right now! I hope that guy rots in prison for what he did."

Jaymie didn't respond, her face hidden by the wooden headboard of the bed she was pushing around on the thick carpet. Finally, she stood, dusted her hands off and said, "I hope they have the right guy."

"They do, trust me on this! I called Lori this morning and talked to her for a while."

"How is she doing?"

"About how you'd expect. Poor girl can't talk without crying. It was her son who saw Cody and Shelby together fighting."

She moved the bed again, farther away from the wall. "But he didn't see Cody do anything, right?"

"What happened was, Lori got separated from her kids while she was talking to someone, and when she caught up with Travis he was alone. He told Lori that Shelby had gone off, I guess with Cody. She found Shelby and suggested they go home—"

"She went off with Cody?"

Pam stood and squinted. "I don't know. That's what Travis said. Anyway, Shelby had something she wanted to do. So

Lori gave Travis a lift home and she never saw Shelby again. Cody must have tracked her down and dragged her off to that shed."

"But that doesn't make any sense," Jaymie said, straightening and staring at Pam. "Did Travis tell her that that same night? That Shelby went off with Cody *before* she met back up with her mother?" The timing just didn't seem possible, given that she saw Cody at the band shell at almost the last minute of the evening.

"I don't know if it was that night or later that he told his mom about the guy. Why?"

It made a difference to the timeline, but her mind was a little tangled. She just shook her head.

"Look, this is all real clear to anyone who cares to see it; I've been hit around," Pam said, her tone hard and cold. "I know how it goes. Shelby stayed with Cody because every time he hit her, he'd say it was the last time. Well, he did hit her again, one last time."

Pam started up the vacuum cleaner, so Jaymie went to the next room to move the bed so they could get a head start there. One of the Queensville Historic Manor pamphlets was sitting on the bedside table, and for the first time Jaymie realized she was going to have to get the other batch she had ordered. The rest were in the storage room of Bill's workshop, off limits because of the murder.

It was looking grim for Nan as far as her son's innocence went. The simplest explanation, that Cody's simmering anger toward Shelby had boiled over and he beat her to death, was likely the true one. She wondered how Nan would handle the reporting of Shelby's death in the newspaper when her son was the prime suspect.

Pam got a phone call and had to rush through the rest of the vacuuming; her son was in some kind of trouble at a friend's house and she had to run to pick him up. Jaymie returned to her own peaceful home. There were times when she just wanted to draw the shades and pretend the world, with all of its violence and trouble, did not exist. But she called herself an optimistic realist; she would acknowledge violence and glare at it with an unflinching stare, but she would also see all the wonderful people and the kindness that there was in the world as a counterbalance, hopefully tipping toward all that was good and right.

She called the newspaper office and got the weekend service. They accessed the printing floor, the staff of which was working through the weekend printing sale flyers for local businesses, to ask about the fresh order of Queensville Historic Manor pamphlets. When the answering service operator came back on she told Jaymie that the printers were almost done with her pamphlets and she could come pick them up the next morning. She hung up, thankful that she didn't have to face Nan. What did you say to someone whose son had been arrested for murder, and who you feared was guilty?

The day went on and she did a few hours at the historic home, which was closing early since it was Sunday, then rushed home, gobbled down some dinner and headed out in her cloak for the Dickens Days walk. She didn't have much to do, since she didn't have access to any of the pamphlets, though there were still some available at the cider booth, which was manned by two gentlemen from the heritage society that evening, with Mrs. Bellwood in charge. So she just walked, talking to folks, trying to stay upbeat and positive. Many hadn't heard about the crime that happened just steps away from the queenly elegance of the festively decorated main street, so it actually cheered her up to hand out candy canes and goodies to children as she told the adults about the manor house.

But then she noticed a news crew from Detroit interviewing Bill Waterman, who looked intensely uncomfortable in the glare of the camera light. She had no illusion that they were asking about the Dickens Days festivities, though they would mention that as a gruesome twist, she was sure. She was torn; if she approached, they would quickly release him once Jaymie was pointed out as the one who found poor Shelby. Bill would be grateful for the rescue, but the last thing she wanted to do was bring more notoriety to their Dickens Days celebration for all the wrong reasons.

She slipped over to the cider booth and muttered her reasoning to Mrs. Bellwood, who agreed with her. She had no pamphlets to give out anyway, and her earnest desire was not that the murder be swept under the carpet, but that it be viewed for what it was, an isolated incident that had nothing to do with their lovely seasonal festival. That would never happen if they interviewed her about finding the body while she was gowned in her Dickens Days cloak and bonnet.

She returned home, her heart heavy, and let Hoppy out into the backyard. He wobbled and bounced the perimeter, sniffing and barking at a foraging squirrel in the semidarkness. She brought him back in, wiped his muddy paws and made sure both Hoppy and Denver had dinner and treats. She then retreated to the front parlor of her beautiful old Queen Anne home and built a fire, settling on the sofa with a cup of tea and the phone.

She called her Grandma Leighton. After the initial chatter about family—Jaymie's mom and dad were coming up for Christmas, but her grandmother was hoping that Rebecca would bring her down to see the house where she was a wife and mother for forty years before all of them headed back to London for Christmas day—her grandmother got down to business.

"I heard from Becca all about this fuss with that poor girl. I guess she heard it from your friend Valetta. It's awful. How are you, my dear girl? I know how sensitive you are."

Sensitive? "I'm okay, Grandma. Please don't worry about me. I'm concerned about my friend Nan. It's her son who is accused of beating the girl. He says he's innocent, but I just don't know. I think he probably did it."

"That'll be her cross to bear, chickadee. But if it's not

him, then it means some fella got away with it. That's not a good thing. Why don't you try to sort this one out?"

"I don't think it's up to me this time. The police have it well in hand. The detective doesn't like me, and she's warned me not to mess in the investigation."

"Well, then, maybe you'd better just stay out of it. Try to get your mind off of things. I hear you have a new boyfriend. Tell me all about him."

She told her grandmother about Jakob and Jocie, but warned that it was early yet; they had just met a few weeks before and he was *not* her boyfriend!

There was something about the conversation with her grandmother, so accepting and sure that Jaymie could solve anything if she put her mind to it, that was soothing and helped her get perspective. By the time she hung up, she was feeling much better and could breathe. Yes, Cody was in jail and accused of the crime. But the detective was no fool. Mrs. Bellwood had mentioned to her that the police were still asking questions in Queensville, trying to account for every second of Shelby's evening. If there was any chance it was someone else, there ought to be evidence.

She called Becca then, with some last-minute plan changes. "Grandma does want to come to Queensville and see the house. Do you think she can make it upstairs to a bedroom to stay over?" Jaymie asked. "The stairs are kind of long and steep."

They decided that their grandmother would come to the house for a meal, but if they decided to stay over, she would be housed at the Queensville Inn. "That is an awesome idea," Jaymie enthused. "Maybe you can put it to her that it'll give her a chance to visit with Mrs. Stubbs. She's been asking about Grandma and would love to see her."

"That's a good idea," Becca said. "I don't generally tiptoe around her, but I don't want her to feel that she can't do what she wants."

"It must be hard to get older," Jaymie mused.

"She's pretty philosophical about it," Becca said. "She told me that the compensation for losing some ability to do stuff is that she doesn't want to do much anyway, other than read and visit. But I know she'd like to see the house again, and visiting with Mrs. Stubbs, Mrs. Bellwood and Mrs. Frump would be a great idea."

"I'll set up a luncheon at the inn for the ladies." Jaymie jotted a note to herself on her ever-present notebook, her lifeline, as she thought of it.

After hanging up, she climbed the stairs to her little refuge, her lovely bedroom, with a calmer heart. She still felt sorrowful for Shelby, who had lost her life, and for Lori, who had lost her child, but there was nothing she could do but help in any way she could.

As she settled in bed with Hoppy on one side, Denver on the other and one of the old Mary Balogh traditional Regencies in her hand, the phone rang. She picked up the receiver without looking at the call display. "Hello?"

"Jaymie, how are you?"

"Jakob!" She sighed, and snuggled down under the covers, setting the book aside. "I'm all right. It's been a busy day. For you, too, probably."

"That's an understatement." He told her about a shipment from an auction house to the junk store, stuff that hadn't sold at their last auction, and about a full day of Christmas tree sales. "I think next year I'm going to add some events at the Christmas tree lot, like a hot cider stand and that kind of thing. I'd love your input. Your rental picnic basket idea is so great, but I just don't have that kind of vision."

"I'd love to help," she said. "I can already think of half a dozen ideas. How about 'Party Like It's 1899'? You'd look so handsome in a tailcoat."

He chuckled. "Love it already." He was silent for a moment, then said, "I thought you were going to phone last night. You get busy?"

She took a long breath, and then decided she needed to

start as she meant to go on, and in this case it was with complete honesty. "No, I didn't get busy. Last night I heard that Shelby died. It was so awful. I feel so bad. I didn't want to end up weeping in your ear. I'm not a weepy woman, but I did cry buckets. We don't know each other very well, though, and—"

"You were afraid I wouldn't understand, or that I'd decide you were too emotional."

She held the phone away and stared at it, then brought it back up to her ear. "How did you know that?"

"I put myself in your shoes," he said.

"Really?"

"Well, yeah, that and I asked my sister-in-law—that's Helmut's significant other—at church this morning."

Jaymie felt laughter burble up from her heart and tears well in her eyes. It was so exactly what she needed to hear, and spoke so well of him that she was touched and warmed. Her heart, never the frostiest organ in the world, melted.

"It doesn't bug you that I talked to my sister-in-law about you, does it?" he asked, a touch of anxiety in his husky voice.

"It doesn't bug me at all. About the opposite, actually." Because it told her so much. First, that he had a positive relationship with his brother's common-law wife, which was a good sign. Next, that he could ask for help, another good sign. And finally, that he cared; that was the best sign of all. "I was afraid I would scare you off with my weepiness."

"You could never scare me off. What does your day look like tomorrow? Can we get together for coffee?"

"I have to go in to Wolverhampton to pick up some more pamphlets at the news office. Can you get away?"

"I have to be in Wolverhampton for . . . well, for something. I don't know what, but I'll make up a reason to be there."

She smiled. It made her feel special that he would go out of his way for her. "Maybe we can have coffee together, then?"

"I'll meet you at Tastee D's at ten."

"You've got a date." She hung up the phone with a sense

that life would go on. Though she was sad about Shelby and felt deeply sorry for Lori, she hoped that justice would be served so Lori could eventually move on and heal from such a devastating event.

And she realized, though she had talked to her grandmother and Rebecca, it was her conversation with Jakob that made her feel more hopeful. She wasn't *sure* why, but she hoped that in her heart she knew.

❋ Ten ❋

SHE SLEPT BETTER than she had the night before, better than she had expected, certainly, but still awoke with a sense that something was deeply wrong. It took a moment to remember; poor Shelby Fretter was dead. A mother was devastated and a family would never be the same.

But with just under two weeks until Christmas, life sped on. Jaymie drove to Wolverhampton and parked in the lot behind the newspaper office, where the print shop stretched out, long and low, an old redbrick building. She normally would go through the main entrance to speak to Nan, but today she was hoping to avoid her editor and just deal with the printing foreman.

She buzzed at the back loading dock door.

A fellow lifted the garage-style door with a grating rattle. "Yup?" he said, making it a question and hollering it over the noise of the print room floor. He was dressed in green workpants and an ink-stained T-shirt that stretched over a moderate potbelly.

"I'm here to pick up an order of pamphlets for the Queensville Heritage Society. It's to be billed to them. I'm kind of in a rush, so can I just back my van up and get the boxes?"

"Wait a sec," he said, grabbing a clipboard from a nail by the door. He squinted at the print, then grabbed a smudged pair of close-up glasses from a shelf. He scanned down the page, then glanced up at her. "Hold on, there's a note attached."

"A note?"

"Yup. Wait just a sec." He grabbed a phone receiver off a hook, punched one number and turned away. When he turned back and hung up, he said, "Boss lady wants to see you up front before you get your order."

Jaymie sighed, blowing air out through pursed lips and jamming her hands down in her coat pockets. "Okay. When I'm done, can I get some help to load the boxes? I don't know how heavy they'll be."

"Sure."

"Should I just go to Nan's office through the plant?"

"Yup. Straight ahead until you see a glass door and windows, then go on through."

Jaymie made her way through the noisy print shop to the offices and found Nan, who sat at her desk with her head in her hands. She felt ashamed of herself in that moment for trying to avoid the woman who had given her the opportunity to write a food column, and in the last few months had become a friend. She stood in the door for a moment, then said gently, "Nan? You doing okay?"

The woman looked up, her face ravaged by pain and anguish, wrinkles that had been mere hints now deep grooves and dark circles under her eyes. "Jaymie, come on in and sit for a minute. I have a favor to ask."

Jaymie took the chair indicated. Nan's working office was a cubicle surrounded by half walls and frosted glass to the ceiling, with just a simple desk and computer, as well as file cabinets and a printer. It was undoubtedly a step down from the role she had played in a lifestyle magazine in New

York City, but it was one she performed with fierce attention to detail. The guest chair was on the same side of the desk as Nan's chair. "Are you okay?" Jaymie repeated.

Nan shook her head briskly, but it wasn't an answer, it was her shaking off the question as immaterial. "I'm crappy, but that doesn't matter." Nan had a whiskey voice, with an attractive burr in it. She had smoked for years and it had left her with damage on her vocal chords, she once told Jaymie. Regardless, her voice had a smoky attractiveness, a rasp that was interesting. "I'm more worried about Cody. He didn't do this, Jaymie."

Jaymie was silent.

"Nobody believes me," Nan growled. "He didn't *do* it. I know he's not perfect, but he could never beat a girl so badly she'd die. He told me he didn't and I believe him."

This was painful, facing her editor and friend like this when she believed it was possible that Cody was guilty. "He's lucky to have you believe in him," she said, skirting the issue.

"If you would talk to him you'd believe him, too," she said.

Psychopaths were often charming, she had heard, and very believable, able to manipulate people's perception of them with their charisma. "You know he was seen talking to Shelby? And that he lied about it?"

"He says he never saw her that evening and I believe him."

"But Shelby's brother—"

"I know, he says he saw Cody with Shelby, and that they were fighting. It's a load of crap, Jaymie," she said, tapping the desk in front of her in time with each of the last few words, color coming into her cheeks. "Cody says that's not true. He got a text message to meet her at the band shell but she never showed up, so he just went home."

"Why would Travis Fretter lie?"

"He wanted to make Cody look bad," she said, sitting back in her chair, which squawked in protest. "He never liked my son."

"Do you think he'd lie about his sister's murder just to get Cody in trouble?"

"Who knows with that family? Travis is a menace. He's been in more trouble with the law than Cody has ever been."

Jaymie was unconvinced. Would Travis lie about the facts of his sister's murder? Wouldn't he want the perpetrator caught, and not to muddy the investigation with lies? Of course, if he had killed his sister himself he would welcome a ready-made fall guy. Or . . . She thought it through. More than one person had lied to make sure the person they thought had committed a crime was arrested.

But the simplest explanation was that Cody was guilty.

Nan had been moving things around on her desk, shifting papers and pens and paperclips. Every movement was hasty and jerky; she was agitated and upset. Finally, she looked up at Jaymie. "I said I have a favor to ask. I've put you on Cody's approved visitor list at the jail where he's awaiting arraignment. All you have to do to see him is go and sign a permission slip."

Why would she visit Cody, who she despised for his treatment of Shelby and his mother both? "I have no reason to visit Cody."

"You do now," Nan said, and slid a plastic swipe card along the desk. It had the *Wolverhampton Weekly Howler* banner across the top and Jaymie's ID photo from her employee file in one corner. "You're an accredited member of the press now. I want you to follow this story."

"But—"

"Hear me out," the editor said, one hand help up in a *stop* indication.

Twenty minutes later Jaymie backed her van out of the newspaper parking lot feeling like she had been hit by a truck named Nan. She parked in the donut shop lot; it was a small modern stand-alone building on a busy street corner in downtown Wolverhampton. As she locked her van, light flakes drifted down and she huddled in her parka. The chill was becoming more bitter, and she was shivering as she jammed her hand in her pocket, her fingers brushing against the new press card.

Jakob was at a window booth. He waved to her as she walked along the building and entered through the glass doors. She greeted him and slid into the booth.

"What's wrong?" he asked, reaching across the table and grabbing her hands, chafing them.

She sighed and looked down. He had broad work-roughened hands, and she curled her fingers around his thumb. "I'm not sure how to handle something." As she shed her parka, she told him what had just happened, and how she felt like she was being pushed into investigating because of her friendship with Nan.

"Did you tell her how you feel?" he said.

He had taken both of her hands again, across the table. As the waitress approached he pulled away, and her hands felt instantly cold. She ordered a coffee and chocolate croissant, needing both warmth and comfort food.

"I didn't know how. How could I say, 'Nan, I think your son is a creep and that he likely did it.' It's just . . . I don't know what to do."

As they got their coffee and fixed them up—he took two sugars and cream, she noticed—he was silent. When they were done and Jaymie had taken a bite of her croissant, he said, "Do you in general respect her opinion?"

She nodded, chewed and swallowed.

"Do you think that her love for her son would blind her to his faults?"

"I don't know. I've never seen her in this state. He's her son; she's not going to believe he's guilty. *You* know him. What do you think?"

"I've known him such a short time. We've worked together a few hours, but most of what we talked about was hockey and craft beer. Based on my knowledge of him I'd say no, but . . ." He sighed and sat back, staring out the window at the traffic. When he looked at her again, it was with some decision in his expression. "I think you need to take the emotion out of it. I'm troubled by his behavior, but I actually did get *one* chance to talk to him about some of this stuff. It was Friday afternoon. He had come out early to help me cut a few trees for the ready-cut lot." Jakob paused and frowned down into his coffee cup. "I asked about how he reacted when faced with difficulties; was he violent, did he fly off the handle? He admitted he did. He said he would snap, but it was always over quick, like, his anger didn't last more than a few seconds. I asked him if he wanted to change and he said he did." He shrugged. "I don't know if he was being honest. I intended to follow up that conversation with another."

There was no need for him to say more. That very night Shelby was beaten.

"What exactly did your editor say to you?"

Jaymie recalled the conversation and related it to Jakob as she sipped her coffee and finished her croissant. Nan was sick with worry about her son, not because he was in jail, but for the future. Adamant that he could not have brutalized a girl he claimed to love, she wanted Jaymie to investigate. Jaymie had successfully helped the police over the last few months, and Nan thought it wouldn't hurt if she looked into this case.

"I told her that I'd been warned to stay out of it, but Nan said if I was working for the newspaper Detective Vestry couldn't say anything."

"I don't know about that. I think the police often tell the media to stay out of an investigation. I guess that doesn't mean reporters do, though."

"That's pretty much what Nan said."

"What do *you* want to do? Let your heart and mind and gut be your guide."

"All three? That's quite the mix," she said, with a smile. It was so good to talk to him about it. Daniel had always told her not to get involved, to stay out of trouble. Jakob was more supportive.

And that was the very last time she would ever compare the two men, she promised herself. Making a swift decision, she said, "I want to at least talk to Cody. I feel a certain responsibility, not to him if he did it, but because I was the one who told the police I'd seen him in Queensville, and I'm the one who told them I'd seen him hit Shelby."

"All the truth, Jaymie. It was your responsibility to tell the police that."

"I know, but now I feel tied to the story, and doubtful. Nan is so *sure* about him. I'd like to hear *him* tell me he didn't do it. I'd like to feel in my gut whether he was lying or being honest."

Jakob took her hand across the table again. "Then that is what you should do. Keep your mind clear and your emotions in check and talk to him."

She nodded. "I was straight with Nan to some degree. I asked her what to do if I found evidence that Cody was guilty. What would she want then?"

"I'm glad you asked her that. What did she say?"

"I should do what I needed to do, and she wouldn't interfere. I was afraid she'd expect me to suppress it, and I couldn't."

"But don't be surprised if, in case you *do* find something incriminating, she goes back on that. Right now it's the editor warring with the mother. I expect the mother will win."

She squeezed his hand. "Thank you, Jakob. I can't tell you how much better I feel now."

"I'm glad I could help." He turned his hand and checked his watch, a handsome gold one with a large face nestled in the dark hair that clothed his wrist. "I gotta go. I told Gus I'd be at the junk store by eleven so he could pick up his daughter from day care, and I'm late." He got a ten out of his billfold and slid it under one of the coffee cups, then added some change out of his pocket.

They both stood and before she realized it, she was in his arms and he was hugging her. She relaxed and sighed. This was nice. *Really* nice. He was a solid man, and it felt good to be in his arms. She pulled on her parka and they walked out to their vehicles holding hands. He had a battered pickup truck, and she laughed, because she had parked her beat-up van right next to his battered pickup. He helped her up into the van and squeezed her hand.

"Call me tonight," she said.

"I will."

She drove home happier than she had expected. The house was quiet and still. She left the boxes of pamphlets in her van, since she didn't know where else to store them right then, just taking out a stack to keep in the house. She had already decorated the house for Christmas right after Thanksgiving. The tree was up in the parlor, and she had a pretty pale-blue one up in her bedroom, but the kitchen tree was the one she liked best.

She heated soup as Hoppy sniffed her shoes and Denver stretched and yawned, climbing out of his basket and wandering to the back door. She let the cat out and then returned, gazing at the Christmas tree, a small one smack in the middle of the table. It was real, just three feet tall, and she had decorated it with no lights, but cheerful red ribbons tying cinnamon sticks, little vintage cookie cutters, and doll-sized vintage kitchen utensils she had found in a booth at an antiques mall on her last visit to her grandmother in London. A length of burlap was swaddled around the base. It was Christmas at long last, after an eventful and dramatic year, and her personal life was finally feeling more satisfying.

Not so for Lori and her family; Shelby's murder was an awful event, truly tragic.

And then she thought of Nan, and how her heart was breaking over her son, in jail awaiting arraignment. If he was guilty, he should be found so. But if he was innocent, he should be free. It wasn't up to her to make that decision, but for Nan's sake she wanted to be able to say she tried to figure it out.

She called Nan at the paper. "I am going to see Cody tomorrow morning," she said. "I'm not promising anything, but I'll talk to him."

"That's all I'm asking," the editor said. "He's supposed to be arraigned, but it'll be a video arraignment. You'll still be able to see him. Now go and write me that Christmas Vintage Eats column."

❧ Eleven ❧

JAYMIE WAS WORKING for the afternoon at the Emporium, so after lunch she dressed up in a festive pair of red slacks, a short-sleeved white fluffy sweater and black ankle boots, her hair done up in a ponytail tied with a jingle-bell scrunchy. Her mother would have said it was too young a look for a thirtysomething woman, and that so much red made her butt look big, but she felt just fine about it. In the grand scheme of things, what were a few pounds between friends? Jakob seemed to like her just as she was.

She walked over to the store and took over the cash desk from Mrs. Klausner, who bundled up the knitting she was doing, a complicated blanket for one of her great grandchildren, and walked home. Just a hundred yards down the road, beyond Jewel's Junk and the Cottage Shoppe, was the two-story brick Victorian where the Klausner family had lived since late in the nineteenth century.

It was a busy afternoon, but around four there was a lull; Valetta, dressed in a candy cane emblazoned sweater vest, locked up the pharmacy and came forward with two mugs of hot tea, her footsteps making the elderly boards of the Emporium floor creak and squawk. She handed one to Jaymie. The mug read, *Of course I love retail . . . Can't you see my smile?* with a frowny face beneath.

"I've ordered a mug for Brock to be from his kids," she said, and took a sip. "It has a photo of one of his real estate signs and says 'World's Greatest Real Estate Agent.'"

Jaymie frowned. "But that's not funny."

"Oh come on, Jaymie. I know how you feel about Brock. You probably think it's at least sarcastic."

Jaymie blushed and rolled her eyes.

Valetta smiled and patted Jaymie on the shoulder. "Don't worry about it. I know he's hard to take at times, but he's my brother, the only one I've got. Anyway, Brock doesn't have my sparkling sense of humor, so he wouldn't appreciate a funny mug." She strolled to the front door, her hands wrapped around the steaming mug. "It's coming down out there!"

Jaymie had noticed the snow. It was lovely. She should feel festive and joyful, but there was a gloomy cloud hovering over her, darkening her mood. "Nan wants me to look into Shelby's death," she said suddenly.

Valetta glanced over at her. "Trying to pin it on someone other than her son?"

"It wasn't like that. Not exactly," Jaymie answered, troubled by the implication.

"No? You mean if you came up with proof her son did it, she'd be all right with it? 'Good job, Jaymie'?"

"But I *don't* know if he did it. I saw him hit her, yes. And then days later she was beaten to death. But it doesn't follow that he definitely did it."

"Don't they say that in cases of murder, nine times out of ten it's the significant other?"

Jaymie watched her friend's profile and caught something behind the words. There was a layer of cynicism there she didn't expect from Valetta. "I don't think it's as high as that."

Valetta shrugged and sipped her tea.

"And besides, I heard from Heidi that she was dating some other guy, too. That would make *him* a significant other, as well. But I've been wondering something else; Shelby had on Lori's coat, you know. Could someone have beaten her thinking it was Lori?"

"That's a bit of a stretch. You might hit someone by mistake, but you wouldn't *keep* beating them once you saw who they actually were."

"I guess. I am going to just poke around. I feel like I owe it to Nan. She's been so good to me. If he's guilty, then fine, but if he's not, that means there's someone else out there willing to beat someone to death." She shivered. "What an awful thing to be thinking at this time of year."

"It's a beautiful season, but it's hard on people, too," Valetta said. "So many expectations, so much pressure. Families have more stress this time of year than any other."

Family. Jaymie thought of the argument she witnessed between Travis and Shelby. It had looked fairly bitter, and supposedly was over someone she was dating, but surely a brother wouldn't kill his own sister, would he? It had happened, though, in their own village many years before. "I remember Becca telling me about some guy who killed his sister, back when you were all teenagers."

"You mean Tracy Pratt?" Valetta gulped down the rest of her tea and shook her head. "Becca always thought it was her brother, Linc, who killed her, but I never thought so. Linc and I were friends; he didn't do it. And there was never a body, so we don't even know if she was killed. I always thought she just ran away."

Jaymie turned away from that old village tale. "Anyway, the point is, I told you I saw Shelby and her brother arguing. He could just as easily be the murderer."

"It sounds like grasping at straws to me."

"Come on, Valetta; play along. Travis Fretter's story feels just too conveniently damning, that he just *happened* to see

Cody and Shelby arguing. If he was so concerned, wouldn't he have interfered? Maybe he is lying and not Cody. The timing just can't be right." She explained what she meant, about the tight timing of Cody being at the band shell, nowhere near town, and yet Travis having claimed he saw him arguing with Shelby. "Who else could have done it? Who had motive, means and opportunity?"

"You really want to do this?" Valetta said, eyeing her. "Okay, what about her boss, Delaney?"

"We did see them talking that morning, and it looked like a contentious chat. He's a possibility, I guess, though he doesn't seem likely. But there's more that I haven't talked to you about. I told you there was another guy. Well, this is how I know: Heidi told me that Shelby was dating some pharma rep colleague of Joel's. Heidi didn't like him. She thought he was a jerk."

"If she was dating a couple of guys at once, maybe jealousy was a motive?" Valetta was starting to get into the discussion now. "This other guy could have been jealous, saw her and Cody together and flipped out?"

"Maybe. I'll have to get Heidi to tell me where he lives and who he works for. I guess I can actually approach people with my press credentials, you know, interview them about their relationship with Shelby."

"Be careful about that, Jaymie. You could get people upset at you." The doorbell jangled and one of their wheelchair-bound customers came in. Valetta was alert immediately, and since it was a pharmacy sale, she headed back to her counter with a wave to Jaymie.

There were a few more customers, and then it was closing time. Jaymie did the float for the next day, closed and locked the till and deposited the envelope of cash through the slot in the safe in the back. She went to the front then pulled her coat on and waited for Valetta. They exited together and Valetta turned back to lock up securely.

"So I guess I'll be going out to the jail to interview Cody tomorrow morning," Jaymie said. "I'm a little nervous."

"You'll be fine. Just stay out of the way of the cops!"

After dinner, Jaymie worked on her Vintage Eats column, then retreated to the kitchen to make the no-bake fruitcake. It called for marshmallows softened with apple juice and evaporated milk. She had done that in the largest of her Pyrex Primary Colors mixing bowls, the huge yellow one, before making herself dinner, because it had to sit for three hours. She noted that the marshmallows had not completely dissolved, but maybe that was how it was supposed to be. She stirred it again and set to work on the cookies.

Crushing so many vanilla wafers and gingersnaps was exhausting, bashing and rolling them with a heavy wooden rolling pin, a few at a time in a plastic bag. And of course she had done things in the wrong bowls. The largest of her Primary Colors bowls held the wet mixture, so once she had the cookies all crushed and added the candied fruit, cherries and nuts, she dumped them in the green bowl, the second largest, and added the wet to it, as she was supposed to. It was almost overflowing, so she dumped it all back in the yellow bowl.

As she worked, she tried to come up with a list of questions for Cody in the morning, jotting them down as she thought of them.

1. *What time did he come to the village that evening?*
2. *Did he or did he* not *see Shelby that evening?*
3. *Why did he lie about being in town?*

She had no idea if he would or could answer. Would their visit be taped? Listened to? Was it even advisable, from a legal standpoint, for him to answer questions? It all seemed so weird and foreign, but didn't every new experience?

4. *Did he know or suspect she was dating anyone else?*

This was an important question; did he know about Glenn or not? And were there others?

5. *What was his relationship with Shelby's family like?*
6. *Who did he think could have done it?*

Other than that, she'd just have to wing it.

She eyed her fruitcake mixture. It seemed so dry and crumbly! She mixed and mixed and mixed, but it didn't seem possible that it would come out okay. Had she done something wrong? She checked the recipe again, but no, she'd done everything correctly. Hesitantly, she added another third of a cup of apple juice and another quarter cup of evaporated milk, noting the changes on her printout of the recipe. The mixture melded and held together, and she packed it into the foil-lined loaf pan and tucked it away in the fridge. In a few days she'd get it out, slice it, photograph it and see how it tasted.

She retreated to her office and typed out her recipe notes, including the changes she had made, and saved them on her computer while she did a load of laundry. She then had a hot bubble bath, deliberately changing her thoughts from murder and investigation to how lovely Jakob's hands had felt warming hers, and how she hoped her growing attraction to him was not unfounded. She was cautious but hopeful, an interesting state to be in.

The phone rang as she was helping Hoppy up onto the bed; he preferred a lift to the steps, though he would use them if he had to. It was Jakob. She sat down on the edge of her patchwork-quilt-covered bed. "Hey. How are you?"

"I was just going to ask you the same thing," he said. "How was the rest of your day?"

"Good. I'm going to visit the jail in the morning to talk to Cody."

"I'll be interested to hear what he says. I'm still troubled by him lying about being here. How did he expect to get away with that?"

"I think for some people lying becomes a reflex action. Joel was like that." She had told him about Joel Anderson, as well as Daniel and Zack, just as he had told her about his late wife and a previous serious girlfriend, his first love. "Then instead of fessing up, they tell more lies to try to cover the other lies."

"I'll never understand that. Telling the truth is so much simpler. On to better topics . . . Jocie asked me about you today."

"She did?"

"She asked when you're coming to dinner again. I said I hoped it would be soon."

"I hope so, too." Jaymie crawled under the covers as Denver strolled into the room and leaped up onto the bed in one graceful movement. Hoppy and Denver jockeyed for space close to Jaymie as she lay on her side with the phone pressed to her ear, a pool of golden light from her bedside lamp dimly illuminating her cozy room with the reading nook in the corner, a tall shelf of paperbacks and an overstuffed chair. "This week is crazy, but closer to Christmas it may actually slow down some. Maybe you can come here next time."

"Jocie would love that. She's a very curious girl. She asked me if you lived all alone, and were you lonely." He chuckled.

She felt a warm tingle that he was talking about her with his little girl. "I am sometimes, but talking to you at night makes it better," she said softly.

They chatted about inconsequentials for a while, then said a prolonged good night. She slept better than she had in days and awoke refreshed and ready, if not eager, to tackle her jailhouse visit.

The Queensville Township police department and jail was housed in a modern glass-and-steel building on the highway outside of town. It was bland and official looking, every detail of it. The jail itself was a long low cement-block-and-steel building that jutted off to one side, and was surrounded by high fencing with razor wire looped on top. Because of recent events Jaymie was all too familiar with the police station itself, but the jail was a new experience. Once inside, she was confronted by many layers of officialdom and security. The procedure to get in was intimidating, but the women and men in charge were nonchalant yet professional.

A young woman in uniform manned the first point of contact from an enclosed desk equipped with a speakerlike metal portal in the middle and a single open slot to hand documents and other items through. She was short and young, but strongly built, with a pug nose and freckled cheeks, her streaked hair in a scraped-back bun, wearing no jewelry, just a tan uniform. She glanced at Jaymie's ID, then got the form she needed and made some crosses at various blanks. "Sign where indicated, please. Who will you be visiting today?"

"Cody Wainwright," she said, as she filled in the blanks and gave the form back to the officer. "His mother, Nan Goodenough, had me put on his visitors' list."

The girl's eyes widened. The murder case was notorious, and Cody's name would be well known, especially among jail staff. She nodded, though, then glanced down at the form, which provided Jaymie's name, phone number, address and some other information. "No cell phones in the visitation area," she said.

Jaymie slid her cell phone under the glass as a male guard came out and searched through her purse with gloved hands and passed a metal detecting wand over her. She was then guided through two sets of locked doors, between which was a metal-detection portal. At the end of it all, a portly male guard glanced at a list, then ushered her to number seven of a bank of video terminals in a clinically cold room that smelled of bleach and pine. In front of the bank of video terminals was a long bench and row of bolted-down chairs. Each video terminal was in a kind of booth, sectioned off from one another with laminate-covered fiber-wood barriers. Many others were there, women with children on their laps, elderly parents, or maybe even grandparents, and the odd sketchy-looking male, glancing from side to side. The tired-looking woman to her left had a baby in her arms and was weeping, pressing a tissue to her mouth as she spoke to her loved one.

Jaymie took a seat and waited. The screen blinked to life and a printed warning appeared, then Cody's face replaced it. She wasn't sure what to do, but noted that he had a phone receiver in his hand. She picked up hers.

"Mom got a message to me that you're going to help get me out," he said.

"That's not exactly true."

He frowned and shook his head in disgust. "Then what are you here for? I only get one of these visits a week, you know."

"I had some questions. I'm, uh, investigating the story, you see, for . . . for the paper." Oh, this wasn't going well. She wasn't sure how much she could say. She glanced around. Were they on tape? Being listened to? Who knew?

He looked disgusted and leaned back in his chair, crossing his arms and propping the phone receiver between his shoulder and ear. "I didn't do it. That's my only comment."

"Cody, why did you lie about being at the Christmas tree farm when you were in town that evening?"

Bluntness appeared to work where friendliness hadn't. He sat up and leaned forward, arms on the shelf in front of him and receiver to his ear. His pale face flushed red, from his cheeks to his ears. "I'd heard what happened and knew what the cops would do, pin it on me."

"Why would they do that?"

"That's what's easiest, right? Because some prissypants told them about me hitting her. My beautiful Shelby; I can't believe she's gone!" His youthful face twisted and tears welled up in his eyes. "I would *never* have hurt her."

"But you *did* hit her."

"It was like an impulse, you know?" he said earnestly, as if that explained it all. "She said something awful about my mom. Called her a name. I lashed out, you know? Wouldn't you?"

"No! Cody, *I'm* the one who *saw* you hit Shelby. It wasn't a tap. You hauled off and hit her with your fist." She wasn't sure why she told him, but she was disgusted by his attempt to minimize hitting his girlfriend. Why was she doing this? Why not let the police work it out? She had gotten lucky a few times, but it never escaped her mind that in most cases she stumbled across the clue that broke the case, antagonized the felon until they struck out at her and in most cases the police were just one step away from the answer themselves.

His look was stony. His eyes narrowed, but then he shook his head. "Okay, so what was I supposed to do? What would *you* do if someone said your mother was a disgusting smelly old bitch?"

Jayme gasped. "She *said* that? Shelby Fretter said that."

"It came out of nowhere. We were just walking and talking about something else, and she looked around and stopped. I remember, it was right by a wrought-iron fence near that green area in the middle of Queensville. She began to say crap about my family. At first I ignored it. She said she'd heard my sister was a tramp, and that my stepdad was a lush. It felt . . ." He squeezed up his face and grimaced and eased his shoulders, like they were tension filled. "It felt like she was pushing me, trying to get me mad. Then she made that crack about my mom and I lost it. *That's* when I whacked her."

She watched him as he swiped at the remaining moisture in his eyes and firmed his chin. He looked like he was telling the truth, but he had lied so many times before, how was she supposed to believe him? "So you were scared and lied about being at the tree farm that evening. Didn't you think Gus would tell the police the truth?"

He shrugged.

"Why *did* you come to town?"

He looked conflicted. "Look, my lawyer says I shouldn't discuss this with anyone. You know?"

"I'm here to help, Cody. And this isn't anything you haven't already told the police, right? You don't have to tell me anything you haven't already told them."

"I guess. I got a text message saying to meet Shelby at the band shell, that she wanted to talk, to work things out. I tried to call her, but she wasn't answering my calls or anything. So that was when I told Gus I had to take off, and headed to Queensville and the band shell."

Jaymie didn't know how precise cell phone tracking was. She had seen enough police shows to know that most now used the GPS embedded in cell phones rather than the old system of checking what tower a call pinged from, but how close was GPS? Would it tell them if he was phoning from the park near the river rather than the Christmas tree farm, or the band shell or downtown Queensville? And did that even matter? As she had herself, it would have only taken minutes to walk from the band shell to the shed.

However, one question occurred to her right away. "Are you sure the text came from her phone?"

He looked blank. "What do you mean?"

"I mean, did it come from the number you always use to text her? Did it come up as Shelby?"

He looked blank, then confused. "I . . . don't know. I don't remember."

Lying or telling the truth? It was something he hadn't been asked before, that was evident. "Did the police seize your cell phone?"

"Yeah."

She stowed away that knowledge to think about later. "So what happened when she didn't meet you?"

"I went home."

"Are you *sure* you went home? Anywhere else first?"

"I went home! I was tired."

"What time was that?"

"God, I don't know!" He shifted, restless. "I don't keep track."

"How did you hear about Shelby?"

"I found out in the morning on Facebook. I didn't believe it at first, thought it was a joke. Shelby had a weird sense of humor."

"Do you know her family?"

"Yeah, I've met 'em. I knew Travis from before."

"How do you get along with them?"

He shrugged. "No comment."

That was an odd thing to say, she thought. "So if someone said they saw you in town with Shelby that night, arguing, what would you say?"

"That they were lying."

That was rapid and to the point. "Why did you think she wanted to talk to you? Hadn't you broken up?"

"I was getting mixed messages, you know? She'd say we were done, then she'd call me late at night or text me. Say she was sorry." He frowned down at the shelf and scratched at something on the surface. "She said I was special, that there was no one else like me."

From the conversation she had overheard between him and his mother, Jaymie thought that would draw him in like honey to a bee. He needed to feel special. "Were you two exclusive?" Jaymie asked, intent on not giving away what she knew of Shelby dating other guys.

He shrugged, not looking up. "I *thought* we were."

She couldn't tell whether that meant he now knew otherwise, or if it was just a toss-off remark. "You *thought* you were?"

He rolled his eyes. "Look, I don't know for sure. I kept hearing things. I heard that she was going out with this guy, some jerk in a suit."

That might be Glenn Brennan, Jaymie thought. "And did that make you angry?"

He narrowed his eyes and was silent for a moment.

"Just tell me the truth," she said.

"We kind of had a fight about it. She said it was just business, some client of her boss's."

"Anyone else?"

"I saw her with some biker dude in Wolverhampton once, at the place I met her. But she told me he was just a friend of a friend. I don't know. Some chicks like biker-looking guys, but he was old. Probably in his fifties."

Biker dude. That was a new one. "Anyone else?"

He shook his head. "I don't know."

The screen flashed that they had three minutes left. She had to hurry. "Cody, who do you think did it?"

He leaned forward, staring straight into her eyes through the video terminal. "Her boss, Delaney Meadows. That guy gives me the creeps. I've always thought he had the hots for Shelby, and she didn't like him the same way. He's the guy who beat her to death, mark my words!"

❧ Twelve ❧

THE VISIT TERMINATED abruptly with the screen going blank. She got up and left, retrieving her cell phone on the way out.

Even after such a brief visit, she felt like she was reentering the free world when she escaped from the jail. She circled the police station, heading across the parking lot toward her van and heard her name shouted. Chief Ledbetter, a paunchy gentleman in his late sixties, crossed the parking lot from the other direction with Detective Vestry, who appeared stony eyed and irritated, her lips compressed into a thin line.

As Jaymie approached the chief, she heard him say to the detective, "Go on in, Angela, I'll join you shortly. I have some private business with Miss Leighton."

The woman whirled and stomped into the police station.

"She looks angry," Jaymie said, as she joined the chief by the walkway toward the building. The ground was coated with snow, but it had melted off the sidewalk. There was a flutter of tiny flakes in the air, though, and it was getting colder. She jammed her hands down in her parka pockets.

"She's always angry. Woman's going to have a stroke if she keeps it up. She smokes, you know, like a fiend. And drinks black coffee. Feel like she's trying to live up to some detective stereotype. Course, look at me," he said, patting his belly, which jutted out from his unzippered parka. "I eat too much of my wife's excellent cooking."

"It must be hard to be a female detective on a small town force?"

"Hard to be a female detective anywhere. Won't do for her to try to be more like a man, though, 'specially with me. I think we all bring different perspectives to crime detection, woman or man, young or old."

She smiled. He was unique, Chief Ledbetter. Much smarter than he liked people to know. He had begun to relax and not play off his folksy persona with her, and she often saw the glint of a ruthless intelligence in his small eyes. He had retired from a big city force some years back, moving to Queensville. But found he missed police work and so became chief of Queensville's tiny force. He was going to be forced into retirement for good soon. She wondered what he'd do when he did retire permanently.

"So what's up, Chief?"

"Saw your name on Cody Wainwright's visitor list."

Jaymie shifted from foot to foot. "Nan asked me to talk to him."

He eyed her speculatively. "Ms. Goodenough should just let us do our job. She's been here every single day badgering our desk folks, telling them they're not doing their job, that her son is innocent, that she'll expose us for the idiots we are."

Jaymie grimaced, but it didn't surprise her; Nan had a talent for rubbing many people the wrong way. "It's her *son*," she said weakly.

"I am *well* aware of that. She tells us all the time. Beginning to hear it in my sleep." He paused, his breath coming out in puffs of steam. "I would tell her it's too bad that she raised a liar as a son. We didn't arrest him on a whim, you know."

"But it wasn't your idea; you were out of town for the weekend."

"I stand by my assistant chief's decision," he growled. "I'm not gonna tell you our case against him, but I will tell you that that boy has lied consistently, and I have no doubt he has lied to you, to his lawyer and most especially to his mom."

"Nan is sure he didn't do it. I don't know what I believe. I don't want a guilty guy to go free, but I don't want an innocent guy to pay, either."

He cocked his head to one side, scratched his belly underneath his parka and examined her eyes. "I should warn you away, you know. I'm probably crazy."

"You're crazy like a fox," she said.

He jabbed his finger at her and said, "But you get any info, you bring it to me, you hear?"

"I will do that, Chief. I'm assuming you have his cell phone."

He just looked at her.

She met his gaze evenly. "Cody says Shelby texted him, and I was wondering if the text really came from her phone, or from another? If you have his cell phone, you already know."

"I can't tell you that."

She sighed. "I guess not. But he says he tried to call her back, tried to text her. That should pinpoint when he left Jakob's farm. Travis says he saw them together arguing, but the timing just doesn't seem right to me."

"We are investigating every bit of his story. Leave it alone, Jaymie." He harrumphed for a moment, then screwed up his face and sighed. "I am going to warn you after all. I would prefer it if you wouldn't poke around in this."

"I won't cause any trouble, I promise. You know me . . .

I tend to go down different avenues than the police can or will. He's not the only suspect. I saw Travis Fretter arguing with his sister. If anyone had motive, *and* motive to deflect attention by lying about seeing Cody and Shelby together, it's him. I don't mean to load any more trouble on that family, but that's what *I* saw."

"I'm asking you to leave this alone, Jaymie."

"I *promise* I won't get in the way of your investigation." She waited. What could he do? Maybe have her arrested for interfering in an ongoing investigation? She didn't know enough about the law to know.

He sighed wearily. "You know what? It's fine. I don't think you'll get in any trouble this time because we've got the right guy locked up."

"Maybe you do," she said blandly. "Maybe you don't."

He chuckled, a throaty, gruff sound rumbling through his barrel chest. He turned and walked toward the police station. "Stay out of trouble!" he shouted over his shoulder, his words puffed out on breaths of steam that trailed behind him like steam from an old-fashioned train chugging down the tracks.

She headed to Wolverhampton and parked behind the newspaper printing plant, went around to the office, waving to the receptionist and going directly to Nan's office. She tapped on the cubicle half wall. Nan looked up.

"Jaymie! I was just framing an editorial piece to explain how we'll handle my son's arrest."

Nan looked somewhat better but still disheveled, with her coarse hair sticking out and the bags under her eyes only slightly less puffy. But her wry tone was intact, a good sign.

"I was just talking to Cody."

The editor waved her in, peeked up and down the aisle to check that the other staff were a ways away, then pushed Jaymie to sit down in a chair. "And?"

"Nan, he's lied about a lot." She watched the editor's eyes, but there were neither tears nor anger. So far. "I just don't know if you truly want me looking into this."

"Why not? You're the one who always seems to stumble over the body, and then the culprit."

Jaymie forced herself to be calm. She didn't just *stumble* over the answers, she asked questions and figured things out. But she was determined not to take offense.

Nan eyed her when she was silent. "What did you and Cody talk about?"

She relayed most of the conversation. "He says that Shelby texted him to come meet him in the park near the band shell. I asked if he was sure the text came from her cell phone, but he wasn't sure, and the police have his cell phone now, so I'll never find that out."

"I'm not sure I get the distinction you're going for."

"He said he got a text telling him to meet Shelby at the band shell, that she wanted to straighten things out or something like that. But if he's not sure the text came from her phone, then maybe someone else used it to get him to the park and incriminate him. Lots of people knew he had hit Shelby."

"You're a smart cookie to think of that. Did you ever think of journalism when you were in college?"

"Nope. Not once. I did get a liberal arts degree, but had no clue what I wanted to do. I think it's taken me this long to figure it out."

"What have you figured out?"

"That I don't need a care r to fulfill me. Some people do, but not me."

"I would have gone crazy without a career," Nan said. "I couldn't have stayed home with the kids." She shrugged. "It's all good as long as you know what you want."

"I do now," Jaymie said. "I did talk to the chief in the parking lot. He wasn't in town when the arrest was made, but he's standing behind his assistant."

"He's always looked like a hick to me."

"He likes people to think that. I asked Cody who he thought did it, and he said Delaney Meadows, Shelby's boss.

I don't get that, but I'm willing to look into it. Do you have anything on him?"

Nan grabbed a phone, punched in one number, muttered something then hung up. She clicked her desktop computer on, glanced at it, then turned back to Jaymie. "What else?"

"Well, Cody mentioned some older biker guy that Shelby had been seen with, maybe a guy she was dating? I don't know who it is, and I'm not sure how to find out."

Nan thought for a moment, sitting back in her chair, which squealed in protest. "We may have a contact in that community. I'll have someone look him up and see if they know anything about a biker guy seen with Shelby Fretter."

"I have an idea of another guy Shelby was dating at the same time as Cody, and I already have a connection, so I'll be looking into that today." She paused. "You know, Nan, I don't know the first thing about investigative reporting or anything like that."

"I don't actually want you to write a story, I want you to dig for information. You've done plenty of that in the last seven months or so, haven't you?"

"I guess."

"Then just do whatever you've done in the past that's successful. But you can tell someone you're writing for the *Howler* if you get stuck and need to give a reason why you're poking around." Her computer bleeped, and she looked at the screen then hit a button. The printer on the file cabinet sputtered to life and printed off a few pages, which she handed over to Jaymie. "This is everything we have on Delaney Meadows." She went back to the screen and scanned the information. "Moved to Queensville three years ago. Started small, now runs a thriving white-collar headhunting agency. Involved in the chamber of commerce."

"Anything from before he came to Queensville?" Jaymie asked.

Nan stared at the screen then back to Jaymie. "There's more there, maybe some about his past before Queensville.

I'll have something for you on the biker guy by tomorrow morning, or even later today. I'll email it to you."

She was decisive and swift, as always. Jaymie stood, folding the papers and sticking them in her purse. "I'll do my best, Nan."

"I know you will. You can't help yourself." With that cryptic remark, Nan waved her away.

Jaymie drove back to Queensville, thinking about the visit with Cody and her conversations with Chief Ledbetter and Nan. For better or worse she was becoming known as an investigator of sorts, or, as the older ladies of her acquaintance called it, a nosey parker. But in this case it was not her idea, she was being pushed into it. She could have said no, but she was so grateful to Nan for all her help in achieving her goals of becoming a food writer, and hopefully eventually a cookbook writer. How could she say no when she was asked a favor? And that was one of her problems; she had trouble saying no when someone asked her to do something or give them something.

That would be her New Year's resolution, she decided, to learn how to say no if she didn't want to do something. But this time, though she was hesitant, she *did* want to do this, for Nan's sake, but also for justice. There was just enough doubt in her mind that it would bug her until she settled it with herself. Three days, she decided. She'd give it until Thursday, and if she was no further ahead, or still thought Cody guilty, then she'd tell Nan she couldn't find anything to help Cody. She heaved a sigh. A goal and time limit was good. Three days.

But she had to fit everything else in during this busy time of year. She parked in her spot in the parking lane behind her house. The snow had melted off except in the shaded parts by hedges and fences. She entered through the summer porch to the kitchen and was greeted by one happy puppy and one sleepy cat. Hoppy bounced and wobbled out to the yard to piddle and bark. He had started barking more lately, and Jaymie didn't like it, but it was hard to get him to stop.

She called Valetta, filled her in on what had been the upshot of the meeting with Nan, then decided she needed to buckle down to work. Lunch was a bowl of soup and half a sandwich eaten at the kitchen table with her to-do list and calendar in front of her. She had arranged to help both Cynthia Turbridge and Jewel Dandridge at their shops. She filled in whenever they needed an extra pair of hands, and both did before the next onslaught of Dickens Days tourists later in the week. She had to check her rental picnic baskets at the Emporium, which would allow her to see Valetta. She would then head out to the manor house to help with the cleanup that she had, after all, committed them all to.

Pondering her picnic baskets made her think of Jakob, though to be fair, almost everything seemed to make her think of Jakob these days. He had talked about getting her ideas for expanding and changing up his Christmas tree farm for next year's holiday, and she could think of a half dozen, one of them being involving him in her picnic basket rental. She wondered if he had room for an open bonfire and make-shift outdoor kitchen near the tree fields. If he did they could have folks come out, drink hot chocolate, eat an outdoor picnic lunch, and if there was snow, have snowman building and sleigh or cart rides. Then the family could choose their tree and take it home.

She rested her cheek on one hand and stared out the back window, through the summer porch to the yard. She was becoming alarmingly mushy, her insides like warm pudding when she thought of him. He was good-looking in a sturdy Teutonic way. Jaymie was feminist to the core; she felt that men and women should be treated equal and must receive equal pay for equal work. The world wasn't there yet, not by a long shot, but being a feminist didn't stop her from *deeply* appreciating the wonderful differences between men and women. Jakob Müller made her feel beautiful when he held her in his arms. She sighed and smiled.

However . . . time was fleeting. She told herself to stop daydreaming and, after consulting her purse appointment calendar, wrote down her itinerary for the next few days. One day at a time, she told herself, with regards to Jakob; that was how she took everything in her life. She hustled through making some more brownies to give out when she did the pamphlet walk for Dickens Days again, and thought to call Heidi.

"Hey, Heidi, how is it going?"

"Pretty good. Bernie came over today and we made cookies. She's been practicing what you taught her."

Jaymie had given them both a few cooking and baking tips, but Bernie was the only one of the two who had put them into use.

"We made the cutest cookies shaped like little men."

"Gingerbread cookies?"

"Uh, yeah, I guess."

"That's good! I wondered if you were helping at Dickens Days this week?"

"I'll be there!"

"Good. I'm going to be at the manor Thursday, Friday and Saturday until seven, but I'll be heading straight to hand out pamphlets for Dickens Days from there. I'll see you then, I guess."

"I'm going to the manor today to help with the cleaning," Heidi said.

"Really?" Heidi was wealthy and had a cleaning service for her own home, even though she didn't have a job or any real responsibilities. It was heartening that she had volunteered to help with the unglamorous and largely thankless task of cleaning Queensville Historic Manor. "I'm doing the same a little later today, at about three o'clock. Can I meet you there? I have a question slash favor to ask."

"Okay. What about?"

"Glenn Brennan."

"Yuck. Why?"

"I'll tell you when I see you," Jaymie said. The moment she hung up from that call, Becca phoned with questions about getting their grandmother into their Queensville home. Grandma Leighton was a little unsteady on her feet, but Jaymie thought if she took up the throw rug in the front hall there shouldn't be any trouble. "I'll make sure the path is cleared so it isn't too difficult for her, but the bathroom is upstairs. What can we do about that?"

"I know Mimi and Grant are opening their house for the holidays, too," Becca said, about the Watsons, next-door neighbors who were longtime friends of the Leighton's. "They have a powder room on the main floor, so Grandma can get to that one if she needs to go before we return her to the Queensville Inn." The Watson's house was indeed very close, because homes on their street were not separated by lanes.

After that they went through their to-do lists together, but finally Becca asked, "So, are you really looking into the death of that poor girl?"

"How did you hear about it?" Jaymie asked, astonished.

"How do you think? I called Valetta to ask if she could look down the road to see if the work on the house is going ahead," she said, talking about the house she and Kevin were converting into an antiques and fine vintage china shop. "I would have asked you, but Valetta is right there. I guess the roofers are patching up the problems, even in this weather, so hopefully it won't leak anymore. Then she told me about that editor of yours asking you to investigate. I think it stinks that she's put you in such a position, and at this time of year, when you're busy. You should have said no. You've already got too much on your plate, and it could be dangerous."

Jaymie stiffened, took in a deep breath, then let it out without saying what she wanted, which was for big sister Becca to butt out. "Nan has been good to me, and I know I *could* have said no. I decided to go ahead, but I've given myself a time limit; if after three days I don't feel I'm getting anywhere, or I still feel that her son is probably the killer, then I'll tell her I'm done."

Becca was silent for minute. "I guess. If that's how you want to handle it."

"That's how I want to handle it," Jaymie said firmly. Her whole life Becca had been stepping in, trying to tell Jaymie what she should be doing. It was, she supposed, left over from many years before when Jaymie had needed her almost as a surrogate mother. Fifteen years older than Jaymie, Becca had stepped up, giving four-year-old Jaymie the safety net she had needed when their parents went through a rough patch, bickering constantly and almost separating.

"I've made you mad," Becca said, a rueful tone in her voice. "I just can't help it. I still feel like I should tell you what to do."

Jaymie laughed out loud. "As long as you don't mind me pushing back, we'll be just fine."

"I don't mind. Kevin says I boss you around too much. Maybe he's right."

"Give Kevin a hug for me and tell him he's about to become my favorite brother-in-law of all time," Jaymie replied, and they hung up on laughter.

The week and a half before Christmas would be organized chaos, so she wrote a timeline for the next few days, with places she had to be penned in, and the duration of the event. That afternoon she had Cynthia and Jewel down for two hours, then the manor for two hours to clean. The evening was hers to write her no-bake fruitcake recipe and column, and get it in to Nan.

She put the rest of the soup away, fetched her coat and boots and was just ready to don her winter gear and leave the house when the phone rang. Hoppy danced around and she nearly tripped, but she got to it and answered. "Hello?"

"Is this Jaymie Leighton?" the youngish woman said, her voice breathy and nervous.

"It is. Can I help you?"

"You shouldn't be trying to help that newswoman get her son out of jail, you know," she said, her tone hardening. "He's a jerk, a murderer and he killed poor Shelby. I have inside information. You probably don't know this, but Cody Wainwright was seen following her that night."

"Oh?" Jaymie was trying to place the voice . . . Had she heard it before? Where did she know it from?

"Yeah, *oh*! Why don't you ask him how he got Shelby Fretter's blood on his coat? Let him try to explain *that*." Click.

❧ Thirteen ❧

THE DIAL TONE hummed in Jaymie's ear.

Who *was* that? The voice sounded hauntingly familiar. But she had interacted with several young women over the last couple of days and it could have been any one of them. In a thoughtful frame of mind she pulled her boots on and grabbed her cell phone, pulling the charger cord out and checking her text messages. Nothing from Nan yet on the biker. She stuck it in her purse, pulled on her coat, and headed out to the van. She was driving because right after Cynthia and Jewel, she was going to the historic manor and she just didn't have time to walk, even though she had promised herself to get enough exercise and eat right over the holiday season.

The voice on the phone nagged at her brain; she knew she had heard it recently, but when? And where? Was it . . . Ah! She pulled up to the curb between Jewel and Cynthia's shops, but before she got out she texted Nan to ask her a question. It had taken a few minutes, but she was almost certain that the voice on the phone was the girl at the jail who had checked her in. Nan might know who she was, or might be able to find out.

She sat thinking for a moment, staring across the road, examining the cottage Becca and Kevin had bought as a joint venture. They didn't have a name for it yet, but it was going to be an antiques boutique, filling a gap in Queensville's growing antiques-and-vintage-destination profile. Becca and Kevin's store would sell vintage and antique china, and early-to late–nineteenth-century fine antiques: sideboards, etageres, dining room furnishings, Turkish rugs, chandeliers and elegant knickknacks.

But there was a lot of work to be done on the cottage before then. When Jaymie first heard about the venture, she was afraid Becca would ask her to run it. With the number of commitments she already had, she didn't want to be tied down to a six-days-a-week shop. But one of Kevin's sisters who already lived in the States would be moving to Queensville. She would have an apartment in the back and run the store.

In the background her mind had been working; she was sure who the caller was, and disturbed by what she had said. Should she call the chief? Or was that going too far? She'd wait until Nan returned her text before deciding.

Jaymie climbed out of her van and turned, transfixed for a moment by the sight of the yellow fluttering crime scene tape on Bill's workshop behind Jewel's store. It was a forlorn sight, and took her right back to that moment of finding poor Shelby Fretter, her hours on earth numbered, though no one knew it then. Overwhelmed with sadness as she was, Jaymie still felt so alive, the cold crisp air filling her lungs, the energy coursing through her. Poor Shelby would never again experience all the joy and sorrow, drudgery and excitement, loveliness and awfulness that was life. She deserved to have her true killer found and convicted, whether it was Cody or someone else.

Jewel stepped out her front door with a long twist tie in

her hand and wrapped it around the railing, fastening a bit of the sagging garland. She caught sight of Jaymie and followed her gaze to the workshop. "Bill is beside himself," she called out as Jaymie headed toward her. "The cops won't tell him when he can have access to his workshop again." She crossed her arms over her chest, tucking her hands under her arms. "You'd think they could let him have his place back."

"It can take anywhere from hours to days to clear a site," Jaymie said. She followed Jewel into her store and they set to work on a display that the shopkeeper was changing up.

After about an hour Jaymie headed over to Cynthia's Cottage Shoppe, where she helped do much the same. When they were done, Cynthia insisted on making Jaymie a cup of tea, so she waited in the living room display, smiling at the look of the place. There was a puffy sofa with a gorgeous soft white cover and chintz cushions, and in front of it a coffee table cobbled together from reclaimed wood and the legs of a broken chair, painted aqua and sanded to have a weathered look. It was rustic and charming, perfect for a cottage. Shelves lining the walls held old birdcages painted white and filled with flowers, as well as cutesy knickknacks like china poodles in tutus and little girls with sun umbrellas. It was Valetta's kind of kitsch, but Jaymie's friend preferred hunting for those items at thrift stores and junk shops rather than paying the inflated prices Cynthia's chichi store demanded.

It was overwhelmingly claustrophobic, every surface covered, every item painted white or a pastel, everything made over into something else. She liked a lot of it, but her taste ran to using vintage items as they were meant to be used. Her cell phone chimed and she read a text message from Nan. It addressed both what Jaymie had texted her about and her previous request about the biker dude. Jaymie was frowning down at it when Cynthia came in with a tray bearing tea in Christmas mugs and a plate of mint green–tinted spritz wreath cookies adorned with pastel and silver sprinkles.

She took a cup and sipped. "Cynthia, are you still . . . uh, friends with Johnny Stanko?"

The older woman blushed. Cynthia was a midfifties elegant big-city transplant who had recently suffered an addiction relapse, her past drinking problem rebounding after a broken heart. But she was working through it now, and had made unexpected friends with a rough-hewn shambling late-thirties fellow by the name of Johnny Stanko, who treated her as if she were a delicate piece of china he was not fit to touch. They were dating, though most dates were, it had been whispered, attending twelve-step addiction meetings together. "I *am* friends with him. We do a lot of things together, actually."

"Does he still work as the busboy and bar back at that place on the highway?"

She nodded, with a hint of suspicion in her blue eyes. "Why?"

Jaymie filled Cynthia in on the bare bones of what she was trying to do for Nan. "I just got a text saying that one man Shelby had been seen with is a biker fellow who frequents the bar where Johnny works. He'd probably know him to see him. If I gave you the name, could you have Johnny give me a call when he comes into the bar again?"

She hesitated. "This won't get Johnny in any trouble will it? With anyone? His boss, the biker?"

"I can't imagine why it would. I just want to know so I can catch the guy in a more relaxed setting, not track him down at home." Cynthia still hesitated, so Jaymie added, "All I want is for Johnny to point the guy out. I'll take it from there."

"I'll call him and get back to you tonight."

"Thanks, Cynthia." She gulped back the rest of her tea and nabbed a couple of cookies. "I have to get out to the manor," she said, standing. "I'm going out to do a shift cleaning. Heidi is meeting me there and says she's going to clean, too!"

Cynthia gave a wry chuckle as she followed her to the door. "You may need to follow her around and clean up after her. I have an idea she doesn't know which end of a dust mop to use!"

Jaymie sat in her van for a second, ate the cookies and reread Nan's lengthy text message beyond the stuff about the biker. Nan said that the girl Jaymie was referring to at the jail was probably Mikayla Jones, Travis Fretter's occasional girlfriend. Jaymie's personal information was on her consent form she signed at the jail; that explained where Mikayla got Jaymie's name and phone number. But why the anonymous call to inform on Cody? Given who she was, all this did was pique Jaymie's interest in, and suspicion of, Travis Fretter, moving him up the list of suspects. Unless there really was Shelby's blood on Cody's coat and it turned out he had been following her, verified by another independent witness, Jaymie would set aside that whispered information as useless, motivated likely by a desire to turn Jaymie's attention away from Travis.

Jaymie drove out of town and was happy to see others at the house. The Queensville Historic Manor was only open from Wednesday through Sunday, so some of the heritage society would be taking advantage of today to spiff up the décor and clean. Jaymie entered to the cheery sounds of hammering, chatter and the occasional thud that echoed through the manor. She popped her head around the corner and found Mabel in the dining room resetting the table carefully with the red and white transferware loaned to them by Becca. She had laid a red toile runner, and was centering a red transferware tureen in the middle, brimming with long-needled white-pine branches, threaded with pearls and holly sprays. "That's going to be so beautiful!" Jaymie said.

Mabel turned and smiled. She was a compact little woman, full busted and stocky, but swift and light in her movements. "Thanks to your wonderful sister. She came through for us with this; she loaned me a complete set of Romantic England transferware by Meakin, with the tureen, serving pieces . . . everything! I'm going to do up the sideboard in the same way," she said, waving her hand at the tiger oak mirrored sideboard, mounded with Christmas greens and table linens at that moment, as well as a basket full of china dishes.

"Do you need any help?"

"Oh, no, dear, thank you. This is an absolute pleasure. I have two sets of china and my husband will divorce me if I start any more collections, so this way I can play with other patterns!" She chuckled. "Besides, I like working on my own. I'm getting it done today because my youngest daughter is coming to town early for the holidays." Her vivacious manner dimmed. "She was friends with Shelby Fretter, you know. When I told her what happened she was shocked. She got a text from Shelby just last week saying that when they got together over the holidays she had some things to tell Lynnsey."

Jaymie's interest quickened. "Did she say any more? What it was about?"

"I don't know." Mabel paused and watched Jaymie for a moment. "Do you think that Cody boy really did it? Killed that poor girl?"

"I don't know," Jaymie admitted. "His mom sure doesn't think so."

Tears started in Mabel's eyes and she shook her head, fiddling with a teacup then setting it down. "It's so *sad*! And at this time of year, too. I know it would be the same any time of year, but Christmas! Christmas means family to me. Poor Lori. I can't imagine walking around Queensville, seeing everything so festive and people wishing each other Merry Christmas, and all the while there's this hole in your heart where your child should be."

That was probably the best description Jaymie had ever heard for what Lori Wozny must be feeling. But Jaymie had seen the possibility of that same heart hole for Nan, the same feeling of emptiness if it was proved that her son did it. "I don't know if Cody did it, but he says he didn't. I've told Nan Goodenough I'll see if I can find anything out."

Mabel patted Jaymie's arm. "I would do that for a friend,

too. I don't know which would be worse, losing your child, or knowing that your child committed murder."

"Mabel, would your daughter talk to me about Shelby, do you think?"

"She's pretty upset," Mabel said. "I don't want her hurt."

"You know me. I'll be careful."

"How about I ask her? My husband is already on his way to the airport, and they'll be back by dinnertime."

"Can I call later?"

"Let me give her your number and have her call you."

Jaymie had to be satisfied with that, and went upstairs to lock up her purse and hang her coat on a hook. Someone had done up a chore chart and it hung on the volunteer-lounge wall. Jaymie checked it to see what needed doing, and tackled the job no one else wanted, the volunteer bathroom and kitchen area. She was in a mood to scrub.

She was in the depths of the toilet when she heard a commotion downstairs. Heidi's light tinkling laughter rang up the stairs and through the door. It made her smile.

A light tread echoed up the stairs, and Heidi's voice rang out, "Jaymsie? Where are you?"

"In here, the bathroom." Jaymie swished the brush around the toilet bowl one final time and flushed. She washed her hands and turned as Heidi bounced in. She had to smile; her friend had dressed for cleaning like a prototypical nineteen-fifties housewife in a dress, pearls, and with her long blond hair done up and wrapped in a kerchief. She probably imagined dashing about, feather duster in hand.

"What are you doing?" Heidi asked, eyeing the bathroom with distrust.

It was untouched from its days as a serviceable but not glamorous portal of family hygiene. In other words, the fixtures were sturdy and white, but from its years as a boarding house and then flophouse, they were scratched and stained with rust, iron and other mineral deposits from the hard well water that served the house. "I'm cleaning the volunteer bathroom."

"Why don't the volunteers clean it themselves?"

"I am a volunteer, and I'm cleaning it."

"Oh. You've already cleaned it?" She stepped over and stared down into the toilet, eyeing the orangey stains. "Eew!" She wrinkled her nose.

"It's clean, even though it doesn't look it. Now I just have to wash the floor."

"Let me do that! I want to help, but I just don't know where to start."

Jaymie showed her where the bucket and cleanser was, and left her at it while she went and cleaned up the coffee break area, rinsing out the kettle and descaling it, and wiping down the cabinets. After half an hour she wondered, what could be keeping Heidi? It was just a six-by-six-foot bathroom; the floor should have taken ten minutes at the very most. She poked her head around the corner and saw Heidi on her hands and knees. "What are you doing?"

She looked over her shoulder. "Cleaning the floor!"

Jaymie gawked over her shoulder. Heidi had on rubber gloves and was scrubbing with a brush. She had worked her way down the floor and had systematically erased a three-foot length of yellowish paste wax gunk that had gathered and melded with dirt along the edge of the bathtub. "Wow! Heidi, you have a hidden talent. Who knew?"

She sat back on her haunches, her fluffy skirt pooling around her, and gazed up at Jaymie, blinking in confusion. "What do you mean?"

"I've never been able to get that stuff off the floor. You do know this is just the volunteer bathroom for now, though, right? The public doesn't see this. I think we should utilize your talents in the parts of the house where they can be appreciated."

When they had both finished their tasks, though, Heidi had

had enough of cleaning. They descended to Jaymie's kitchen, since she wanted to check to make sure that everything was all right for the next day. As she rearranged the displays, Heidi sat at the table by the window, drawing the curtain open and gazing out on the darkening day, dwindling toward a five p.m. mid-December sunset.

"Are you and Joel spending Christmas with your parents or his?" Jaymie said over her shoulder.

"Neither," Heidi said.

"What are you doing?"

"We're going to Oahu for a week."

Jaymie turned and stared at Heidi's profile. She sternly reminded herself not to judge. One person's happiness would never be another, as Jane Austen had noted hundreds of years ago. Jaymie couldn't imagine not spending Christmas with family, but Heidi and Joel had their own ideas. Maybe they just needed a break from the drama their engagement had stirred in both camps. "I hope you enjoy yourselves."

"Me, too. I love Hawaii." Heidi turned away from the window. "What was it you wanted with Glenn Brennan?"

"Ah, yes. I'm glad you reminded me." Jaymie sat down opposite her friend and told her what she was doing. "So in my effort to track down whomever Shelby spent time with, Glenn has become important. Can you think of any reason to call him or text him?"

Heidi made a face. "I don't like him, and I think he *knows* I don't like him. Joel was happy when he heard Glenn got fired for something he posted online. I asked if he was the one who turned him in—Joel didn't like the guy's tactics—but he says no, that he didn't even know about it until some guy he works with passed the news along. It was stuff about some girl."

Jaymie's heart thudded. "About a girl? Could it have been something about Shelby?"

Heidi's bright blue eyes widened. "I don't know, but maybe! Is that important?"

Jaymie thought that it could be. It became vitally important to track the guy down, something she'd try to do online. But she wasn't about to share her line of thinking with Heidi. "I don't know. Right now, I just want a reason to talk to him."

Heidi smirked. "I could say I wanted to set him up with my best friend!"

Jaymie smiled, surprised as she often was by Heidi's quirky sense of humor. "You'd have to pick between me or Bernie, then, right?"

"Bernie would have him on the ground in a headlock in one minute if he talked to her like he talked to Shelby."

"Maybe some other pretext. Though I don't need a pretext, do I? Is he kind of a media-hound type, do you think?"

"Uh-huh, especially if he thinks there'll be some opportunity to talk about himself. Honest to gosh, he's worse than Joel, and Joel does like to talk about himself."

"Then can you text Glenn and tell him you have a friend writing a story about the tragedy, and that I'd like to talk to him as someone who knew Shelby? Do you think he'd talk to me, or would it scare him away?"

Heidi paused, frowned but then nodded. "I think he would talk to you. He'd see himself as involved in something big. And I'll say it's a favor to me; he was sucking up to me pretty hard."

"I'll bet he was. So you'll do it?"

Heidi took out her phone, scanned through her numbers, chewed on her lip then texted something. "I don't have his number, but Joel does. I'd want Joel to know what I'm doing anyway. We promised not to go behind each other's backs." They chatted for a few more minutes, then her phone chimed. She got the number and texted Brennan, adding a smiley face after every phrase. She and Jaymie chatted for just a few more minutes when Heidi's cell phone chimed again. Heidi read the message and looked up, an expression of mystification on her smooth face. "He says he'd love to talk to you. He says that he wants the public to know the real Shelby Fretter."

❧ Fourteen ❧

HEIDI HEADED HOME and Jaymie texted Glenn Brennan. He responded immediately, saying he'd meet her for dinner at Ambrosio at six. It was dark by five when she got home. With only an hour to spare before meeting Brennan, she hustled, letting Hoppy out for an abbreviated piddle run, and filling the animals' food bowls. She dressed in good wool slacks and a pretty sweater, swept her hair up in a chignon, all while she tried to figure out how to broach the subject of his behavior toward Shelby and what happened after their dates. She couldn't think what to say, so she'd have to rely on inspiration.

As she let her old van warm up, she remembered that the last time she was at Ambrosio it was for a difficult and uncomfortable dinner with her parents, Daniel and his parents. His mother had tried to sabotage Jaymie from the beginning out of a desire to keep him close to Phoenix, where they lived and where Daniel's business was headquartered. She felt like she had dodged a bullet when they broke up.

She drove out of town and down the highway thinking of Daniel and their doomed relationship, which made her think of Jakob. With Daniel out of her life, her head and heart were clear. She hoped that her next romantic endeavor would end with true love. But she couldn't think of Jakob right that minute, or she'd start float-walking again, and that was not appropriate for the hard-hitting reporter she was supposed to be.

She pulled into the parking lot of the restaurant, locked the van and walked carefully across the icy asphalt in her best boots, the ones with very little tread. Just then a salt truck roared past on the highway, so maybe it would be a little less icy when she headed home. Salt, though not the only product used to deice, was by far the cheapest and most readily available, and so was both the bane and blessing of a Michiganian's existence. It destroyed car body work, wreaked havoc with good suede and leather boots and yet saved countless lives by ridding the roads of ice. She'd rather have the lives than the boots.

Ambrosio was warm and golden in this holiday season, decorated with pine boughs and gilded ornaments, the big windows curtained in gold drapes and lit with twinkle lights. The competing scents were of good wine, spices, roasted meat and perfume. She hung her coat in the cloakroom and stood at the entrance, not sure what Glenn Brennan looked like. There was one lone man at an intimate table for two over in the corner by a gold Christmas tree. The best tables, those by the fireplace and windows, were already taken, but he had chosen well for an intimate chat.

She gave Glenn's name to the host and he guided her to the table in the corner; she had guessed correctly. Brennan, to his credit, set down his rye and cola and stood as she followed the maître d' over. But he immediately lost those politeness points as his eyes clouded with disappointment. She was not his type. She knew that, based on Heidi and Shelby's svelte figures and blond hair, but still, the guy could have been a little more discreet about his chagrin. She was not there on a blind date, after all; this was a news story and she (supposedly) a reporter.

"Mr. Brennan, I'm Jaymie Leighton. How are you?" she said, putting out her hand.

"Just Glenn," he said.

As they shook hands the waiter came over with the wine list, which she waved off, saying, "We'll be on separate checks. Just the menu, please. No wine for me."

"Don't you have an expense account?" he asked. "You asked for the meeting; I thought you'd be paying."

That explained why he had chosen the most expensive restaurant locally, and why he was consuming drinks at such a rate. There was already an empty glass in front of him as he worked on a fresh one. He was a smooth-looking fellow in a navy sport coat and slacks, a white shirt open at the collar, and a gold signet ring on his pinkie, as well as a gold chain bracelet.

"I'm a freelancer, not a staff member," she said. "No expense account."

"Well then, you can write the whole dinner off on your taxes, right?"

"Quite frankly, I don't even know if you'll have anything of value to tell me, Glenn." He looked like the kind of guy who would see that as a challenge.

He tapped his fingers on the table as the waiter brought them menus. Jaymie didn't want to eat with this man, but it would not be the *most* uncomfortable dinner she had ever had at Ambrosio, as she had been reflecting on during her drive. She glanced at the menu, decided on the soup and salad combo, then set the menu aside, mindful of her mission. She watched him as he scanned the list of choices. Like Joel, he was fortyish. He had smooth skin, dark hair brushed into a self-conscious wave and shiny with hair gel. His full mouth had a petulant look, turned down at the corners. He tapped his fingers constantly.

He frowned down at something, but didn't seem focused on the food list he held. After a moment he glanced up at her. "Jaymie Leighton. Why is your name so familiar to me?" He squinted, stared at her across the table and snapped his fingers. "Wait a sec. You're the girl Joel Anderson was living with, right?"

"I am," she said, trying to keep from gritting her teeth. It had been a year since Joel dumped her and she was most definitely over it, but Brennan's manner was frankly disbelieving and he was giving her the once-over again. It was irritating, but she did her best not to assume what he was thinking.

"You are *not* what I pictured when Joel talked about you."

Aaand . . . there it was.

"And you're friends with Heidi Lockland, your replacement?"

"I am."

He went back to studying the menu. The waiter came back and took their orders; a bottle of wine and the salmon Wellington for him, just the soup and salad for her. He gathered the menus and departed.

"Heidi tells me you went out with Shelby Fretter a few times. How did you meet?"

"Dating website."

That was surprising. "Did you choose her or did she choose you?"

"Why does that matter?"

She shrugged.

"As a matter of fact, she chose me," he said, with a smirk. "She was tired of dating losers and bozos like that kid Cody, the one who killed her."

"Did you know about Cody at the time, that she was dating him, too?"

"Of course not, but it's all over the news now."

"Did you know she was dating others, even if you didn't know who they were?"

"I figured. She was gorgeous. Chicks like that don't stick

to one guy for long. That's what I keep telling Joel. Heidi will get bored with him and move on soon enough."

Maybe to him, his manner seemed to suggest. The penny dropped. *That* was why he so readily agreed to meet with her; he was trying to curry favor with Heidi. That was good. He was likely to not suspect her line of questions, since he was so wholly consumed with himself.

"So it didn't bother you that she was dating others?"

"Why would it? So was I. We only went out a few times, for crying out loud."

"As a salesman, you're accustomed to making sound and rapid judgments on people." Flattery will get you everywhere with certain kinds of people, Jaymie knew. "What was she like? I've been trying to get an idea of her personality, but it's a little difficult."

He shifted in his seat, toying with his glass and looking pensive. "That's what I said to Heidi. I want people to know the real Shelby Fretter, not the sweetie pie she pretended to be. She was moody as hell. If I was a few minutes late picking her up, she'd do this not-speaking-to-me routine. And that was after only a couple of dates."

"Did it bother you?"

"Of course. You women are all alike, you know. Men are all different, but every woman I've ever met has been moody and possessive. Look at another girl in a date's presence and she gets all crazy and gripes at you."

Translated, that meant he liked to ogle other women while out on a date and not be called on it. She took in a deep breath, let it out slowly, and tried not to judge. *Stay impartial. I'm a reporter, I'm a reporter*, she made herself repeat in her thoughts. "Did you like her?"

"Sure." He sat back and crossed one leg over the other, taking a gulp of his drink. "She was easy on the eyes and bright enough to know how to behave, but not so bright she fancied herself smarter than me, you know?"

"She worked for a headhunting agency, right?"

He smirked. "That's what Delaney wants to call it."

"What do you mean? What else is it?"

"What *isn't* it? The guy's into everything. I told you, I met her through a dating site. A *dating* site," he said, with heavy emphasis, leaning toward her across the table.

What was he trying to say? "Do you mean the dating site is Delaney Meadows' business? And you emphasized *dating* . . . Are you calling it something else? Like an escort service or something?"

"You didn't hear it from me," he said, dropping a heavy wink.

"Did you pay to go out with Shelby?"

"No way! I've never paid in my life. Others might have, but I sure didn't pay her."

That was a little confusing. "Glenn, the site is either a dating site or an escort agency; it can't be both."

"Look, I'll write it down and you have a look." He wrote down a URL on the back of a business card and slid it across the table to her. "I'm just sayin' . . . it seems odd. For one thing, guys pay to join the site and women don't. What does that tell you?"

"That's odd. So you paid to join the site?"

He shrugged. "They had photos of *gorgeous* girls, all local!"

"Did you date anyone else from the site?"

"A couple, both beautiful. Look, why are you asking all this crap? I thought this was about Shelby."

"You met her on the site, right? So I'm just covering every aspect of her life."

"Okay, I get it."

"Why did you stop going out with her?"

"She was too much effort; moody, bitchy and sarcastic. She thought I didn't get her little quips, but I'm no idiot."

That was debatable. She leaned forward and smiled across the table at him. "You have such a very unique way of putting things."

He chuckled and drained his glass, ordering another rye

and cola when the waiter brought their dinner and the bottle of wine. "And you're getting more attractive with everything you say. Maybe old Joel knew a thing or two." He winked.

"Glenn, did Shelby ever speak of Cody Wainwright?"

"Why would she talk about a creep like that?"

"You know he's a creep?"

"Well, sure, from what I've heard. He's in jail, isn't he?"

"It was a vicious crime. You must have been shocked when you heard."

"It was awful. A real shame."

"You mentioned that she could be a little much, though, right? Can you see that driving someone to hurt her?"

He paused and stared at her. "Are you suggesting she *deserved* what happened to her?"

"Of course not!" Jaymie said, flustered. She wasn't being as subtle as she'd hoped, obviously.

"I hope not. If every snarky and difficult woman in the world got murdered there'd be no women left."

She watched him as he ate. His behavior baffled her. His attitude toward Shelby was hard to read, sometimes complimentary, sometimes critical. "So how is work?" she asked. "I understand you work for a competitor of Joel's."

"I'm taking a break."

"You left the company?"

"We had a parting of the ways. I was getting bored anyway."

"When did that happen?"

"Last week. I'm not gonna worry about it until after the New Year." He smiled. "I'm a gentleman of leisure right now."

"What brought it on? Heidi told me that she heard you were fired over something you posted online, something inappropriate about a girl. Was it something about Shelby?"

"Why did she tell you that? What is this?" he asked suddenly, his voice underlain by a tension and anger that was a warning. He stared at her, his tone changing to puzzlement rather than anger as he asked, "What do you want? What are you looking for?"

"I *am* just trying to find out about Shelby Fretter, everything about her, even if it's something you said online or something someone else said." She had flash of insight as to what would appeal to someone like Brennan, and leaned over, lowering her voice to a confidential murmur. "I want the dirt, the inside scoop. Everyone is so *disgustingly* positive when someone is killed. You only hear about the good side of them. I want everything else."

Glenn calmed. His eyes glistened with interest. "I could tell you things," he said, his words slurring softly. He knocked back the rest of his drink and the remainder of his wine, then held up his hand to the waiter to signal for another. "Shelby Fretter was a gold digger, just like the others. They only ever get with a guy for free meals, or they ask you for money for plastic surgery, then they dump your ass and move on. I don't know what the hell she saw in that Cody kid, but it must have just been sex, 'cause she liked a guy with money and she didn't care where the money came from."

Stunned, Jaymie only managed to murmur, "Oh?" It seemed she had blown up the dam that had been holding back his venom.

"She *pretended* to be high-class, but I heard she was dating some biker guy who made his money from drugs and a protection racket."

"Really?"

"She was none too particular. Heard she was dating around a *lot*."

His tone was vicious, and she felt queasy. "But you had stopped dating her before she died, right?"

"Oh, sure!" he said, waving one hand and almost knocking over his wine glass.

"Have the police talked to you yet?"

"Why would they?"

"They want to talk to anyone who knew Shelby. Maybe they haven't gotten to you yet. This just happened last Friday evening, after all. Were you at the Dickens Days event?"

"Crap, no! Christmas is overrated."

"Were you on a date maybe?"

He squinted across the table. "What?"

"Last Friday night. Were you out on a date?"

He shook his head, a little confused looking. "Can't remember."

"Glenn, that was only four days ago."

"Maybe I was out of town . . . yeah, out of town, working."

"Working? But you'd left your job."

He shrugged and stood as the waiter approached with another rye and coke. "I gotta go."

"Glenn, wait, you can't leave yet," she said, shaking her head to the waiter, who turned and took the drink away. "You have to pay for your meal."

"Oh, yeah." He summoned the hapless waiter who returned, this time with the tableside debit-credit machine.

It was a confusing few minutes. While Glenn tried to remember his credit-card PIN number, Jaymie jumped up and found the maître d', taking him aside. "Between the rye and the wine, Mr. Brennan has had way too much liquor. I don't want him driving away from here."

The man looked alarmed, his thick brows raised. "But the wine was for you, was it not? Mr. Brennan was drinking rye."

She shook her head. "I didn't drink anything. I just met the man tonight. Did he arrive in his own car?"

"I *think* he drove here." He wrung his hands, then tugged at his suit jacket sleeves. "I must do something. We can't risk trouble."

"I'm sure you'll figure it out," Jaymie said.

The maître d' bustled off, had a whispered conference with another very well dressed gentleman, then came back to the table just as Jaymie was sitting back down and Glenn was returning his credit card to his wallet and sliding it into his jacket pocket.

"Mr. Brennan, as a courtesy of the restaurant we would like to offer you a taxi cab ride home, or to the destination of your choice."

Glenn's alcoholic funk had worsened. He protested that he was perfectly fine to drive, but he wasn't. He searched his pockets for his keys, then stared at them in mystification when he dug them out. Between them, the manager and maître d' got his satin-lined cashmere trench coat from a hanger in the cloakroom, helped him into it, hustled him out to a waiting taxi and sent him home to his condo in Wolverhampton, the address obtained from his driver's license.

Jaymie paid her portion of the bill, tipped generously, and gathered her things. But before she left, she spoke to the maître d' again. "Has Glenn Brennan been to this restaurant before?"

"Oh yes, he's a regular."

"Have you had this trouble with him before?"

He appeared hesitant, but finally said, "We usually establish a limit with him. The wine tonight fooled us."

"Do you know if he was here last Friday evening?" He gazed at her blankly, and she continued, "He's, uh, dating a friend, and she's just wondering where he was. He didn't show up for their date."

"I don't believe he was here."

"Okay. Thanks so much!" She headed outside in a thoughtful frame of mind. Where was Glenn Brennan at the time of the murder? How could she find out?

She sat in her van and checked her phone. There was a text from Cynthia. Tuesday was pool tournament night at the bar, and the biker in question, Clutch Roth, always participated. Jaymie could probably catch him, Johnny had told Cynthia. Jaymie was faintly uneasy about it, but she had sworn to investigate. Johnny would be there at any rate, in case she ran into trouble.

She drove directly there instead of going home first. The bar—called Shooters, a reference to both drinking and pool playing, Jaymie assumed—was a low-slung joint on the highway about halfway between Queensville and Wolverhampton. Jaymie pulled into the parking lot in front. During the day the place was nondescript brown shingles and dark windows, but at night it blazed with a shooting star neon light over the false front. The doors were lined in blinking red and green holiday lights, and tinsel garland striped the posts that held up the overhang. A festive OPEN sign blinked, as well as neon ads for beer and liquor. Jaymie had been there once or twice with Bernie and other friends when they wanted to play pool. It wasn't her kind of scene, but it certainly wasn't dangerous, even if it did have a bit of a reputation for being a biker bar.

She pushed through the door and let her eyes adjust to the darkness punctuated by a blaze of neon everywhere: lights over the long wooden bar, glowing liquor ads and a retro jukebox in the corner howling out Def Leppard over the rumble of chatter and laughter. She spotted Johnny with a bar rag slung over his shoulder. He was carrying a bus tray, clearing a table in the corner of foam-flecked glasses and empty bottles. She slipped through the crowd and approached him. "Hey, Johnny," she said, tugging at his rolled-up jean sleeve.

"Hey, Jaymie," he said, smiling but seeming uneasy.

Johnny was a big fellow, long limbed, shambling, always looking like he hadn't grown into his height yet, even though he was in his late thirties. He had a rough life growing up, Valetta, who babysat him as a kid, had told her, but Jaymie knew he was doing his best to stay on the straight and narrow now after a stint in prison. He was keeping up with meetings, going now with Cynthia Turbridge, and though a bar might seem like a rotten job for a recovering alcoholic, he appeared to be making a go of it.

"Do you have a minute to talk?"

He glanced around. All the tables were clear. "I'll dump this, check with the bartender, and we can sit here for a minute. Can I bring you something?"

"Just ice water with lemon, if you could?"

"Sure." He swiped his rag around on the table, hoisted the bus tray on his shoulder and headed behind the bar.

She slid into a banquette seat with her back to the wall and examined the room, wondering if her quarry was already there. Shooters was long and low-ceilinged, with a bar along one side near the front, banquette seating along the other side, tables for those who wanted to sit and a big square area at the back with six game tables: four for regular pool and two snooker tables. Some folks gathered, but they were mostly chatting and casually knocking a few balls around, no actual games yet.

Johnny returned, set the ice water on a coaster in front of her and sat down, keeping his eye on the barroom. He was busboy, bar back—responsible for refilling ice and fetching items from the storeroom for the bartender—and bouncer.

"Is he here yet?" Jaymie asked.

"Not yet." He checked his watch. "It's just seven thirty. He's usually here about now." He glanced over at her. "This isn't going to get him in trouble, is it?"

"No, not at all. He's just been mentioned as going out with Shelby Fretter and I'm wondering if he knows anything that could give a hint as to who killed her."

"Going out with her? I don't think so. He's got an old lady, you know," he said. "Does this mean that you don't think that Cody joker is the guy?"

She examined Johnny's rugged face, twisted in a skeptical expression. "Have you met Cody?"

"Sure. He was in here a few times."

"What's he like? I only know him through Nan."

Johnny sighed, leaned back and crossed his feet at the ankles, sticking his long legs out in front of him, his size-thirteen boots like small rafts. "He's like the other college kids who come in here slumming, trying to pick up the hot biker chicks, biting off way more than they can chew. He got in a fight one night and he's been banned ever since. The owner doesn't take that crap from anyone."

Uneasily, Jaymie thought that was just the kind of hothead who would fly off the handle and beat a girl who sassed him.

"That's Clutch there," he said, nodding toward a tall skinny guy with graying hair pulled back in a ponytail and ample gray stubble on his chin. The biker ambled in, followed by a careworn-looking woman in jeans, a tee and a leather bomber-style jacket that did not look warm enough for a motorcycle ride in subzero temperatures. She shivered. Clutch had on jeans and black leather boots, and over it all he wore a caped duster. The woman slipped behind the bar where a pot of coffee was at the ready and poured herself a mug, but the man took a spot at the bar, one foot up on the railing. "He looks like one tough dude, and he is. But I've never seen him disrespect a lady."

Jaymie nodded. Johnny lived by the same code, she knew, and that was his attraction for someone like Cynthia Turbridge. Another guy might seem smoother, more sophisticated, more elegant, but when it came down to brass tacks it was how a man treated a woman that was important. That was what told you everything you needed to know about him, in some respects, anyway.

Jaymie wondered how she should approach him. It might be dicey asking him if he dated Shelby when he had his lady with him. She asked Johnny his opinion.

He stood and whipped the bar cloth over his shoulder. "Let me send him over. I'd be straight with him, if I were you. He doesn't like it when folks lie to him. It makes him mad."

Jaymie felt a shiver down her back, and decided to take his advice. "Thanks, Johnny."

She watched while Johnny spoke to the guy, who turned and assessed Jaymie with a piercing gaze. He nodded, picked up his longneck beer and strolled over, sitting down in front of her.

"Jaymie Leighton?" He stuck his big hand out across the table. "I'm Clutch. You want to talk to me about my acquaintance with Shelby Fretter."

She shook, examining his pale crystal-blue eyes, the skin around them seamed by years of life and a squinted view of the road through a helmet visor. She felt an odd surge of amity. There was something about this guy that she liked, and she wasn't sure what it was. "I do. How did you know her?"

"She was a friend," he said shortly.

"I'm sorry," she said gently. "It was awful, how she died. I'm the one who found her. I wish I could have done more than just call 911."

"You did what you could," he said.

"They have a fellow in jail right now charged with her murder, did you know that?"

He nodded, watching her and frowning. "You think they got the wrong guy?"

"I don't know, but I'd like to make sure. I don't want the wrong guy locked up and the right guy—or girl—walking free."

"How old are you?"

Jaymie startled, said, "I'm thirty-two."

He nodded. "Just a little older than Natalie."

"Who is Natalie?" Jaymie asked. The name was familiar. Could it be—?

"That's my daughter. Shelby Fretter was trying to help me find her. She's been missing for six weeks."

❊ Fifteen ❊

THERE WAS A moment of stunned silence on Jaymie's part. Then she asked, "What happened? And what was Shelby's part in it?"

He hunkered forward, his elbows on the table, and stared into Jaymie's eyes. "You working for that newspaper lady?"

She hesitated and examined him, trying to decide if it was in her best interest to admit that she was. Then she remembered Johnny's advice to be honest. "Kind of, but kind of not. I'm a columnist for the *Howler*, a food columnist. Vintage Eats."

He quirked a smile. "Hey, my lady reads that. Reminds her of the old days, she says."

Jaymie nodded. "Nan is a good woman. She, of course, is convinced her son didn't kill Shelby, and wants someone other than the police looking into it. I've been successful in the past just poking around, looking into things. I've given myself three days to decide if I want to pursue it or not."

He nodded. "So if I tell you something and ask you not to spread it around, you'll keep your mouth shut?"

"Of course! Or at least . . ." She hesitated, picking at a scratch on the wood table as she tried to frame what she needed to say. "Clutch, I don't care about anything but what pertains to this case. But if there is something that I think the police need to know about, I'll tell them. I have a friend on the Queensville force and Chief Ledbetter is kind of a friend, too."

He nodded, and his gaze slipped around the room. Someone waved to him from the pool table in the back and he returned the wave. "They're waiting on me. Hold that thought a sec. I want to tell them to get on with it." He stood, straightening to his full height, and ambled to the back, where he had a brief conversation with a potbellied fellow in jeans, who was chalking his cue stick.

Jaymie glanced around. Clutch's lady friend had donned a bar apron and was serving patrons, hoisting a large tray full of beer glasses and empties. She threaded through tables easily, as more folks entered and took seats or strode to the pool tables. The biker returned and straddled a chair, leaning his arms on the back of it.

"I don't want anyone railroaded. If that stupid-ass kid didn't kill Shelby, then he ought to be freed. Anyway, I'm going to tell you about my daughter." His voice broke, and he glanced around as he cleared his throat and swallowed. "Natalie is a good girl. She's smart as a whip, but she sure does like money. So anyway, she was working at the bank in Wolverhampton but quit when some other job came up, something that would let her travel, she said, and make a lot of dough."

"Sounds ideal," Jaymie said, privately thinking it sounded far *too* ideal.

"Sure, but she wouldn't tell me exactly what it was. I was worried and told her to be careful, but she just laughed." He cleared his throat again. "She said, 'Dad, I know what I'm doing! You know I'm no idiot.' And that's true, God love her. She's a smart cookie. But man, she has the worst taste in guys! I didn't like the fellows she was dating, and I didn't like the guy who hired her, neither. He's a pissant little piece of crap." He shook his head. "Natalie is smart, but she has blinders when it came to men. Don't get why. She keeps getting her heart broke, but she won't smarten up."

Jaymie digested what he said, but still didn't get what it had to do with anything. "So where does Shelby come in?"

His mouth twitched. "I know her mom real good. Lori's a good friend of my lady. Natalie disappeared six weeks ago. Just poof, gone. She called me and said she was going out of the country for three weeks for her new job. I told her to be careful and let me know when she got back. She's traveled alone before, loves the Far East. Spent a year in Japan in her twenties teaching English and traveled some after that, so she knows her way around. She told me she was going to South Korea to work, and then for a little vacation."

"And?"

"I didn't think nothing of it. She's a grown-up, can take care of herself. But three weeks later when I didn't hear from her, I went to her place and banged on the door. No answer. Her car was in the parking lot out back. I texted her, called her, nothing. So I called her friends—the ones I know, anyway—and nothing. They hadn't heard from her and she hadn't posted online. She wasn't much into that online stuff anyway, and I'm not on there neither. Too much crap, you ask me. But I did find out she'd told them the same thing, that she was going to Korea, but she told them other stuff she didn't tell me. She said that with this new job she got to travel for free and all she had to do was appear at promotional events, that kind of thing. Sort of like modeling, she said."

The posters about Natalie were up all over town, including in the Emporium, but it hadn't said anything about her disappearing in Korea, or on her way to Korea. There had to be more. "What do the police say? Have you tried your congressman, or the state department?"

"Hold on a sec," he said, putting up one big hand and rolling his shoulders, anxiety etched on his long face. He scruffed the bristle along his jaw. "I went to the cops. At first they didn't do anything. She's a grown woman, they said, all that crap. So I broke into her place and looked around. When I proved to the cops that she told everyone she was going on a trip, but she never left home and didn't even take her purse or passport or credit or ID, *nothing*, they finally took it serious."

That was bad; no woman would go on a trip—or anywhere—without her purse. Jaymie felt a thread of anxiety start in the pit of her stomach for Clutch and his missing daughter. "So how was Shelby helping you?"

"Lori told me Shelby worked for the fellow that was Natalie's new boss."

Jaymie sat back. "Do you mean Delaney Meadows?"

He nodded. "That's him."

"Did Shelby and Natalie know each other, then?"

"Yeah, like I said, Lori is my old lady's friend, but the kids didn't know each other before. I guess they met when Natalie came in for the interview for the modeling job, and they talked when she came back for other appointments. Natalie even went out with Shelby's brother a couple of times."

"Have you tried talking to Meadows?"

"Sure have. I called and even showed up at the office, but all he says is that Natalie never left America, wasn't on the flight she was supposed to be taking, and that he doesn't know anything else. Second time I showed up he called the cops. I don't want no hassle with the police, not when I need them to help me find Natalie. So I can't contact him. He's got an order of protection out against me. Says I threatened him."

"Did you?"

He shifted and squinted. "I may have," he said evasively. "I was severely irked. But the jerk won't tell me where Natalie was going or why, or what she was doing working for him. I talked to Shelby. She told me there's something weird going on, and she'd try to help me out."

"Have you talked to the police since Shelby was killed?"

He sighed, shook his head and looked off toward the front door, his face bathed in the blinking light from the Coors Light sign. "What if I got that poor girl killed?"

"You mean, what if Shelby was murdered because she was looking into what happened to Natalie?"

He nodded, his expression grim.

"Clutch, even if that is what happened—and I'm not saying I even think that's likely—you didn't coerce her into looking into it. It's probably not even connected, but you should talk to the police about it."

"I'll do that, and I'll call Lori, too, see if I can do anything for her."

"I'm going to be talking to her boss, and I'll try to find out more about Natalie's disappearance."

His face cracked, his expression like the tragedy mask, his mouth twisted into a grimace as he tried to keep his emotions in check. "I know the truth, Jaymie. I *know* she's dead. There's no way on earth she wouldn't have contacted me if she's still alive. But I can't let it go, can't rest, don't sleep. She's my baby girl and I need to know what happened." He squinted and pinched the bridge of his nose. "If you find out anything, I'll be beholden to you for the rest of my days. I won't rest until I know the truth and bring her home, wherever she is."

His lady friend seemed to feel his emotion and approached, putting one hand on his shoulder, a question in her eyes. He looked up at her, covered her hand with his own and introduced them. "This is my backwarmer," he said, squeezing her hand. "Gabby, this is Jaymie Leighton. Gabby's my old lady, but not Natalie's mom. *She's* been gone for years." He told her what Jaymie was going to do. Gabby nodded, offered a fleeting smile then went back to work.

Jaymie stood. "I just know I'm going to have more questions for you, but my mind is reeling and I can't think of anything." She felt the weight of his loss strongly, and knew she had just added another investigation on top of Shelby's murder. His pain was raw. If she could help, she must. "Can I call you?"

"Sure can," he said. He took out a card and scrawled a number on the back. "I'd appreciate it."

"I haven't ruled out that Cody Wainwright did kill Shelby Fretter," she said, but explained her doubts. "I'm not a trained investigator, though; I just snoop around and follow my gut. I may not find out a single thing about Natalie."

"I know. Don't sweat it."

It was nine by the time she got home. Hoppy dashed out the back door, Denver ambled, and Jaymie sat down at the kitchen table after putting the kettle on. She desperately needed a cup of tea. The light was blinking on the phone, so she grabbed it and hit the message button.

"Hi," a young woman said. "My name is Lynnsey Bloombury, Mabel is my mom? I guess you want to know something about Shelby?" Everything she said had a question mark at the end of it. "So I have to go to the Queensville Inn tomorrow morning, right? Would you meet me there for a coffee? About ten?" There was a pause. "Okay, that's it."

Jaymie took her cup of tea up to her tiny office, just a cubbyhole on the second floor, and sat at her desk, checking her email. One long one came in from Becca with details of everything from her upcoming wedding: the bridesmaid dresses Jaymie, Valetta and Dee would wear; the cottage shop renovation; their grandmother's health and their parents' planned schedule. Hoppy barked in the backyard, so Jaymie scooted downstairs, let him in, followed by Denver, who shivered and huddled into his basket by the stove. The night had descended into a bitter cold.

Jaymie trotted back upstairs. Valetta sent an email—unusual, since she preferred the phone—but this one contained only photos she had taken of the two of them working at the Emporium in their gaudy Christmas sweaters on Christmas-sweater day, an annual tradition for them on December first.

Then there was one from Nan. Jaymie had learned a lot about Nan over the last five months. She was the kind of woman whose brain never truly stopped functioning, even when asleep, and she was capable of holding multiple conversations at once even while she was typing something. She was so type A, her husband, a mild-mannered newsman with a soft voice and strong constitution, had been known to go away on "fishing weekends," though he never did more in the boat than drift lazily on the river and read Dick Francis and Harlan Coben novels while smoking cigars.

Her email was very much in her frenetic voice: fast, full-on, faintly angry, impatient. She attached several pieces from the newspaper about the Fretter/Wozny family. Jaymie saved them to her desktop and a flash drive to read later. It seemed that the newspaper had covered a lot of the family's legal woes, from a drug bust and break-in arrest of Travis Fretter—was that where he had met and started dating Mikayla Jones, the girl from the jail, Jaymie wondered?—a DUI traffic stop for Lori Wozny, to a charge against Shelby for threatening, most recently, a reporter for the *Howler*. They seemed to have a bitter enmity, the Fretter/Wozny family and the newspaper. It was no wonder Nan had been warning her son about going out with Shelby, even if it was none of her business who her adult son dated.

Nan also rattled off a lot of random information she had gleaned.

From an inside informant at the police station, *not* Mikayla this time: Lori's and Travis's accounts of where they were and when the evening of Shelby's death apparently differed dramatically.

Both agreed that Shelby had said she was meeting someone to talk about something, but that it wouldn't take long. Travis, when asked, said he got the impression her meeting was personal, while Lori claimed Shelby said it was business. Travis told the police that he last saw Shelby at about nine, but there was no mention in the official report that he saw her arguing with Cody, and indeed, Jaymie knew that they had Gus's statement that Cody Wainwright was at the Christmas tree farm until about nine thirty or so when he gave the tale about a family emergency and left. Travis stuck with his mom, he said, and they looked for Shelby after a little while.

Lori had expected her daughter to meet her and Travis at their car at about ten; it was parked at the feed store down near the docks. The village had been advertising free parking for those who wanted to take in the Dickens Days festivities. Lori, though, said that she and Travis got separated. She thought he had gone off to find his sister, and didn't see him for about half an hour, until he reunited with his mother at the car. He told her he hadn't been able to find Shelby. Both of their stories agreed from then; she gave him a ride home and came back to find Shelby, since she was her daughter's ride.

Jaymie sat back; that was an interesting variation. Lori admitted she and Travis had gotten separated, and were not together the whole time, but Travis's statement didn't mention that. Why, unless he was responsible for her death? She skipped back to the list of violations the police had investigated the family for; yes, there was the one she had noticed. Travis Fretter had apparently threatened his sister, Shelby, in a public place, a party at a friend's home. The police were called by the homeowner, who was alarmed when Travis Fretter left the party, then came back with a two-by-four and threatened to kill his sister.

Jaymie shivered. Had he managed to carry out that threat? Was he the type to use his fists if he couldn't find a two-by-four?

She jotted some notes. She would have liked to know what Travis and Shelby were arguing about when she caught sight of them that evening. Would Lori know? Would she tell

Jaymie? Probably not. Reflecting on the discrepancies between the mother's and son's stories, she wondered if anyone else that evening saw Travis alone and noticed where he was heading. She jotted down a note to ask Valetta, who had a bit of a bird's-eye view from her position on the porch of the Emporium. And if Valetta had seen nothing, maybe she could suggest others who may have.

She took her empty tea mug downstairs, turned down the thermostat and locked up, then headed back upstairs and changed into pajamas. She returned to the computer, though, and began to scan local social networking sites established on Google and Facebook. She quickly found names of many of the major players in the murder: Travis and Shelby Fretter; Delaney Meadows; Lori Wozny; Glenn Brennan; and even Clutch's daughter, Natalie Roth.

There was a lot of discussion about the tragedy. Many openly mourned Shelby, calling her an angel, a sweetheart, the best friend in the world. But the young woman had her detractors, too. Some said they were sick of people trying to make her out to be an angel when she was well known to steal boyfriends, trash talk friends and go behind people's backs. Jaymie felt faintly sick, like she was watching violence done to the girl who was unable to defend herself.

And then there were a few who hinted darkly at what dangers she was facing. She had told one friend she had information that would bust the town wide open, if he was to be believed. Jaymie jotted down his name and noted his place of business. Austin Calhoun worked for a call center in the same building as the headhunter company Shelby worked for. Since Jaymie was going to the inn in the morning to meet Lynnsey Bloombury, she'd head directly after to Delaney Meadows' business, which was just down the street, and she'd look up Austin Calhoun at Queensville Direct Call Center.

As she looked farther back in time on social networks, she found some troubling passages, bits and pieces Shelby posted that almost seemed like threats. She openly complained about young guys who thought it was okay to hit a woman, and used initials, CW, as an example. Cody Wainwright. Another in particular made her blood run cold. A "gentleman" who had gone out with her, Shelby said, told her that she was mouthy and disrespectful. She should shut up and behave like a lady if she wanted to be treated like one. He apparently told her he was tired of mouthy brats expecting men to pay for everything and then getting huffy when he wanted a little sugar. She ought to behave herself, he said, or someone was going to spank some respect into her.

The man who threatened her was Glenn Brennan.

❧ Sixteen ❧

S HE TRIED TO be mindful that this was as reported by Shelby, but still . . . it was a telling remark, like words from beyond the grave. How far was "spank" from "beat"? She looked back and found more references from a few days before she died about someone harassing her online, but Shelby didn't actually say that it was Glenn Brennan who was cyberstalking her, so it was unclear. It was entirely possible that Shelby had reported Glenn Brennan for his behavior online toward her to his company, and that was why he had been fired. That would undoubtedly make him angry.

He was a suspect, in Jaymie's eyes, and she'd make sure Chief Ledbetter knew about him, too.

She should have gone on to investigate the dating site, but she was tired and uneasy about it all. Jaymie crawled into bed, her mind reeling with all the pain and fear and violence of what she was investigating. She picked up the phone and dialed the number she now knew by heart, and Jakob answered. The gruff but mellow gravel in his voice soothed her better than the sweetest music.

"What are you doing?" she asked.

He chuckled. "Reading a report on the specific rates of growth of the various conifers in Michigan and how to maximize it. Oh, and joining an online discussion about common pests in the Christmas tree industry."

She laughed. "Fascinating!"

He asked about her day, and she told him some of it. As they talked, she began to feel better. "It's such a sad thing to be focusing on this time of year," she said. "But I feel bad for even saying that."

"I get what you mean. It's this sense that even at what is supposed to be the most wonderful time of the year something just isn't right. It's because you feel for people, Jaymie. Some folks could forget it, but it stays with you. That's probably what makes you good at looking into things."

"I guess. I wish I was a little more like those who can just forget about people and move on."

"Don't say that. You're who you are and I love that you care about people."

It warmed her and she snuggled under the covers, petting Hoppy's head where it rested on her knee. "I have a bunch of stuff to do tomorrow, but if I come out to the tree farm, will you be there?"

"I'll be there for part of the morning, then I have to go to Algonac, bounce back to Marine City, take some stuff to the store and unload, then be to Jocie's school in time for their annual concert. Her and her tumbling troop are doing a routine." There was a pause. "Would you like to come?"

Her heart thudded. She was about to say yes, but realized his whole family might be there, and she was just not ready to meet his parents and or brothers yet. Anyway, she was going to be so busy she might not even be able to fit it in. The last thing she wanted was for his family's first impression of her to be a hurried and late one.

"I think I'm going to be running around so much tomorrow I wouldn't be able to guarantee I'd be there." She took a deep breath and let it out. "And, Jakob . . . I assume your parents will be there, right?"

"Sure."

"I do want to meet them, but not when I'm rushing in and out. I want to make a good impression."

"You couldn't make a bad impression if you tried," he said gently. "But I understand."

"Thank you. Sleep well, Jakob."

"Sweet dreams, Jaymie."

SHE SLEPT BETTER than expected and awoke with a clear vision of some avenues she wanted to explore. Shelby had a troubled relationship with several people, but she had friends, too, and Jaymie had some names of her supporters from the social media she had explored the night before. She was also going to pick up where Shelby had left off, and find out what had happened to Natalie Roth. Clutch's pain and loss was so potent it affected her still. It seemed impossible that the incidents were not connected, and yet, they were so very different.

The first thing she did was report what she had learned to Chief Ledbetter. Maybe it was wrong to tell him about Glenn Brennan's words as reported by Shelby, but Jaymie was not going to hold anything back from the police, not when it was this important.

Then she said, "Chief, I have some information that leads me to believe that Lori Wozny's and Travis Fretter's stories about what they did that evening are substantially different. I know you already know that, but it made me wonder . . . Why would Shelby's brother lie about where he was that night, during a period that Lori says he was apart from her? I wondered if you were investigating him as a potential suspect in her death."

The chief harrumphed. "We are reviewing all statements for irregularities. I wouldn't answer your question even if we were just talking as police chief and citizen, but you are now working for Nan Goodenough. I won't be quoted in the press, Jaymie."

She was silent for a long moment, then said, "I understand, Chief. But I do find it interesting. There's more, though." She told him about the call she received, explaining about the blood on Cody's coat that was purported to be Shelby's. She hesitated, then gave the name of the girl she suspected, Mikayla Jones, and told him her reasoning. "I'm not one hundred percent certain, but it sure sounded like her."

He was silent, but it was the quietude of rumination, not anger.

She said tentatively, "And, Chief . . . I know you probably have this, but I've been thinking about something I noticed that night, the fabric caught in the splinter in the table. It wasn't from anything Bill would wear, I'd swear to that. What it looked like to me was the lining of a suit jacket."

"You do notice a lot, don't you? We had already figured that out, and that's all I'm going to say."

It was all she needed, as it confirmed her guess.

"And, Jaymie, I suppose you'd want to know this, if you don't already. We've released Cody Wainwright for the time being. We didn't arraign him on the murder charge."

Jaymie was stunned into silence.

The chief chuckled. "Sounds like Mrs. Goodenough hadn't told you yet."

"You seemed so certain, Chief; what changed your mind?"

"Where'd you get the idea I was certain of anything? The arrest was premature; the DA decided against arraigning him on murder right now. Doesn't mean it won't happen, just that it's been deferred." He harrumphed. "Hasty, that's what the arrest was. That's what happens when I go out of town."

After she hung up the phone she called Nan, who was happy but cautious. Until the true killer was behind bars, she wouldn't rest. Jaymie hung up, made a cup of tea and wrote an organized list of her day. She performed all her usual morning tasks and took care of the animals.

She then packed a little bag of goodies and dressed carefully in business-appropriate clothes. For her that meant a skirt, boots, sweater and her best winter coat, a cream wool trench handed on to her by Becca, for whom it was now too small. Pinned to the lapel was her favorite seasonal pin, a vintage Christmas tree with pearls and red and green stones as decorations. She walked through the village, saying *happy holidays* to those she knew, smiling and nodding to those she didn't. Queensville meant so much to her. It was home in every sense of the word, and though she didn't understand how her parents could move to Boca Raton and love living there so much, she went to visit them at their condo once a year in March. Still, she didn't get the attraction— the older she got the more she understood the saying "to each his own."

For her, that was Queensville.

The Queensville Inn was formerly the largest Queen Anne style home in the village, but when it was converted to an inn it had been expanded. A two-floor addition housed the more luxurious modern rooms and suites. She was meeting Lynnsey Bloombury in the coffee shop through the double doors and just off the main entrance. She waved to one of the waitresses she knew and found a table, carefully hanging her coat on one of the coat trees sprinkled throughout the restaurant in the winter. There were many people, tourists and locals, having their morning coffee, and some were breakfasting. Queensville didn't have any other real restaurants, so the inn provided one of the few places for folks to meet for business or pleasure.

An auburn-haired young woman entered, glanced around and spotted her, and crossed the room to stand by the table.

"Jaymie Leighton? I'm Lynnsey Bloombury." She stuck out her hand and they shook. She took off her long parka, slung it over the back of the chair and sat down with a sigh opposite Jaymie. "I'd forgotten how different it is looking for a job in Queensville than San Fran," she said, rolling her eyes.

"You're here looking for a job?" Jaymie was surprised, given that Lynnsey had a good job in the tech industry, from her mother's report.

"Yeah, I'm kinda lonely on the coast. I was coming back anyway for Christmas, but this thing with Shelby hit me hard. I miss my folks and my friends. I thought it wouldn't hurt to look around while I'm here."

"But the Queensville Inn?"

"Hey, you gotta start somewhere. Any job to start is better than no job."

Jaymie nodded, appreciating that attitude. "What do you really want to do?"

She shrugged. "I just don't know. All my friends in school seemed to have some goal, some idea of where they were headed." She gazed out the window as the wind blew across the outdoor patio, now shrouded in covers over the wrought-iron tables and chair sets. "I never did. And I still don't. I'm a receptionist slash gofer at the firm where I work. They keep saying they don't know what they'd do without me, but . . . it's just not enough. They're all so driven and into their work. I can't hang out with them, because work is all they talk about and I only understand a quarter of what they say, if that. I feel like a fish out of water."

"I know exactly what you mean," Jaymie said, and explained her own lack of an identifiable "career," and how she was finally at peace with it. "I've just decided I'm not a career kind of person, and that's okay. I like working, but I get bored easily . . . Funny to say that, when I live in a small town, with no excitement . . . or what other people would call excitement."

The waitress came over and she and Jaymie exchanged

pleasantries, then they ordered coffee and pastries. "The pastries are to die for," Jaymie said. "The chef is French Canadian. I run a picnic basket business, among other things, and his pastries are always a hit. I guess I'm lucky," Jaymie went on. "I have several jobs and hobbies and I'm always running, but I love my life."

"You *are* lucky. I did that in school, a variety of things, I mean. I took office admin and secretarial, organizational classes. After leaving school I worked at a high-end boutique, a cooking school and then in a real estate company. But I just get restless. I moved on to the tech company I work at now, but I'm already bored out of my mind. At least here I'll be restless among friends."

They shared a chuckle, but Lynnsey's expression grew serious. "But first, I want to help you find out what happened to Shelby. She was my BFF, you know? We went to school together. I lost track of some of the others, but Shelby and I just clicked and stayed clicked, you know?"

"I understand." The waitress brought their coffee and pastries, and Jaymie poured cream in her cup. "I still stay in contact with the girls I went to university with in Canada and we meet at least once a year no matter what. I email them all the time." Jaymie examined the other girl. Lynnsey was a tidy, smartly dressed redhead with a pretty, small-featured face and bright hazel eyes. Outwardly she didn't appear to have much in common with Shelby, who was harder edged, more intense, but as friends they may have filled in each other's empty spots. "I've heard all kinds of stuff about Shelby, but if I'm going to figure out what happened to her, then I need to know more from an insider, someone who truly knew her."

"That's me," Lynnsey said, her eyes brimming with unshed tears. "I miss her already. We were going to get together when I came back for Christmas and moan about our boyfriend troubles."

"Boyfriend troubles?"

"I can never find a nice guy and she was bored with dating really off guys lately. Said they were all dogs."

Odd, considering she kept dating, but maybe . . . Jaymie tilted her head to one side as an idea began to form. Were there reasons other than a desire for a love life that kept her dating several men? "Did she mean Cody Wainwright in particular?"

"That's the guy who's in jail for killing her, right?"

Jaymie didn't correct her; that Cody was now out of jail was neither here nor there.

Lynnsey frowned down into her coffee cup and took a long swig. "He was your typical young guy, she said."

"But he knocked her around. Did she ever tell you that?"

"Did he *really* do that?" Lynnsey, eyes wide, stared at Jaymie. "Look, you gotta understand something. Shelby was . . . different. She sent me a few emails telling me that she was scared of Cody, but still she kept him around. I didn't get it. And then she emailed me that if anything ever happen to her, I ought to look at Cody. I called her, scared out of my mind, but she kind of brushed it off, said she was half joking. It made me crazy. It was one of the things I intended to talk to her about over Christmas. I wanted to know what was going on."

Jaymie stirred her coffee. "I'm surprised you even question his guilt, given the emails. Most people are assuming he's guilty, and they don't even have that insight."

"Shelby was getting more erratic; I was worried. Cody killing her just seems . . . I don't know. Too easy," Lynnsey said. "Nothing in Shelby's life was ever that simple and clear cut."

"What do you mean?"

She shrugged. "Just that she complicated everything."

"How?"

"You had to know how her mind worked. She's like me in some ways . . . easily bored. So she would deliberately complicate things."

"How do you go about complicating your life?"

"She thought it was fun to make people a little crazy . . . Like in high school, she deliberately pitted two best friends against each other. It started as an experiment of social science, or at least that's what she *said* it was. She was good at justifying her own brand of crazy. She wanted to see if she could turn close friends against each other just using social means, like gossip and innuendo."

"That sounds . . . pardon me for saying it, but it sounds cruel."

Lynnsey shrugged. "She figured they deserved it. Trust me, those girls were the queen biotches of the school, so Shelby was just having some fun with them. She managed to have them at each other's throats in no time. They had a huge fight in front of everyone. Even when they found out it was all based on lies, they were never friends again after that."

Trust was such a fragile thing, and once broken it was difficult to mend. Jaymie was horrified but stifled her personal opinion since Lynnsey didn't seem to think it was such a big deal. It did offer a revealing insight into Shelby's character and gave Jaymie food for thought. "So you don't think Cody killed her?"

She knit her reddish brows. "I didn't say that, I just said it seemed too simple an explanation. She was done with him, though, so who knows?"

"She was *done* with him? Did she tell you that? Was she serious?"

"I think she was. She had some plan for getting rid of him once and for all."

"What was the plan?"

"She didn't tell me. Said she'd tell me all about it at Christmas. I was going to stay with her." The tears resurfaced but she dabbed at her eyes with her paper napkin and went on. "She was thinking dating older men might be the way to go: money, security, better sense. I said, yeah, but what about all that baggage, you know, children, ex-wives . . . and she said,

'Who said anything about *ex*-wives?' Weird comment. But she wouldn't say any more."

"Lynnsey, did she ever mention anyone named Natalie?"

The young woman's eyes brightened and she leaned forward. "She sure did. She told me she needed someone to talk to away from the village about something. Natalie Roth is the girl who disappeared."

Jaymie nodded.

"Shelby had an idea she knew what happened to the girl, and she was going to take that information to the police!"

❧ Seventeen ❧

"WHAT DID SHE know? What did she tell you?" Was the mystery going to be solved as easily as that? She'd love to be able to tell Clutch what happened to his child.

Lynnsey shook her head, her mane of auburn curls bouncing. "She told me some, but not all. We got interrupted. She had phoned me from work, I think, maybe from the cafeteria or lunchroom. I'm not positive of that; it could have been some other coffee shop, I guess. I could hear other voices in the background. Anyway, she told me that Natalie was mixed up in something real nasty, and she was killed so she wouldn't talk."

"Did this have to do with her boss, Delaney Meadows?"

"I don't know. We got cut off before she told me much."

"You must have had an impression, though. Could you tell anything?"

Lynnsey bit her lip, a streak of pink lipstick smudging her teeth. "I just don't know. She just said 'something real nasty,' those exact words, but like I said, we were cut off. She said she was hoping it would solve the case, but that she was sure of one thing; Natalie was dead. She was going to have to tell Natalie's father."

This was awful, but Clutch himself believed Natalie was dead. Jaymie sighed and stifled tears. It was going to be devastating to him, another family torn apart.

Speaking of which . . . "Lynnsey, if you knew Shelby in school you must know her brother, Travis."

Lynnsey rolled her eyes. "What a jerk he is! Those two hated each other. When he was a kid he was one of those mean little boys, throwing frogs at cars and spinning kittens by their tails."

"Literally?" Jaymie said, gasping.

"Literally! I guess he stopped doing crap like that, but I still couldn't stand him. When we were teenagers he was always hitting on me and trying to get a peek at me in the bathroom."

"So she hated him? In, like, a brother-sister kind of way? Or something deeper?"

Lynnsey paused and thought as she drained her coffee cup. "I don't know what he felt about her. He creeped me out, so I spent as little time as I could with him. But I do know she *hated* him. Lori made excuses for him, saying he didn't have a father figure growing up, blah, blah, blah. She was always bailing him out of trouble. Shelby told me that someday he was going to do something so terrible he'd end up behind bars."

Maybe he had fulfilled his sister's worst fears, Jaymie thought, considering the lies he'd told about his evening and the mysterious half hour or so he was missing. Natalie Roth's fate could be tangled in there, too, considering that Travis apparently dated Natalie.

They were finished with their coffee. Lynnsey had to leave, as she was looking into other job opportunities in Wolverhampton. One place she *wasn't* going was Delaney

Meadows' headhunter business. When Jaymie asked why, she just said from talking to Shelby she didn't have a good opinion of the guy. Nothing concrete, just an icky feeling.

"One thing I trusted was Shelby's gut," Lynnsey said. "She had been hit and beat up all her life, especially by her mother's boyfriends. She was angry . . . *really* angry deep inside. I always thought she'd do something important, like work at a battered women's shelter."

"Maybe she was making a start by looking into Natalie Roth's disappearance, especially if there was something fishy about it," Jaymie mused.

"I guess we'll never know what she may have done," Lynnsey said, tears welling in her eyes. She gave Jaymie a quick hug, grabbed her parka and speed walked out of the coffee shop.

Jaymie didn't leave the inn. Instead she headed past the main desk, with a wave at Edith, the owner's girlfriend, who was sitting behind it, then down a familiar hallway to a main-floor suite. She tapped on the door.

"Come in!"

She entered. Mrs. Stubbs was sitting in her mobility wheelchair by the window, where the light was best, reading a large-print mystery novel.

"Jaymie!" Mrs. Stubbs cried, sticking her finger in the page she was reading. "Thank goodness. Someone interesting to talk to. Despite my books, I've been suffering from boredom." She patted the bed with one arthritic hand, indicating she wanted Jaymie to sit. As usual she was wearing a jewel-colored velour pants and jacket set over a T-shirt. "Come in and tell me what you've been up to."

Jaymie crossed the floor of the comfortable bedsitting room where the woman was cosseted and taken care of twenty-four hours a day by her devoted son and his live-in girlfriend. She drew out from her purse the plastic bag of treats—some brownies, shortbread cookies and fudge—and set it on the bedside table for Mrs. Stubbs to pick through later. She perched on the bed and the friends discussed family plans for Christmas, which was creeping up so quickly Jaymie didn't know if she'd get everything done.

Mrs. Stubbs looked wistful, riffling the pages of her book while she stared out the window. "I remember being that busy, when the boys were kids and my husband was alive, and my parents, too. I didn't think I'd ever have enough time to do everything that needed doing. I used to imagine a time when I could just sit and drink tea and read a book." She chuckled, but it was a mirthless sound. "I guess that's now; I have all the time to read I could ever want. What I wouldn't give to go back and have some of that busy time to do over."

Jaymie's heartstrings plucked, but she knew she needed to distract her friend. They talked about her Grandma Leighton's upcoming visit and that she would be staying at the inn and would be visiting with Mrs. Stubbs. That cheered the other woman immensely. Inevitably they spoke of Shelby Fretter's murder and how Jaymie was investigating it, semi-officially this time, at the request of the suspect's mother.

"I'm just not sure how I'll handle it if I think he's guilty."

"Cart in front of the horse, Jaymie. Are you truly going into this with an open mind?"

"I hope I am now. Cody has been released, but Nan won't be happy until he's completely out of the woods."

"Tell me what you have so far."

Mrs. Stubbs was a remarkable woman, elderly, yes, but with a clearer mind than many half her age. She listened and commented, and then was silent for a few moments when Jaymie had told her all. It had helped to go through it all with Mrs. Stubbs, because it made it clearer in her own mind.

"We seem to have a few possibilities here, don't we?" Mrs. Stubbs finally said. "Poor Shelby may have been killed by someone close to her for personal reasons."

"Right. It could be Cody, or her brother, Travis, who has a mean streak, and who I saw arguing with her right before she died."

"Or even her mother," Mrs. Stubbs said. "Don't write her off because she's upset about it. If I was a mystery writer, I'd make the mother the murderess, just once!"

"You do have a gruesome imagination, don't you?" It was a possibility, but remote. "I don't see it being Lori. The other strong possibility, if I discount Cody, is that Shelby was killed because of what she was looking into: Natalie Roth's disappearance and probable death."

"If Mabel's daughter is right about what Shelby told her, that she knew who had killed Natalie and was going to the police about it, then it *seems* likely the two are connected. Two young women dead, and all involved with the same people? Not likely a coincidence." She held up the book she was reading. "In this idiot mystery the stupid girl investigating never figures things out, she just stumbles across answers. And people tell her things for no earthly reason! She doesn't even have to ask questions, they just babble to her!"

Jaymie smothered a smile. The woman was an avid reader, but not an uncritical one. "I wish people would just babble to me. Most of the time people clam up and won't say a word."

"Yes, well, also in this idiot book no one lies to the girl detective, nor does she even consider that folks are lying to her. But people lie all the time. The more important something is, the more likely they are to lie about it. My point is, Jaymie, I know you have a real reason for looking into this, but it doesn't mean those you talk to will be any more receptive to your snooping, nor will they necessarily volunteer information, nor will they tell you the truth. You're going on to this Delaney Meadows' place of business after this, right?" Mrs. Stubbs said.

Jaymie nodded.

"Be careful, dear," she said, putting one arthritic hand over Jaymie's where it clutched the edge of the mattress. "I have some information. I'm a little afraid to share it with you because it may get you in trouble. But . . . I trust your brains. You will do with it what you must."

Jaymie waited as Mrs. Stubbs ordered her thoughts.

"I know Delaney Meadows by sight. His wife is a dear girl, one of the library volunteers that brings me my monthly quota of books. A few days ago when she came with my books, she was later than usual and visibly upset. I made her sit down and asked what was wrong, but she wasn't going to tell me. I winkled it out of her, though. She saw her husband coming out of one of the inn rooms with a young woman. The young woman, she told me, was Shelby Fretter, an employee of her husband's."

Jaymie was stunned, and immediately saw that it introduced another suspect into the spectrum. Many a woman had slain a competitor for her husband's affections. She was silent a moment too long.

Mrs. Stubbs, agitated, moved restlessly. "I know what you're likely thinking," she said, her voice creaky and clogged with emotion. "But Lily Meadows is a darling girl. She could not possibly kill someone. Even with extreme provocation. She's just a tiny little dab of a thing, sweet natured. For heaven's sake, she volunteers to bring library books to shut-ins! That makes her a saint."

"Lily Meadows," Jaymie mused. "Lily . . . I know someone with that name. Ah, she's in my historical romance book club! It's likely the same woman." She thought for a moment more. "I have one sure way of eliminating her as a suspect. Book club met on Friday night, the night Shelby was murdered. If it's the same girl and she was at it, she can't be guilty because it never breaks up before ten."

"I don't need that to know she's not guilty," Mrs. Stubbs said. "She's a sweet girl and even if her husband is a low-life cheating scum, there is no way on God's green earth she would do anything so vulgar about it as murder."

Lost in thought, Jaymie let Mrs. Stubbs ramble. Lily Meadows was a possible new line of inquiry, and she could approach her as a friend. But Lily was not likely to open up about her husband's supposed extramarital activities. However, just because Delaney was at the inn with Shelby did not necessarily mean they were having an affair. Though it did make some sense of Lynnsey Bloombury's remark about Shelby asking who said anything about *ex*-wives. Did she mean she was into dating married men even if they stayed married? And was dating the boss her way of climbing the ladder?

As in every investigation she had been involved in during the last seven months, things got far more complicated before the truth began to glimmer like a faint light in the distance. This was a complication she'd need to explore. She made a mental note to check in with someone else in book club to see if Lily Meadows was there that night.

"When was this that Lily Meadows saw her husband and Shelby Fretter together?"

The elderly woman frowned down at her hands, massaging the knobby joints. "Let's see . . . she always brings me my books on Thursday evenings. This was the last time she brought me books, because she had a Christmas treat she had baked using a recipe from one of the mysteries, so it was just last week."

"Thursday evening, just one day before Shelby was murdered," Jaymie said. "What a coincidence." She would not say it aloud to Mrs. Stubbs, because it would upset her to know the direction of Jaymie's thoughts, but was it possible that Shelby's murder was the result of a woman scorned? Jaymie hugged Mrs. Stubbs good-bye, then left the inn by a back door and headed to the Belcker Building on Munroe Street. It was a converted old house, as were most office spaces in Queensville. This was a large two-story yellow brick, with a glass entrance foyer added on the front and a modern addition on the back, where the property sloped to a ravine.

Jaymie entered and read the business list in the front lobby. There was a chiropractor, a dentist, two law offices, a call center and Delaney Meadows' headhunting agency, Meadows Employment Agency. There was also a café called the Bean & Leaf. She descended the terrazzo tile stairs to the basement and followed signs past the chiropractor and one law office.

The café was tiny and filled to bursting with folks at that time, midmorning. By the door there was a divider with a cafeteria-style counter where sandwiches, soups, coffee and tea were doled out. A plastic Christmas tree was taped to the top of the glass divider and foil streamers were draped from ceiling duct to ceiling duct. She turned and surveyed the room, which was jammed with small tables and iron chairs; at the far end natural light drifted in through a large plate glass window overlooking a small enclosed terrace.

This was likely exactly where Shelby had spoken to Lynnsey from that day. If she was speaking of confidential matters it was not the best place, since the tables and chairs were crammed together with very little room in between. Perhaps someone overheard her speaking of her investigation of Natalie Roth's disappearance. Would that matter? Not unless that someone was involved in said disappearance, or talked to someone who was.

As one of the servers looked at her and was about to speak, Jaymie smiled, turned and left. She found Queensville Direct Call Center upstairs on the main floor. She pushed through the nondescript steel door. There was a long reception desk, beyond which were six-foot-high fabric dividers. She could hear a steady murmur of voices and ringing phones. She approached the reception desk, got the attention of the receptionist, who was hunched over her computer keyboard, and asked if she might have a moment of Austin Calhoun's time. The young woman stared at her with an assessing gaze.

"You wanna complain about a call from the call center? Or service from one of our clients?" she asked.

"No, not at all. I just have a question to ask Austin."

"You a friend? Family?"

"No, he doesn't know me. This is about a mutual friend of ours," she said, skating perilously close to blatant lies. "Could he speak with me for five minutes?"

"Your name?"

She gave it and the receptionist made a call, eyeing Jaymie as she did so. She hung up. "He'll be out in a minute. Have a seat," she said, waving toward three plastic chairs lined up against a wall under a giant poster reminding folks to smile, since a smile came across in your voice.

Jaymie smiled. "Thank you." It did actually come through in her voice, she thought.

Moments later a young man came out from beyond the dividers. He was plump and fair-haired, wearing a pale-blue shirt and argyle sweater with tan pants. She stood and introduced herself.

His eyes widened. "I know who you are," he said, pointing one finger at her. "You're the one who finds the dead bodies. You found *Shelby*!" He covered his mouth with one plump beringed hand and his eyes watered. "Oh, my," he muttered. "Do you want to talk to me about Shelby?"

She nodded, not sure what to say to the effusive fellow.

He turned to the receptionist and said, "Tell Rudy that I'm taking an early lunch. I'll be half an hour, but if I'm more, then he can just dock my pay, the old Grinch." He whirled back, ducked around the open end of the reception desk and grabbed Jaymie's arm. "Come with me." He led her out of the office.

"Are we going to the Bean & Leaf? It's pretty crowded."

"Somewhere more private." He led her down the hallway to a door labeled "Conference Room," and pushed through. It was dark and cold. He flicked a bank of switches that created a pool of light at one end, where there were two black leather retro-looking pod chairs by a wall of faux cherry-wood polished cabinetry. He led her past a long scarred black conference table and pushed her into one of the chairs, then turned to a counter on the wall of cabinets, switching on a single-serve coffee machine. It gurgled and heated up. "Tea okay?" he said over his shoulder. When she said yes, he pulled some pods out of a little drawer under the machine and grabbed some mugs. He made two cups. "Hope you like it black."

"Black is fine," she said, bemused, as he handed her the mug and plunked down into the other chair. It was clear that this was a conference room for the joint use of the companies in the building, but probably not for the casual use of employees. She felt faintly guilty even though this wasn't her workplace, and then reflected that it certainly indicated the difference between her and Austin. She was the kind of person who felt the need to ask consent, and he seemed to be the kind who believed it was easier to apologize than ask permission.

"How did you know Shelby?" she asked.

He curled up in the chair, his hands wrapped around the black mug, regarding her avidly over the rim. "How horrible was it for you, finding her? I can't imagine. It breaks my heart, you know. Did you ever meet Shelby?"

Jaymie thought of her one brief meeting. "Uh, kind of."

"She was just one of a kind." His eyes teared up. "She was like my best girlfriend, you know? We always took lunch together, and gossiped like crazy. I kind of felt like I was living my life through her, sometimes, all the boyfriends and parties, and she was *so* ambitious. She was amazing!"

"I'm so sorry, Austin. I didn't know you were so close."

He slurped a long drink of tea and took in a deep shuddering breath. "I guess I kind of hero-worshipped her. When I came to work for Delaney—"

"So that's how you knew her? You worked for Delaney Meadows, too?"

"I didn't say that, did I? Sure, that's how we met. I worked for him for a few months."

"Doing what?"

He waved one hand. "Data entry, filing . . . whatever! Anyway, Shelby and I got so close during that time, like this," he said, crossing one finger over the other. "Not everyone was so fond of her though, you know?"

Jaymie had questions she wanted to ask, but if there was anything she had learned it was to not shut down a free-flowing tap of information when it was in mid gush. "Why?"

He cocked his head to one side. "She was . . . brash. Yeah, that's the word . . . brash. She'd tell you the truth, no varnish, and if you didn't like it, then, buh-bye!" he said, waving one hand.

"Sounds like the type who would make enemies."

"I guess." He examined her. "I never did ask . . . What do you want with *me*? I guess I just ran off my mouth and didn't even think."

"I'm looking into it, informally." She explained her work for Nan Goodenough. "She, of course, doesn't think her son did it. I'm investigating just to see if there are viable alternatives, and maybe get at the truth. I was reading online postings and I saw your name. You were defending her, and seemed to know her. I thought I'd talk to you."

Austin's blue eyes widened. He looked remarkably like a baby, with a round cherubic face and a lick of pale hair that curled on his forehead. He was only about twenty, Jaymie judged.

"People are awful! But she could get a gal's back up. She was not afraid to tell you where to get off."

"You hinted online that she was investigating something dangerous, that she was into something dark and she was gotten rid of. What did you mean?"

He shifted uncomfortably and his cheeks pinked as he rolled his eyes. "I may have been just . . . you know, exaggerating. I can be the teensiest bit dramatic at times. She was very mysterious, was Shelby, but when I think back I wonder if she may have been teasing me, you know, about being into something dangerous."

"You said you talked about her boyfriends. I've heard she was dating more than one guy." This was part test; did Austin really know Shelby, or was he a publicity hound attaching himself to a sensational murder case?

"She liked Cody, but thought he was way too attached, like . . . *scary* attached. She was afraid of him."

Jaymie recalled how passionate Cody was in his defense of Shelby to his mom. Yes, that may have been too attached given their actual relationship. It didn't bode well that a friend knew she was afraid of him; it sure wouldn't look good in court if Austin was called as a witness. "Did she talk about that, about being afraid of him?"

He nodded. "Said he was the kind who flew off the handle too quick. She said she never knew what would set him off, that he was unpredictable. She had a bruise on her cheek one day, and said he'd done that. She told me one of these days he would hit her hard, and she'd never know it was coming."

Jaymie shut her eyes. That sounded scarily close to what probably happened. But was it not odd that she would put up with it, given what Lynnsey had to say about her being angry at those who beat women?

"She was going to break it off with Cody," Austin said. "She was seeing some other dude, too, though, some pharma representative. I remember that because I joked that there was this new weight-loss drug out, and could she get me some."

That had to be Glenn Brennan. "What did she think of him?"

He shuddered. "She said he was creepy . . . handsy. I asked was he sexy, and she said no, he was a jerk. I asked why she kept seeing him, but she wouldn't say."

Interesting. "Anyone else?"

"Maybe." He took another sip of tea and watched her. "Look, if I tell you something in confidence, will you tell your boss or the police?"

This was one of *those* moments, the ones you look back on and wish you'd handled differently, Jaymie thought. What could she say? "I probably won't unless it exonerates Cody, how about that? That's the only thing I'm interested in, ultimately."

He was silent. "This has been bugging me, and I have to tell someone. Maybe you can tell me what to do about it."

"What's up?"

"It's true, what I said online; I *do* think that Shelby Fretter was involved in some deep stuff, and I *think* that she was writing it all down. She was always reading a novel—she liked thrillers—or writing. She wrote in some kind of journal or diary every single day, and she always hid what she was writing when I joined her. And sometimes . . . *sometimes* she had this smile on her face. It was haunting. Like she was enjoying something shady *waaay* too much."

❧ Eighteen ❧

H E COULDN'T EXPLAIN more, just that there must be a diary or journal somewhere with something written in it. Jaymie made a note of that. She had a sense that it could be the one thing that would crack the investigation wide open, so . . . to tell the police about it or not? Not at this point, she decided, since she didn't actually know it held anything more than shopping lists for Christmas.

"Austin, what was Shelby and Delaney Meadows' relationship like?"

His hand jerked and he spilled some tea on his sweater. "Crap!" He jumped up, went to the wet bar and got a paper towel and blotted the tea stain. "That surprised me. I didn't know anyone else suspected. I had a feeling they were involved, but she told me no way, that she didn't like him that way." He shrugged and sat back down, picking up his mug. "I don't know. I just saw them together outside of work way too much, and him with that vindictive cat of a wife of his."

Vindictive cat? Didn't sound like the same saintly

book-deliverer-to-shut-ins that Mrs. Stubbs spoke of. "I've heard of Lily Meadows," Jaymie admitted. "What makes you say she was vindictive?"

He paused, eyeing her, then said, "She's the one got me fired. She looks like the kind who wouldn't hurt a fly, but she heard some joke I made, and that was it. Delaney fired me. Shelby tried to stick up for me, but little miss wife-of-the-boss wasn't having it."

"What was the joke?"

He hung his head in mock shame, then looked up at Jaymie, his blue eyes sparkling with malicious humor. "She had a new dress, Chanel couture, and all I said was, Matthew six, twenty-eight. A meadow is a field, right? Who knew she'd know her Good Book so well?"

It took Jaymie a moment, as she did not know the Bible nearly as well as she supposed she ought, but she finally clued in. "Oh, wait . . . something about the lilies of the field, neither do they sow, nor . . . uh, I'm not sure of the rest."

"Good Lord, you're practically Bible illiterate," he said, with an eye roll. "King James version is, 'consider the lilies of the field, how they grow; they toil not, neither do they spin.' Though Lily does spin; I've seen her at spin class. She's Queen B at the gym."

What a different perspective one got speaking about someone to two different people. She'd have to remember that. The truth was likely somewhere in between Mrs. Stubb's saintly version of Lily and Austin's venomous view. "You got fired because of that?"

"She made a big deal out of it. I guess she doesn't like that anyone would think she doesn't earn her way. But I mean, they don't have kids. Why should the woman not work? Everyone else does. She does all these little volunteer things that make her feel worthwhile, and she's on every board and in every volunteer group, but *really*!"

"Don't you think that's between them?" It all sounded

fishy, she wasn't sure why. Had that been all there was to his being fired from Delaney Meadows' business?

He shrugged and finished his tea, then got up and took his mug over to the sink, sitting it down in the small stainless steel basin. "Speaking of . . . I have to get back to work or Rudy will have my butt on a platter. I sure do hate the call center, but I don't want to get fired this close to Christmas."

"Just one more question," she said, and he turned back toward her. "Did you know anything about Shelby looking into the disappearance of a young woman?"

His expression blanked. "I don't know what you mean," he said. "I have to go. Toodles!" He waved his fingers and headed out at a brisk pace.

Jaymie sat a minute longer, looking at the door. Why was Austin Calhoun lying about that? She was convinced that he did know about Shelby's investigation into Natalie Roth's disappearance. She took her mug to the sink and washed the ones they had used, turned off the coffee machine and dried the mugs. She heard footsteps and turned just in time to see a fellow enter; she recognized him right away, even only having seen him from a distance. He had a stooped stance that was familiar. It was Delaney Meadows.

"Oh, I'm sorry," he said. "I didn't know the conference room was in use."

"It's not. I'm just . . . tidying up after a private interview," she said, realizing he wouldn't know if she was an employee of one of the firms in the building. "Do you need it?"

"I'm setting up some interviews for an executive assistant and I don't have anywhere to do it but here." He seemed at a loss, staring around as if he didn't know where to start.

"Let me help. You're Mr. Meadows, right?" She got a paper towel and wiped out the sink, then tossed the balled-up paper into the garbage.

"Do I know you?" He was tall, slim and nicely dressed, with glasses and sandy thinning hair brushed carefully over his domed head. But the stoop, from rounded shoulders, appeared to be habitual.

"No. I'm sorry about Shelby Fretter. Is that whose position you're interviewing for?" Her mind was tumbling at full speed, but this was a unique opportunity to ask questions without him having his defense shields in place, so to speak.

"It's a terrible thing. I feel so bad for her family," he said vaguely, still standing at the door and staring.

He did *not* sound sincere. "So, if you're interviewing . . . will anyone be interviewing with you?"

"No."

"Then the long table is too formal," she said decisively. "How about over here?" she said, sweeping her hand toward the chairs she and Austin had just vacated. She moved back to them and pulled a small round table between them. "How many do you have coming to be interviewed? And are these folks your own agency has already interviewed for other positions?" She eyed him.

His gaze sharpened. "You know what my company does; I'm surprised."

"Why wouldn't I?" she said.

He shrugged. "I've got three girls coming."

"Staggered by how much time?"

"Uh, half an hour between each."

"And you've got someone in your office sending them here?"

"Yes. I just didn't . . . The police have been wandering in and out of my office and I don't want to have that interrupt me. Or . . . or scare the girls off."

She turned one of the chairs and shifted the table a few inches. "Understandable. I imagine they've searched her desk. Did they take stuff away?" she asked, wondering about the journal Shelby was writing in. It was possible she kept it with her, possible that she left it in her work desk and possible it was somewhere else entirely.

"I think so. I didn't pay attention. I mean, it was her boyfriend who killed her, right? Nothing to do with me or her work."

"What was her job?"

"My assistant." He set his sheaf of papers down on the conference table and started looking through cupboards. "Should I ask them if they want coffee? Or . . . I don't know. I'm a little perplexed. Shelby had been with me awhile and I guess I got to rely on her. Maybe too much." He stopped and turned, eyeing her. "You're not looking for a job, are you?"

"Me? No. Not right now, anyway. I have a few jobs."

"Sounds like the kind of gal I'm looking for, eager to work. I have one girl working for me who wants the job. I've got her on reception and phones right now, but there is no way I could rely on her."

"Why not?"

He shrugged and his gaze slid away from Jaymie. "She's just not . . . That isn't her forte, I guess you'd say. She's more interested in taking the easy way out of things."

Interesting. "What were Shelby's job responsibilities? I can't say I'd rule out her job without knowing."

"She kept my schedule straight. I have a couple of companies and the needs are very *very* different."

"I know one is a white-collar headhunting agency, but what is the other?"

He eyed her and squinted. "Well, I, uh, supply models to companies that want a spokesperson for their auto show, or, you know, a booth model for a tech show. A pretty girl to stand around, hand out pamphlets and attract attention."

"Around here?"

"Anywhere. Here. Canada and other countries."

"There is actually a call for that?" Jaymie asked, thinking of Natalie Roth. This was getting interesting. Clutch had already told her that Natalie was excited about her new job working for a company that sent models to other countries, and this was the confirmation that she was indeed working for Delaney Meadows' modeling agency. Was Shelby investigating her boss in connection to Natalie's disappearance?

"Sure. The world loves a pretty girl."

She suddenly remembered what Glenn Brennan had said the evening before. "I thought I heard you ran a dating agency or something? Some guy I met said he found someone on there."

He licked his lips. "It's . . . Well, yes, I do run a dating website, but a classy kind, you know, for professional men to find suitable girls. But that's not a profitable business, at least not, ah . . . not yet."

"So the dating website and the modeling agency aren't the same thing?"

He stared at her. Clutch had called him a pissant piece of crap; she wasn't sure what to think yet of Delaney Meadows.

"What'd you say your name was?"

"I didn't."

"Who do you work for?"

"A lot of people."

"What's your name?"

"Jaymie Leighton."

His lips firmed and he pointed an accusatory finger at her. "You're that snoopy girl, the one who found Shelby's body. Why are you here? Are you following me?"

"No, of course not, I—"

"Yes, you are. You're following me. I don't like that. I think you ought to go."

She remembered how he had had Clutch thrown out and obtained a protection order against him. He was more than a little paranoid. "This is just a chance meeting, Mr. Meadows. I'm so sorry about Shelby. It sounds like you relied on her a lot."

There was a tap at the door and a young woman stood in the doorway. "Am I early?"

He glanced down at his clipboard. "No, you're right on

time. This girl was just leaving." He turned and glared at her. "Weren't you?"

She knew when she was beat. "Yes, I was. I'm sorry, Mr. Meadows. Maybe we can talk another time."

"I doubt it."

She hastened from the room, but didn't leave the building. This was the perfect time to do a little snooping at the Meadows agency. It was just down the hall, a rather nondescript office, with a partial glass door and a sign with the company's name on a plaque beside it. She pushed open the door and went up to the reception desk.

"Hi. Uh . . . Lizzie Bennet to see Mr. Delaney Meadows," she said to the girl at the desk, who was doodling on a notepad while twirling her hair and chewing gum, the trifecta of reception duty. This must be the unsuitable replacement for Shelby.

She stared at Jaymie a moment in mid hair twirl. "You have to go to the conference room, that's where he's interviewing, you know. Not here."

"I'm not here for the assistant job. I'm here to interview him for the *Wolverhampton Weekly Howler* business section," she said, fishing out her press pass. She realized belatedly it was in her real name, flashed it and stuffed it back in her purse. "I have an appointment at . . ." She checked her watch. "Right now, actually."

The girl looked like a deer caught in the headlights, confused and unsure. She had a strand of hair pulled out to the side of her head like a long piece of blond cotton candy. "But . . . he's in the conference room."

Jaymie sighed and moved from foot to foot. "I hate to have come all this way and then not be able to get the interview. It's going to do his business so much good, but we're coming down to the wire. Were you the one I spoke to last week about the article?"

"Oh, no, that would have been Shelby. I'm surprised she didn't write it down for him. She was so efficient."

"Shelby . . . Oh! That's the poor girl who was killed in this village, right?" Jaymie watched the young woman's eyes. "I heard about that. You knew her?"

She nodded.

"What was she like?"

"She was nice," the young woman said.

How descriptive. Jaymie leaned in and said, "I heard she was involved in some kind of run-in with another employee, a guy named Austin. Is that true?"

Her eyes widened, and she leaned forward, dropping the strand of hair. "Did that get out? I thought everyone had passed it off. They told some story around the office about him getting fired because of poor Lily, but it wasn't Mrs. Meadows' fault. I mean sure, she was mad at Austin for teasing about her expensive taste in clothes, but it was him making that crack about Shelby and Mr. Meadows dating that got him fired. I mean, Shelby was so mad! I've *never* seen her that mad before. She told Austin that he had a big fat mouth and that he should close it before she decided to tell everything she knew about him!"

Jaymie acted suitably awed, and her mind clicked through the information swiftly. "What did she mean? What did she know about Austin that she could reveal?"

The girl shrugged. "I don't know. I guess she died before she could say."

Jaymie asked a few more questions, but the girl didn't know anything more. "Look, can I just sit in Mr. Meadows' office until he comes back?"

She looked reluctant. "He'll be gone for a while."

"Then maybe I can go back and leave him a note?"

"I can do that," the girl said. She got out her pad of paper and a pen and looked up at Jaymie with a bright expression.

"Okay." Jaymie thought for a second, then said quickly, "Tell him that I'd like to interview him to get his opinions on the government regulatory conference in Flint that will discuss the implications of the foreign trade agreement section two one oh subsection three seven one on companies that have international travel mandates as a part of their substructure. I'd also like to get his views on the oversight committee in gubernatorial electoral college voting procedures." She stopped to take a breath and was gratified to see the completely overwhelmed and mystified look on the girl's face. She hadn't gotten beyond writing down "Interview" on the sheet.

"Could you repeat that, please?" she asked plaintively.

Not if her life depended on it, Jaymie thought, with only a dim recollection of the gobbledy-gook nonsense she had just spewed. "It's vital that this not be messed up. Just let me go back and leave a note on his desk, and I'll be out of your hair in three minutes."

The phone started ringing just then. The girl hesitated, but the ringing phone beckoned. "Okay, but just for three minutes!" She picked up the phone and in her best reception voice said, "Meadows Employment. How may I direct your call?"

Jaymie circled behind the reception desk and ducked around the hall, getting her bearings. It was a tolerable office space, radiating off a central office lounge with a square of couches facing a television tuned silently to Fox News Network. She could hear voices down the hall, and she veered away from them, not sure what exactly she was looking for. But she soon spotted one possibility; there was a desk in a cubicle with a photo of Lori Wozny and Shelby by the blank screen of a desktop computer monitor.

She only had a few minutes, so Jaymie hastily searched the desk. There was the usual desk rubble: paper clips, ball-point pens, felt markers, elastics, a stapler, staples, stickers and erasers. But more tellingly there were travel brochures, too, and some notes that Jaymie couldn't figure out. It almost looked like an itinerary, or a list of steps to do something or get somewhere. There were short forms and initials, but she didn't have time to puzzle it through. She looked over her shoulder, ripped the page off the notepad, and stuffed it in her purse, deciding to look at it later.

Not finding anything else, Jaymie skipped down the hall until she found Meadows' office, which was unlocked. She slipped in and stood, looking around. It was modest, almost blank, offering no hint as to its owner's personality other than a bland landscape on the wall and a calendar of kittens. But his planner was open on the desk. She flipped back through to the day of Shelby's death. He had a full load of work and appointments, and some notes jotted down for that day, but most telling and interesting to Jaymie was a notation for the evening.

"Dickens Days—SF," it simply said.

❧ Nineteen ❧

HAD HE THEN been at the event, and was "SF" Shelby Fretter? Had he met with Shelby for a lovers' rendezvous? Or had he followed Shelby and her family, lured her away and beat her to death?

Why *would* he?

Or why *wouldn't* he?

The amount she still did not know was overwhelming. In the short space of her morning she had added significantly to the list of possible suspects in Shelby's murder. Austin Calhoun or Delaney Meadows could have killed her. Maybe they were unlikely, but they were possible. Lily Meadows, too . . . she was a possible suspect.

Footsteps in the hall alerted her, so she tore a blank piece of paper from the notepad and scribbled some random words, then looked up as the receptionist came to the doorway.

"I don't think I ought to leave you back here," she said uneasily. "Mr. Meadows has been cranky, what with the police here a few times and such."

Jaymie straightened. "Look, I've decided not to leave a note. It's too complex. How about you just forget it for now, and I'll catch up with Delaney later. I know where he lives and I know his wife, Lily, very well, so I'll give her a call and we can meet at his home later, when he's more relaxed."

"Okay," the girl said, looking confused.

"Don't worry one little bit about it. My goal is to make this easier for everyone, so don't even worry about telling him I was here; I'll take care of everything, trust me!" Jaymie smiled and stuffed the gibberish note in her pocket. If the girl knew Jaymie she'd recognize the feverish tone of someone who had trouble lying convincingly.

But the girl actually smiled and nodded, with a big sigh of relief for one thing she didn't have to worry about in a position that was clearly beyond her ability. "Okay. That would be better. Thanks. What did you say your name was?"

"Don't even worry about it," Jaymie said, patting her arm and slipping past her. "So long! I have to hurry. Got another meeting."

She sped out and headed down to the Bean & Leaf, shaking from nerves, got a cup of tea and sat at a table by the window overlooking the courtyard. This was all getting terribly confusing, and she had a lot of leads but no organization. In the last hour Austin Calhoun, Delaney Meadows and Lily Meadows had zoomed up the list of suspects, and she wasn't sure how to go about eliminating them.

She knew one thing; she needed to speak with Cody again. She remembered something he had said in the confrontation with his mother, that Shelby had told him Nan was out to get the Fretter family, and had a vendetta against them. Did Shelby really think that? He seemed to agree. She needed to speak with him about it. She got her notebook out of her purse and wrote that down, then pondered what else she needed to ask.

Shelby's journal or whatever it was she was writing in: that nagged at her. She got out her cell phone and texted Nan to have Cody call her. She needed to ask him if he had ever seen Shelby writing in a journal and where it might be. She was curious about what Shelby was writing.

She also texted Jakob, remembering that she had planned to drop by the tree farm to see him, but he texted back that he was already on his way to Marine City and wouldn't be back until late afternoon. It looked like she wouldn't get to see him after all. She sent him a frowny face and said she'd call him that evening, after he was home from Jocie's winter pageant.

Nan texted back, telling Jaymie to call her house, where Cody was staying, whenever she wanted. She then made a note to track down Lily Meadows and find out if she was at the book club meeting on the Friday night of Shelby's death, and anything else she could discover about Delaney's wife, about whom two people had vastly different opinions. The note in Delaney's planner about Dickens Days and "SF" nagged at her. If Lily was at the book meeting she could at least eliminate one person from the pool of suspects.

She sat back and sipped her tea, and accidentally tuned in to a conversation at a table behind her. What caught her attention was the name Natalie. It wasn't an especially uncommon name, but Queensville was a small town; not that many Natalies around. Two women were talking in hushed whispers.

"(*Unintelligible*) . . . but *I* know the truth. She was scared, so she left town."

The other young woman said, "I don't think so. I think she's dead."

"You don't . . . You can't know that for sure. Who knows?"

"I think she got in trouble with . . . (*unintelligible*) . . . and took off, and got in bad company and died."

Jaymie shifted to hear better, but the girl gave her a look. Sighing, she turned in her chair to face them. "Pardon me, but I couldn't help overhear you talking about Natalie. That wouldn't be Natalie Roth, would it?"

The girl facing her, a pretty blonde not more than twenty-one or so, blinked and started, then said reluctantly, "Why?"

Jaymie hesitated, but then said, "I know her father. He's so upset. He doesn't know if she's alive or dead, and you can imagine how awful that is."

The other of the two girls, a brunette with olive skin and almond-shaped eyes, turned in her chair. Her dark eyes were clouded with doubt. "No one thought anything of it when she said she was working for Delaney and going to Korea. I know another girl who did it, and came back okay."

"Actually, she never left Queensville," Jaymie said. "Her passport and ID are all still in her apartment."

The first girl's expression cleared and she sighed in relief. "Well, that's good! She probably took off on a vacation, or with some man!"

"For six weeks?" the brunette said. "No, this is worse. Much worse. Someone would have found her or she would have contacted someone in that time. When the police came around asking questions I couldn't think of anything to tell them. I mean, I don't *know* anything. But this is bad." She met Jaymie's gaze. "She's gone, isn't she?"

"Maybe, maybe not. I'm Jaymie Leighton. How do you girls know Natalie?"

The girls were Dawn and Honey. They both worked at the call center and knew Austin Calhoun. He was bitchy but fun, they agreed. Yes, he was friends with Natalie; they saw them together quite often. *They* only knew her from lunches at the Bean & Leaf, but she had talked about her new job, though so far she had only done an auto show and a convention. She was excited about the opportunity, both agreed, to travel to Korea. She liked travel a lot.

"If she had a good experience I was going to try to get the same job," Dawn, the pretty blonde, said.

"Honey, you said a few minutes ago that you thought she got in trouble with—and I couldn't hear that part—and took off, got in with bad company and died. Who were you talking about? Who did she get in trouble with?"

She exchanged a look with her friend, who shrugged.

"Just tell me; I'm interested, and it won't go any further, I promise."

Honey looked round the room, then bent forward. "I just don't trust Delaney Meadows. There's something wrong there, don't you think? Does he look like the kind of guy who'd start a modeling agency?" She sat back. "I *did* say I thought she took off, got mixed up in bad company and died. But . . . that's all."

Jaymie watched her for a moment, but she remained calm. "What is it about Delaney Meadows you don't trust?"

Honey frowned down at her cup. "He's just kind of . . . weird. I don't know what else to say. Just this feeling, like, he watches you with these cold eyes, like he's taking inventory."

"And he's around at all hours," Dawn added. "I've seen him sneaking in here at midnight."

"What were *you* doing here at midnight?" Honey asked, eyeing her friend.

The blond girl giggled. "I was meeting a friend on the sly. He had something I wanted." She widened her eyes and pinched her fingers together, taking a hit off an imaginary joint.

"And you saw Delaney?"

"Yeah. He was sneaking into the building."

"Sneaking?" Jaymie said. "He has a business here. He could have just remembered he needed to do something."

Dawn nodded. "I guess."

"Was Natalie dating anyone? Was she worried about anything, or upset? In any kind of trouble?"

"Well, actually . . ." Honey blinked once, calculating, it appeared to Jaymie. Then she nodded. "Okay, I'm not sure if this means anything, but I know one thing; Natalie was dating, for a while, at least, Shelby Fretter's brother, Travis. When she dumped him, he showed up here and said he wasn't leaving until she talked to him. Shelby had to come out and calm him down. Natalie wasn't even in the building that day—she only came in when she had to talk to Delaney—but Travis was really upset."

AS JAYMIE WALKED home, she considered what else Honey and Dawn had to say. Natalie, like Shelby, dated a lot, several different guys. She was a gorgeous girl and once told Dawn that she should consider doing what she did, date guys who could offer some financial reward for the time and trouble. Both girls knew about Meadows' dating site, but were divided on their opinion of it. Dawn thought it was harmless, but Honey was leery, saying it felt like a scam to her. She had logged on once, and when it said that girls could subscribe free but guys had to pay, she said it felt off.

Jaymie agreed with her. She was familiar with ladies' nights at clubs, when women got in free and men had to pay a cover charge. Club owners knew that guys were generally more likely to attend if there were large numbers of girls to hit on, and would buy more drinks for themselves and girls. But this felt kind of like the men were paying for introductions to girls, which was one step away from some very unsavory dealings.

The information about Travis was interesting: that he had been upset when Natalie stopped seeing him. Did Shelby suspect he was behind Natalie's disappearance? Is that what they were arguing about the night of Shelby's murder, that she was going to turn him in? She had to find a way to meet and talk to him, as well as to connect with Lori Wozny. That was going to be tricky, but she only had a very short time left before her self-imposed deadline, though she knew enough for her to make one decision right now, actually. Cody was not the killer. There was more than enough doubt to go around, and several viable suspects with more motive than he had. She wanted to know, both for Nan and for herself.

Once home, she made a to-do list and sat down at the kitchen table with the phone to work her way through part of it. She made some business calls for the picnic baskets as well as for Dickens Days. She touched base with Mabel and Dee, then called Valetta quickly.

"Can you answer me one question?" she asked. "The night of the murder, did you, from your angle, see Delaney Meadows that evening? At all?"

There was silence for a moment, then Valetta said, "I had to think for a second, but yes, I did see him. I'm trying to pin down what time." She was silent for a moment, then said, "It was probably around nine or so; I saw him scurrying off down the road."

"Scurrying?"

"Like a rat will do."

Jaymie chuckled. "Nine, you say . . . and scurrying."

"Do I sniff a mystery?"

"Just developing alternate theories. It's possible that he killed Shelby for reasons I'll explain at some point, and that was why he was scurrying. I'll have to work out the timing, but it sure does seem possible to me. Now . . . did you at any time see Travis Fretter alone?"

"I can't say that I did."

"Darn. Okay. Gotta go." Valetta was protesting that Jaymie couldn't leave her hanging like that as she clicked the off button on the phone.

She then settled down in the parlor and called Cody. He sounded groggy at first.

"I didn't sleep much in jail. Uh . . . thanks for getting me out."

"I didn't have anything to do with that. Chief Ledbetter and the DA decided there wasn't enough evidence to prosecute you. The only way to ensure that you don't end up back in trouble is to figure out who did this."

"I want the cops to find out who killed Shelby." His voice cracked as he said her name.

"Good. I have a lot of questions, Cody. How did you and Shelby meet?"

He shrugged. "A bar. How else do you meet girls?"

"Did you approach her or did she approach you?"

"Neither. I mean . . . a mutual friend introduced us."

"Who was the friend?" Jaymie asked.

"Her brother, Travis."

Interesting how Travis's name kept popping up. "How do you know him?"

"Just from playing pool at Shooters."

Easy enough to set up if it was not by chance. She wasn't sure why she was suspicious of Cody and Shelby's relationship, but it was odd that Shelby would go out with Cody when he was the son of a woman she despised. And it was even odder that she would *keep* going out with him when he apparently hit her. "Are you and Travis still friends?"

"We never were *really* friends. The guy's a punk."

"Did you know a girl he was dating, Natalie Roth?"

"I've heard her name; Shelby talked about her. But I never met her."

"You said to your mom that Shelby thought Nan was out to get her and her whole family."

"Yeah, she bitched about that a lot."

"But was there a single thing your mother's paper reported that wasn't true?"

He paused, then said, "I don't know. Shelby thought they couldn't catch a break, that's all, and that everything they did was reported, while other stuff wasn't."

"Did she ask you to get your mother to back off?"

"No. I just figured she didn't want to come between us."

Interesting that she never tried to get him to interfere on her family's behalf. What was the purpose of befriending him and dating him, if not to get Nan to stop her supposed vendetta against her family? "Do *you* think that your mom had a vendetta against Shelby and her family?"

"I don't know. I tried to defend Mom, but Shelby just wouldn't listen."

"Did you ever see her writing in a journal or diary?"

"A journal? She did have this book that she kept in her purse all the time, and she wrote in it. I figured it was just a date book, you know, so she wouldn't forget stuff."

So she kept it in her purse. Did the police have it, Jaymie wondered? She'd give a lot to know what was in it. "Was there anything suspicious, or odd, about her behavior? Anything you felt she was hiding or lying about?"

"Oh, yeah, *that's* what I wanted to talk to you about," he said, his voice clearer, more awake. He shifted like he was finally sitting up. He told her that he stayed at Shelby's apartment for a couple of weeks after Nan kicked him out. "I saw Shelby a couple of times haul this duffel bag out of her closet and root around. When I came close she kind of shielded it. I asked her what was in it, and she just said old clothes."

"But you thought she was lying?"

"I don't think it, I *know* she was. She would never let me stay home when she wasn't there . . . She said I should be out looking for a job anyway. But one day when she was out, I went back to the apartment and got the bag out of the closet. I opened it and it was full of stuff."

"But not old clothes, I'm assuming. What kind of stuff?"

"I only saw it for a minute because she came back in. I thought she was gone for the day but she'd just gone to the store for milk before work."

"And?" Jaymie asked impatiently.

"It had a stack of bills, like fives, tens, twenties; a lot of them. There were a couple of cell phones, those cheapie pay as you go. They were still in their packaging, you know? There were *some* clothes, like underwear and pants and T-shirts, and a thick stack of gift cards: Visa, Mastercard, Walmart, Walgreens and cell phone minutes."

Jaymie was silent for a moment. "Was she planning to leave town?" Though that did not seem like typical packing for a vacation or moving; it felt more like . . . well, it felt like a runaway's bag.

"Not that I know of. I mean, it's not like there was

anything keeping her, if she wanted to go, right? Why hide it? I asked her if she was going anywhere."

"What did she say?"

"She didn't answer."

She filed that thought away for future reference and pondering. "So is that all? You rooted through the bag, and then what?"

"Like I said, she caught me. I told her I was just looking for something of mine I lost, but she didn't believe me. She tried to act like she was cool, that she was just mad I was looking through her private stuff, but she took the duffel with her and stashed it elsewhere. I never saw it again and she kicked me out of the apartment two days later."

Jaymie had an uneasy feeling. She asked Cody a few more questions, her mind teeming with ideas and worries. Most important, she asked where he thought Shelby took the duffel bag. Possibly to a friend's or to some kind of storage place?

"The gym," he said promptly. "I'd bet on it. She wouldn't want to leave it with a friend. She was real suspicious of everyone, and she'd want access to it whenever. And I have the extra key."

❧ Twenty ❧

H E WOULDN'T TELL her how he got the gym locker key, and didn't have anything more to say. She told him to stay away from the gym and her locker, whatever he did. The last thing he needed was to look even more guilty. He couldn't go in there anyway, he said, because it was an all-female gym. He pled his innocence, repeated that he'd never do anything to hurt Shelby. He loved her, even if she didn't love him.

Jaymie was uneasy about the bag, but curious. And yet . . . it didn't feel right. Cody's refusal to tell her how he got the locker key sat in her gut like a lump of something tainted. Since he wasn't kicked out of her apartment until two days later, Jaymie assumed he had searched and found the extra key, because Shelby certainly would not have given it to him. The duffel bag was the murder victim's property and what was in it could have some bearing on the case, could even exonerate Cody! It would be worthless if she or anyone else tampered with it. Any DA or defense attorney worth his or her salt would argue that Jaymie could easily have put anything into the bag, so whatever was found in it would be useless as evidence.

But the other side of the argument was this: Cody had the key to her locker, and thus access to her duffel bag, despite his claim that the gym was for women only. Wasn't the bag useless as evidence anyway because he could have tampered with it at any point? In that case her looking into it wouldn't matter one way or the other.

It might just be time to talk to Chief Ledbetter about the case again, and all she had uncovered. For all she knew they already had this info, but Jaymie doubted it. First, she needed to get her ideas organized, and she needed to talk to Lori Wozny and Travis Fretter.

The phone rang just then.

It was Valetta again. "Are you up for anything this evening, even just a movie night . . . before the madness that is the last week before Christmas?" Valetta asked.

"Maybe. Starting tomorrow I'm crazy busy; Dickens Days, Queensville Historic Manor, working at the Emporium and then family. Grandma Leighton is coming to town for the first time in years. And then . . . there's Jakob."

"I'll understand if you'd rather spend this evening with Jakob, you know," Valetta said.

"No, they've got a school thing this evening. Jocie's gymnastics group is doing a tumbling routine during the winter pageant and the whole family will be there. Jakob asked me if I'd like to go, but I'm not ready for that, I don't think."

"Oh, I think *you're* ready, but you're not sure his family is ready."

"Maybe. I'm afraid to rush things with them. Look how it worked out with Daniel's mother! I do *not* want a repeat of that."

"I don't think that will happen with Jakob's family, but there's no rush, right? You've got time," Valetta agreed.

"What I need is someone dispassionate to help me hash out this stuff with Shelby. Would you be up to coming over for dinner? And talking about the case?"

"Done and done! I'll always come over if you're cooking."

"You might end up eating a ten-pound brick of sticky-sweet no-bake fruitcake," she joked. She had peeked at the so-called fruitcake and it didn't look too good.

"May as well glue it directly to my hips," Val joked.

"It wouldn't need glue," Jaymie replied.

She had an hour before Valetta was to come over, so she sat down and made notes for the fruitcake article, then took the loaf out of the fridge, where it had resided in foil-covered mystery since she made it. It was actually as heavy as *several* bricks. She peeled back the foil, and it was, as she had worried, sticky.

"Dang." She called her grandmother and fretted about the recipe.

"Jaymie, you have to follow the recipe exactly!" Grandma Leighton said, her tone warm with suppressed laughter. "I remember that cake, made it for the Christmas of . . . let me see . . . 1963? It was soon after Alan and Joy married. It was pretty darned good, if I'm remembering the right stuff, but when you first mix it up, it seems like it's going to be dry and crumbly. You have to trust the recipe and do exactly what it says. Just do it over again!"

"I don't have time!" Jaymie wailed.

"Yes you do. Just give it a try."

"Thanks for talking me off the ledge, Grandma," she said. "I'm looking forward to seeing you. Mrs. Stubbs is *so* excited that you'll be staying at the inn! She gets kind of lonely, and having you there to talk to will be nice."

"I don't know why we never thought of this before," she said. "I know what you're all worried about; that the stairs at the house will be too much for me and the bedrooms and only bathroom are upstairs. I know my limitations; I wouldn't be able to climb them. But the inn will be perfect. Maybe we can do that in the summer next year."

More relaxed and able to see the funny side of her fruit-cake fail, she cut some sticky pieces and photographed them anyway. She might feature them on her blog under "what not to do."

Valetta tapped on the back door as Jaymie was about to fold the failed fruitcake back into its foil tomb. Hoppy yipped once, while Denver slunk under the table. She opened the door and let her friend in. Valetta unwound her scarf and pulled off her boots, setting them on the mat by the back door as she stared at Jaymie's concoction.

"Don't ask," Jaymie said with a laugh, entombing the fruitcake and returning it to the depths of the fridge to languish and perhaps die.

"I won't. A rare moment for you, a failure?"

Jaymie explained and got her friend a cup of tea. "While I make dinner we're going to make up a list of suspects and figure this out."

"So you really don't think Cody Wainwright did it?"

Jaymie frowned and got out a frying pan, set it on the burner and turned it on with a poof of flame. She drizzled some olive oil in the pan. "I guess it's still possible, but I don't think so." She explained the timeline and why it didn't work. "That's why they released him. There's nothing to make the charges stick. The assistant police chief jumped the gun while Chief Ledbetter was out of town." She opened the fridge and peered into it. "Is corned beef hash okay?"

"Crack a couple of eggs on top and you've got me. Why are you unsure, then?"

"He's lied so many times. And he hit her. He says he lashed out when she called his mom names, but why should I believe him? And that's no excuse anyway, even if she called his mother names until the end of time."

"Hey, *I'm* certainly not going to defend him. But is lashing out at someone in anger once the same as methodically beating someone to death?"

"You may have a point." She got boiled potatoes, corned beef, onions and mushrooms out of the fridge and set them on the counter. "I know one thing I have to do before we even make a list." She turned the stove off and got the phone.

"Who are you calling?"

"Book club president." She got the president of her historical romance book club on the line. "This may seem strange," she said to her, "but I have a question to ask . . . actually, a two-part question. First, is the Lily who is in our book club Lily Meadows? I've never heard her full name. And second, was she at the meeting last Friday night?"

She listened intently, then asked a couple more questions. When she hung up, she turned the stove back on and diced the onions, tossing them in the sizzling pan. She turned back to slice mushrooms and cube potatoes. "So, Lily Meadows does not make it onto the list of suspects because she was indeed at the book club meeting, after which she stayed and chatted for another hour, long past the time of the beating. On to other suspects, including her husband, who you saw scurrying down the street at the right time!"

Jaymie went over all that she had learned, filling her friend in on everything so far. Valetta pulled her clipboard over to her, writing down the names as they discussed them in order.

Glenn Brennan. He was a jerk, yes, and had been nasty online concerning Shelby. He had also lied to Jaymie about where he was that evening. "He doesn't seem too bright. He told me he left his job the previous week, then said he was out of town on a work trip. By then he was too drunk to question further." He was certainly a contender, and she needed to find a way to talk to him again, though she wasn't sure how.

She said as much to Valetta, adding, "How can I find out where he was that evening?" The onions were translucent, so Jaymie dumped the sliced mushrooms into the sizzling pan, sautéed them, then added the diced potatoes and turned up the heat to get a nice brown crust on the bottom. She shredded some corned beef and added it to the frying pan.

Valetta thought for a moment, then said, "Didn't you say he belonged to that dating site that Delaney Meadows started? Would they have a chat forum or something for the members to connect? Maybe there's some info there."

"That is why I call you all the time; you have the best ideas! I'll do that later. I intended to look into that site anyway, but I'll be sure to check it out with him in mind. I'm still trying to find out if there's any connection between Shelby's death and Natalie's disappearance."

"Do you think the two are connected?"

"Part of me thinks they have to be, and another that there is no real reason to think they are. They knew each other, Travis Fretter was dating Natalie, and Clutch asked Shelby to look into her disappearance; that she was murdered just a short while later seems like it has to be connected."

"I think I heard a 'but' in there somewhere."

"But . . . I believe in the randomness of coincidence. Shelby certainly had other things going on in her life, including her toxic relationship with Cody. I wonder, too, was she looking into her boss's business, the one that had Natalie Roth about to fly off on some modeling job? And speaking of that . . . Delaney Meadows, his wife is out of the picture, but he sure isn't. Remember, I saw him arguing with Shelby that day after she was in the store. It did not look like a friendly relationship, and he was certainly evasive at his office."

"And we know that his wife was at the book club and he was in Queensville."

"That notation on his calendar about Dickens Days and SF . . . Did she meet Delaney and it led to something nasty? I'm still trying to figure out if they were having a relationship, or if it was purely business. Why were they at the Queensville Inn the night *before* she was murdered?"

"And in a room, no less, not even just at the restaurant. It's odd."

"It is. I don't get it." Jaymie continued to fry the onions, mushrooms, corned beef and potatoes until they were crispy and brown, then seasoned with a sea salt and freshly ground pepper medley. She made four wells in the hash with the back of a wooden spoon and broke eggs into the wells, putting a lid on the frying pan. Valetta had already gotten Corelle plates down from the cupboard and grabbed cutlery as Jaymie got out the milk carton.

"I think I need to talk to Delaney Meadows again; this time I'll be a little blunter, and more honest."

"You be careful," Valetta said, pouring milk into two vintage glass tumblers as Jaymie took up their dinner.

"I will. I think I'll track down Austin Calhoun again, too. The more I think of it, the more evasive he seems. I'm not sure he was telling me the truth about anything, particularly about why he was fired from Delaney's agency. In fact I know he wasn't telling the truth about that, but I'm not sure why he lied, except he's afraid, maybe?"

"Like Shelby's murder scared him?"

"Could be."

"What do you think about Travis Fretter?" Valetta asked, then took a long gulp of milk. She dabbed at her mouth with a paper napkin. "He is one person you know was there that evening, when she was killed."

"*And* he lied about the sequence of events, making it seem like he was with his mother the whole time, when he wasn't." She thought a moment. His name kept coming up. "He was the one who introduced Shelby to Cody, too, and he had also dated Natalie Roth. A lot of connections there." She told Valetta what she had thought about Shelby and Travis's argument, so swiftly followed by her death.

After dinner they washed and dried the dishes. As she hung up the damp dishcloths over the stove handle, Jaymie said, "On another subject, I think I need to follow my grandmother's advice about something," she said. "It's going to haunt me if I don't do that no-bake fruitcake right, but I need a bunch of stuff: vanilla wafers, gingersnaps, marshmallows. Do you feel like making a run to the grocery store in Wolverhampton with me?"

"I'm up for it if you are. Let's go. I'm ready."

Jaymie eyed her; for someone who had suggested a movie night she seemed awfully eager to go shopping. They took Jaymie's van, since Valetta had walked over, and Valetta griped all the way about how cold the van was, and how torturous the passenger seat. They parked, did their shopping in a nearly empty store and exited to the van. Jaymie started it up, let it run for a moment and backed out of the parking space.

Valetta said, "Do you mind making a side trip?"

Aha, and now the real reason Valetta hadn't minded venturing out into the cold night. "Not at all. Where to?"

Valetta glanced over at her, her face shadowy in the dim parking lot light. "Believe it or not, Eva is in that pageant at the same school as Jocie." She looked at her watch, pressing the button to make the dial light up. "I know her number is third, in just about fifteen minutes."

"If I show up there it'll look like I'm stalking Jakob!" Jaymie objected. "Especially after saying no to his invitation!"

"He won't even know. I just want to stand at the back and watch Eva so I can tell her I was there. I didn't think it was important to her that her old aunt was there, but when she found out this afternoon that I wasn't coming she sounded really bummed. I feel awful, and I'd like to be there. I was going to ask if you minded just peeking in on it. C'mon . . . what can it hurt?"

Reluctantly, Jaymie gave in and headed out of town to the side road the school was on. They parked in the lot and entered, moving down long hallways adorned with cutout snowflakes and snowmen, as well as bulletin boards detailing upcoming events in the New Year. The school was the one Jaymie had gone to, but Valetta and the others—Becca and Dee—had gone to an older school that had been sold and was now an office and light industrial space.

They made their way to the auditorium and snuck in the back. It was a big room that doubled as the gymnasium, with a small stage at one end. Tonight the lighting was low, and the floor, marked with borders and foul lines for basketball and other games, was full of rows of folding chairs, mostly taken. Someone was plunking away on the piano, playing some ubiquitous winter song, as a school ensemble sawed away on screechy violins and twittered on off-key recorders.

Valetta grabbed Jaymie's arm and hauled her to sit down in seats near the back. Eva's solo was next, and Jaymie was surprised by how sweet she sounded, singing a song about a snowman who fell in love with a snowlady, and how they got married and were together until they melted in spring. The message was that though nothing lasts forever, it was important to enjoy the good things life has to offer while they last, a surprisingly deep message for one so young.

"Sounds original. I wonder who wrote it?" Jaymie whispered, as the audience applauded.

Valetta grabbed the program that was lying on a chair in front of her and adjusted her glasses. "Eva said they had a volunteer who was helping with the pageant and she was writing all the songs. Let me see." She ran her finger down the page and stopped. She looked up at Jaymie. "Talk about your coincidences? Guess who the volunteer is who wrote the song?"

"I can't guess."

"Lily Meadows!"

"Austin said something about her volunteering at a lot of things!" The next act was announced, and it was the Fun Time Tumblers. That was Jocie's team! Jaymie watched the little girls and boys, aged five to eight, tumbling and dancing, moving confidently about the stage. She easily picked out

Jocie because of her short but sturdy stature. The little girl was so very confident, doing her tricks and then standing front and center for applause.

It was spellbinding. When Jaymie was a kid she was awkward and afraid to take up space in the world. That lasted through the teenage years and well into her twenties. It was lovely to see children of all different body types and abilities who were so sure of themselves, with radiant smiles and laughter.

Jaymie leaped to her feet and clapped, cheering enthusiastically, completely forgetting herself in the moment. And then she saw Jakob; he was standing, too, and turned to see who the other cheering nut was. When he saw her, he smiled, his grin huge and warm, like a warm hug from a distance. He bent over, spoke to someone beside him, then sidled out of his row and made his way down the aisle and toward her.

"Hey," he said, hugging her. "You came after all!"

She could feel the heat in her cheeks, and saw, with a side glance, how Valetta was watching with a grin on her face. Jaymie introduced them, Jakob taking Valetta's hands in his for his special kind of warm handshake. "We had to run to the grocery store in Wolverhampton," Jaymie explained. "Valetta wanted to stop in to see her niece, Eva, who sang just before Jocie's tumbling troupe came on."

A woman a couple of rows ahead turned and shushed them. Jakob took her arm. "Can we talk for a minute? Maybe out in the hall?"

"I'm going to find Brock," Valetta whispered. "I just want to say hi, and tell him how great Eva did." Valetta made her way down the aisle, scanning the audience for her brother.

"I don't want to take you away from your family," Jaymie said.

"It's okay. My mom is backstage already. She volunteers with the troupe to make costumes. It started because they couldn't find ones to fit Jocie properly, and my mother is a great sewer, so she now makes all of their costumes. It gives her an excuse to buy pretty fabric, she says." He took her arm and they retreated into the hallway. Once there, he took her in his arms and hugged her again. "It's so good to see you," he murmured into her ear. "And to hug you."

"Mmm, I agree."

They stood like that for a few long minutes, then he released her. "Do you want to meet my folks tonight?"

She felt her heart thud again. "I'm not prepared, Jakob. I'm kind of a mess; we just had dinner and then scooted out."

He looked disappointed, but nodded. "But soon, okay?"

"Soon," she agreed. "I just want to make a good impression."

"You couldn't *help* but make a good impression."

She smiled up into his warm brown eyes. "Jocie was so good! She has so much confidence and joy; you're doing wonderfully with her."

He nodded in satisfaction. "She needs to know she can do anything she wants: math, art, singing, dancing, writing."

"How do you negotiate it all? I mean, society telling you your little girl needs to be smart and pretty and successful. What if she just wants to be a princess?"

"Then she can be a princess."

Jaymie nodded. "That's good, that freedom. She can be a princess or an astronaut or—"

"No, not *or* . . . she can be a princess *and* an astronaut, a fashion model *and* a baseball player." He paused and smiled down at her. "I hope that one day, if I ever have a boy, I will teach him that he, too, can be a cowboy *and* a fashion model, a truck driver *and* a florist. I don't want my little girl limited by any imaginary lines in the sand. I don't think I'm saying that correctly, but . . ." He shrugged.

"You're saying it perfectly, Jakob," she said, touching his arm and looking up into his eyes.

Just then, a door down the hall swung open, hitting the wall behind it with an echoing thud. Lily Meadows stormed out, then stopped and furiously tapped a message into her phone.

Jaymie started away from Jakob. "That's Lily Meadows," she said under her breath, and explained that she was looking into Delaney Meadows' possible involvement in Shelby's death. "I just don't know what to think, whether he's involved or not. I wish I had a way to get into his office alone."

He chuckled and hugged her close. "You are a never ending source of wonderment," he said, then let go of her. "I'd better go back to my brothers," Jakob said, stroking her arm. "Can I see you one evening?"

"Let's talk tomorrow. I'd love to see you, but I'm doing the Dickens Days walk for the next few nights."

"I can meet you there!" he said, with a quick smile. "Gotta go. You be careful."

As he ducked back into the auditorium, and the sound of a guitar and warbling voices echoed out into the hall through the open door, Jaymie watched Lily. The slight woman gave up texting and hit a series of numbers. She paced, her arms folded over her bosom, the phone held up to her right ear.

Her neck and cheeks were red, and she seemed on the verge of tears. Jaymie started down the hall toward her as she talked to someone, then hit the hang-up button and threw the phone down the hall. It smacked against the wall and some plastic chipped off the case. It all skittered down the hallway with an echoing clatter.

"Lily!" Jaymie said, approaching her. Lily was indeed a tiny woman, as Mrs. Stubbs had said, tonight wearing a long skirt and blouse with a cardigan and floral infinity scarf. In book club she rarely spoke up, preferring to let the bigger personalities take over meetings and discussions. But when she did speak it was to make deeply felt observations. Books mattered to her; that was something she and Jaymie had in common. "Are you all right? Can I help?"

The woman turned, her eyes clouded with tears. She dashed them away with the sleeve of her cardigan and crossed her arms over her stomach. "Jaymie, what are you doing here?"

"I'm here to watch a friend's niece. What's up?"

"It's nothing."

"You don't throw a cell phone for nothing. Come over here. Sit down." Jaymie led the woman over and pushed her down on a bench in a pool of light outside the auditorium doors. She then retrieved the cell phone and the broken piece, brought it back and set it on the bench, then sat on the other side of Lily. "Tell me what's wrong," she said, her hand on the other woman's arm.

Lily broke down into tears and wept, covering her face with her hands. Jaymie let her sob, then got a tissue out of her purse and dampened it at one of the water fountains in the hallway. She brought it back and handed it to the woman without comment.

Lily took a deep shuddering breath, blotted her eyes, and said in a hopeless voice, "I think my marriage is over, that's all."

"Why do you think that?"

"Because Delaney is a jerk, that's why!" Her words caught on a sob. "You don't know my husband, but the guy is a class-A jerk, a cheating, lying, misogynistic *bastard*."

Jaymie wouldn't have pegged him as a woman hater, but who knew? "Are you better off without him, then?"

She took a deep shuddering sigh and shrugged. "Maybe. He's been acting so weird lately, shifty, whispering in the phone, spending hours on his laptop, which, by the way, he has changed all the passwords and codes on. Who does that unless they're hiding something?"

Jaymie decided not to ask how she knew about the changed passwords if she wasn't trying to snoop into her husband's private business. "Lily, I'm good friends with Mrs. Stubbs. She's worried about you. She told me you caught your husband with Shelby Fretter at the Queensville Inn the evening before she was murdered. You thought they were having an affair?"

Lily's head had snapped up. It was like a fawn at the water's edge when they sense danger. "I didn't *catch* him, I *saw* him."

Any moment the pageant would be over, the audience would stream out, and Lily would have duties to take care of. What did Jaymie need to know from this woman while she had her? "Did you have any reason at all to think that your husband was having an affair with Shelby Fretter?"

Responding to the direct questioning, Lily sat up straighter. "I know I said it, but Delaney just wasn't . . . I never thought he'd be the type to cheat. You know, he doesn't like sex very much. It's money he wants, and he's always trying to figure out some way to get it."

"Like how?"

She shrugged. "Some new business or venture that would pay off big-time."

Or some *crooked* venture. Jaymie wondered if his meeting with Shelby was simply business, or something else entirely. There were possibilities, including extortion on one side or the other. "Did you know Shelby?"

"Sure. She'd been to our house for dinner. At first I just thought she was a nice girl. But in her own way she seemed as ambitious as Delaney. I always thought they'd make a perfect pair, not a single human or affectionate thought between them, completely goal oriented."

"So if that's true, you never did feel that he was going to leave you for her?"

"I guess not," Lily said, her voice weary. "But something is up, I feel it in here." She struck herself in the chest, near her heart.

Just then the auditorium doors opened. There was a flood of noise, chatter and people, streaming into the hallway in a cheerful thunder. Someone sang a snatch of "Let It Snow," and someone else groaned; laughter followed.

"I gotta go and see the kids!" Lily said, jumping to her feet and grabbing the broken cell phone. "They've worked so hard. I'll see you at book club, Jaymie!" She sped away, down to another set of doors and through.

Jaymie caught sight of Valetta and hauled her away before

Jakob's family could catch up with them. She was not ready to meet his mother, especially, and she wasn't sure why. In minutes they were on their way back home. She dropped Valetta off at her cottage.

"You get some sleep, kiddo," Valetta said, looking up at her in the dome light of the van. "You seem kinda jumpy. And it's going to be a busy haul from here to Christmas."

Jaymie returned to her home and parked the van, retrieved her groceries from the back and headed up the flagged walk that bisected her backyard, but saw a figure hunched on the back step. She paused, until the figure looked up. It was Nan Goodenough!

"For heaven's sake, Nan, you must be freezing!" Jaymie said, surging forward again. "How long have you been here? What do you want?"

Her editor stood, hefting a bag under her arm. "I needed to talk to you, but not on the phone. I didn't want to talk until I saw you in person."

Jaymie eyed the duffel bag uneasily, but unlocked the back door. Hoppy charged out and swiftly retreated to a piddle spot in the corner of the yard. Denver blinked up at the light, then curled back up in his basket and tucked his face under his winter-thick tail, sighing deeply and retreating back into a catnap.

Nan plunked the duffel down on the trestle table and looked Jaymie's kitchen over with interest. She pulled off her ski parka and tossed it aside, rubbing her bare hands together then tucking them under her armpits. "It's freezing out there tonight."

"I'll make tea," Jaymie said, still eyeing the duffel. She knew what it was. And she couldn't have been more nervous about it if it had contained a nest of vipers.

"You do love all this stuff, huh?" Nan said, eyeing the vintage tins lined up on the cupboard tops among an antique weight scale, sets of bowls, vintage choppers and other utensils from the last century, and even some from the century before that.

"I do." She pulled out a chair and indicated it. "So, Nan, let's not beat around the bush. That is Shelby's duffel. Cody told you about it, and you retrieved it. Why? And why did you bring it here? Have you looked in it yet?"

Nan sat down and gave her a withering look. "Of *course* I looked into it. That's why I want you to hide it somewhere the cops can't find it. Bury it if you have to."

❊ Twenty-one ❊

WITH SHAKING HANDS Jaymie unzipped the duffel bag as Nan looked on. They both had a mug of tea, but Jaymie's stomach was doing flips and there was no way she'd be able to down any before she knew what had Nan in such a panic. The woman wouldn't say, she just wanted Jaymie to find out for herself.

Inside was a jumbled mess of clothes, mostly casual exercise wear along with panties and sports bras. An elastic band was tight around a stack of cards. Jaymie slipped it off and flipped through Walgreens, Walmart, Visa and MasterCard gift cards. There was cash, too, a lot. Jaymie riffled through the bills and estimated there was more than Cody had implied, easily ten thousand dollars or more. Maybe she had added money since he saw the bag. There were also the two so-called "burner" cell phones still in the packaging.

"She was planning to run for some reason," Jaymie mused.

"That stuff is not what's got me worried," Nan said. "Look harder."

She dug farther through the clothes and at the bottom was a small leather-bound journal. Inside was Shelby's name and the date September eleventh. Jaymie looked up.

Nan, her face set in a grim expression, said, "Read."

So Jaymie sat down and did, skimming through much and reading only occasional entries all the way through. When she was done all she said was, "*Gone Girl.*"

Nan nodded. "She was planning to disappear and make it look like Cody killed her. Why? What did he ever do to her?"

"Besides hitting her?" Jaymie said bluntly, closing the book and slapping it on the table. "I saw that Nan. He *did* hit her. Nothing she said to him could have excused that. But I'm not sure any of this is about him. This was aimed squarely at you and your newspaper and how you had targeted her family. Or at least how she perceived that you had targeted her family."

"Oh my God. Do you mean that?"

"Just wait." She thought for a long minute, tapping the leather cover with her fingernail. "So she wrote a malicious journal, saying that Cody was threatening her daily, had hit her repeatedly and was systematically cutting her off from friends. A lot of that can be disproved easily enough. He certainly was not cutting her off from anyone; in fact she kicked him out of her apartment and had complete freedom apart from him. I didn't know her, but the entries feel fake to me, clumsy . . . like she was having too much fun with it."

There was no real fear in the lines, not that Jaymie noticed. It felt like some of the first-time novels, self-published before they were ready, that she had read, by authors who badly needed an editor. She wrote that Cody had the heart of an evil beast, and that "blows from Cody's fist rained down on me like a monsoon," that he "hurt me so bad I wanted to crawl away into a hole like a frightened little bunny rabbit." Metaphors and similes were apparently a favorite technique, and she used them copiously.

Jaymie had Austin as a witness to Shelby's writing in the

journal, and the smile she had as she wrote the passages. But despite that, it was terribly true that Shelby Fretter's life had ended, as the diary forecasted, violently. That was why Nan wanted Jaymie to hide the duffel bag. She feared the impact of the journal on the police case against Cody.

But Jaymie also knew what Nan didn't; others attested that Shelby had spoken about being afraid of Cody, and that he had hurt her. Also, there were the emails from Shelby to Lynnsey claiming Cody hurt her, which she then contradicted in phone calls. What was going on? Something felt off to Jaymie about those reports, but the police wouldn't see it that way, especially not with the additional testimony of the journal to Cody's physical battering of Shelby. Though she figured it was impossible for him to have killed her if the cell phone supported his timeline, she couldn't be sure of that, and the journal could be viewed as a kind of "dying declaration," which was sometimes used in evidence at murder trials, from what Jaymie had read. Like a statement from beyond the grave, it spoke to her fear of a certain person, and since she had died in much the same manner as she forecast, it could certainly be used as supporting evidence against Cody.

"Why was she leaving town, Nan? I don't believe it was fear of Cody."

"It certainly was *not*! I get that he hit her once—I confronted him about that—but he swears to me that was it, and never again. And he *never* did any of the things she concocted in this piece of trash!" Nan said, putting one finger under the edge of the book and flipping it over in contempt.

"Okay, all right," Jaymie said sternly. "Nan, calm down. Why did you kick him out of the house? He told me that's why he went to stay with Shelby."

"We were fighting all the time. I told him he needed to get a grip and get a job. I was fed up, and told him to get out. I didn't expect him to take me seriously."

"Okay. So . . . Shelby seemed to be planning a life on the

run. Why? Shouldn't there be some reason why she wanted to leave town and disappear? I feel like the plot to finger Cody was just an added bonus in her mind. And if that's the case, maybe whatever she was running from was the real reason she was murdered." Jaymie frowned down into her full cup of tea. "Or not. She was looking into the disappearance of Natalie Roth and was somehow involved with Delaney Meadows. Whoever is responsible for Natalie's disappearance, and, I'm afraid, death, may be Shelby's murderer, too."

"Then who did that?"

"I don't know. I'm looking into it."

The editor sighed dramatically. "Then just hide this stuff until you figure it out."

"No!"

Nan jumped at Jaymie's forceful manner.

"I appreciate your worries," Jaymie said, staring right into the older woman's eyes. "But you asked me to look into this, and I'm doing it. Cody told me about this bag, and I was trying to decide what to do about it, but you retrieved it and brought it here. This puts me in an awkward position, and I'm not willing to go to jail for obstruction of justice."

"You and the chief are buddies. He's never going to arrest you."

"Don't bet on it," Jaymie said. "His lead detective on this case does not like me and thinks we're too close." She had made her decision and crossed the kitchen, grabbing the cordless phone. "I have to call Chief Ledbetter."

Nan left in a huff as Jaymie made the call. As bad as it made her feel to be at odds with her editor, she was doing the right thing. She hoped it didn't get Nan in trouble. She called Chief Ledbetter at home and he heard her out, grunted once, and said he was on his way. She wasn't surprised when he showed up with Bernie Jenkins—her friend but also an ambitious officer on the police force—as his driver and note taker.

The chief settled at her kitchen table. She told him that Nan brought her the duffel bag and asked her what to do about it. He opened and laid everything out as Jaymie turned on the overhead light and shooed Hoppy away. Bernie catalogued the items and cash as he examined the bag. He shoved his glasses down on his nose, peered at what appeared to be some hand stitching in the dark lining, and tugged on a loose end. As she watched he unraveled the thread and reached in. And pulled out tickets.

She gasped, as did Bernie.

"Where are they to?" Jaymie asked.

The chief shook his head. "Sorry, part of an ongoing investigation."

"You wouldn't even *have* this bag if I hadn't called you!"

He grinned and stared at her over his glasses. "I guess it doesn't matter if you know, but don't let it get around. They're bus tickets to Clearwater."

"Clearwater, Florida? In the US!" Jaymie exclaimed. "Wait . . . something just clicked." She fetched her purse, dug in it and took out the piece of paper she had stolen from Shelby's desk. She scanned it, then handed it to the chief. "This was in Shelby's desk at the employment agency." Sheepishly she explained what she was doing there and how she happened to look in Shelby's desk. "I guess Detective Vestry overlooked it. It's pretty cryptic, and at first glance not important. I wasn't even sure what it was, but I get it now. This is from a phone call she made, or online searching; it's a rough schedule of buses to Clearwater, where they stop, and what times of day they run. But why Clearwater? Why not fly to the Bahamas or . . . I don't know."

"Tougher to book plane tickets out of the country. Easier to trace, too," Bernie said. "She may have been planning to go somewhere else from there, though."

The chief nodded.

"But why was she planning her disappearance? That's what I haven't figured out yet," Jaymie said.

"So this duffel was hidden in her gym locker," Bernie said. "I'm a member of that same gym."

That wasn't surprising, since it was the only women's gym in the vicinity. Heidi was a member, too, and both kept trying to get Jaymie to join. But she preferred walking Hoppy as exercise. "Lily Meadows is a member, too," Jaymie said, remembering what Austin told her. "Apparently she takes the spin class?" She described Lily to Bernie.

"I think I've seen her there, and Shelby, too. It seems to me . . ." Her dark eyes went blank for a moment, and Chief Ledbetter watched her with interest.

"Whenever she gets that look," he said to Jaymie, "I know she's going to come up with something." He was a staunch defender of Bernie's bid to make her way to detective someday, and was, in essence, mentoring her.

Bernie nodded. "It took me a minute to make sure I was remembering it right, but I saw Lily and Shelby talking once, and it wasn't friendly. Lily said something to her, something mean, and then threatened her."

"What did she say?" Jaymie asked.

She thought for a moment. "It was a while ago now. If I remember it right, Lily said something like, 'I don't know what you and my husband have cooked up, but if you get him in hot water I'll make sure you go down.'"

"And you didn't think to tell us that?" Chief Ledbetter said, an expression of disappointment on his pouchy face.

"We had a suspect under arrest in the murder," Bernie said, frowning across the table at her boss. "How could an extraneous conversation overheard between the victim and some random tiny little woman who uses two-pound weights in the gym mean anything?" Her cheeks flushed a darker tint and she ducked her head. "Besides, I'd forgotten about it until now. That was almost two months ago."

"I know for sure Lily Meadows didn't do this," Jaymie said, and told them about the book club meeting that Friday night. She then told them about meeting Lily earlier that evening, and what the woman said. "I find it interesting that she said she knew Delaney and Shelby were up to something. She's definitely worried about her husband."

Bernie and the chief exchanged looks, but said nothing. Jaymie knew from experience that they could be looking into any number of things that she would never know about until the end. They left, taking the bag with them. Jaymie had made it clear that the key to the locker was in Cody's possession in the editor's home, so *Nan* didn't do anything wrong, though Jaymie didn't know how he got his girlfriend's gym locker key.

It was late. Jaymie got ready for bed in a fog, all the information she had received jumbled like a trash heap of clues. And like some trash heaps, she had a feeling there was a valuable piece of information there if she could just search through the junk and find it.

But there were so many loose threads.

Why did Travis Fretter lie about being with his Mom the whole time that evening, and where was he when he wasn't with her?

Why did Glenn Brennan lie about being away on a work trip that same evening?

Where was Delaney Meadows scurrying to or away from that night?

Were Natalie Roth's disappearance and probable death tied to Shelby Fretter's murder? What did Shelby know about it?

Curled up with Hoppy and Denver, she first leafed through the file of information on Delaney Meadows that Nan had printed off for her. She just hadn't had time until now, and wondered if she'd missed something. First were the usual congratulatory "new business" stories, and employment figures. But then there were some questioning letters to the editor. One was a lengthy question about Meadows Employment Agency and its connection with DM Models. There was an odd veiled reference to "luring" young women in to work for them.

The author wished to remain anonymous, but also wanted

to hear from any young women who had interviewed with or worked for DM Models, and asked that responses be sent to a post office box address. Jaymie, familiar with Shelby's writing style from perusing the journal, thought she detected the same tone and even similar wording in the letter. That made sense, if Shelby was beginning to suspect her boss in Natalie's disappearance and thought it was connected somehow to the modeling agency.

From there Jaymie got her laptop and went to the dating site Delaney Meadows admitted to starting. The only way to sign up was to create a profile. The whole process felt weird, not because there was anything wrong with dating sites or meeting someone online, but because there was a distinctly odd feel to this one. The interface was sophisticated looking enough, but with the men paying and women not, and wording that implied that the more attractive the woman was, the more likely she was to hook up with a quality man on the site, it was off-putting, to say the least. But she was not there to meet someone, she was there for information.

So she built a bare-bones profile using a fake name, lying about her interests and uploading a free-use photo of an attractive redhead she found on a stock-photo website. The last thing she needed was for someone she knew locally to see her picture on the site. "Okay, Lizzie Bennet," she said aloud, referring to her fake namesake, "let's see what you find." She started looking through members. Since she had never been on a site like this before, she was just feeling her way around at first.

She easily found Glenn Brennan's profile, and the amount of puffery was astounding. She bookmarked his page, then moved on. There were forums, a variety of them. Some were for general chat on different dating topics, while others were shout-outs and advice, or seeking the same, but one topic interested her right away. The topic was "Creeps." There was a hard and fast rule that names could not be mentioned on the forum, but right away she recognized someone just by description.

One girl complained about a guy she called TDL; it took Jaymie a while to find out that stood for The Drug Lord. He was a jerk, she said, who took her out once and expected her to put out. Another young woman chimed in that she had the same experience with a guy who claimed he was a pharmaceutical salesman. "Aha!" Jaymie said. "Sounds like our friend Glenn." Hoppy, fascinated by Jaymie talking out loud, had wriggled his way up to having his front paw on her knee, watching her face intently.

The forum complaints went back months. If it was indeed Glenn—and Jaymie believed it was—he was a very busy dater, with a similar method of operation every time. Lavish spending, over-the-top gifts of roses and champagne, then a veiled reference to spending the night together . . . all on the first date. By the end of the date his hints had turned to demands. A rejection brought insults that questioned a girl's character and motives for dating him.

The kindest comments called him a loser and jerk. The cruelest suggested his ancestry was more closely connected to the common simian origin than most. Not one hinted at any physical altercation with him.

From there she went back to the social network sites where she had found comments that led her to Austin Calhoun. He claimed he truly loved Shelby, that they were besties, creatures of a like mind. However, as she reread his comments more closely, she realized that some gave hints that when he left Delaney Meadows' employ, it was because of some problem that originated with Shelby. She had missed that last time, but now understood, from the receptionist at the employment agency, that Shelby had become angry when he had hinted she and Delaney were having an affair.

Then Austin made a few snarky comments about Delaney, along with the hints she had noted before about Shelby being into something dangerous. In his conversation with Jaymie at the office building he had brushed off those online hints as himself dramatizing, but was he really, or was he just reluctant to confess what he knew or surmised? Austin Calhoun was definitely worth another interview, one that wouldn't be interrupted by work. She also made a note to call Heidi in the morning, to touch base about anything else she might know about Shelby and Glenn Brennan's relationship.

For the first time she wondered about all the money in Shelby's bag. Where did it come from? That was a *lot* of money, and Jaymie knew from experience how hard it was to save when there was a car to pay for, health insurance and in Shelby's case probably, an apartment, nice clothes, shoes. How did she get together that much money?

Hoppy whined, and she put out one hand to scruff behind his ears. The journal Shelby wrote bothered Jaymie a great deal. While the premise of the novel and movie *Gone Girl* was evidently behind her plan, her journal writing was spitefully clownish. Was it mere ineptness, or just that she didn't intend to be gone forever? Perhaps she had her revenge on Nan planned as a few weeks or months of Cody uncomfortably eyed as responsible for her disappearance before she returned with some explanation. Her acquaintance with Shelby was too superficial for her to know. She needed to talk to those who did know her, including Lori and Travis. Was Jaymie right when she imagined the journal and its implication of abuse by Cody was part of a plot to destroy, or at the very least discomfit him, and therefore his mother?

That would be one of her tasks for the next morning. She shut off her laptop and turned out the light. It was going to be a sleepless night. She had a nagging worry that Shelby's plan to disappear for a while may have led to her demise as someone got wise to it and decided to use it in their own plot to murder her. It was a leap, maybe, to think that, but it fit all of the facts, and explained a lot. And if she didn't do something about it, someone could just get away with murder.

❧ Twenty-two ❧

EVEN AFTER ALL she had uncovered the night before looking through the Internet chat rooms and other forums, Jaymie was still confused. If her supposition was right, and whoever killed Shelby was aware of her toxic relationship with Cody, then maybe they were also aware of her plan to leave town and finger Cody as her "murderer." Their altercations had occasionally been public, as she had witnessed herself. But Shelby's plans? Who knew about that? If Jaymie was right, that inside knowledge could be the one thing that pointed to who did it.

Jaymie was fairly sure that Shelby didn't ultimately intend for Cody to be convicted of any crime. She may have meant him to have an uncomfortable few weeks or months after her disappearance. After a time she likely planned to resurface, saying she was just on vacation, or taking a break, or even that she had to get away because she was afraid of him. All to avenge the perceived persecution of her family by the newspaper.

Did Lori Wozny know about Shelby's plot? Jaymie thought that she must have. What woman would disappear without telling her mother? Jaymie wanted to ask her, but wasn't sure how to go about it without harassing someone who was in a great deal of pain. This was delicate ground with a genuinely grieving mother.

Even given that, it didn't explain who took Shelby's plan and ran with it, if that was the case, killing her in such a way that Cody Wainwright was fingered as the assailant. That would require knowledge of Shelby's plan to implicate Cody in her disappearance, knowing she was going to be in Queensville that night, and that Cody was, too. If that was true it made Travis a logical suspect. But according to the note in his planner Delaney Meadows knew where Shelby would be, too, and since she wrote in her journal a lot at work, he could easily have had a look at it if she left it lying around her desk. Maybe he planned to have it discovered as a part of the plot to finger Cody, but Shelby didn't leave it in her desk. Would Delaney know Cody would be in town? Or did he care?

It was confusing and so far, just speculation. Was Shelby Fretter the chatty sort who regularly confided in girlfriends? Was she closemouthed? Or did she share her plans, but only with family? Whatever theory she came up with that excluded Cody still had to take into account that poisonous relationship. As annoyed as she was with Nan for dragging the duffel to her place the night before, Jaymie knew it had garnered her crucial information. She never would have seen the diary if the editor hadn't done that; Jaymie intended to just tell the police about the bag. They would have seized it, and the contents would have remained a secret. Having read them, she could tell that the journal entries were as phony as a three-dollar bill, as her grandmother would say.

Christmas Eve was in one week. There was much to do, but while she had been running around investigating, her normal life had fallen into disrepair. The house looked a little shabby, the animals were beginning to look at her with those mournful "you don't love me anymore" glances, and she still had wrapping and baking to do. Fortunately she at least had all her Christmas shopping done, and Becca and her mother were taking care of the plans for their Queensville reunion. The women in her family were planners as well as doers, thank goodness. But Jaymie did need to go out to the Queensville Historic Manor and check in on her kitchen, and see if any cleaning needed to be done. She had been the one to suggest they take the load off Lori while she mourned her daughter's tragic passing, and yet she hadn't been keeping up with her end of the bargain. So after walking Hoppy and feeding him and Denver, she got into the van and headed out to the manor.

She shed her boots and coat at the door and padded through the house in her sock feet. There was the usual bustle of heritage committee people there. Mabel Bloombury was in the dining room futzing around with her vintage china display yet again. Becca had loaned them so much that she had some stored in the sideboard and was taking out a green transferware tureen to center on the table. Jaymie headed back to her domain. To her surprise, she found Lori Wozny on her hands and knees in the kitchen, scrubbing the floor. She stood for a moment, her stomach twisting in concern: How to approach her?

But Jaymie's usual manner was to just say what was in her heart. "Lori, hi." The woman turned and looked up at her. Her face had the ravaged look of someone in excruciating pain. Jaymie sank down onto the floor by her. "I'm so sorry about Shelby. I just can't imagine what you're going through. You know you don't need to be here, unless you want to be. We'll take care of it until you feel better."

Her mouth worked and a tear leaked from the outer corner of her right eye. She swiped it away with her arm and shook her head. "If I don't get out of the house I'll go effing crazy. I mean it; sometime I feel like I'm going to crawl right out of my skin, then other times I want to hit something. Or someone. Like that ass-wipe son of your precious editor. I see they've let him off. He's going to get away with it."

Ah, the opening she had been half hoping for and half dreading. Carefully avoiding the topic of Cody, Jaymie said, "I wish I had been able to help Shelby that night. She was still alive when I found her."

"Did she say anything?" Lori asked, turning and sitting on the floor to face Jaymie.

It was dreadful to kill that hope in her eyes. "No, I'm sorry. She was unconscious."

"So at least she wasn't in any pain," she said hollowly. She sat cross-legged on the damp tile, her skinny jeans showing holes at the knees that were more fashion statement than wear and tear, Jaymie surmised.

"I wish I had known her. I've met a few people who did in the last few days. Sounds like she was quite the girl," Jaymie said. "Her brother must be horribly broken up."

Lori shook her head slightly, then said, "Sure. Of course."

Was she mistaken, or was there a flash of uncertainty on her face, along with the negative shake of her head? "He was with you both that night, right? I think I saw you all together. I hope he was there to help you when you found out?"

"He was home. Or at least that's where I took him. He should have stuck with her! He never should have let her out of his sight. Then that piece of crap couldn't have gotten his hands on her!"

"I understood she was meeting someone there that night," Jaymie said. "Did she tell you that? I mean, not that she was meeting Cody, but someone else?"

It was as if Lori froze in place, she became so still. But far from blasting Jaymie, as she had half expected, the grieving mother muttered, "She said she was meeting up with someone, that she had some business to take care of. I didn't think anything of it, but . . . yeah, she did say that."

"Did she ditch Travis then? Is that what he said?"

"I guess," she said, pulling off her rubber gloves and tugging at a ragged fingernail.

Shelby had parted from her mother and walked on with her brother, which meant that Travis may have seen who she met up with. But in that case, he would presumably have told the police. Not that Jaymie knew everything the police had learned.

"Lori, I know you know Pam Driscoll. She's actually my next-door neighbor and friend."

Lori eyed her, now chewing on the ragged fingernail.

"Pam said you told her that you got separated from your son and daughter, and when you caught up with Travis next he was alone. He told you that Shelby had gone off with Cody, but the police know that at that time Cody was still at the Christmas tree farm working. That's why they released him."

Lori's expression was cold, and she had stopped working on the ragged nail.

"Pam said you found Shelby after that but that she had something she wanted to do, so you gave your son a lift home, then came back to meet up with her. But . . . but you never saw her again."

"I . . . That's not quite . . . I think Pam got it a little wrong." She resumed work on the nail again, tore it off and picked it out of her teeth, depositing it in the pail of water with a flick. "Shelby did say she was meeting someone. I don't care what anyone says, that was Cody. Or maybe he was stalking her and got her alone."

"But *did* you see her again, after you took Travis home?"

She shook her head. "I never saw her again."

"What time was that?"

She shrugged. "I don't know . . . around nine, I think."

"And you never saw Cody."

"Travis did."

He said, Jaymie thought. She was stubbornly clinging to her son's assertion, but it just couldn't be true. Nobody else saw Shelby and Cody together, and the story had changed, subtly, the order of things, the timing, when they parted from each other. It was still possible that Travis himself had had a disagreement with his sister, beat her to death, and that was why he lied at first that he was with his mom the whole time. "Do you know who she was meeting? Was it business, or personal?"

Lori narrowed her eyes and scrambled to her feet, beginning to pack up her cleaning supplies. She tossed the damp rubber gloves and sponge in a nearby empty bucket. "I don't know why you're asking these kinds of questions and I don't know who she was meeting. Maybe it was that jerk who killed her."

"But what if he didn't do it?" Jaymie got up, too, and touched Lori's bare arm. "Lori, think about it for just a moment; what if it *wasn't* Cody Wainwright who killed her?"

The woman froze again. There was a struggle indicated by her expression. Hatred toward and suspicion of Cody was warring with a dawning fear that Jaymie's words held some truth. "But he *did* do it. The police arrested him." Her tone held less conviction.

"They've since released him."

"You're just trying to get him off the hook for that editor woman, your boss!"

"Lori, that's not true," Jaymie said, urgent to convince the woman of her sincerity. "I *am* asking around, looking into it. But from my heart believe this; if it is true that Cody Wainwright killed Shelby, I want him to pay. I *loathe* those who kill. They deprive an innocent person of the awesomeness of life and deserve whatever they get from our legal system." She took a deep shaky breath. "But I've seen people persecuted wrongly, too. It matters to me that the right person is caught, and it should matter to you, too."

"What do you want from me?" The words were resentful, but she seemed almost curious.

"I'm trying to find out what *else* was going on in Shelby's life." This was the dicey part . . . *Tiptoe, Jaymie, tiptoe,* she thought. "Was she planning any major moves, or did she have any thoughts of leaving town in the near future?"

"Why do you ask that?" she said, her tone wary, her eyes squinted, her mouth drawn, purse-string wrinkles seaming it.

Jaymie considered just telling the truth about the duffel bag, but decided against it. "There were indications that she was planning to take off, maybe to Florida. Did you know anything about that?"

She was silent. That answered Jaymie's question more certainly than any words.

Finally, Lori cautiously said, "I have a sister down in Florida. Shelby thought she might hang out there for a while."

The ticket to Clearwater! So, it was probably *not* a permanent move, just part of her plot to punish Nan for a time by incriminating Cody. "Why leave her friends and family? And a great job, by all accounts, one she was good at!"

She snorted, suddenly energized. "Great job? With that scam artist Delaney Meadows? You mark my words," she said, shaking her finger in Jaymie's face. "He's the one who'll be leaving Queensville, any day now, before folks catch up with him. Oh, I know *lots* about him; Shelby told me everything. He tried to give her money to shut her up. Hah!"

Money! Was that the answer to the money in her duffel? "What did she tell you?"

Lori shook her head and said, "Never mind. I have to go."

"What was Meadows hiding? Lori, wait—"

The woman put up one hand, palm facing Jaymie. "No, you know what? You don't have a clue about Shelby. No one does! She was smart. She was a little crazy, but she was . . . she was a good daughter!" She started to sob, grabbed the full bucket, which sloshed water on the floor, and stomped out of the room.

Jaymie was about to go after her, but Lori shouted as she left, "Just leave me alone!"

That was unmistakably her cue to stop harassing the poor

woman. Jaymie got out a towel from under the cupboard and mopped up the spilled water. So Lori knew Shelby was planning to take off. What was more interesting, though, was what Lori said about Delaney Meadows. She'd give a lot to know what Shelby told her mother, and what Delany was hiding from the world.

She had intended to call Heidi and ask her about Glenn Brennan and Shelby. Too bad she hadn't done that right away in the morning, but Heidi didn't get up that early, so she never called before ten. Which it was now. She moved out the kitchen door and sat down on the stoop, huddling in her coat as she dialed her friend and waited. When Heidi answered they went through the usual salutations, then Jaymie got down to business.

"Heidi, you and Joel went out with Glenn and Shelby, right?"

"Longest evening of my life. Shelby didn't like me at all."

"You said she appeared bored and didn't seem to want to be there. So what was your impression of why Shelby was out with him?"

"Beats me. They hardly said two words to each other. When they did it was just her pressuring him to meet her alone for a coffee the next day, like she had something to talk to him about, but not in front of us."

"I don't understand why she was out with him. This was an attractive girl who could have done better." Unless . . . Did she have some reason to think that he'd gone out with Natalie Roth at some point? Was he a suspect in the girl's disappearance? That was something to consider.

"I don't know why she was out with him. *I'd* never date him. I mean, Joel can be impossible, but Glenn is a swine!"

"You said he was hitting on you, right?"

"He did while Shelby and Joel were both away from the table. After that he kept calling the house, like he was looking for Joel, you know. But then he'd ask what I was doing, and did I want to go out for coffee."

"How did you get rid of him?"

"I told him to leave me alone or I'd tell Joel."

"Simple enough."

"I've been told I'm not very subtle."

"And why should you be?" In the last moments of the conversation Jaymie had noticed a familiar car pull up the drive. A young man got out, slouched against the far side and lit a cigarette as he stared off over the fields.

Travis Fretter. Everything she knew and had heard rushed in on her. It was Travis and *only* Travis who claimed to have seen Shelby and Cody together, arguing, the night of her murder. Cody said that wasn't true, though he'd lied before, many times. But Travis had lied, too, saying he was with his mother the whole time when Jaymie knew he had been apart from her for at least half an hour. According to what Lori had told Pam, the siblings went off together, but got separated. When Lori found her son, he said Shelby had gone off alone, but Lori caught up with Shelby, who told her mom she had something she needed to do. A lot hinged on that tale; if Lori saw Shelby alive, and *then* gave her son a ride home, it virtually exonerated Travis, but the story kept shifting, like a sand bar in a storm on the lake.

Why was the simple truth always layered under blankets of conflicting stories? It must drive the police mad.

"I gotta go, Heidi. I'll talk to you later." She put her phone in her pocket and stood, took a deep breath and approached the car. "Travis?" she said. "Travis Fretter?"

He turned and eyed her. "Yeah?" A puff of smoke came out with the single word.

She eyed the smoke in his hand; it was not a cigarette, and the unmistakable whiff of pot drifted on the frigid breeze. "I'm Jaymie. I knew your sister. I'm so sorry about what happened. You must be devastated."

He nodded and took another drag, holding it in his lungs, then letting the smoke slip out of his mouth and into the frosty air.

"I'm actually the one who found her that night," Jaymie said, hoping to see a crack in the tough-guy veneer. "It was terrible."

He nodded, and Jaymie started to get angry. What was wrong with a guy who couldn't express even the simplest of emotions regarding his sister's murder? "I saw you two together that evening, and it looked like you were having a violent quarrel," she said, needling him. "You must not have gotten along."

He took a long drag from his joint, then carefully stubbed it against his boot heel and stowed it in a small metal box, which he slipped in his coat pocket. "What do *you* know?" he said, the inhaled smoke drifting out with his words.

"I know you lied to police and told them you saw Cody and Shelby together. I'm not sure why, unless . . ." She paused for dramatic effect. She was going to be intolerably rude, but she was sure he was lying, and somehow he needed to be confronted. He was eyeing her uneasily. "Unless you were just intent on nailing Cody Wainwright. I'll bet that's it, right? It all goes back to your family's vendetta against Cody's family." She paused, but could see he was getting more uneasy. It was interesting that he didn't jump right in and defend himself, though.

Feigning concern, she watched him and said, "Cody never met up with Shelby that evening; I know that for a fact. As soon as you're in court as a witness, saying you saw them together, they're going to question you every which way. Perjury—lying to the court after being sworn in as a witness—is a federal offense. You could get ten years."

"I didn't swear to it," he said, shifting uneasily. He shook his head and turned away, moving toward the house.

Jaymie watched him. He was clearly tense and wanted to get away. "I know you must be upset about Shelby's death. Do you have any idea who did it? Was she mixed up in anything shady to do with her boss?"

He whirled. "Why are you asking me all these questions?"

"Travis, whoever did this stole Shelby's future, her *every-thing*: marriage, children, love. Life. And the killer stole from you, too, and your children. They'll never know their smart, fierce, beautiful Aunt Shelby. Even if you didn't get along with her a hundred percent of the time, I know you loved her."

For the first time he looked conflicted. "When we were kids we got along all right, not great, but just like any other brother and sister. But lately . . . she was so uptight. I couldn't even make a joke without her going off on me. That's what happened that evening, you know, why we were arguing. I was teasing her about her boss and she just snapped."

"What did you say?"

He frowned down at the uneven ground and scuffed a frozen rut in the mud with his boot. "I knew she was looking into why Natalie disappeared. I said maybe Delaney had her stashed somewhere, like he was keeping babes all over the place, and she'd be next."

Interesting that that made Shelby angry. Did Delaney have something to do with Natalie disappearing after all? "I know you dated Natalie."

He shrugged. "Just a couple of times. She dumped me."

"And I know that you introduced your sister to Cody Wainwright. Did she ask you to do that?"

"Sure. I knew him, she said she wanted to meet him, so I set it up."

"Why did she want to meet him?"

He looked at her and shook his head. "Nuh-uh. I'm not going to . . . I don't know. It was none of my business."

"You knew about her plan, I'll bet. You knew she was going to take off and get Cody blamed for her disappearance, all to upset Nan Goodenough, didn't you?"

He shook his head, but didn't speak, his eyes wide.

Just then Lori came out the kitchen door, slamming it behind her. "Don't say a word to her! She's working for that Nan woman!"

"That's how this started," Jaymie admitted, turning back to watch the woman approach. "But I told you the truth, Lori; all I want is for the guilty one, the one who murdered Shelby, to pay. That's all I care about."

She expected the bereaved mother to get in the car with her son and drive away, but she stopped dead. "Have you found anything out? I want to know."

Jaymie felt her heart thud; Lori was actually listening! "I've found out a lot."

"Like what? What have you learned? About who?"

Shaking her head, Jaymie said, "That's not how this works; I can't just tell you everything I know. I don't like Cody Wainwright. I saw him hit Shelby, and I don't condone that. But I do *not* believe he killed your daughter. Look, Lori, I know she was planning on pinning him with her disappearance. Maybe it seemed like a trick or a prank to her. But I believe that someone used their intimate knowledge of her intention to finger Cody so they could get away with her murder."

Lori's eyes filled with tears. She hugged her purse to her chest. "I *told* her not to do it, told her it was stupid. But she was smart, and tough, and she hated how Nan Goodenough always managed to make it seem like we were dirt."

Jaymie held her tongue. It wasn't up to her to get into that, to defend Nan. "Someone knew all that and used it. I'd be mad, if I were you. I'd be furious."

"I'll think about all this," Lori said, her voice full of doubt and trepidation. "I'll think about it and call you if I decide to talk to you." She had clung to her hatred of Cody and her suspicion of him for so long, letting go was proving to be a feat.

Jaymie had done all she could. As the mother and son got in the car and drove away, she muttered, "I hope you decide you can trust me."

She went back in, told Mabel that she'd be back to do her

kitchen part later then left. She stopped off at home, walked Hoppy, answered an email, made a phone call then headed to the call center, intent on finding out whatever it was that Shelby felt Delaney Meadows was up to and what she may even have blackmailed him over. To do that Jaymie needed to talk to Austin Calhoun, as well as Honey and Dawn, and she needed to stop worrying about stepping on toes. This was getting critical.

The phone rang just as she was getting her coat and purse.

"Is this Jaymie Leighton?"

"This is she." It took Jaymie a moment, but she recognized the voice. "Is that Glenn? Glenn Brennan?"

"Yeah. I'm glad I got you. Uh . . . I wanted to apologize for the other night." He sounded sheepish. "I don't usually get drunk like that but this whole thing has upset me way more than I let on. Can we get together? I need to talk about it to someone."

"About Shelby?"

"Yeah."

Jaymie paused. "I don't have time today. I'm pretty busy."

"Are you sure? I'll meet you anywhere you say."

"I'm running around all day and this afternoon I'm volunteering at the Queensville Historic Manor, but I'm going to be working at the Dickens Days festival this evening."

"That goes from dinner 'til about ten, right?"

"Pretty much. Did you have something specific you wanted to talk about?"

"Actually, yes. Shelby told me some stuff."

"Have you told the police?"

He was silent for a moment, then said, "It's about her family. I just . . . I don't want to get them in trouble if it's nothing. I was hoping you could tell me what to do."

"Can't you just tell me on the phone?"

"I would like to explain in person."

Jaymie was torn; on the one hand she wanted to find out

what he had to say, but she was intent on checking out other things she could only do during the day. "Okay. I'll be there this evening. We can talk then."

She walked through the downtown of Queensville, just one street with the Queensville Emporium at the top and Jewel's Junk and the Cottage Shoppe along it, and the Knit Knack Shack as the last shop. Soon Becca and Kevin's new venture would be open across from those businesses, and there was a rumble among those in the know that there might be a new bakery café opening in the now-vacant cottage just on the other side of it. Jaymie stopped at Becca's new shop and looked through the door, where the plasterers were smoothing the walls, preparing for paint and wallpaper as a radio blasted Christmas music.

But it was late December; no one was working that hard. Everything in the business world seemed to shift gears as Christmas approached. There was still a week to go before the big day, but for some folks no more real work would get done between then and Christmas Eve, when the whole town would shut down for at least one day. Jaymie continued on, wending her way through her beloved town until she got to the Belcker Building. She entered the glass foyer, then made her way down to the Bean & Leaf. It was time enough for an early lunch. She was hoping that Austin and the two young women would also use it for their lunch dining.

She got a cup of consommé and half a smoked turkey and brie grilled sandwich, with a mug of tea. It wasn't long before her wishes were answered. Austin came in with his lunch bag and a fashion magazine. He got a coffee from the lunch counter and turned, looking around for a free table. She waved, and he hesitated but then joined her, sliding into the metal and plastic chair opposite her.

"I was hoping I'd see you here," Jaymie said.

"Oh?" He took out a plastic tub of carrot and celery sticks, while he looked enviously at Jaymie's sandwich. "That looks

good. I'm trying to lose some weight, but it's such a struggle."
He sighed in dramatic fashion and chomped on a carrot stick.

"I know what you mean. It's kind of hopeless before
Christmas, though. Do you want half?" She cut the half brie
and turkey sandwich in half and offered him the quarter sandwich on a napkin.

He took it and bit down, rolling his eyes. "So good! I haven't
had bread in a week."

"I'm trying portion control," Jaymie said sympatheti-
cally. "I'm always waging the battle of the bulge. I write a
food column, and that makes it tough! So much good food,
so little time."

He chewed and swallowed, eyeing her. He reached across,
picked up her cup of consommé and took a long drink.
"Mmm . . . good with the sandwich, right?" he said.

She smiled and pushed it back across the table to him.
Though she wasn't especially germaphobic, she never shared
a cup with anyone, especially not at cold and flu season, but
she'd just as soon let him have it anyway. "Austin, I wondered
after we talked, how well did you truly know Shelby?"

He looked affronted and crunched down on a celery stick
with vigor. "What do you mean by that?"

"Nothing bad. I just thought you only knew her a few
months, right?"

"That's true."

"You seemed alarmed when I asked about her and Delaney's relationship."

"I just . . . I wasn't sure what would happen. I get myself
into trouble sometimes, with things I say or do, and I wasn't
sure you should be nosing around Delaney Meadows. I was
afraid you'd say I told you they were going out together."

"And later, you just brushed me off and seemed in a hurry
to get away from me when I asked about Shelby looking into
Natalie Roth's disappearance."

"Yeah, about that." He eyed her speculatively. "Look, I

loved Shelby like a big sister, but she could be cray-cray, you know what I mean? She was like this gorgeous diva doll sometimes. She came to work full on dressed to the nines, like she was a businesswoman, even though she was just little old Delaney Meadows' receptionist. Called herself an 'executive assistant.' Puh-leeze!" He rolled his blue eyes.

"About Natalie?"

He drank down the rest of the consommé and leaned across the table, checking around the restaurant first to make sure no one was close. "I knew about the 'investigation,'" he said, sketching air quotes. "At first I thought Shelby was kidding when she asked me a bunch of questions about Natalie Roth. But after a few weeks, I got kinda scared. Natalie and I were close, like, BFFs, you know? We met at a party. She was gorgeous! Dark haired, dark eyed, exotic, you know. We went to a fashion show in Detroit together in September. That's where she got the bug to be one of those spokesmodels, so when I told her about Delaney starting up DM Models, she set up an interview, got the job and quit her bank position in Wolverhampton."

"She disappeared in early November, right?"

He nodded. "I didn't know where she went. Or what happened."

"Shelby started looking into it for Natalie's dad. So what scared you off when I asked?"

He shrugged and crunched on a celery stick. "Something odd about that whole thing. I was afraid it had to do with Delaney. He's kind of strange, you know? Secretive and suspicious. He's hiding *something*. What if that something is that he killed Natalie? And what if he killed Shelby because she found out that he killed Natalie?"

"That's exactly what I want to know."

"Yeah, well it scared the bejeebers out of me to think it. Is he some psycho nut, like Norman Bates cray-cray? Made me uncomfortable when you asked a bunch of questions."

"What if I told you I'd heard that Shelby was mad at you for implying she and Delaney were having an affair? And that she had told you to butt out, or she'd tell people what she knows about you?"

His cheeks turned bright pink and his eyes teared up. He swallowed hard. "That was . . . that was hurtful."

"What was she referring to?"

He sniffed back the tears and told her what happened. Austin had apparently thought someone at work was into him, but he was wrong. "I made an idiot of myself," he whispered, glancing around the crowded café. "Shelby was threatening to spread the tale wide over social media. She could be a real biotch sometimes, you know?" He pulled a tissue from his sweater pocket and dabbed at his eyes. "You won't say anything, will you?" he asked, a catch in his voice.

She put her hand over his on the table. "Not a word, I promise." He was so young, and so vulnerable.

"That's why I miss Natalie. She loves me for who I am. I wish I knew where she went!"

"That's one thing I'm trying to figure out, and if I can just find out what happened to Shelby, maybe they're related. The other day after I saw you, I got into Delaney's office. I wanted to poke around, but I didn't have enough time. I believe that he had the opportunity to kill Shelby. I'm not saying why I think that, but trust me . . . he *could* have done it. I don't know if he did, though, and I didn't have time to check out his files." She smiled across the table. "I'd *love* to have a peek at them, and I wonder if you have any ideas of how I might get into the office when there is no one around."

Unexpectedly, Austin grinned, his eyes gleaming with mischief. "Sweetie, you came to the right place. You want it, you got it." He dug in his sweater pocket and brought out a ring of keys. "You could say I'm a collector." He jingled them. She reached out, but he snatched them back and looked around the café. "One of the things I've collected lately is keys, and I just *happen* to have a key to the Meadows agency office." He slipped two keys off the ring and held it out. "The big silver one is mine to the back door, and the gold one is to the employment agency. I'll give this to you to on one condition."

"Yes?"

"If you get caught, don't tell them the key came from me!"

She smiled and took the key. "No problem at all."

❧ Twenty-three ❧

ONCE HOME SHE toyed with calling Glenn Brennan back and arranging to meet him somewhere that afternoon, but she had too much to do. Instead, she called her friend. "Valetta, feel up to some snooping before the Dickens Days stuff this evening?" Jaymie asked, holding the phone against her shoulder while stirring brownie batter.

"You know me well enough to know the answer. Where do we meet?"

Jaymie explained about Austin loaning her his key to the employment agency, and her plan to look at the files and computer to figure out what was going on with the Natalie Roth case and Shelby's involvement, and whether it all led back to Delaney Meadows.

"Sounds cool. You want to meet there?"

That was the great thing about a friend like Valetta; no need to convince her, she was up for anything. Even trespassing. "Yeah. Just at dark. What time is that?"

"This time of year? About five."

"I knew that," Jaymie said, with a chuckle. "But they'll still be open then. Six o'clock; I know the offices in the building close down at five, even the call center."

"You got it. I'll wear my cat burglar outfit."

The afternoon went quickly, but not quickly enough for Jaymie. She spent three hours at the manor, playing the part of an early twentieth century housewife, and baked cookies in the antique oven, which she was beginning to get the hang of. A couple of classes of kids from the elementary school came through; one of those last-week-of-school outings that keep excited kids interested. She did her best to make it sound interesting and everyone got to try a cookie, which they enjoyed. She left as soon as she could and sped home, changed, ate a sandwich and called Valetta. "Meet you there, fellow burglar?"

"Will do."

As soon as the sun sank, it became bitterly cold. She stuffed her mitted hands in her parka pockets and walked briskly through the quiet streets, the way to the Belcker Building familiar now. Austin had told her that his key was to the back door of the building, so when she saw Valetta, dressed similarly to her, she motioned for her to follow her down the lane and around to the back. The parking lot was not quite carless, but just then a group of stragglers came out chattering and laughing together. Jaymie and Valetta turned toward each other, as if lingering while waiting for a ride, or to chat before departing the workplace.

Once the last two cars had cleared the parking lot, Jaymie looked at Valetta. "Ready, partner in crime?"

"I am if you are. And it's not a crime, it's a worthwhile enterprise to find out who killed a girl. If it wasn't, I wouldn't be taking part."

"Thanks for those pearls of wisdom," Jaymie said, her chuckle coming out on puffs of steam. She pushed the first key into the lock and turned, and the door opened readily. They were in. Jaymie led the way upstairs to the Meadows

Employment Agency. The door key worked, and they entered the dark office.

They stood inside for a moment, getting their bearings. "Are there any windows to the outside?" Valetta asked.

"I don't think so. Why? And why am I whispering?"

"We can turn on lights, right? If there aren't any windows to show the light on the outside?"

Jaymie felt by the door, flicking on a light switch. The reception area leaped in to brilliant relief and she blinked, let her eyes adjust to the bright light then led the way around the desk and into the office. "Let's snoop in some of the offices, then go to Delaney's. I have to think that's where we'll hit the jackpot."

Together they carefully searched the offices along the corridor. It appeared that Delaney's employees mostly worked on the employment agency end of things. It was legitimate, as Valetta had conveyed with her story of Brock finding an assistant through them. They discovered references to placements of local graduates with Fortune 500 companies in the airline and tech industry, as well as an international hotel chain. Delaney Meadows was, to some extent, who he said he was.

"But I find it odd that no one else in the office seems to be involved in this DM Models business."

"And the dating business," Valetta added.

"Yeah, he shrugged that off when we talked, saying it was just starting. It's time to look into his office," Jaymie said, checking her watch. "We've got another half hour or so before I have to go and work the Dickens Days. Glenn Brennan phoned me earlier today; he has something he wants to tell me about Shelby's family, something Shelby told him. I wonder if it has anything to do with her brother, Travis. Oh, and Jakob texted me earlier; he wants to meet me at the band shell at nine."

Valetta smiled. "He's the real deal, isn't he?"

"I'm not saying a word! Let's get a move on so we can get

out of here." She led the way to Delaney's office. "I keep thinking that maybe Shelby found something out about his involvement with Natalie Roth's disappearance, and that's why she's dead. Because of that notation in his planner I know he was supposed to be at the Dickens Days event, and probably meeting with Shelby. And I have independent verification that she was intending to meet someone there and didn't want anyone else around when she did it. I suspect, too, that she was blackmailing him. That's where the money came from, the dough she was using to finance her disappearing act to Florida."

"But what made him kill her?" Valetta asked. "What happened with Natalie Roth?"

"I don't know. I'm hoping I find something out."

She led the way into his office, pulled off her parka and sat down at his desk. She flicked on his computer, wondering if it was password protected, but it wasn't as far as she could tell. Sloppy or lazy. And odd for someone who she had heard was secretive. "Maybe you could start going through his personnel files, if they're on paper?" Jaymie said.

"Will do." Valetta tossed her coat aside, grabbed a rolling chair from another office and sat down by the wooden file cabinet.

Jaymie took some time to puzzle out his filing system on his computer. He had compartmentalized his files so that the employment agency was up front, with the DM Models business buried in anonymous file names. The dating website info was buried even deeper. No wonder he didn't worry about password protection. Once she figured out how to search the appropriate files, it got her nowhere. It would have helped if she knew what she was looking for, but she was randomly trying to tie him into Natalie's disappearance, so she was searching any file attached to her name. So far she had found her digital resume and a list of emails in the modeling business files.

She sighed deeply. Was she going to have to read through the emails one by one? She'd start in reverse chronological order, beginning with the last ones first. "Finding anything?" she asked, looking over at Valetta.

"I think so, but it may not mean anything."

"What is it?"

"It's just an oddity. I'm in the dating website paper files. Did you know that he printed out the file and application of every person who has signed up?"

"Why would he do that, I wonder?"

"I don't know. But what's weirder is, I'm looking through these just after looking through his DM Models file, and noticed that there are an astonishing number of the girls from the DM Models site who are apparently also looking for love . . . but under a *different name.*"

"What?" Jaymie turned and eyed her friend, paying closer attention. "What do you mean?"

"I mean, I've looked through the DM Models profile pages and seen lots of the headshots given. Gorgeous girls and a few gorgeous guys, all local. Then, when I leafed through the dating profiles, I'm seeing the same photos crop up. So, either all these gorgeous model-type folks want to work, and also find love under assumed names, or the dating profiles are fake. I suspect the latter."

Jaymie sat back in her chair and thought about it. "I suppose they could be doing online dating, too, but it feels off, doesn't it? Why would every one of them choose a fake name?"

"They wouldn't. Something is wrong."

Jaymie randomly typed in some key words in the computer search box, and one of the results looked promising. She clicked on it, and there popped up a spreadsheet with a list of names and variations on those names. There was a list of Ashleys with last names starting at Anderson and going down to Washington. There were men's names, too, like John, which had last names exactly the same as Ashley. "Very strange," Jaymie said aloud, and explained what she was finding.

She backtracked and looked at the file the spreadsheet was in. There were photos in it, all headshots of young to middle-aged men and women, all attractive. And then she found a list of document files labeled Contact 1, Contact 2, and so on. She brought up Contact 1. "Listen to this: 'I hope you don't mind me writing to you. I came across your profile and was immediately struck by your beauty-slash-good looks. Your smile is enchanting-slash-handsome. Would you consider corresponding with me?'" She looked up from the monitor. "What the hell is this about?"

"It sounds like every scam letter I get in my email or on Facebook that starts, 'Dear one, I saw your profile and was attracted by your smile,' meanwhile, my profile is of a kitten with a ball of yarn."

"I get those, too, and my profile pic is an old eggbeater. Sure, nice smile."

Valetta laughed out loud.

"This is the one labeled contact two," Jaymie said. "It reads: 'Thank you so much for responding to my bold email. I'm new at the whole online dating thing and a little shy. Maybe we can take this conversation to email instead of the dating site? I'd love to share my deepest feelings with you.'" She looked up, wide-eyed, at Valetta. "Does that sound like anyone you've actually talked to in real life? And here is contact three: 'I'd love to come visit you, but I'm afraid I just can't afford to take time off work. I'm supporting my elderly mother who has Alzheimer's-slash-cancer-slash-blindness, and her care is very expensive. I would so love to meet you though, and worship you the way you deserve. Those who have let you go must be fools not to value you, your smile, your warmth, and your beautiful—*brackets* blue brown gray—eyes.'"

"Okay, let me guess. I'll bet contact four is a plea for a loan so he—or she—can come visit and yet still pay for the care of his poor aged mother with Alzheimer's slash cancer slash carbuncles!"

"It's a dating scam," Jaymie said, sitting back in the squeaky chair. "That's what Delaney Meadows has set up."

"And he's using the pictures he's gotten from the models as the profile pictures. Why not just look online for pictures?"

"Maybe he's afraid those will be noticed. I know some scammers have been caught that way, by using someone's photo who finds out."

"Yeah, but local would-be models? I wonder if—"

"Shh, Valetta, what was that noise?" Jaymie said.

They were both silent for a long moment. Nothing.

"Probably just the heating system or something," Valetta said. "Anyway, I've read a lot about these romance scams. Brock sends me links about them all the time. I think he's afraid I'll fall prey to it. As if!" She snorted a laugh.

"But how does this connect to Natalie's disappearance and Shelby's murder?" Jayme mused. "I *feel* like the two must be connected, but I guess I should keep an open mind. They may not be."

"Let's start with Natalie. She was working for DM Models, right?"

"Right. According to her father she had just started and had a job set up in Korea, but we know she never left the US."

"We don't know why, though, or where she went, or with whom, or how."

Jaymie sighed, discouraged. "We know next to nothing."

"But we do know what happened to Shelby."

"Sure; she was murdered by someone who likely knew about her plans to disappear and place the blame on Cody. That's why I was thinking it could be Travis, her brother, but she may have confided in others that I don't know about. One thing I *do* know is she was writing in that journal here, at the Bean & Leaf and probably kept the book here while she wrote in it. Someone that she worked with, even Delaney Meadows, could have read it and gotten the drift. If they had a reason to get rid of her it would be ideal to use the journal's hints to place the blame on Cody and away from the real perpetrator. Someone texted him to get him to Queensville that night, if I'm to believe him."

Valetta had been flipping through the dating profiles and frowned suddenly. "Wait, I saw *this* picture in the DM Models."

"Yeah, you already figured Delaney was culling photos to do a romance scam on guys using the model photos."

"But this one," Valetta said, flapping it in the air, "happens to match up with someone you know."

Jaymie snatched it away from her friend. "That's Natalie Roth!" she said, "But the profile name is Ashley Nash. And it says . . . it says she had been corresponding with a guy named—"

"What are you doing in my office?"

Jaymie gasped and almost fell off her chair as she looked up to find Delaney Meadows standing in the doorway. The noise she had heard must have been him letting himself into the office! There was no clever way out of this. She stood and faced him, shivering, the nerves hitting her in a wave. Valetta looked scared out of her mind, too. "I'm trying to find out what happened to Shelby Fretter."

He looked startled, and she worried that she had stupidly tipped her hand. If he killed Shelby, he was dangerous. If he didn't, then he should have no reason not to let them walk out of there, or call the police to charge them with trespassing. But he wasn't going to do that; they had uncovered enough already to at least know he was involved in a scam. She was paralyzed by fear as she watched him slip his hand in his trench coat pocket.

He brought out a gun. "You just had to keep being snoopy, didn't you?" he said, shaking his head. "You just couldn't leave me alone. I'd hoped I had at least until the New Year before everything went belly-up."

"Meaning before you were caught?" Jaymie asked, her voice trembling.

He nodded. "You're worse than Shelby," he said. "You," he said, pointing the gun at Valetta. "I know you. You're that gabby pharmacist, aren't you? Lily goes to you all the time for her meds."

Valetta nodded. "She needs them to cope with *you*."

"Me? She's the one who's impossible, demanding, whiny . . . Anyway, shut up and get down on the floor with your back to the wall. Sit cross-legged, hands where I can see them."

She obeyed.

"And you, Miss Troublemaker, you I don't want anywhere near her." He looked around his small office. "Just sit over there," he said, waving the barrel of the gun toward the other wall. "And take that wheeled stool, turn it upside down and hug it. *Now!*"

Jaymie did as she was told, sitting across the office from Valetta, hugging the small upside-down stool. She thought his next move would be to tape her wrists together, but instead, he paced the office for a long minute, silent. What was his game plan? He didn't seem to have one.

He looked panicked, his eyes darting from Valetta to Jaymie and back and around the room. Nothing made sense yet, as much as she tried to figure it out. It was like a collage of random facts sewn into a crazy quilt of happenings with no discernible pattern. Except for what she had just learned about who Natalie was supposedly dating, matched on the dating website.

"What are you going to do?" she asked Meadows as he paced.

He turned to her, wild-eyed. "I don't know. Everything is a mess now. And all because of you," he said, pointing the gun at her. It trembled with every movement of his hand.

Almost fainting with fear, Jaymie met Valetta's gaze, her eyes wide.

"Delaney, it's okay," Valetta said, her voice calm and steady. "Should I call Lily for you?"

He whirled and pointed the gun at her. "Good *God*, no! Why would I want you to call that impossible drag? I know what I have to do now," he said, his voice becoming steadier. He pointed his gun at Jaymie. "You, get up."

❋ Twenty-four ❋

"GO INTO THE drawer," he said, pointing the gun at Jaymie as she set the chair aside and stood, then at the desk drawer. "And get out a file that says 'Plans.'"

"Plans?"

"Yes, *Plans*! Get it!" He was almost shrieking with tension, his face a sickly color under the fluorescent lights.

Her hands shook from the surprise of his screeching at her, but she leafed through, found the file and pulled it out.

"Give it to me," he said. When she went to hand it to him it dropped instead and spilled its contents on the floor. There was a passport and some other cards that looked like pieces of identification. "Idiot!" he fumed. He had lost his cool manner, and was now a nervous bundle of furious energy, his movements jerky and uncontrolled, his sallow cheeks starting to blotch with red patches.

The gun waved wildly, his trench coat flapped open, exposing the silky lining, and Jaymie remembered the fragment of silky fabric she had seen in the workshop. Coat lining; why hadn't she thought of that before? She exchanged frightened looks with Valetta. But feeling afraid made her angry, and being angry made her want to get to the bottom of everything she had been investigating in the last week. "So did Shelby come right out and ask you if you had anything to do with Natalie's disappearance?"

He pushed the last papers into the file and straightened, staring at Jaymie. "She threatened me! Told me that she was going to tell Natalie's dad I killed her." He shivered, and it was clear that Clutch terrified him. "I never did anything to that girl and I told Shelby that. Natalie was doing some work for me, learning the ropes, setting up a mark. She had a great phone voice; sexy, sultry. She was ambitious and saw the benefit of what I was working on and how quick we could make some money. Not like Shelby, who was a little prig!"

Jaymie was taken aback; she had never thought of Shelby as a prig. He didn't seem remotely aware of her plan to take off, but she couldn't be sure yet. "So you were grooming Natalie to take part in your con?"

"I was already doing pretty good, but just on the email aspect, you know, getting stupid lonely hearts to send me money to come see them." He paused in his jerky movements. Talking about the business appeared to calm him, and he took a deep breath. "She had some new ideas to expand," he said, as if he was talking about a legitimate business venture. "I used her for catfishing a couple of times when I needed a female voice on the phone. She was going to try a little romance scam or two of her own on the side. For her the scam cash was just to live on while she established herself in modeling. I tried to tell her she could make more money on the romance scam than modeling would ever bring her, but . . ." He shrugged, seemingly puzzled why she'd want to work a legitimate job when she could make a living conning lonely men. "I set her up on a legit modeling job. Last I knew, she was supposed to be boarding a plane for Korea."

A romance scam of her own . . . *hmmm*. Jaymie was

intrigued, especially given what she saw in his files before he caught them. "But Natalie never got on the plane. We know that because her passport was still in her apartment."

"Maybe she got scared and took off," he said, looking uneasy. "How do I know? That's what I told the cops when they came sniffing around a month ago."

"Did Shelby confide her own plans to you?"

"Plans?" He stared at her, brow furrowed. "What do you mean?"

Jaymie thought he was either telling the truth or he was an extremely good liar. He *didn't* know about Shelby's plan to take off and finger Cody as culpable in her disappearance.

"You," he said, pointing the gun at Jaymie. "Sit back down on the floor, grab that stool again and shut up. Everything's gone to hell now because of Shelby. It was such a sweet setup!" He leafed through the reassembled file, pocketing the passport and some other papers.

The gun was wavering in his hand, and Jaymie was afraid it would go off while he was not paying attention. She sat back down on the floor and grabbed the stool, wrapping her arms around the cold steel base, wondering if she had the nerve or strength to throw it at him and dislodge the gun. It was too risky. "So did the romance scam work? Did people actually send you money?"

He eyed her uneasily as he tossed the empty file aside and shoved the ID in his coat pocket. "You'd be surprised what people will do if you tell them what they want to hear. If dopes will give money to a complete stranger for a few kind words, then I'm willing to profit. Natalie agreed. There was a fortune to be made." He stomped his foot. "*Damn* Shelby for getting in the way!"

"How did she get in the way?" Jaymie asked.

"None of your business. I gotta get out of here."

"But you didn't kill Shelby, did you?" Jaymie said.

"*God*, no! How many times do I have to say it? I'm a lot of things, but I've never laid a finger on a person, man or woman, in my life." He glanced at Valetta, then Jaymie. "Okay, look . . . you want to know so bad why I'm in trouble? Shelby, damn her, called the IRS and the FBI about what she found in my files."

"The IRS?" Jaymie said. "Why them?"

He shrugged. "There may have been some . . . irregularities in my bookkeeping. That's why I do all my own accounting, but Shelby just *had* to snoop! Of *course* the IRS paid attention. Those guys are worse than the feds! I think that's what she was going to tell me that night, that she had turned me in to the IRS."

"Did you meet her in Queensville like you planned?"

He shuddered, then shook it off. "No, we, uh . . . we never met, but I'd bet she was going to blackmail me some more. I already gave her cash to get her off my back, hoping it would buy her silence. Fat chance!" He snatched up a few things from his desk, including a cell phone and notebook, and stuffed them in his pocket while keeping the gun trained on them. "I'm getting out of here. Have a ball going through my files, because you're going to have all night to do it." He thrust out his free hand and snapped his fingers. "Hand over your cell phones."

"I don't have mine with me," Jaymie said, as Valetta reluctantly gave him hers.

"You expect me to believe that?" he snarled.

"You can believe it or not; I don't have it."

He glared at her and she steadily returned his stare.

"Fine," he said, pocketing Valetta's "I'll leave this one outside. Have fun overnight, girls. The cleaners come in at six in the morning; they'll let you out."

He backed out of the office and closed the door after him. Jaymie heard the lock snick into place as she stood and set the chair aside. She tried the door but it was indeed locked. Valetta got up and shifted her sweater back down around her hips.

"So call the cops," Valetta said.

"I told the truth," Jaymie said with a grimace. "I didn't bring my cell phone. It's in my purse."

Valetta sighed, but then brightened. "Well, duh! We'll just use the office phone. How dumb can he be to lock us in with a landline?" She sat down at the desk and picked up the phone, then made a face. She looked over at Jaymie and waggled the silent receiver in her hand. "It's dead."

"He must have had a way to turn it off at the reception desk."

"Now what?" Valetta said.

"We can shout? Bang on walls?"

"We already made sure there was no one else in the building. I guess we're stuck here until the cleaning crew comes, unless you've developed a skill for lock picking?"

"I can try," Jaymie said. "They make it look so easy in the movies."

She tried to pick the door's lock with a straightened paperclip but gave up after ten minutes. Resigned to their fate of spending the night in the office, she and Valetta then searched the dating and modeling files, both on the computer and in paper, compiling the information they needed to prove their case.

"I think that Shelby Fretter went through these files herself and discovered what we did, that Natalie Roth had gone out with one of the guys who signed up with the dating website, but not as Natalie, as Ashley Nash. Now we know Natalie was running her own little scam." Jaymie shook her head. "I just can't figure Shelby out. On the one hand she was planning to nail Cody to the wall by disappearing, leaving evidence behind that would point to him murdering her."

"Like *Gone Girl*; that was a creepy book."

"Exactly. But on the other hand she was going after Delaney, first when she maybe thought he had something to do with Natalie's disappearance, and then for tax evasion and illegal practices. I'm pretty sure she was also going after the guy she suspected did something to Natalie Roth." She heard a noise and jumped up. "What is that? Do you think Delaney's coming back?"

"Jaymie?"

"That's Jakob!" She ran to the office door and rattled the doorknob. "In here, Jakob!" she said, slapping the office door with her open hand. "The inner office labeled Delaney Meadows! He locked us in."

"Stand away from the door," he said.

They moved back to the desk and heard a smash as the door shuddered. The doorknob on their side fell to the floor and the door swung open. Jaymie rushed into his arms, feeling the enveloping hug like a balm to her heart. "How did you know where we were?"

"You didn't meet me at the band shell. I asked the ladies at the booth, who said you didn't show up to do your Dickens Days walk. Everyone was worried. They said you *never* miss an appointment. I called your house, I went by there, and called your cell phone . . . nothing. I remembered that you talked about Delaney Meadows and some of your suspicions. I figured you may have wanted to snoop around his office, so I came by here and found Valetta's cell phone on the top of the garbage can behind the building." He pulled it out of his pocket and handed it back to Valetta. "Sorry, I had to look into it to see whose it was. Once I figured that out, I knew you two *must* be inside, so I took a chance and busted in."

She heard more voices. "Who's that?"

"I called the police, too, but I didn't want to wait for them. Not when you might be in danger."

"I sure am glad you thought of it!"

Chief Ledbetter arrived, along with Detective Vestry. "Now, Jaymie, you're going to tell me everything you know or suspect."

Jumping from foot to foot, agitated, Jaymie said, "Yes, I will, I will, but Delaney Meadows is on the run, so I'd advise you to get him as fast as possible. The IRS is after him, but he's also broken probably a dozen laws that I know of."

The police chief huffed and squinted his eyes. "He's one of our prime suspects for killing Shelby Fretter. He was in the right place at approximately the right time."

"I don't think he did it, Chief," Jaymie said, taking a deep breath and calming herself as the detective looked on with a disapproving stare. "But I think I know who did. I can give you his name, his address, even his phone number." And she did just that, writing it on a piece of note paper and handing it to him.

Detective Vestry had stiffened. "We can't just—"

"I'm going to trust you on this and take the guy in for questioning," Chief Ledbetter said, interrupting his detective and sending her a warning glance. "I want to see you later to answer some questions."

"Anything you say, Chief," Jaymie said, as Jakob stifled a smile and Valetta chuckled.

"You say some of the information is here, in this office?" He turned to Vestry. "We need to seal this up and get a search warrant. Have Ng handle it. But first, get on the radio and put out an APB on Delaney Meadows. And we'll have to find *this* guy and figure out how we can detain him until we get a warrant," he said, waving the piece of note paper with the culprit's name and address on it.

Jakob took Jaymie on one arm and Valetta on the other, and they walked out of the Belcker Building, through the dark streets to downtown, as Jaymie filled him in on what they had discovered. It was all such a relief, but she was still unnerved, hoping and praying she was right. Valetta joined Brock and her niece and nephew, who were strolling toward the Emporium.

Mrs. Bellwood was tending the cider booth and waved heartily as she saw Jaymie. "You found her!" she said to Jakob. "Where have you been, Jaymie?"

"I was unavoidably detained."

Mrs. Frump called out, "There's someone else looking for you."

"Someone looking for *me*?"

"A nice young man said he was meeting you here."

Jakob looked over at her, his brows raised.

It took her just one second, and she realized who it was. "Good grief, I didn't think he'd still be here or I would have told Chief Ledbetter!" Jaymie said.

"That's him," Mrs. Frump said, pointing to a retreating figure.

Jaymie grabbed Jakob's arm. "That's him, the guy I told you about, the one who killed Shelby Fretter!"

Jakob bolted after him, grabbed his arm, and said, "Hey, just a moment, buddy."

Glenn Brennan pulled his sleeve out of Jakob's grasp and started to walk away quickly, but Jakob raced after him and got a handful of wool coat sleeve again, holding him fast in the faint pool of light shed by the lamppost. "Now wait a minute, friend. I think you ought to stick around."

"Let him go," Jaymie said, her voice shaking. She didn't want anything more to do with Brennan than to tell the police he was in the village and needed to be apprehended.

Jakob caught her eye and she stared at him. He tightened his grip and said, "It's okay, Jaymie, it's under control."

Glenn pulled and tugged at his sleeve, eyeing Jakob. "Listen to the lady and let me go! I've got a hot date waiting."

Heidi and Joel approached, eyeing the tense tableau with uncomprehending gazes. Mrs. Bellwood whispered to Heidi, who pulled out her phone and hurriedly punched in three numbers.

"I don't think you should make your date, Glenn," Jaymie said, mustering up her courage. "Not after the last couple have ended so badly."

"I don't know what you mean," he said, pulling at his

sleeve, his dark wool trench becoming flecked with white as the snow thickened.

But Jakob grabbed him more securely by the upper arm, his grasp strong after so many years of manhandling Christmas trees and massive antiques in his store.

"You killed Shelby Fretter," Jaymie said, her breath coming out in rapid puffs of steam.

"You're out of your mind," he snarled, tugging harder, trying to jerk his arm away. "Tell your boyfriend here to let go of me, or I'll have him written up on assault charges!" He twisted suddenly, the rapid movement wrenching his arm from Jakob's grasp. Instead of running he turned and launched himself at Jaymie.

The force of his attack made her stumble sideways, but he was no match for Jakob, who roared his anger and grabbed him in a bear hug, jerked him off his feet and wrestled him easily to the ground. Other people had run to see what was going on. Brock, seeing the attack on Jaymie, came running. "Who's in the wrong, Jaymie?" he cried, dancing back and forth from foot to foot.

"The guy in the trench coat is a murderer; Jakob is trying to keep him subdued until the cops come."

Brock leaped into the fray and sat on Glenn's flailing feet as Jakob pinned the killer's torso. A siren sounded from somewhere, and a police car rocketed up onto the grass near them. Bernie, Jaymie's police friend, bolted from the car, gun drawn, and shouted, "Separate, everyone, and stay where you are with your hands locked behind your head!"

Jakob and Brock obediently knelt, hands clasped behind their heads, but Glenn Brennan leaped to his feet and took off, skidding and tripping down the walkway across the village green.

"He's Shelby's killer, Bernie!" Jaymie shouted, hands on her head, grasping her hair in handfuls. "Don't let him go!"

Bernie shouted to the junior officer with her, "Radio in; the chief is already on his way. Contain the scene!" She sprinted after Glenn and tackled him, taking him down and effectively containing him even as he struggled and shrieked. Backup arrived and Brennan was arrested.

Jakob clapped Brock on the back and the two men shook hands. Jaymie joined them and hugged Jakob tightly. "I was so scared! I'm glad you're safe."

More charges would follow, but Chief Ledbetter had enough now to hold Glenn Brennan without applying for a warrant. While the snow thickened, officers interviewed Mrs. Frump, Mrs. Bellwood and Jakob. Chief Ledbetter took a brief statement from Valetta and Jaymie and told them to come in to the police headquarters in the morning.

The crowd that had gathered dispersed, as it was already ten. The Dickens Days evening was finished. Valetta said, "Everyone over to my place for cocoa and snacks!" She gathered up her brother, his kids, Heidi and Joel, and invited Jakob and Jaymie. "I think we have a lot to talk about."

Jaymie was exhausted. In Valetta's tidy living room, lined with knickknack shelves that held her collection of kitsch, they related what had happened, but she let her friend do most of the talking. She just leaned against Jakob, with his arm around her, holding her up. At long last he stood and pulled her to her feet. "I'm going to walk Jaymie home, Valetta, if you don't mind."

Joel, sitting on the floor beside Heidi, began to clamber to his feet. "I can give her a ride. My car's just at the curb."

Jaymie looked up at Jakob. "I'd rather walk home with Jakob," she said, noticing Heidi yanking Joel's arm and giving him a look.

After hugs all around and wishes for sweet dreams and sound sleep they donned their coats and exited into the cold, crisp night air. It was a sparkling evening with icy crystalline snowflakes fluttering in the air. The slap of frigidity woke Jaymie up. They walked arm in arm back to her home and up to the front door. The cedar garland around the door and the fairy lights in the iron urn topiaries were aglow with silvery light. "Do you want to come in?" she asked, turning toward him.

"I wish I could, but Jocie is at my mother's and tomorrow's a school day. I want to get her home."

"I understand," she said, looking up at him in the faint illumination of the twinkle lights. She leaned against his chest and sighed deeply, the most relaxed she had been in over a week, since the awful murder that had started it all. "I'm so relieved Glenn was caught. Thank you," she said, her voice muffled against his coat front.

He put one finger under her chin and turned her face up to his, then pulled her close and kissed her, softly at first, but with unmistakable passion. She shivered in pleasure; *this* was the missing ingredient, what had been lacking with Daniel. The rub of his whiskers, the cold of his cheeks, the smell of his soap, the soft warmth of his lips; it blended to become Jakob for her. There would be more to come, but for now, it was enough to have this.

"I have to go," he said, regret in his husky voice.

"Good night, Jakob," she whispered.

He thumbed her cheek and kissed her lightly again. "Good night, Jaymie."

❧ Twenty-five ❧

NAN WAS ECSTATIC to have her son completely cleared in the murder. Jaymie was happy for her. Though she didn't like Cody, he wasn't a killer.

When she went to the police headquarters the next day with Valetta to give their statements, she was greeted with the news that they had found Natalie Roth. Their investigation of Glenn Brennan had uncovered a storage locker on the outskirts of Wolverhampton that he had rented just after her disappearance, and there was the poor young woman's body stuffed into a large plastic tote.

Unexpectedly and against legal counsel, Glenn would not shut up, spewing forth his story in graphic and minute detail. Chief Ledbetter told Jaymie in confidence that it appeared that Natalie Roth, encouraged by Delaney Meadows, had indeed been working on a romance scam as Ashley Nash, and under another few names. After a carefully worded call in the newspaper for more information they had been contacted by a couple of men who told police that she had been dating them—under different names—and had asked for money. One gave her a thousand dollars so she wouldn't go to his wife, but the other refused and never heard from her again. Neither had realized she was the girl in the copious "Missing" posters around the area because she wore a blond wig, which was found in the tote with her body. According to a confidante, Natalie had wanted the money to fund her burgeoning modeling career and pay for some plastic surgery.

But she had worked the scheme on the wrong guy when she tried Glenn Brennan. After a few dates and some intimacy, she pressured him for money, telling him she'd go to his boss at the drug manufacturer for whom he worked and reveal his violently kinky side. He killed her in a rage and stowed her body in the locker that he rented the next day. Shelby, suspicious of her boss's dating website dealings, had gone through the dating and model files and come to the same conclusion Jaymie had come to about Delaney's con, Natalie's involvement and how she had met her end. Jaymie remembered what Shelby had said that day at the historic house, that she could investigate rings around Jaymie. It appeared she had made the fatal mistake of trying to emulate Jaymie's recent investigative forays and pin Glenn Brennan down herself. That's what she meant when she told her friend Lynnsey that she thought she knew who had done it and was going to the police.

It was a mystery how she knew where the key to Bill's storeroom was until Cody admitted that in a brief phone conversation with Shelby he may have told her where to find it. She was probably seeking somewhere warm and private to confront Delaney about his scam and get more information from him on what she suspected about Glenn Brennan's part in Natalie's disappearance and presumed death.

But it was too late. Her increasingly pointed questions had tipped Glenn off, and he followed her to the storeroom. Shelby was confrontational; in Glenn's confession he admitted that she told him she had proof he killed Natalie. He beat

her, leaving her for dead, but he left a little shred of evidence
behind; the bit of fabric caught on the bench was likely from
the lining of one of Glenn's overcoats. It would take time for
the lab to confirm it, and that the splatter on the coat was
Shelby's blood, but it was apparently the right color according
to Jaymie's inside source, also known as the chief himself,
and there was a tear, with material missing. Valetta's information that she had seen Delaney hustling away from the
area that evening made the chief wonder if he had found her
and was frightened he'd be blamed. Unless Delaney gave
them that information they might never know, but he'd come
very close himself to being arrested on suspicion of killing
Shelby.

Chief Ledbetter hoped he'd be able to charge Brennan with
premeditated murder, and that was where the text to Cody
came into play. Glenn had admitted that Shelby got tipsy one
evening and told him all about her plot to avenge her family's
honor by screwing the son of the *Wolverhampton Weekly
Howler* editor to the wall with a smear campaign. It hadn't
taken much to figure out who her target was, since Shelby
had openly dated Cody, and rumors were rampant about the
Fretter family's run-ins with the newspaper. As Jaymie had
suspected, the text to lure Cody to town, supposedly to see
Shelby at the band shell, had come from a burner phone that
Glenn set up to emulate one from Shelby, with a photo of her
as the ID. Glenn was just smart enough to pull off the decep-
tion that had worked on Cody so well, texting him moments
after he had beaten Shelby so severely she appeared dead.
Ultimately the timing had not worked as Glenn had hoped,
but it wasn't for lack of effort on the killer's part.

It was over, and the right guy had been apprehended. In
the week before Christmas, Clutch buried his daughter. In
her memory he and his buddies were arranging a fund-raiser
for the New Year, the proceeds of which were going to a
domestic abuse group in Wolverhampton. Lori, Travis and
the rest of her family buried Shelby. One of the random facts

that came to light during the investigation was that Travis's lies about his timeline that night were simply because he was meeting with his pot dealer.

Delaney Meadows was apprehended and charged with fraud and tax evasion, but there would likely be more charges before it was all over. Lily told Mrs. Stubbs that her husband was cooperating in the Natalie Roth and Shelby Fretter murder cases, establishing how the two women ended up the victims of such heinous crimes. In return he was hoping for a more lenient sentence. She was standing by him, hoping he had learned his lesson.

Jaymie sped through the next days, busy with Dickens Days, the heritage house, work and a holiday party at Heidi and Joel's with Bernie and a few others. Jakob attended and got along easily with her friends, but then, he was the kind of guy who never seemed at a loss among company. He could talk to anyone about anything. Joel, at first oddly protective toward Jaymie, ultimately backed off.

She saw Jakob a few more times with and without Jocie. The kiss wasn't repeated, but still . . . it kept her warm and tingling whenever she thought of it. She talked to him every night, the intimate sound of his voice in her ear a promise of things to come. It was time to meet his family. Her hesitation came from her fear that his mom especially wouldn't like her. In a late-night conversation she confessed all to Jakob, who chuckled warmly.

"*Liebling*, my mother is already half in love with you because of how Jocie speaks!"

Jaymie was silent for a long moment, stunned by any number of things: his pet name for her, that Jocie spoke of her to her oma, that Jakob's mother was predisposed to like her.

"Jaymie?"

"What does *liebling* mean?"

"Uh, it's German for *sweetheart*. If you don't mind."

"I don't mind," she said softly.

"Does that mean you're ready to meet my family?"

"I am," she murmured.

"Good. Your family is coming down when?"

"Day after tomorrow," she said. "The twenty-third. We're planning dinner together, and then Christmas Eve day we're driving to Canada."

"Can you bring them to my place for a dinner on the twenty-third?"

She thought about it. Her mother and father, Becca, Kevin, Grandma Leighton, all of them, meeting at the same time his mother, father, brothers, sisters-in-law and nieces and nephews. And Jocie and him, most important of all. "Are you sure *you're* ready for that?"

"I've been ready for weeks," he said.

She took a deep breath and let it out slowly, petting Hoppy's head gently. "Okay. Let's do it."

After that, her life was on fast-forward. She had three million things to do, including going out to Heartbreak Island to make sure the cottage was secure before the river froze up completely, doing laundry, shopping, cleaning and cooking. She remade the no-bake fruitcake with the ingredients she bought and put it in the fridge, hoping it turned out better than the trial one, since she had sent the recipe with her notes in to Nan. It would be in her December twenty-fourth column, a little late to make, but done, at any rate.

She talked to Becca, her mother and her grandmother on the phone half a dozen times, and Valetta was invited to join the family get-together at Jakob's cabin home. On the morning of the twenty-third Becca and Kevin brought Grandma Leighton to Queensville, taking her directly to the Queensville Inn. There she settled in, and looked forward to lunch with her old friends Mrs. Stubbs, Mrs. Frump and Mrs. Bellwood, then a nap before dinner at Jakob's. Becca and Kevin were staying at the inn as well. Alan and Joy, Jaymie and Becca's parents, arrived about noon at the Queensville house in a drift of luggage, hailstorm of kisses, blizzard of gifts and a flurry of complaints from Joy about the long drive from

Florida and her father's insistence on keeping to a modest fifty miles per hour.

Jaymie, through it all, felt like she was going to jump out of her skin. What had she gotten herself into? What if it all went terribly wrong? And what if Jakob realized he'd made a mistake and decided he could never love her? That was her real fear beneath her worries, she acknowledged. This relationship had become frighteningly important to her.

Her father cast her questioning looks, but all she could do was smile so she wouldn't cry. He hugged her. "Nervous about tonight, pet?"

She nodded into his chest.

He smoothed her hair and kissed her forehead. "We'll all be with you."

That was what she was worrying about.

But finally the time came and they drove through the dark of early twilight, Jaymie sitting in the backseat of her father's car and directing him, with Becca, Kevin and Grandma following in Kevin's luxurious sedan, his GPS guiding them. Valetta was going to be a half hour late, she said, as she had a pharmaceutical emergency, someone who had come down with the flu and needed meds delivered.

It was during the car ride that Jaymie caught on to how nervous her mother was, too. She had a gift for Jocie, even though Jaymie had assured her it was not necessary. She had three books, one a children's cookbook, a second adventure story and also *The Velveteen Rabbit*. When Jaymie protested that the book might be a little young for Jocie, who was a very intelligent little girl, her mother just primmed her lips and shook her head. "Maybe someday she'll have a little brother or sister to read the book to," she said softly. Jaymie had no answer for that.

Joy clutched the prettily wrapped parcel on her lap all during the ride. When Jaymie ducked her head over the backrest to talk to her mom, she saw that the package was somewhat the worse for wear, clutched too tight against her mother's narrow bosom. Jaymie put her hand on her mom's shoulder. "Jakob is a lovely, amazing man. His parents have to be as wonderful as you two to have raised such a great guy." She squeezed.

Joy Leighton put her hand over her daughter's and caressed it. "I just hope they like me." Her voice caught.

Jaymie's heart squeezed in sympathy. Her mother was as nervous as she was. "Mom, they're going to love you, just like I do."

They pulled up to the log cabin. The curtains were drawn back and electric candles winked and glowed in the windows, a welcoming light. There was hustle and bustle, of course, as Becca and Kevin helped Grandma out of the car and up the three steps to the cabin, with Jaymie's father anxiously watching every move. As they got to the door, it was thrown open and Jakob stood, the brilliant light framing him and throwing his features into darkness, chatter and music pouring out from beyond. And under his arm stood Jocie, her sturdy little body pressed against her daddy's legs, his red plaid Christmas sweater clutched in her fists as she avidly examined the newcomers.

Grandma Leighton regarded her gravely. "Hello, child. What's your name?"

She ducked out from under her father's arm. "My name is Jocelyn Eleanor Müller, ma'am. What's yours?"

Grandma Leighton bent over slightly and met Jocie eye to eye. "I'd like you to call me Gramee. Would that be okay?"

She nodded. "Would you like to come in?" she asked, taking the elderly woman's hand.

"Lead the way." Jaymie's grandmother tottered forward, supported by her cane and Jocie.

Jakob gestured to the others. "Come, come in out of the cold, everyone. Introductions can wait until you're inside."

It was long and involved, of course, and done with much laughter and promises that there would be a quiz later. Jaymie's father stood and held Jakob's hand in a handshake, regarding him thoughtfully. He clapped him on the shoulder finally and nodded. Then Jakob took Jaymie's hand and led her to a woman sitting in one of the wing chairs drawn close to the fireplace.

"Mama, this is Jaymie," he said softly.

Mrs. Müller, a heavyset woman, struggled to her feet and pulled Jaymie into a warm, soft hug. "I'm so happy to meet you," she said, her guttural voice full of feeling. She held Jaymie's face between her hands and stared at her.

Jocie pelted over to them and grabbed Jaymie around the legs, looking up at her. "Oma, Jaymie likes to cook. And her mama brought me a present. Did you see? She got me a cookbook!"

Jaymie glanced over at her mother and smiled; the gift was a success. But she was caught by the expression on her mother's face in the flickering candlelight. It held so much hope, but some worry. She beckoned her over, and Joy hesitantly approached. "Mrs. Müller, this is my mom, Joy Leighton. I know Jakob introduced everyone, but I hope you'll have a moment to talk and get to know each other."

Mrs. Müller's round face creased in a big smile. "Come, Joy, sit by me and we will talk," she said, taking Jaymie's mom's arm and pushing her to the chair beside her.

Valetta arrived and Jakob introduced her to everyone. The women began to take up dinner, but Jaymie stole away to stand in an alcove by the stairs for a moment, just to get a breather and look over the crowd. Jakob's father was a calm, soft-spoken man, handsome and rough-hewn, plagued lately by a bout of heart trouble. He, Jaymie's father and Jakob's oldest brother stood by the fireplace talking golf.

Mrs. Müller had made sure to give Grandma Leighton a comfortable seat away from the worst of the noise but close to Joy and herself, so the three women were quietly chatting, letting the younger women and men take charge. Valetta and Becca were in the kitchen with Jakob. He showed them where everything was, then got dishes and glasses down from his cupboards. Jocie was sitting on her oma's lap, looking at the cookbook while Joy pointed out recipes. The gift was a rousing success.

Sonya, Helmut's live-in girlfriend, a pale Scandinavian-looking natural blonde, approached, sipping a glass of wine. "Overwhelmed?" she asked.

"Just taking a breather."

"I know *I* was overwhelmed when I met his family for the first time. They're kind of boisterous, being all boys. There's more, too; we're missing Franz, his wife and their four kids. Your sister's fiancé is a great guy," she said, nodding across the room to where Kevin had Sonya's children on his lap, both at one time. "He's telling them a story about a troll."

"I was a little concerned about adding my whole family into the mix, but it seems to be working out."

"The Müllers are wonderful people," Sonya said, patting Jaymie's arm. "And now, I suppose I should help with the food, though the extent of my cooking is opening takeout containers. Helmut does most of the cooking, and Oma Müller, too."

Jaymie smiled. "Not everyone likes to cook, but I love it. I brought a baked pasta dish you might like to try for your family. Super easy. I never met a kid who didn't like pasta."

They joined Becca and Valetta in the kitchen, just off the big open living area, while the men carried in a long folding table and set it up for dinner, buffet style. With so many people, it just wasn't practical any other way. Everyone ate, the mix of dishes everything from Jaymie's pasta to Oma Müller's traditional German potato salad, a huge ham, salami and salads, made and bought. After their big meal, desserts replaced dinner items on the table. Among the pies and cakes, Jaymie hesitantly brought out her platter of trial number two of the no-bake fruitcake. She made sure her grandmother tried a piece, and Grandma Leighton's face lit up. "It's delicious, Jaymie! I made this in 1963, for Alan and Joy's first Christmas as newlyweds."

After dinner Sonya and Kevin sat at the piano and played some Christmas songs. Some sang along, while the others talked or just sat in quiet contemplation. Jocie and her step-cousins were playing by the hearth with the train that had circled the big Christmas tree in the corner.

Jakob snuck over to Jaymie, took her arm and pulled her through the kitchen and out to the porch. "Look at the stars," he whispered to her, wrapping her in his arms and a plaid blanket he had brought out. The night was inky black and clear, twinkling stars like Christmas lights blinking down upon them.

They stood just like that for a few minutes, her back to him, his arms wrapped around her. But then he turned her around and stared down into her eyes. His were dark in the low light, mysterious. She reached up and touched his cheek, cold in the night air, scruffing his whiskers, and he bent down and kissed her, long and slow, lovely and warm. The tingling warmed her all the way to her toes. She felt like she was on the cover of one of the kinds of contemporary romances she read, the Christmas specials, but this was better than any book; *so* much better.

He held her close. "*This* is my favorite Christmas memory," he whispered into her hair.

"Mine, too," she murmured, then tilted her face up for another kiss.

"Mine, too," a little voice said, ending on a giggle. Jocie raced out the open door and joined them, pressing herself to them both.

They let her in between them, making a family sandwich, and squeezed until she was giggling. This was a Christmas that Jaymie would never forget.

later some Christmas magic will have turned it into a slightly sticky but moist fruitcake that kids will love.

The original recipe called for pecans, not walnuts, and seedless raisins, not dried cranberries, and if you prefer, go ahead and use those original ingredients.

Serve it up to friends and family and enjoy! And remember what my Grandma Leighton always says: "Fruitcake is like family; it's just not the same without a few nuts."

VINTAGE EATS BY JAYMIE LEIGHTON

Time flies during the holiday season, and everybody is desperate for some easy homemade treats to serve guests. Cookies, bars, tarts, pies, cakes: most folks have a few staples that they make every Christmas. But the lonely, lowly fruitcake, if served, is most often the bought variety. Who has time to make it ahead and wait until it's properly aged, as a fruitcake should be?

You do! Even if it's just a few days until Christmas or your gathering, you have time to make this moist, delicious, kid-friendly no-bake fruitcake! Maybe the kids or grandkids can even help make it; with marshmallows and nuts, it's a surefire winner.

No-Bake Fruitcake

Makes one 9 by 5 by 3-inch loaf.

INGREDIENTS
48 (¾ pound) marshmallows
¾ cup undiluted evaporated milk
⅓ cup apple juice
4 ¾ cups (about 14 ½ ounces) crushed vanilla wafers
2 ½ cups (about 7 ½ ounces) crushed gingersnaps
2 cups broken walnuts
1 cup dried, sweetened cranberries
1 cup mixed candied fruit
1 cup halved candied cherries

METHOD

1—Cut marshmallows into quarters, pour evaporated milk and apple juice over them and let stand for 3 hours, stirring occasionally.

2—Combine crushed vanilla wafers and gingersnaps, nuts, cranberries, fruit and cherries in a large bowl.

3—Add marshmallow mixture and mix well.

4—Pack firmly into a foil-lined loaf pan, cover top with foil and store covered in the refrigerator for several days.

You can turn this loaf out on a platter and top with slivered almonds and candied cherry halves, if you like. It looks pretty just as it is, though!

A Word from Jaymie:

A few notes about this recipe; you will think it's too crumbly, and will be tempted to add more liquid. Don't do it! Pack it firmly in the loaf pan, make a wish, and a few days